Murder. Betrayal. Aluminum.

Recycling, once a gangly, wide-eyed youth, all arms and legs, has grown up and now faces those pesky problems that come with adulthood, like making money. And the big garbage companies that once sneered at recycling, like Consolidated Scavenger, now want to take over.

Rookie investigative journalist Brian Hunter, seeking to reinvent himself in midlife, covers the "recycling wars" in Berkeley, where Scavenger seeks to crush its competitors, like Re-Be, a scrappy and idealistic recycling collective. Brian finds the body of his friend Doug crushed in an aluminum bale, and hunts down the murderer, all while trying to win the heart of Barb, Doug's former lover, who's become a suspect in his murder.

But *Wasted* is not just another trashy mystery. Set in the gritty and malodorous world of garbage and recycling, the novel is rich with resonant themes of reinvention, transition, and discarding that which no longer serves us.

Part mystery, part love triangle, part midlife crisis, and part political satire, *Wasted* asks the age-old question: How do I act with truth and integrity, make the world a better place, and still get laid?

"Waste isn't waste until it's wasted."
— Daniel Knapp and Mary Lou Van Deventer,
founders of Urban Ore in Berkeley

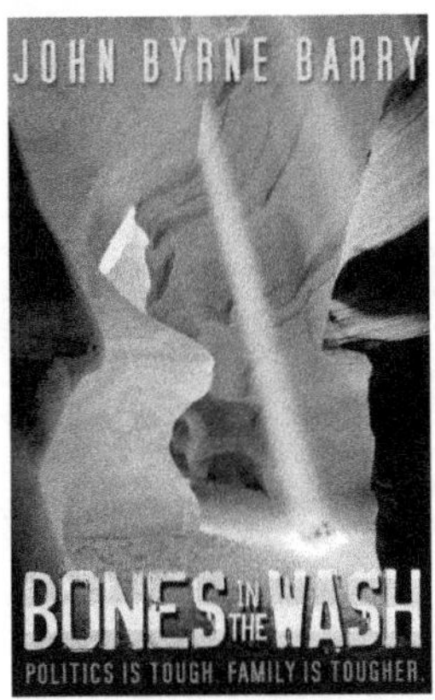

Praise for

Bones in the Wash

Politics is Tough. Family is Tougher.

One of those unusual novels where you end up talking about the characters as if you knew them well. Set during the 2008 presidential campaign in New Mexico, and complicated by the romance, rage, and lives of two fabulously dysfunctional families. A wonderful read.

—Bob Schildgen, author of *Hey Mr. Green*

Albuquerque Mayor Tomas Zamara understands that politics is like playing football on a muddy field. If you don't get dirty, you're not giving your all. But gutter politics is not his style.

The Democrats' Barack Obama is drawing adoring crowds with his soaring speeches, and Zamara's GOP bosses are pressuring him to do "whatever it takes" to deliver New Mexico's five electoral votes. Challenging him every step of the way is fierce, young Sierra León of the Democracy Project, who calls on him to listen to his better self and reject his party's dirty tricks.

Mayor Zamara is also grappling with being a suspect in his wife's murder; fending off his father, who wants to rescue his failing business with city money; and satisfying his demanding new woman, the radiant and volatile Tory Singer, who may not be who she says she is.

bonesinthewash.com

More Kudos from readers:

"Remarkable how the author so completely understands the characters."

"Entertaining and addictive."

"Finished reading at 4 a.m."

"Couldn't put it down."

WASTED

MURDER IN THE RECYCLE BERKELEY YARD

John Byrne Barry

a 'green noir' mystery

ISBN: 978-0-9967262-0-7

For my mom and dad.

1.

Berkeley Scavenger

In the beginning, we threw our garbage away by throwing it. In the corner of the cave. Outside the door of the hut. In the street. Rats, dung beetles, and bacteria did the rest.
> —Brian Hunter, "The Garbage Shortage,"
> *East Bay Beat,* September 30, 1998

I'm tired of taking showers at the Y. The skin between my toes is itchy and cracked. Maybe it's time to get a real place with my own shower, live like an actual middle-class person instead of sleeping illegally in my office, on a sorry-ass sofa bed that only unfolds if I hang my chair on a hook.

Or rather, not sleeping, as is the case now. I'm studying the fat ventilation tube clamped to the high ceiling. The moonlight paints a gash on it, as if all the air is about to spill into my studio.

I could get up and work for my bookkeeping clients, but every hour crunching spreadsheets is as deadening as a day in a coal mine, without the black lung disease to hasten my demise. But that's a good thing. I may be depressed, but I'm not looking to end my life. I'm looking to start it.

OK, I'm getting up. I'm going to head out into the darkness with a shopping cart to steal bottles and cans. I'm getting up. Now.

Yesterday, my friend Doug told me that every month in

Berkeley, poachers "steal" $15,000 worth of recyclable aluminum, glass, and cardboard from Re-Be's apple-green curbside bins. (Re-Be is what everyone calls Recycle Berkeley, the collective where Doug works.) He encouraged me to go undercover as a poacher to see what I might discover. The pickup schedule he gave me is tacked to my bulletin board. Today's route is in the flatlands, about ten blocks away.

Determined to reinvent myself as an investigative reporter, I now seem to be covering what Doug calls the "recycling wars"—the fight between the recycling true-believers and the corporate come-latelies, like the giant multinational Consolidated Scavenger. Which Doug, not so affectionately, calls "Con."

I maneuver a shopping cart from the furnace room through the dark and narrow corridors. Donning my disguise—jeans with a hole in the seat, a stained Microsoft Excel t-shirt from a trade show, crusty garden gloves, and a St. Louis Cardinals baseball cap I've had since high school—I can't say if I look the part, but I feel it. My throat is scratchy, my stomach churning with two cups of truck-driver strength coffee, my eyes bleary.

Walking up Ninth Street, I start seeing the bins at Delaware. The shopping cart keeps veering right because one front wheel doesn't touch the ground. I have to stop every few minutes to tilt up on the back wheels and reposition. I'm sure that's a metaphor for something, but I haven't worked it out yet.

There's no one around, but I feel jumpy. It's not like I've never walked these streets in the dark before, but there's something unsettling about the hours before dawn. I have to fight the urge to go back to my studio and burrow back under the covers.

Once bottles and cans are placed on the curb for pickup, they legally belong to Re-Be. When scavengers in their shopping carts rummage through the bins, take the cans or cardboard or whatever they can get a good price for, they're technically stealing.

The first block has been picked clean—there's only newspaper and mixed paper left. Heading east on Virginia, I find a block no one has scavenged. After half an hour, I've barely covered the bottom of my cart. Already I smell of stale beer and soda.

As I bend over a bin, I feel a tap on my shoulder. I jump. Hovering over me is this big black guy maybe fifty years old, with a scraggly white beard and yellow gloves.

"Hey, how's it goin'?" I say as nonchalantly as I can. "I'm, uh, Brian." I'm not alert enough to lie.

"I ain't see you before," he says, in a soft voice. One of his eyeballs rolls around inside the white of his eye, like a marble in a funnel. He's at least six four and two hundred fifty pounds. In his right hand, held partly behind his back, is a long flat piece of weathered white wood with a pointed end, like he's pulled a picket off a fence.

I consider running. His shoelaces are loosely tied and he does not look fleet of foot. With a head start, I can surely outrun him. At the end of the block, I eye a couple of shopping carts. I didn't hear them. Maybe he's oiled the wheels. Mine squeak. What's that advice I heard? If it moves and it shouldn't, use duct tape. If it doesn't move and it should, try WD-40.

I stay put.

"First time in this part of town," I say. "Used to do Oakland right near Piedmont. Got hassled too much." Doug told me poachers in the Piedmont neighborhood of Oakland were being routinely harassed by the police and "advised" to go to Berkeley.

"You gotta find somewhere else, boss. This here's mine. You got a sponsor?"

He takes a step back and unscrunches his neck. I think he's reading me right. I'm not going to challenge him.

"How do I know what territory is left?" I ask. "I'm new in town."

He squints at me as if he's trying to read the small print on a medicine bottle. "You look like you be new all total," he says. "You sure you done this before?"

I look up and down the street. "Just a couple times," I say. "Back east, St. Louis, when I was really broke. Like I am now."

Without warning, he swings the picket and hits my thigh.

I howl. "Oh shit, shit, *shit!* What the—" Before he swung, I was nervous and measuring my words, but stunned and emboldened by the pain, I yell at him fearlessly. *"You're fucking nuts!* Why the fuck did you go and do that for?"

"You were after my shit," he says.

I grit my teeth, hold my leg. Nothing's broken. But he swung his picket hard on the meat of my quadricep. I look down the block at his carts.

"No, I was *not* going to take your shit," I snarl. "If you weren't so totally *stupid,* you'd see I was going to do whatever you wanted me to."

"You were going to run off with my carts."

"No, run *away* from you, maybe, but not with your *stuff.*"

"Oh." He pauses. "But you *was* lying to me."

A few blocks away, a train passing through blares its horn. The 5:30 commuter run to Sacramento.

"I have to sit down," I say.

"Here, you want a beer?" He reaches into a frayed canvas shoulder bag, the kind I wore as a kid delivering newspapers on my bike in Dogtown, and pulls out a can of Weltanschauung. My stomach is sloshing from the coffee, but I mutter thanks, and sit on the curb. A couple of birds chatter, but otherwise it's quiet. Early birds. Daybreak is an hour away.

The big man folds his legs and squats beside me, holding onto the handle of my cart. "I'm Wilson," he says. He pulls out another can, opens it, drinks.

The beer is warm. That surprises me, but I don't know why. Did I think he had a cooler on his cart?

"Thanks for the beer, but it doesn't make up for the fact that you whacked me without provocation."

"Without provocation. Without pro-vo-ca-tion." He draws out the word. "You were looking at my carts."

He pulls himself to his feet, guzzles his beer, and tosses the empty in my cart. "Next week Friday at four in the a.m., meet me here," he says, pointing to his carts at the corner. "I'll be your sponsor. Get you started."

"Started?" I ask, staring at him, trying to look tough and skeptical.

"But you gotta follow the rules," he says. "I'll get you a map. You can't have this one. This is mine."

He unfolds a worn piece of paper and holds it in front of me. It's the Berkeley route map from Re-Be, but with dotted red borders drawn in various places. I try to pull the map closer and tilt my head to read it under the streetlamp, but Wilson grips it tightly in his fist. His thumb covers the top of the map, but at the bottom, I see a list of buyback centers. I recognize several of them. He yanks the map away, then reaches into his pocket, gives me a couple of crumpled dollar bills.

"Get yourself some donuts."

"No, I can't—"

He pushes the bills into my palm, and closes my fingers around them. "Next week," he says.

He walks back to his carts. A pair of raccoons poke their heads out of a sewer grate after he passes, then they retreat.

I plant my feet, fold my arms in front of my chest, and look him in the eye.

"Doug, attacking me, attacking my integrity is *not* OK. I thought we were friends. I—"

Shaking my head, I leave it at that, and snap a photo of a nearby stack of aluminum bales. In the breeze, I smell the bleach disinfectant that Re-Be workers scrub the pavement with at the end of each workday. I also catch a whiff of curry from the Indian takeout place up the street that's always so crowded on weekends.

"OK, I'm a little out of control." Doug steps back, holding his palms up, fingers curled, as if carrying two melons. "But these people are criminals, *predators*. This isn't just about holding onto our jobs, our twenty worker-controlled, democratic, non-hierarchical jobs, by the way. It's about the fucking chain ganging of Berkeley. It's about community control, resisting domination by corporate criminals. It's about recycling creating six times as many jobs as landfilling. Look what Re-Be's doing: We're teaching third graders about worm composting. We've spun off three salvage yards that are doing good business. We're not just picking up the cardboard packaging, we're getting people to question whether they need to buy the fucking product in the first place. You think Con is going to do that?"

His voice softens. Again, he leans towards me, but without the aggressive stare.

"Hunter, what you write *matters*. The stories you publish make a difference. Con's expansionist intentions are out there now, seeping into the public consciousness."

I hesitate, disarmed. This is the Doug I know, even admire. Relentless, yes, but passionate too, with a hint of graciousness.

Clunk. Startled, we both turn towards the storage shed where it sounds like a rock has dropped on the roof. A seagull swoops down and lands on the eave.

"Feeding time," says Doug. "The gulls bring shells from the bay, drop them on the roof to break them open. It's cool. That's why I work Sunday mornings when we're closed. The gulls don't visit much during the week when there's people and trucks everywhere. Plus I get to play with the machines."

A foghorn in the marina blares. Doug turns back to me, bites his lip.

"Oh, one more thing."

He pulls a folded piece of paper from his pocket and casually hands it to me. In the middle of a computer printout are two lines highlighted in yellow marker.

James Wilcox, $500
Lynn Brady, $500

"What's this?"

"Like Deep Throat said, follow the money. These two jokers don't even live in Berkeley and here they are making the max donation to Womack's council campaign."

"So these are campaign contributions?"

Doug nods. "Five hundred for a council race? This is from the city clerk's office. It's not their money, it's Con's. Wilcox is the floor chief at the transfer station. He can't be pulling in more than about forty large. And Brady, that's his wife, home with the kids. They live in Emeryville in a shithole handyman special. Old beater up on blocks in the yard. These people are fronts. Womack and her council buddies want to shut us down, let Con swoop in."

I stare at the printout. Doug bites his thumbnail, spits it on the ground, then turns and strides back across the yard toward the cavernous football-field sized warehouse, open on one side, where the sorting and baling take place. He doesn't ask me to follow him, but I do.

Against the center wall of the warehouse, bales of cardboard are stacked ten feet high. Paper swirls on the concrete floor. Doug climbs up three steps into the cockpit of the baler, and sits in front of the silver control panel, with its colorful switches and buttons and levers. In the center a big red circular button says "EMERGENCY STOP."

He flips a switch and the cans sitting in a pit on the floor start their ascent up a sloped conveyor belt. At the top, they drop fifteen feet into a hopper and a steel ram squeezes them into a block about four foot by four foot by three, like a wide file cabinet on its side.

I stand on the concrete slab the baler is mounted on, my head at Doug's knees, and study the folded paper again. Re-Be's two-year $2 million contract with the city to collect recyclables is up for renewal in May. Doug is afraid the council will open it up to competitive bidding and Consolidated Scavenger will lowball the bid and pluck it away. Con has done that elsewhere.

Election Day is a month away. At stake are five council seats, and which of Berkeley's political parties will control the council and decide Re-Be's fate.

"Talk to them," barks Doug, jabbing his forefinger at the highlighted names. "Grill them. I'll be damned if I'm going to let Barb take over what we built here."

"Barb?" I say, with surprise in my voice. "She couldn't have anything to do with this, you know that. She just started."

Barb had been Doug's lover for ten years—she and he had been the matriarch and patriarch of Re-Be. Then, over the summer, with the quickness of a kitten, she broke up with him, quit Re-Be, and took a job as recycling director in Consolidated Scavenger's Oakland office.

Doug scowls at me, his eyes narrow. "You don't know her. She'll fuck us over, they'll promote her, and then she'll blush and trot out her 'oh, little old me, I'm just trying to make the world a better place' bullshit. I'll kill her before I let that bitch sell us out again."

Pause.

"That's off the record."

I watch the cans roll uphill. "Sounds like the breakup hit you pretty hard." I'm careful to sound as neutral as possible.

He snorts. "She was just a crack I fell into. It was understood from the beginning that she would bail." He shrugs. It's a common gesture of his, but this one is so quick, it's more like a twitch. "But taking the Scavenger job. That was hateful, man. Poison. She did it to spite me. Not only do I not want to be with you anymore, she's saying, I want to destroy what we built together."

A compressed bale of aluminum clatters out the baler's side door, then the chute at the top of the conveyor belt opens, and a new batch of cans falls into the hopper.

A gull glides to a ledge below the metal ceiling and squawks.

"Doug, you're wrong. Barb had changes she had to make. She didn't do these things to spite you. And she was not just some *crack* you fell into. That's *mean*."

"You've got the hots for her, don't you?" he says, jabbing his finger into my chest. "That's it, you're hot for her."

"Hot for Barb?" I say, pretending to be confused. Then I decide not to be. "I like Barb. I've always liked her." Truth is, I've lusted after Barb since the moment I met her, but I keep that to myself.

"You stay away from her, Hunter, I'm not finished with her."

"She apparently is finished with you."

"It ain't over until it's over."

"Yeah, right," I say.

He jumps out of the cockpit and lands on the ledge a foot in front of me.

"You shit," he says. "You weasel. You're pussy-whipped. *That's* why you're scared to expose Con. You're afraid to piss off Barb."

"OK, Spaulding," I say, "I've had enough of your shit. Barb leaves, you can't deal with it, so you vent your spleen at her and the company she works for. That's a lot easier than looking inside, because you know you drove her away—"

"Hunter with a left jab," Doug sneers, but I won't let him talk. I get in his face.

"This witch hunt you're on." I keep my voice low and measured. "You're tearing Re-Be apart, calling people cowards, ripping into Barb in front of her friends, accusing hard-working board members of being bought off. Re-Be's an embattled place, mostly because of you. You can't blame that on Scavenger." I take a breath. Downshift.

I drank beer one night at the Albatross with Doug and he told me his parents took him to the courtroom when he was a kid to watch them defend Black Panthers and union leaders and criminal defendants, and that that inspired him to work for justice and fight for a better world. Fight was the key word. That's what he learned from his parents, he told me. How to fight.

"Doug, please. Listen to me." My tone is soothing, earnest. "You and Barb were together for a long time. Tight for a long time. Her leaving must mean quite an adjustment. People understand that, they do, but you've turned their sympathy into animosity. If you'd let up on all this demonizing, tell people you're hurting, they'd come around."

Doug leans over me until his nose is an inch from mine, and snaps his words as if they're darts.

"Don't. Analyze. Me. If I want a shrink, I'll steal $100 and rent one."

I can't hold his stare. It's too vicious. I pull back. I've never seen him this unhinged before.

"A therapist wouldn't be a bad idea," I say, looking down at a black stain on the concrete.

He pauses, then crinkles his nose and bares his teeth. I lift the camera to my eye and snap the shutter. He flinches, then swipes at the camera.

I recoil, but then he shoves me into the pit on top of a rickety pile of cans. I land on my back. The camera bangs my cheek. The cans cushion my fall, but a stab of pain rips my right shoulder. My scream echoes off the warehouse roof.

All of a sudden, I feel the surface under me moving, and I'm being carried up by the slanted conveyor belt that feeds the baler. I try to climb out, but can't get a foothold. I sweep the cans off my legs, plant my foot on a ledge and push myself upright, twisting to grab for the side wall. But my feet slip on the slick surface and I fall face first. I flip myself around and I can see the end of the belt a few feet above me where the cans fall into the hopper.

I catch the wall with my hand and then, summoning some primal gymnast within, yank my body to it and throw my legs over the side. I brace for the impact with the concrete slab, but instead fall on Doug and we tumble with our arms and legs entangled, sliding in a puddle of oil and water.

I leap to my feet.

"You fucking lunatic," I shriek. "You could have killed me. You're fucking—" I can't find the words. Doug sprawls on the ground with a pained look on his face, rubbing his elbow. Blood smears his forehead. I look around for a shovel, a two-by-four, something I can swing.

"You know I wasn't going to hurt you." Doug winces as he sits up. I hope he's hurt. "I was just letting off steam."

A shaft of sunlight reflects off a chair and scorches my eyes. Bile blisters my throat. I have to get out. I don't trust myself.

Doug gestures to the control panel behind him. "I was about to push the stop button. We've got all sorts of safeguards. I wasn't going to let anything happen. I wouldn't. You know me."

"No, I don't know you at all."

3.

Follow the Money

The most pivotal city council race in Berkeley pits challenger Sarah Gluckman, a lawyer/child-care-worker advocate backed by the left-liberal Peace and Justice Coalition (PJs), against incumbent Sheila Womack, supported by the more moderate Neighbors and Families for Berkeley (NFBs). At stake are downtown development, rent control, and the future of Recycle Berkeley, the embattled organization that runs the city's curbside recycling service.
—Daria Reeves, *San Francisco Chronicle*, October 12, 1998

The next morning, I follow the money to Emeryville.

I call James Wilcox at work, but he's out, so I decide to try a face-to-face interview. I learn more in person. That's because I look unthreatening—put me in a UPS uniform with a package and all anyone will remember is the brown uniform.

I'm not striking like Doug, who's nowhere near handsome, but memorable with all his sharp angles and jerky movements. I'm five nine in hiking boots, skinny as a sapling. Back when I played guitar in a hard-driving acid-folk-rock, Afro-Cuban Clash-wannabe band, I could get down and dirty, but one friend used to say I was too white. Hey, I am what I am, a northern European mutt. I do have a nice thick mop of hair—though it's poorly cut, according to at least one source. A month ago, at a lunch meeting of the West Berkeley Business League, I overheard two women talking about me. "He'd be pretty cute if he got a decent haircut and some nice clothes. He's got a kind, bouncy quality."

I'm not feeling so bouncy this morning. The gash on my cheek is small enough I don't feel like a pirate, but I'm tense in the crick beneath my shoulder blades, and I can't seem to untie the knot tightening between my temples. And I wasn't doing so great *before* my fight with Doug.

I don't want to ascribe too much meaning to being attacked and hurt twice in three days, but I don't want to ignore it either. If the trend continues, I'm liable to get gunned down in an alley.

But I give myself some credit. I wouldn't be getting myself into trouble if I were sitting at my desk, tracking debits and expenditures. (Yes, some of my clients are in arrears in their bills, but not enough so that they, or their bookkeeper, are likely to get whacked by a picket. Or shoved in a baler.)

It's eerily quiet as I head out. My office is in a low-slung wooden 1920's warehouse, a warren of art galleries and furniture-makers and there's often a toxic-sweet scent of petroleum products wafting through the low-ceilinged hallways. No one seems to be stirring this morning, at least in my wing of the building.

I know that Maya, my glass-blowing neighbor, spends the night here sometimes. Now and then when I pad to the bathroom around midnight, I see her stove burning orange through the partly ajar door. But she doesn't live here. This sleeping in my office is temporary. I'm just trying to save some money and get my bearings back.

The bustling, post-industrial West Berkeley neighborhood I walk through from my studio toward Emeryville is an area in transition. Most, but not all of the old steel foundries and manufacturing plants have flown off to Kuala Lumpur or Tijuana. Dozens of retrofitted industrial shells now house an eclectic mix of software startups, yoga studios, consumer boutiques, rug importers, pottery collectives, and publishers.

On the block next to mine, the 19th century collides with the 21st—the Berkeley Brass Foundry, a brown-brick fortress erected in 1895, squats across the street from a sleek glass and steel cube that houses a biotech startup. There are still enough railroad tracks, workers with hard hats, and peppy ladybug-like forklifts zipping to and fro to give the neighborhood a gritty feel, but you can also find a good cappuccino within four blocks in any direction.

Maya hates it. "Frigging Starbucks'll be here soon," she snarls.

I second that snarl, but secretly I like the mix, wish I could freeze the moment, savor it, like those last chapters of a satisfying thriller.

That's why they're called transitions. They don't last. Except for mine.

Emeryville, ten minutes from my studio, has already "gone over to the dark side," as one friend says.

When I first came to the East Bay in the mid-'80s, this little city of 5,000 residents was invisible. Now it's bursting with cranes and construction. Berkeley and Oakland want developers to pay mitigation costs, build responsibly, create public spaces. Emeryville says, come on in, do whatever you like. From the abandoned factories and vacant lots sprung sprawling software campuses, high-rise apartments and hotels, shopping malls, and a shiny new Amtrak station. IKEA is building a giant store by the freeway. A planning commissioner I know says dourly, "I failed to prevent the Emeryvillization of Emeryville."

The block where Brady and Wilcox live didn't get the memo. The row of shabby one-story townhouses has the charm of Army barracks, only less so. The Brady/Wilcox place is not as ramshackle as Doug described, though there is a house with knee-high weeds and a clunker on blocks down the street.

I don't hear anything when I press the doorbell, so I rap loudly on the door. With each knock there's a thin metallic ring, as if an empty coat hanger is rattling on a hook.

A woman with fluorescent red hair opens the door a sliver. Doug didn't describe Lynn Brady, but I imagined a sugary hillbilly housewife in an apron. Not even close. Tall, late twenties, pink complexion with black horn-rimmed glasses, she wears her hair crew cut short in front and long in back. A silver stud pokes through her nose. I hear the Beatles' "Ob-La-Di, Ob-La-Da" playing behind her.

"What?" she asks.

"Hi, my name is Brian Hunter. I'm a reporter for a weekly newspaper in Oakland called the *East Bay Beat*. I'm writing about the upcoming election and I wonder if I can ask you a few questions."

"I don't know anything about politics."

"Are you sure about that? It says here on the Candidate Contribution Compliance Report from the city clerk's office in Berkeley that you and your husband—is that James Wilcox?"

"Uh huh," she says, gripping the door as if she's ready to swing it closed. All I can see is her face and neck.

"It says here that Lynn Brady and James Wilcox each made a contribution of five hundred dollars to Sheila Womack and five hundred to Chris Wass, both running for Berkeley City Council."

"Must be something my husband took care of."

She starts to close the door, but I slide my foot in its path. "I'm not trying to get you into trouble," I say through the four-inch gap. "It's just that making an illegal campaign contribution is a felony under California law and you could go to jail. Two of the checks are from you. Could they have been made out in your name without your knowledge?"

The color drains from her cheeks. Her eyes dart from side to side, as if looking for an escape route. I nudge the door open with my knee.

"You and your husband made the maximum contribution to a city council candidate in a neighboring city when it doesn't appear that you have a lot of extra money. You don't, do you? Have a lot of extra money?"

She doesn't answer.

"Ma'am, are you registered to vote?"

"I've got to go," she says, withdrawing behind the door. I reach in and give her my card and ask her to have her husband call me. As I remove my foot and she closes the door, the Beatles start belting out "Bungalow Bill."

I'm used to professionals like the Scavenger press reps, who never flinch, so it feels unsettling to scare someone. I could get to like it though.

Next I visit the third floor at City Hall.

I've never met Sheila Womack or Chris Wass. I try Wass first, but no one answers.

I approach Womack's office cautiously. Doug blasted me for not being partisan enough. Womack is likely to feel the opposite.

The door is open a few feet and I hear two voices.

I recognize the first as Gill Sykes, Womack's aide. "I can run my own life, sweetie," he says. "I don't need you playing Lady Macbeth."

Then comes a woman's voice, cool and measured. "I hear hesitation where I want to hear enthusiasm."

I don't know who it is, but it's not Womack. I crane my neck to get closer. All I can see is a wall of bookshelves and a motorcycle helmet.

I met Sykes once at a solid waste commission hearing. He wore a double-breasted suit and a diamond earring, and the other six of us were in jeans. Doug described him as "ambitious with a capital A." He's a slight African American man about the same build as me, maybe thirty years old.

"I'm just looking both ways before I cross the road," he says. "Lots of dangerous drivers out there—"

"You didn't look both ways before jumping into my *bed*," she says, sounding disparaging and seductive at the same time.

"Oh, I didn't think you were dangerous." I hear a wink in his voice. "Lucky for me, I was wrong about that. *Very* wrong. And *very* lucky."

Then comes a thunk on the floor, like someone dropping a heavy bag, followed by the slurpiness of a kiss. Then whispers. The hallway is empty. I edge closer to the opening. Suddenly, the door opens and she walks out.

I twist quickly to my left and scoot over to the bulletin board. The woman, tall and thin with shoulder-length blond hair and a glint of emerald earrings, catches my eye before I turn. I arch my head toward the board and study the agenda for the upcoming meeting on off-leash dogs.

"You were listening, weren't you?" she says. I put my finger on the board as if to read the notice better. Pretend I don't hear her. But I feel her stare boring through my back. *Go away. Please.*

But I've been yapping to myself about not being timid, and she's not carrying anything hard to hit me with. So I turn to face her. Wow, she's gorgeous. Delicious lips with a whitish-pink gloss, long pale legs with a sparkling ankle bracelet.

"Hi, my name is Brian." I offer my hand and give her a warm smile.

She hesitates, more anxious than angry. I keep my hand outstretched.

"Abby," she says, and gives me a tepid handshake.

"Abby, hi. Um, this is going to sound weird, I'm sure, but—" I stop and look at my shoes. "It's sort of embarrassing."

She looks at me with suspicion, then opens her hands as if to say, go ahead, out with it, but I'm skeptical.

"Well, I saw you walk up the stairs and I was so *captivated* by you and I was hoping to talk to you and get your phone number, but then you ducked into that office, and I was waiting, and, well, can I call you?"

I grab a pen and notebook from my pocket and stand poised to write her number.

She relaxes her face, then squeezes out a tiny smile, as if someone were twisting her arm behind her back. She pulls sunglasses out of her enormous purse. The smile disappears. "Stop stalking me, or I'll call the police." She hurries down the stairs.

I grin to myself, pleased with my impromptu performance. Not only did I disarm her, I managed to practice my flirting. So unlike me. The *old* me, that is.

From the stairwell railing, I follow Abby's head as it gets smaller and she flits through the first floor lobby to the Milvia Street entrance. I turn back to Womack's office, but Sykes is headed out the door. I walk next to him, tell him I'm a reporter for the *Beat,* and ask him if he can answer some questions about contributions to Womack's campaign.

"Not now. Hunter, right?"

"Right. Brian Hunter. Tell me about James Wilcox and Lynn Brady. They've each given your campaign five hundred dollars."

"It's a big city," he says, walking fast. We're halfway to the second floor. "Sheila has supporters she's never met, people who like what she stands for. Now, if you'll excuse me."

I race down the steps to get in front of him. "I have evidence that it's Con's money, Consolidated Scavenger, and that Wilcox and Brady are fronts. Which means their contributions are illegal."

He stops with one hand on the railing and his feet on different steps. Is he going to answer me, slip around me, or plow through me?

He folds his hands across his chest and his frown melts into a smirk.

"If you're so concerned about corruption," he says slowly, "you might ask around about the Re-Be slush fund."

"Tell me more."

"Simple. Re-Be is illegally diverting funds it receives from the city for recycling work and funneling them to the PJs for election activities."

"Really? Is there proof?"

"We're assuming the auditors will find it. They're looking."

"And who is 'we'?"

"We? 'We' would be the law-abiding citizens of Berkeley, California."

4.

None of Us Will Ever Forgive You

"The name Re-Be came first as a standalone name, Re-Be as in 'becoming again,'" says Barb Genessee, former Re-Be staffer, now Consolidated Scavenger's director of recycling operations for Oakland. "Later someone suggested it could stand for Recycle Berkeley. Everyone assumes it was the other way around."
—James Tate, "Garbage Giants Recruit Recycling Veterans,"
Bay Business, October 13, 1998

I fell in love with Barb the first time I met her, nine years ago, in the middle of another Indian Summer. My band, the Burning Bridges, performed a benefit concert in the Re-Be yard to support a city ballot measure calling for a five-year moratorium on garbage incineration. (It won.)

When she introduced the band, she thanked us so profusely for our support, as if we were some high-flying superstars who commanded a princely sum for performing. It wasn't just the words she used, it was her enthusiasm and sincerity, how personally touched she was by our generosity.

The sun was scorching and Barb wore a skimpy spaghetti-strap dress with sandals. After our performance, I flirted with her shamelessly, which I could somehow do with a guitar strapped around my shoulder. I was dazzled by how her face gleamed in the sun, how she stood close to me and touched my arm as we talked, how her sparkling eyes held mine so intently.

We were babbling about nothing, mostly about the weather, but it was all subtext. For me, anyway. She said something about how rarely it got this hot in Berkeley, and very quickly, we figured out we'd grown up in the same state—she in Kansas City, me in St. Louis.

"Well, I like it hot," she said, twisting her hair around her fingers. Then this lanky, longhaired guy with close-set eyes came up behind her and put his arm around her waist. "This is Doug," she said, taking a step backward. Doug nodded.

"Righteous tunes, man." Then he led her away.

A few years later, the band was ancient history, Eileen and I were married, and I was making a modest, albeit dull living counting money for various businesses and nonprofits. One day, I walked into Re-Be looking for work and ended up volunteering, working with Barb to get Re-Be's books on the computer. I told myself it was for a good cause—giving back to the community and all that—and maybe other people believed that. All I wanted was an excuse to be near Barb.

Last winter, I ran into her on a gloomy night at a political poetry slam at the Bolshevik Café and we hung out afterward, drinking beer and commiserating about how unhappy we were in our relationships. I remember telling her that Eileen and I had "retreated into our private disappointments."

Doug is the one who urged me to write about the recycling wars. But would I be chasing this story if not to reconnect with Barb? Of course, if I'm successful exposing Con's misdeeds, Barb's not likely to be thrilled with me, so who knows how smart this whole idea is?

Monday afternoon, after lunch, I bicycle down to Barb's office in downtown Oakland. I lock my bike to a parking meter and climb the stairs, two at a time, to her fifth floor office, pushing off my knee with one hand, pulling on the railing with the other. I didn't notice the pain from Wilson's picket on my ride, but I do now.

At the fourth floor landing, I stop to catch my breath and peek out a narrow window across Lake Merritt toward the bone-dry Oakland hills. I lift my arm and sniff. A hint of the locker room, but only if I jab my nose in there.

I'm nervous. I'm going to ask Barb to dinner. Slip the invitation into the conversation casually, as if it just occurred to me. This is the first time I've seen her one-on-one with both of us unattached.

When I walk into her office, she grins at me from her chair, gesturing in a self-mocking manner. Like the Pope greeting the masses in St. Peter's Square. "Welcome to my palace," she says.

I make eye contact and hold it. I smile and rotate my head slowly to take in the spacious office.

She pushes her chair back and comes out from behind her desk. I bend on one knee and take her hand with a light grip. "May I kiss your ring?" I say.

She waves me up and gives me a hug, then motions me to the group of chairs in the corner. She *seems* happy to see me. Neither of us says anything until we're seated. "If I let them," she says, "they'd have someone bring me coffee in the morning, do all my faxes, make all my copies. 'That's why we have support staff, Barb.' I'm not used to all this queen-bee stuff, and they're starting to understand that."

She pauses.

"The good news is I don't have to fix any trucks."

Barb has never played the queen-bee role, despite her many accomplishments and leadership. She's always been less a tada-here-I-am person and more oh-there-you-are. She was stamped with the same midwestern modesty template as I was, but working at Re-be certainly magnified that. Stars not allowed at the egalitarian Re-Be.

"How are you handling your transition?" she asks, reaching

over and touching me on my wrist.

"Well, I'm no longer 'living in my office.' I've reframed it as a 'live-work loft.'"

"That's good. You know I ran into Eileen at the gym. We had a nice talk."

"Venting about your exes, I suppose."

"Actually, no. She said she was sad that you two couldn't work it out, and she wishes you the best in your next chapter."

"Oh."

"But you're not doing so great, are you?"

"No, I'm fine. Well, fine might be stretching it. But how do you know all this?"

"Lucky guess." She leans forward in her chair, her eyes wide and inviting.

"Well, I'm OK," I say, "but I still find myself having all these conversations with Eileen, as if something doesn't happen unless I tell her about it. I write letters I never send. I—but I didn't come here to blather away about myself, I wanted to see you, to interview you for my story, give you a chance to balance some of the crazy things Doug has been saying."

And ask you to dinner. But that gets caught in my throat.

On that night we ran into each other at the Bolshevik Café, Barb drove me home and we kept talking in her car across the street from my house. The lights were out. It was late. Eileen had gone to bed. After about five minutes, Barb turned the engine off, and that was when I took off my seat belt, and leaned over so my head was on the steering wheel, looking up at her. I made a silly face and she smiled, and then I pulled her to me, but my back was twisted and when I tried to kiss her we bumped noses.

I sat back up and made like an airplane with my index finger, taking a dramatic dive and detaching her seat belt buckle. This time when I leaned over the emergency brake lever, she leaned toward me.

We were making out long enough that the windows steamed up, and I kept going because I was excited and because I assumed she was going to call a stop to it any second. I had never had sex in a car before and I was starting to think maybe this would be the first time. But I couldn't help thinking that Eileen might look out the window and recognize Barb's car, so I stopped, said I had to go. Barb said she did too.

Many times since then, I've wondered how far we would have gone if I hadn't stopped, and kicked myself for my timidity. But stopping was the right thing to do. My relationship was crumbling at the time, but it wasn't over. Neither was Barb's.

I called Barb to have coffee a few days later and she said that it wouldn't be a good idea.

That was more than a year ago.

Barb gets up from her chair and walks over to the wall next to me and straightens a slightly askew Ansel Adams print, that one with the full moon over New Mexico.

"Well, I'm sure you'll figure it out," she says. "You've got a lot going for you."

I tell her about my visit with Doug yesterday, how agitated he was, how he pushed me into the baler. "I felt like I'd been transported into one of those after-school black-and-white TV shows where Batman is about to be crushed or impaled in some devious death trap by a cackling villain. I only had a few seconds to get out of there."

I leave out Doug's spiteful comments about her, but I do say I'm concerned about the intensity of his anger, with me and with her. She closes her eyes and rubs her forehead.

"I don't mean to suggest that you're responsible or anything," I say. "I'm not part of the firing squad. I respect what you've done."

"Do you?" She sounds skeptical.

No one at Re-Be has questioned Barb's decision to leave Doug. "What took you so long?" is the most common reaction.

Some, however, are giving her grief for taking a paycheck from Scavenger.

She walks over to the window, adjusts the blinds to block the bright afternoon sun.

"Brian, what am I *supposed to do?*" Her voice is quivering with despair. "Don't you think *I know* how he's acting? He's stuck. As if his shoes are nailed to the floor."

"Look, I'm doing this story like I said on the phone, but I really came because I wanted to see you."

"Here I am."

She wraps her hair in her fingers, looks down. She ties her thick hair back, but strands are always getting loose and hanging in her face. She's constantly twiddling with her hair, pushing it behind her ear.

"As for your stories, let me say that I have read them with great interest, and feel like you capture the core of what's at stake, with colorful and compelling prose, but, and here I shift from the Re-Be Barb to the Scavenger Barb, you give far too much, far too much credence to Doug's paranoid ravings. His demonization of Scavenger. You've been around Re-Be. It's inefficient, unimaginative, rigid, trapped in the past, and that's for starters. I take some responsibility for that, but it was also part of the Re-Be zeitgeist, this efficiency-is-corporatism, discipline-is-fascism bullshit."

"They're struggling without you. You know how important you were."

"Unfortunately, my colleagues did not make me feel very important when I was there, but that was then. Voilà, the new me."

"I'm working on that too. A new me. Still a work in progress."

"Aren't we always? Works in progress."

"I'd like to think so, but I've been stuck and sometimes

there's no progress at all. No pain, no gain, I get that, but pain is no guarantee of growth."

She looks up, but past me, her eyes unfocused, tired. "It took me years to break up with Doug, but I'm still not free. I am determined not to give him the satisfaction of seeing he's getting to me. But I fear that one day I'm going to snap."

She glances toward her desk, then back to her hands.

"I don't want to be a victim. I'm too privileged to embrace victimhood. I've got a lovely place to live, meaningful work, enough to eat, too much to eat even. But somehow because Doug was so headstrong about this collective principle, and, I don't know, threatened somehow by my competence, I found myself feeling like a victim. Unappreciated. Feeling sorry for myself. That's not who I am, not who I want to be. But that's what I was becoming. I had to leave to save my life."

"Amen. And you have."

"I have." She nods, her lips pressed together in a pout that seems to say that saving her life is more a goal than an accomplishment.

"You don't look like a victim," I say. "You look great."

"Thanks," she says, and then comes an awkward silence, until I ask her about work. She begins explaining how she's redesigning the commercial recycling program in Emeryville and Oakland, a spiel she clearly has trotted out before. She relaxes, relieved that we're onto something she can talk about with ease.

She talks with undulating hands, like her Italian forebears, punctuating her sentences with fingers spread wide. Despite her weariness, she looks absolutely lovely, with her lithe, graceful gymnast's body, her Mediterranean face with a hint of olive. Her black hair, lightly streaked with white and gray, gives her gravity and elegance. Her face is too angular to be classically beautiful, but she's "handsome" in a hardworking, modest, comfortable-in-her-own skin way. She looks stronger and more fit than when I worked with her on Re-Be's bookkeeping three years ago, but it's jarring to see her wrapped in a business suit. I'm used to seeing her in simple jeans and t-shirts with colorful earrings and bright Guatemalan shawls. She's done a lot of work on herself in the past few years—running, modern dance, therapy, swimming, yoga, juice fasts, and so on. I heard from someone at Re-Be that one reason Barb wanted a better job was so she could afford more therapy and bodywork. I've heard her summer's been a dramatic one, full or tears and late-night calls to friends.

As she launches into Scavenger's plans to collect food waste from restaurants, her phone beeps. She holds up a finger to put us on pause, then walks to her desk and punches a button on the phone.

"There's a Doug Spaulding here in the lobby," says a female voice over the speaker. "He says he'll wait as long as he needs to until you see him."

Barb rolls her eyes. She presses the button, holding her finger there, and says, to me, "Stay."

I nod. "Send him up," she says.

She shakes her head. "This is the third time he's showed up. I've avoided him twice. I'll feel safer with you here."

"Are you afraid he's going to hurt you?"

"I don't know," she says. "You know the story, right?"

I nod. "Second- and third-hand."

She opens the door, then sits down behind her desk and takes a few deep breaths.

I see Doug ambling down the hall, all legs and elbows, looking out of place in his denim work shirt and ponytail. Though he's pushing fifty, he still moves with the gangliness of a teenager during a growth spurt. He squints as he enters, nods at me. Not a hint of surprise.

She points to an armchair. "Have a seat."

Doug marches directly toward her until the desk stops him. He pushes, but the desk is heavy and doesn't budge. Then, his thighs against the edge of the desk, he leans forward, and glowers at her. She meets his stare without flinching.

He steps back and starts pacing.

She straightens a stack of paper that's already straight. At Re-Be, her workspace was never this neat and uncluttered.

"We're watching," he says, hands folded behind his back. He's casual, low-key. With little affect. "You step on our turf and it's war. And we don't play by the rules."

"Do we have to go over this again, Doug? This turf business is so tedious. It's like the crazies saying Re-Be gets its marching orders from Havana. Do you really think Con is going to—?"

"Damn fuckin' straight I do—"

"Let me finish." She brushes her hair behind her ear, holds it there with her fingers. "We have our hands full jumpstarting the commercial program. Residential is not that lucrative, you know that. You have to trust me on this. If I thought for one nanosecond that working here would endanger Re-Be, I wouldn't be here. Period."

Doug's fists clench by his side. "None of us will ever forgive you."

"*You* might never forgive me," says Barb. "That's your problem. But I talk with Kisa, Shannon, Miguel. They understand. They—"

"They don't have the guts to call you traitor to your face. I do."

"How brave of you."

"You know Con is using you."

"That's why they pay me. That's why they call it a job. They pay me money and they expect me to accomplish something in return. It's called the real world, Douglas, it's something—"

"You're contemptible. You're a whore. You—"

"Cool it, Doug." I jump up. "Barb's not the enemy. She's—"

"Oh, Hunter speaks his mind," snaps Doug, turning his glare on me. "That's right, I forgot. You're sweet on Barb, aren't you? That's so *touching*. You two would make such a *cute* couple, you with—"

"Enough!" Barb says. She turns to me, in a quieter voice. "Brian, I can defend myself. I've been doing it for years. Too many years."

I ignore her. "Doug, get yourself some help. Put some boxing gloves on and swing at a punching bag or something. You're way out of line."

"She betrayed us," says Doug, addressing me and pointing his finger at Barb. "And she doesn't even know it." He can't hide the weariness and distress under the hostility. For a second, it almost seems he's about to roll up into a ball and cry. Behind the turf war bluster, his message to Barb is unmistakable. "How could you leave me?"

He regroups, turns back to Barb, raising his voice to a saccharine snarl. "Let's see. How do we take over?"

He counts off with his fingers. "First, we steal their best people, bribe them, put them up in fancy offices, with vacant postmodern *crap* on the walls. Second, we lowball the bid to get the contract. Third, we squeeze out the competition and bury them in—"

Barb stands, leans on her palms. "Don't talk down to me." Her voice is even and controlled. "My eyes are wide open. What's so revolutionary about collecting bottles and cans in 1998? We won that battle. Why not let a mainstream company handle it? Get Re-Be out there on the cutting edge with something no one else will do."

"Only Con is not just some mainstream operation," Doug says, "it's a mother-fucking global criminal. You've got a trail of blood and toxic waste all over South Asia. You're dumping radioactive stew in the Ganges River, shipping incinerator ash full of dioxin to Burma where they put it into concrete construction bricks—"

"I know, child slavery, organ trafficking, genocide, the list goes on—"

"Oh, I almost forgot," says Doug. "Step four. Jack up recycling rates by threatening poachers and sending them to Berkeley, with a fucking map of the Re-Be routes."

Barb sighs, then picks up the phone and punches in a number. "So, are you going to leave now or do you want me to call security so you can make a scene? Whine about how you were manhandled by the badass corporate criminals? Your call."

"Believe it," he says. "I've seen the maps."

I decide now would not be a good time to say that I may have seen the map, too.

Doug pushes up against the desk again and glares at her. This time he rams his legs into the desk with such force that it lurches an inch toward her. With the phone in her left hand, she sits down and writes a note on a pad of paper. As calm as if she were alone in the office.

As he turns to leave, he shoots me a squinty-eyed sneer. "You'll regret this," he says, loud enough for most of downtown Oakland to hear. At first, I think he's talking to me.

When Doug leaves, Barb stands up and exhales, as if she's been holding her breath for the past ten minutes. I take a tentative step toward her. She moves behind her chair and tightly grips the blue fabric of its back and breathes in and out. Then she takes a drink from her light blue mug and moves toward me. I open my arms wide and she leans into them, but she still has the mug in her hand and it gets stuck between us and spills. She holds on. I can feel her trembling.

"Thank you for being here." She pulls away and points at the wet spot on my shirt. "I'm sorry."

"It's only water. Hey, let's sit down."

I take her hand and lead her to the chairs in the corner. We sit. She squeezes my hand for a second, then lets go and jumps up.

"Look, I need to earn my mercenary paycheck, bring this program in on budget and how am I supposed to do that without busting my ass?" She's mumbling now.

"We underbid to get the contract, just like he said, and somehow I'm supposed to make a profit. But the numbers don't add up and well, you don't want to hear about it."

"Actually, I do."

She leans her head back, closes her eyes. "Another time. And that's off the record, the lowballing."

"Another time. I'll call you. I'd love to see you under better circumstances. To have fun."

"Fun," she says. "I forget what fun is."

"He's really being an asshole," I say. "But he is right about one thing—I am 'sweet on you.'"

On my way down, through the window in the stairwell between the third and fourth floor, I see Doug climb into his battered bread truck and scream up San Pablo toward Berkeley with a squeal of tires.

5.

Add Sex and Stir

According to Solano County Assistant District Attorney Maria Gonzalez, several small waste haulers complained they were being harassed and followed by Consolidated Scavenger trucks and that their customers were "blitzed"—that is, offered below-market rates for garbage hauling. Pretty soon, says Gonzalez, Scavenger had all the contracts and the small haulers were out of business.
—Glenn Fontana, "Monopoly Mania: How Two Garbage Companies Came to Dominate California's Solid Waste Business," *Corporate Crime Quarterly*, Spring 1998

Maya lends me her car and Tuesday morning I head out to Diablo Landfill before the sun comes up. Owned by Scavenger, Diablo is set deep in East County near the delta, surrounded by treeless ridges lined with wind turbines. Cows and sheep munch on the dry grass. I've arranged to interview James Worton, the chief engineer, but when I arrive, it's Julian Allard who gives me the tour.

Interesting. He's a P.R. guy, not an engineer, based in Oakland, in the same office building as Barb, so he may have risen as early as I did to get here. He says Worton had to testify at a hearing. Maybe. I'm flattered that they're afraid I might knock Worton off-message with the punch of my questions.

When Allard and I climb out of the truck to look over the hillside where the "possum-belly" trailers empty their cargo, the odor slaps me in the face.

"Ah, the smell of money," he quips.

For years, the so-called garbage crisis read like a variation on an old joke: Landfills are much too dangerous, and there aren't enough of them around. A decade ago, we were ready to strap garbage trucks onto the space shuttle and blast them into orbit. Then, big players like Scavenger built huge regional landfills like Diablo, a new generation of waste-burning incinerators came online, and recycling took off. So for garbage companies in California, the real crisis today is that there's not enough garbage to go around.

It makes sense for cities to divert as much waste as possible from going to the landfill, but landfill operators live for the dump fees, so recycling hurts their bottom line.

Looks like Diablo is getting its share today. A procession of trucks rumble up the hillside and dump their loads into the hollow below. Allard points to a nearby area that's been capped and landscaped. "You go down ten feet there and there's hardly any decomposition. It's like an Egyptian tomb. You could find a hot dog from ten years ago, still all there. That keeps leaching to a bare-bones minimum."

When I ask Allard why Scavenger has racked up so many fines, he says it's because it purchased companies that didn't have the capital to meet all the environmental standards.

"It's like you buy a house that's got dry rot. It's your house now, the dry rot is your responsibility, even though it was there before you arrived. That's how it is with garbage. There's lot of figurative rot in these companies we've purchased. Some of them were downright criminal in their negligence."

I edge closer so I can watch the bulldozers covering up the dumped garbage with dirt.

"I understand you were one of the early recyclers," I say. "Founder of the El Cerrito program. How did you end up here?"

like this. How could I have convinced myself otherwise? Doug was clearly the aggressor in the story and Barb was tenacious in fending him off, but I guess it looked ugly regardless.

I write down what Barb is saying. Not that I am going to publish it, though I note she hasn't said that I misquoted her or got my facts wrong. I didn't "create" the truth. I reported it.

"I know Con has gobbled up other companies," she says. "I know they pushed for higher landfill standards to drive the little guys out of business. I know I'm not working for Mother Theresa, though she has her dark side too. A lot of those little fly-by-night companies that Con bought were corrupt. Thanks to Scavenger—and Re-Be—landfill regs are stricter, recycling goals are higher. We fought for those things at Re-Be. What were you thinking? 'This time it's personal.' Unfucking believable."

"I wasn't thinking, Barb. About you anyway. The story. It was stronger with the personal stuff. But I lost sight of how you would feel, and you always seem to be so tough and impervious to being hurt."

"That is an act. I bleed like everyone else." Her voice doesn't sound tough or impervious now.

"I admired how you defended yourself against Doug," I say, "how calm you were. I'm trying to be less timid. Err on the side of being an asshole."

"That makes it OK to turn my life into the Jerry Springer show? You get your personal growth by humiliating me, is that is? How dare you? How *dare* you?

"Barb, I'm sorry. Really."

"Stop groveling. It won't unwrite the story."

"You told me you'd be used as an example by people who wanted to trash Con."

"I didn't expect it would be you. I thought you liked me."

"I do like you. I always have. I think you're amazing."

"So what is this, sixth grade? You like some girl so you tell her she's ugly."

"I like you a lot, Barb. I really do. You're an engaging and beautiful woman. Inside and out. I'd like to go out with you."

"Can you run that by me again?" she says. "I must have missed something."

"I'd like to take you out. To dinner. Dancing too."

"Now why would I want to do that? Why would I even want to be seen in public—with you—after you humiliated me in your goddamn newspaper?"

I rub my eyes, press my palm to my chest. "Because you're bigger than that. Because you accept my heartfelt apology and because you know I will never *ever* tell your story again without express written permission in triplicate. Because you believe in redemption and reinvention. Because you and I have both been through the relationship wringer and we can maybe provide some comfort and healing to each other. Because we can have some fun together. Remember, you said it's been a long time since you had fun."

"I don't think so."

"Didn't we have fun together that night at the Bolshevik Café. I know I did."

Silence. It sounds like she's holding her breath.

"Because next time, I'll engage in more traditional courting practices, like bringing you flowers."

"Well, flowers would be an improvement," she says, with hesitation in her voice.

"How about if I throw in some chocolate?"

Another long silence. I resist filling it.

"This going out. What did you have in mind?"

"I was thinking we might get together someplace quiet for a drink, then go dancing at the BFD club in the city—they've got swing dancing on Thursdays—then we go back to your place and make out for an hour or two, then make love until the

"*I* was uncomfortable," I say. "I'm sure it was more unpleasant for you."

"Why didn't you say something?"

I gulp. "Next time I will. Can I take you to dinner? I know that won't make up for me standing by silently, but it's better than apologizing." She does a double take.

"You scared me, you know. About the insurance."

"Your insurance is fine. I am sorry. Didn't you ever pretend to be someone else when you were a reporter? And aren't there, like, a million Chinese restaurants right up the street?"

She hesitates, looks away, then says, "OK," stretching out the word so it sounds like she's not sure. We go to a small Schezuan place a block away.

I ask her about her time at Scavenger, but she twitches her nose like she smells something bad, and suggests we order first. Then I ask her about her current job instead.

"It's OK," she says. "I love the creative part, but it's such a cynical scene. No one believes in anything."

She talks about a potato chip campaign. I encourage her harangue, interject a few times, but mostly restrain myself. She seems happy to have an attentive listener.

It's not until we're on our main course—mu shu vegetables for me and broccoli with chicken for her—that she slows down and the perfect opportunity for a segue presents itself.

"Who knows where I'll be working in five years?" she says. "I certainly—"

"Speaking of transitions," I jump in, "watch this seamless one here—where were you working five years ago? Consolidated Scavenger?"

"I was there two years, a little more."

"Tell me about it."

She bites her lower lip and looks at the broccoli balanced on her chopsticks. "You already know more than I do. I may not be the normal reader because I worked at Scavenger in the press shop, but I am able to step back and read a story like an outsider, and you did a superb job of making me interested in that world, making me care that Scavenger might be a threat to this homegrown recycling collective. I don't know that I could tell you anything new."

"The way you described the advertising world just now—skeptical and questioning. Like that, but about Scavenger. You know, any criminal activity, scandals, cover-ups—that sort of stuff. Like that price-fixing episode in Solano County a few years ago."

She holds up her chopsticks. "It's just that, well, I've been doing all the talking and you're finished eating. I have to catch up. How did you get interested in garbage in the first place?" Then she smiles.

I tell myself that no self-respecting, hard-boiled reporter or detective would let a dame distract him, but of course, in the movies, it happens all the time.

I don't intend to blab away, but I do—about how I want to reinvent myself as an investigative reporter and to make a difference, which she calls "refreshing." She keeps nodding her head, and saying things like "wow" and "interesting," and before I know it, I've walked her through my sinuous path from songwriter to the guy who counted the pitiful money the band made to hanging out my shingle as a bookkeeper to writing book reviews and then stories for the *Beat*.

I tell her I stumbled into the waste world by reviewing a book by an archaeologist who excavated American landfills and analyzed them as if they were clues to some ancient civilization. She says she knows the book.

By the time I pause for breath, Donna has finished her dinner, the check's on the table, and a waiter is sweeping the floor. We're the only customers left. So much for my crack investigative skills.

She hasn't said more than a few sentences about Scavenger.

I suggest we get some coffee. She says she's tired, but I remind her that she said she would tell me about Scavenger. (Though she never *exactly* said that.)

It's almost seven. Already dark. Cooling off, but still balmy. She hesitates long enough that she makes it seem like a big concession, but then she agrees.

We walk up to North Beach, and once we're settled at a table by the window, she with her mineral water, me with my cappuccino, I ask her again to tell me about her Scavenger job. She starts talking instead about her experience in Lodi, a sleepy farm town seventy miles from San Francisco, working for the daily newspaper.

"It could not have been more square—school board meetings, 4-H shows, kids breaking into cars. It was a slower life. Nothing like San Francisco. I might have stayed if I had been married with kids. But I met most of the eligible men in town my first year, and didn't have many friends. I had great neighbors though. The old lady who lived across the street—I could go over and knock on her door any time day or night. Sometimes I did."

"I'd love to talk more about that some other time," I say, surprising myself with my resolute, almost demanding tone, "but right now I'd like to hear about your experiences at Scavenger."

"I told you I don't know anything useful."

"Oh, but you do. Otherwise, you wouldn't feel so reticent, as if you're betraying Scavenger."

"I'd like to change the subject," she says. "There are many things you don't know about me, one of which is that I am a competitive Scrabble player and I play almost every day, and I haven't played in days, and how about this: You play a game with me, now—I have a travel set in my bag—and then I'll tell you what little I know about what I did at Scavenger. You're a writer. You're comfortable with words."

"You're going to crush me, right?"

"That's possible."

Two-thirds through the game, when she is ahead, but only by fifteen points, she lays out the word "equinox" along the right side of the board, a triple-word score, with the "Q" on a double-letter square.

"You had all those letters sitting there waiting for this?"

"I was pretty lucky. I've been holding onto the "Q," waiting for a "U," and then I got the "O" and the "X.""

Her insurmountable lead grows until we run out of tiles, and then she seems lighter and I don't even have to remind her of our deal. As she collects the tiles, she starts talking.

"One of my first jobs was to research all the other waste haulers and recyclers in Contra Costa and Alameda counties. Lot of public records searches, some driving around West Oakland where the mosquito fleets are. I learned who the owners were, where they lived, what kinds of loans they held. I got credit reports. As first I was innocent enough to not really know what I was doing, but soon enough I figured out I was digging for dirt that Scavenger could use to undercut its competition. Nothing illegal about that. It's business. Pretty common, I was assured."

She meets my eyes when she comes to the end of a thought, but while talking she looks up, her neck tilted to the right, her eyebrows squinched up, as if seeking inspiration from the ceiling lights or some higher power.

"Scavenger also encouraged employees to join environmental groups, in my unit anyway. So I joined Greenpeace and South County Toxics Network, the Save Alameda Creek Association, the Sierra Club. We'd get reimbursed for our membership dues, we'd sign up for newsletters and action alerts, and bring in all the mail we got to meetings. My job was to summarize these materials for the managers, tell them what the enviros were

to say "wow."

"You can see why the cynicism of advertising doesn't faze me."

"That is a fascinating story," I say.

Then she goes to the bathroom. I have a moment to reflect and I realize I've been so present with Donna that I've forgotten about everything else.

It helps that Donna is "way cute," like her pal Neil said.

I walk her to her bus stop. "One more question," I ask. "Who organized these astroturf groups? It wasn't just you, was it?"

"It was all of us."

"Who was all of you?"

"I suppose you want names."

"Yeah, names. You're a reporter. Names are good."

But she won't give me names.

When she climbs on the streetcar and flashes her pass to the driver, she gives me a big smile. "You know, I can be more fun when I'm not talking about work."

8.

Night Swim

"If all you do is collect bottles and cans, you're not recycling," says Barb Genessee, Consolidated Scavenger's director of recycling operations for Oakland. "Recycling doesn't happen until you turn those collected materials into new products."
—Brian Hunter, "Recycling Rivalry: This Time It's Personal," *East Bay Beat,* October 14, 1998

I bring Barb a dozen red roses. A peace offering, and only $6 from the farmers' market. "The chocolate is coming." I hand her the flowers. "I'm having it flown in from Belgium."

She grimaces. "Brian, I don't mean to be picky, but for me, it's Swiss or forget it."

"Oh, did I say Belgium? I meant Switzerland. You know, with the Euro coming and all that, it's hard to tell those little countries apart. Especially the ones that don't have their own language."

She grins, though she's got this what-am-I-going-to-do-with-you look in her eyes. "Let me put these in some water."

In the center of her dining room table is a big orange mosaic vase full of Peruvian lilies. She puts the roses in a navy blue glass vase, then adjusts the vases so the roses are centered in front of the lilies. "Thank you," she says, turning down the volume on her stereo. She's playing Cesaria Evora, a smoky blues balladeer from the Cape Verde Islands. Barb's apricot-colored t-shirt has the word "breathe" across the top in bold white type and a yoga pose underneath.

I've been at her house twice before, when Doug lived here with her. Once I arrived early for a party and she put me to work getting dishes and utensils to the table. I remember finding, in a cabinet under the counter, a cardboard box of dirty dishes labeled "to wash."

The house is much cleaner and more open this time. With lots of greenery and flowers.

"You were here for that Re-Be bash last spring, weren't you?"

"Yeah, that was toward the end with Eileen. So I don't believe I was truly present."

"Are you present now?"

"I couldn't be more present if I were gift-wrapped," I say.

"Huh," she says. "Oh, yeah, gift-wrapped. That's good. You want some tea, beer, wine?"

"Beer would be great. It's hot."

It *is* hot. Unseasonably so. Well, not really. When it turns hot every October without fail, it's not unseasonable. We forget Indian Summer is coming. But this year is hotter than most. And it's holding on, day after day.

Einstein, Barb's goofy and playful golden retriever, bounds into the living room, wagging his tail. "I was wondering where you were," I say, scratching him behind his ears. He looks up at me with his big brown baleful eyes, his head tilted to one side and his tongue hanging out. He's usually good for a laugh, especially when he rubs his butt up against the couch to scratch himself or rolls on his back on the floor and snorts with abandon.

"He doesn't hear so well anymore," Barb says.

We sit on the couch with our drinks.

"I suppose you're still pissed at me."

"I've calmed down. I'm glad you're here." She takes a long drink. "Still pissed, yes."

"How is it living on your own? That's new for you, isn't it?"

"At first, I could not wait for him to be gone, but once he was it was like I was missing my arm. Sometimes it's too quiet around here. I'd just as soon talk about something else."

She finishes her beer quickly and gets another one. When she sits back down, she takes a quick sip, then starts peeling the label off the bottle.

"Can I ask you something about Re-Be?" I ask. "One question."

She hesitates, nods.

"I know this is out of left field, but someone who dislikes Re-Be told me there's this 'slush fund' Re-Be has to help get the PJs elected. You know anything about that? This is all off the record if you want it to be."

"Brian, you ought to write about something you're not so close to, where you don't know anyone." She stands and raises the window another few inches, as high as it goes.

"I ought to, I will," I say. "But first I have to finish this one. Didn't you pretty much run Re-Be? Or at least held things together? It certainly seems that way, now that you're gone and they're struggling."

"Re-Be is a collective. No one person runs the place."

"Right. And you were just a worker bee."

"I've said enough. Please. I forbid you from splashing my fucked-up relationship with Doug all over the front page again."

"Again, I sincerely apologize. For the record, it was page 3."

She frowns at me.

"Not that it matters."

She puts her beer down on the coffee table, its top surface a faded, crackled turquoise, then slides a pillow behind her, and leans back against the arm of the couch.

"You know, Brian, it would be a lot easier if you'd accept the fact that I'm petty and irrational and contradictory, just like everyone else. You see my strength, I like that, but you don't see my failings. Of course, I know about the slush fund. But it's not my place to tell you about it."

"You knew about it?"

Through the open window, I hear a motorcycle roar down the street.

"Brian, how could I have *not* known about it? If I was the mother hen everyone made me out to be."

"It just seems like something you wouldn't want to be part of. It has Doug written all over it."

"Oh, Dougie and I fooled everyone. I was the good girl, he was the goon. But it wasn't that simple. I have my dark side, but Doug carried it for me all those years, so somehow I got this reputation as a saint, which I don't deserve. And don't *want*. That's why everyone is giving me grief about selling out, going to Con to make a few bucks. They can't believe I'm not this altruistic do-gooder to the core."

"It's just that—forgive me for sounding like an innocent rube—the slush fund is corrupt, illegal. It looks bad. How could—"

"Brian, it *is* bad. But it's tiny. It's a bug." She leans forward, holds her finger and thumb together in front of her face and squints.

"You've got this distorted picture of me. On the one hand, you treat me like I'm Superwoman, able to lift recycling trucks and crush cans into bales with my bare hands, hold together a band of crazy anarchists. And then you treat me like I'm some innocent victim of Doug's evil schemes. It's patronizing and idealizing all at the same time."

"At the risk of being earnest, I guess what I'd like is to get to know the real you."

She walks to the window, turns to face me. Her hair falls across her face and she pushes it behind her ear.

"Earnest is good. I'm just a regular person who's going

through changes and trying to make something of my life. Like you. I'm probably not going to have the kids I wanted, so maybe I'd like to have some stuff. A couch that costs real money instead of a thrift store special. There was no 'slush fund' per se, but we did have several thousand of overhead that we devoted to keeping ourselves politically viable. For PR. Lobbying. No one was ever enriched by it. That's all I'm going to say. It's petty, like stealing office supplies. Especially compared to Neighbors and Families' big pot of dirty money from the landlords."

"You could go on the record and say that."

"No, I could not." She's agitated now. "I don't work for Re-Be. It would hurt Re-Be if you wrote about it. Don't get all impulsive and reckless again."

"Can I ask you a question about Con? Have you heard about Con employees joining community groups to, like, gather information?"

"Brian, is this why you came here, to grill me?"

"No, no, I definitely did not." I walk to the window next to her, leaning my nose against the glass. "I came to see you, hoping to kiss you. I got a little nervous and started talking shop. How about if I go out and knock on the door and start all over again?"

"Just pretend you did."

I fog up the window with my breath, then scrawl, "Barb is human" with my finger. Then I wipe it with the back of my hand.

"I know I told you that I liked you the first time I saw you," I say, but when I look in her eyes, she looks away. I lean against the window jamb. "But actually, it wasn't seeing you as much as hearing. You were pretty darn cute standing there, but when you were talking, your quick wit and fierce intelligence shone through. You dazzled me. You still do."

"That's more like it," she says.

"That time with the city council with your burlap bag theatrical revue, that really blew me away. And, at the risk of repeating myself, I have savored that time after the Bolshevik Café many times. It was special with a capital 'SP.'"

"Just don't be putting me up on any pedestals, Mr. Hunter. I know you like that I get dirt under my fingernails. Fine and good. But that dirt's not just from fixing the trucks. I've got more metaphorical dirt clinging to me than you can imagine."

"Try me. Shock me."

She smiles, holding my gaze now. "So are you going to kiss me or what?"

I lean toward her, blocking what little light there is from the lamp next to the couch. She leans against the wall, her face in shadow. I take the beer bottle from her hand and place it on the windowsill, lift my hands to her face, my fingertips lightly grazing her ears, and, as if I'm trying to touch a soap bubble without bursting it, I guide her head to mine.

She kisses back as tentatively as I kiss her, then puts her hands on my shoulders and looks in my eyes. Her eyes are big and brown. In sunlight, there's a hint of green, but I can't see it now. Her face is smooth except for some wrinkles around her eyes.

"My lips are dry." She reaches for her beer bottle. When I kiss her again, with my hand on her cheek, she kisses back hard and presses against me. Then she jumps away.

"I've got an idea," she says, sounding like a little girl. "Let's go skinny-dipping."

"Swimming? It's dark. It's October."

"We can go to Lake Anza. How often is it hot like this? And Einstein gets to come. He'll love it."

So swimming we go. She drives us up through Strawberry Canyon above the Cal campus and we walk around the lake, towels over our shoulders, to the big boulders on the far side, across from the beach. The air is still, the weather reminiscent of

Missouri summer nights, though not so muggy. It's one of maybe three nights of the year when it's almost too warm. Einstein bounds ahead, looking back at us to be sure we're following. Barb walks in front of me, laughing, playful. Ahead, we hear muffled voices and a splash. We keep going past a cove that's already staked out to the next outcropping. When we get there, Barb peels off all of her clothes and with only a second of hesitation, dives into the dark water.

"How deep is it here?" I ask when she bobs to the surface. Einstein paddles beside her, looking as happy as a dog can be.

"Plenty deep. I've jumped off this spot many times."

I take a shallow dive, skimming the surface. I chipped my tooth on the bottom of a pool once—I'm not taking any chances. The water's cold, but I stroke hard for a minute to warm up, then make my way to Barb and her dog. They swim toward me, Barb with the breaststroke, Einstein with, well, it must be the dog paddle.

A few stars are visible, but the moon hasn't yet risen. I can make out Barb's head above the water, but can barely see her face, even up close.

"I want to kiss you again," I say. "You look scrumptious."

I lean toward her, treading water. My first attempt lands on her nose. She wiggles away, then comes closer. I find her lips. She giggles. Einstein swims between us.

"Someone is jealous," she says.

"We could maybe figure out a role for Einstein here. Could be fun."

"He *is* spayed."

"Maybe he could videotape us."

She mock-slaps me, then swims away and climbs up on the rock and wraps herself in the towel. I swim for a few more minutes, feeling alive and happy, then join her on the rock. She puts her clothes back on. So do I. I sit next to her and pick up her hand and kiss it.

"I like being with you," I say.

Einstein has joined us on the rock and is shaking himself, spraying us with water.

I kiss Barb again. The rock is sharp under my butt. I slide a few inches closer.

"I like you, Brian, so don't take this the wrong way." She hesitates and looks down.

"That's not an auspicious beginning."

"I'm not ready for anything serious," she says. "I know most boys like to hear that, but I don't think of you as most boys."

"Now you're the one idealizing me. I like meaningless sex as much as the next guy."

"I doubt that." She takes my hand and looks up at me. "That's a compliment."

9.

We're All in This Together

Berkeley's innovative "Recycle and Win" program will receive a "best practices" award from the California Recycling Association at its annual banquet this weekend, a black-tie event at the Re-Be yard in West Berkeley. The program, designed by former Re-Be doyenne Barb Genessee, picks one household's garbage can at random every week and if it has no recyclables, the residents get a $100 check and their name in the paper.

—Brian Hunter, "Recycling Rivalry: This Time It's Personal," *East Bay Beat,* October 14, 1998.

From across the yard, through my telephoto lens, I spy Barb chatting with her Consolidated Scavenger colleagues.

Wow!

She looks incredible. I can't keep my eyes off her. She's wearing a simple black gown, more revealing than anything I've ever seen her in. With her hair pulled back, long dangling earrings, a flat silver and black necklace, and a maroon scarf over her shoulders, she has a touch of gypsy to her. She doesn't just look sexy, she looks glamorous. I don't know exactly what it is—the cleavage is a lot of it, but I've seen her in a skimpy tank top before. Must be the high heels, jewelry, makeup. The way the gown hugs her body.

I've never seen her in heels, only heard her scoffing at the idea that a woman would imprison herself in something so uncomfortable and objectifying. All at once, she has become both unforgettable and unattainable. What I've always liked so much about her is how attractive and engaging she is without seeming to try. But here she is trying to be glamorous, and wildly succeeding.

And to think that I kissed her a couple nights ago. I've always thought she was sexy, but in an understated, playful, black lab goofy kind of way. Tonight she's exuding a cool haughtiness and it's turning me on something fierce.

Of course, the coolness might well come from looking at her from fifty feet away through a camera lens, too far for her warmth to travel. I want to go to her, but I'm frozen in place. I'm not in her league.

She's talking with two men, the disagreeable Julian Allard who gave me the Diablo Landfill tour, and Tom Herman, the silver-haired, silver-tongued regional boss of Consolidated Scavenger.

We're in the Re-Be yard, the improbable site of the California Recycling Association's annual awards banquet, under the watchful eyes of seagulls lining the roof of the baling warehouse. Round plywood boards covered with freshly ironed white tablecloths sit on bales of newspaper and aluminum. There's not a plastic utensil or paper plate on the premises.

The asphalt has been thoroughly swept and scrubbed clean and shiny, and is free of the usual broken glass, tin can lids, and plastic bags. A forest green banner with "Recycle Berkeley" in bold san serif type hangs from the tall stacks of bales behind the stage.

This year, it's a formal affair, with about a hundred men and women schmoozing and nibbling hors d'oeuvres just a sniff away from the ripe smelling compost facility next door.

I'm not the only with a camera. Two TV crews are here as well, just as Kisa, the main Re-Be organizer of the event, predicted. "How can they resist?" she said. It's the first time anyone can remember local news covering the awards, but the contrast between the glitzy attire and the gritty atmosphere makes for great visuals. I take photos of the guests as they arrive—when I'm not ogling Barb behind my camera.

Scattered among the starched and formal are some rebels in jeans and army surplus khakis and a couple of women with shaved heads wearing saris. Ah, Berkeley.

Indian Summer continues to hang on, even though October is half over. The day has been still and hot, and by the time the afternoon shadows lengthen and camera operators are setting up, it has cooled to a balmy 70 degrees.

I'm not wearing a tux, as I am part media contingent, part Re-Be hanger-on, but I look more dashing than usual in my white linen wedding jacket. My feet, squeezed into stiff dress shoes, are sweaty and uncomfortable. I can't wait to take them off.

I haven't seen Barb since our swimming adventure.

She said on the way back from Lake Anza that she wants to keep our "relationship" a secret, though since she insists we don't have one, there's not much of a secret to keep. "Doug has a hard enough time with me getting an award," she said. "If he saw me with you, he'd kill me. Or you."

She also told me, again, that she wasn't ready for anything meaningful, and that I should find myself a woman who's available, but I haven't been able to think of anyone, anything, except her.

"Don't go getting attached to me," she said. "It took me years to peel off the last guy who did. It hurt. Him and me. Like pulling tape off my arm. Except that it wasn't over in two seconds. It's still not over."

I focus my camera on Councilwoman Sheila Womack and her aide Gil Sykes, who are sitting thirty feet away, with some other city officials. Just as I'm about to snap the shutter, Kisa waves her face in front of the lens and mugs. Then she plops down next to me and gulps water from the sturdy wine glasses rented for the occasion. She tilts her head, sticks out her tongue in feigned exhaustion, and holds up her crossed fingers. All is going according to plan. So far.

"You hear anything about protesters showing up?"

I shake my head.

"One of the TV guys asked me."

Barb's simple black dress flatters her, but Kisa's long sparkling navy blue gown looks wrong on her—it's too big, too much fabric. Despite an adorable grin on her wholesome and round face, she looks almost comical. But then, she hasn't spent the afternoon dolling herself up either. She's been setting up the tables and stage and negotiating with the caterer. Her curly hair, pinned back, is still damp. She probably just hopped in the shower in the trailer and threw the dress on. I can't remember seeing her without her glasses.

A light-skinned African American, Kisa was adopted and raised by two white lesbian hippies, who are part of Re-Be's extended community. One used to be on the board. Kisa fits right in at Re-Be, but no one expects she'll stay long. She's ambitious, and a sharp, easy-going, "white-acting" black woman is in great demand these days. All the do-gooder groups want, or say they want, more diversity.

She jokingly calls herself a "commodities broker"—she coordinates the sales of collected recyclables—but lately she's been trying to step into Barb's substantial shoes as leader without portfolio. She jumped at the chance to work on the statewide awards committee, and loved the idea of tuxes and gowns. "Hey, we've got recycling professionals wearing business suits now. Let's go all the way, make it a formal event, but hold it here in the yard."

The affair is tricky to manage, not just because of the formal wear and unorthodox setting, but because of the uneasy mix of idealistic veterans and newer corporate types. Kisa isn't *enthusiastic* about the change in the world of recycling, but accepts it. "It's a sign of success when the suits show up," she says.

But mostly it's the controversy over Barb's award, for the "Recycle and Win" program Re-Be started five years ago. Or was it Barb who started it?

The problem is that the awards *usually* go to organizations. Since Barb no longer works at Re-Be, she wouldn't get recognition for *her* project if the award were given to Re-Be. Even though her new employer, Consolidated Scavenger, has adopted a similar program in Oakland, it was during her time at Re-Be that the program started. It wouldn't make sense to honor the big bad wolf that's only recently arrived on the scene, so the awards committee decided to make an exception and give it to an individual. Barb.

The fact that Doug claims it was his idea, and that Barb only "implemented" it, adds another complication.

One of the TV crews is setting up an interview with Barb and I weave through the tables to get closer. The first question is why she's the only *individual* who's receiving an award. She sidesteps it.

"Yes, I understand that's the case. The truth is, this program was designed to raise the rate of recycling and it has. With a simple contest that has captured the imagination of the community—once a week, we pick a garbage can at random, and if there's nothing in there that can be recycled, you win $100. We had ten winners last year. Dozens of other cities are doing this now."

Barb is confident behind the camera, natural. I'm sure if I said that to her, she would say there's nothing natural about it. It's practice. It's being prepared. When she was first pitching the program, she told me she did it all by formula, until it *became* natural. No matter what people asked her, she pivoted to her talking points.

The last question is about Consolidated Scavenger's practice of taking over smaller companies. It's as if the reporter lifted it directly from my story.

"We're all in this together," she says. "The local grassroots groups, the big corporations, the city and county governments. The only way we get to zero waste is by everyone playing their part."

When the interview is over, I start to approach Barb, but David Ginsberg, the Re-Be board president, intercepts me.

"Brian Hunter, got a sec?"

He takes my hand and gives it a friendly squeeze. "Listen, I hear you've been asking around about this alleged slush fund."

Ginsberg is arguably the most bourgeois person in the inner circle of Re-Be, with a wife, teenage kids, a house in the hills, and prestigious medical brokerage job where he, as Kisa says, "hires and fires doctors." He's no Earth Firster, though who knows what he does with his checkbook in the privacy of his home. I've been at Re-Be a number of times when I asked myself, "Where are the grownups?" Ginsberg is a grownup. He's easy to spot at board meetings—he's the only one in a tie. Tonight, however, he's one of many penguins.

"Yeah, one of the things I've been asking around about," I say.

"I'm asking you a favor. Don't follow that trail. Maybe there's a story there, but it's ancient history and there are people I care about who could be hurt. It's small potatoes, very small potatoes, compared to the kind of payola that Con is dishing out to the NFBs. It will be totally blown out of proportion, and strengthen our opponents' hands. Now if there's any other way I can be of assistance, I'd be happy to accommodate you."

Ginsberg's cousin Sarah Gluckman, a vocal Re-Be supporter,

is challenging city council incumbent Sheila Womack, and possibly carrying Re-Be's fate with her.

"Well, Doug seems to think you're an infiltrator from Scavenger."

He sighs.

"I can't figure you out." His voice is calm, but frosty. "I thought you had Re-Be's well-being in mind, but it seems like you're more of a throw-things-out-there-and-let-the-chips-fall-where-they-may kind of guy."

"That is a non-answer. And a non-denial."

I am in fact concerned about Re-Be's well-being, no matter what I say about looking for the truth.

Ginsberg takes off his glasses and with a circular motion of his thumbs, wipes both lenses with the shiny black fabric of his tux. He steps closer and speaks softly, directly into my ear. "Off the record, I did attempt to negotiate with Con. I had coffee with someone who works for the city, someone who went out of his way to contact me, who gave me a heads up about some discussions taking place. That's hardly being an infiltrator, but maybe it's the same thing to Doug. Let me be blunt: if you write about this, or the slush fund, I will see to it that you never set foot in this yard again and never talk to a Re-Be staffer or board member again. Got it?"

I nod. "Doug says you want to fire him."

Ginsberg takes a step back and rubs his forehead. "Doug is hoping I quit in frustration and the anarchists can rule again. But that will be the death of Re-Be. I would love to fire him, that's no secret, but he's got some allies on the board who want to give him a chance to shape up. I'm hoping he does."

He doesn't warn me not to write about that.

It looks like dinner is about to begin, and I haven't connected with Barb yet, so I rush over to her table, where she's speaking emphatically to Herman, punctuating her conversation with fingers spread wide, saying something about catching snails with beer traps. Julian Allard is on the other side of Herman, and I nod at him—it's only been four days since I saw him at Diablo Landfill, though it seems like weeks ago. He doesn't acknowledge me. Neither does Barb. I'm right in front of her. How can she not see me?

But then she does.

"Oh, Brian, I want to introduce you to Tom Herman," She touches my shoulder as I extend my hand. "You've spoken to him on the phone, right?"

Her voice is friendly, but neutral. I could be anyone.

"Tom, this is Brian Hunter," she says, and now she's touching him too. "He's the writer from the *Beat,* and a friend."

I don't like how she buries the word "friend" at the end of her sentence. And why is she acting so affectionate with Herman?

"I always enjoy connecting a face with a name," Herman says, his handshake hearty and vigorous. "I suspect you're not entirely comfortable with Barbara becoming part of our team." His voice is deep and resonant. "But let me tell you, we are *thrilled* to have her. She is transforming who we are."

He lifts his wine glass, tilts his head back, and drains what's left. He doesn't look like he has any trouble sleeping at night.

Barb has turned back to the stage, and her eyes dart left and right.

I ask Herman if he can schedule a time to talk to me. "I've tried contacting you recently, but you have some very effective secretaries running interference for you."

He starts to respond, then a burst of feedback shrieks through the P.A. system and we all turn toward the stage, which is a wooden platform held up on three sides by forklifts.

"Sorry about that," says a bearded man in a tux, leaning on an aluminum-bale podium. "But now that I have your attention, ladies and jellybeans, if you can please take your seats. The food is ready to be served, and we'd like to start our awards presentations by 6:30."

Herman hands me a card. "Try me at this number on Tuesday."

The food is wonderful—your basic gourmet vegetarian fare. Baked butternut squash. Cheese enchiladas with yellow and red grilled peppers. Heaping platters of spinach salad with red onions and olives. Chilled honeydew melon "soup."

I'm working on my salad when the master of ceremonies, a young pony-tailed guy from Santa Cruz, steps to the microphone. "I read some advice today about giving speeches," he says. "First, you tell them what you're going to say, then you say it, then you tell them what you said. I'm going straight to part three. So, in conclusion…."

He pauses for a laugh that doesn't come. "OK, we're recyclers here. We don't like to waste anything, especially our time, so let's get to the awards."

The setting and costumes may be creative, but the awards presentations are not. They drone on. If the event were in a restaurant, it would have little to recommend it. Here in the recycling yard though, with the industrial backdrop and the ever-present seagulls, the festivities take on a campy edge.

On the other side of Kisa sits Ginsberg, and next to him, his wife Lettie. The gossip around Re-Be is that Ginsberg and Kisa are having an affair. At the least, they are "close." Kisa has taken on many of Barb's responsibilities, including being the primary staff liaison to the board. Below the amplified voices, I catch pieces of Ginsberg's and Kisa's whispers. The words aren't important—mostly they're talking about the award winners, but there's an intimacy between them, or so I imagine. Ginsberg seems to flirt with Kisa at one point, whispering in her ear, then grinning at her. Lettie, smiling and talking with another board member to her left, doesn't appear to notice.

When the M.C. announces Barb's award, she pushes out her chair and stands, but before she's straightened her legs, ear-splitting music bursts from the speakers—"the Internationale," the Russian revolutionary anthem.

> *Stand up, all victims of oppression*
> *For the tyrants fear your might*

From behind the orange forklift, five protesters emerge, dressed in bright yellow hazmat cleanup suits and gas masks, marching in front of the stage—and cameras—carrying hand-lettered signs. One reads: "Stop Scavenger Takeover of Independent Recyclers." Another: "Con is a Corporate Criminal." The gulls squawk and fly en masse from the roof of the warehouse.

> *Don't cling so hard to your possessions*
> *For you have nothing if you have no rights*

The marchers weave their way to Barb's table. They're chanting, but I can't hear them above the music, which is so loud, the fabric on the front of the speakers vibrates.

Behind the suit and mask, I can tell that Doug is in front, straining under the weight of a large black plastic bag. No two strides are alike. There's a jerkiness to his walk that makes even the simplest step forward ungraceful. I jump from my chair, grab my camera, and race toward the action.

Barb is frozen, halfway between sitting and standing, her knees bent and her hands on the table.

Behind her, the harvest sun, bleeding red, slips behind Mt. Tam.

When the protesters arrive at the Scavenger table, trailed by cameramen, Doug lunges forward with the heavy bag and heaves it onto the table open end first, scattering the glasses and plates. Halfway out of the bag slides a dead brown dog, shining in the TV floodlights. It's some sort of retriever mutt—like Barb's dog Einstein but darker—its fur matted, its legs stiff.

A wine glass rolls to the edge of the table, teeters for a second on the bunched tablecloth, then drops to the pavement and shatters.

The carcass comes to a rest in front of Barb, who recoils and turns away, her chair clattering behind her. She puts her hand to her eyes first, then her nose. The dog's eyes, open but vacant, touch a white bowl of green salsa. A second later, the smell of decay reaches me. I pinch my nose and focus my camera. Barb takes a deep breath through tight lips, then stands tall, shoulders back, fists clenched.

People at nearby tables scatter. One cameraman wades in closer to focus on the dog. Two others back up to capture the chaos. I take a couple steps forward, then retreat, torn between getting a better view and escaping the smell.

The music cuts off mid-sentence and I hear a whirring of TV cameras.

Doug yanks off his hood and mask and yells, "Hey, Genessee, didja' get your award yet, best performance for a whore in a supporting role?"

He looks totally different, his newly shaved head gleaming in the bright lights. He plants his feet defiantly amidst the broken wine glasses, folds his arms across his chest. Barb strides fiercely toward him, her arms pumping, her eyes narrow with rage. Kisa rushes between them, holding her arms outstretched. Barb ducks to avoid Kisa's arms, then stops and crumples. Her knees wobble, her body sags. Tom Herman comes up from behind and slides his hands under her armpits to keep her upright, but she wriggles free and runs away from the tables, tears streaming down her cheeks, her high heels clacking on the asphalt. Kisa yanks Doug's arm and shouts in his ear, her nostrils flared.

I take photos as fast as my camera lets me. With the scene bathed in TV lights, I don't need the flash. The other demonstrators pass out flyers. One carries a sign that reads: "Find out more at: ConIsCorrupt.com/Berkeley." Behind me, a man yells, "Fuck off, you assholes. Scavenger has union jobs." Then he tackles the one with the sign, grabbing him at the knees. They roll on the ground until someone pulls them apart.

Ginsberg, Kisa, and others herd the demonstrators out of the Re-Be yard. The cameras follow. I hear Kisa tell a reporter. "Spaulding is acting on his own. He is not speaking for Re-Be."

Councilmember Womack is talking into a microphone and gesturing toward the table with the dead dog on it, lying amidst the cutlery and dessert plates. Sykes, her aide, stands by her side, straightening his tie.

Inside the front gate, one of the protesters, a colorful burnout known as Jimmy the Scrap Metal Guy, has taken off his mask and is delivering his rant to the cameras. "Yeah, you know, uh, the big garbage companies, they been fighting recyclers for years, now they want to take over. They want it all, you know, don't want no mom-and-pop outfits. It's stupid. They got the big net, us little guys we get what falls out. Yeah, you know, the scraps."

I peek into the hut, thinking Barb might be in there, but it's empty. I race out the gate and see her down the street, sitting in her car with her hands on the steering wheel, the motor running. When she sees me, she backs into the intersection, makes a U-turn, then lurches off toward San Pablo. I chase her waving my arms, but she doesn't slow down.

By the time I return to the banquet, the dog has been wrapped in a tablecloth, rolled into a cardboard box, and left at the gate, where the animal shelter will pick it up in the morning.

I change into shorts and sandals to help with the cleanup. I volunteer to pile the rental chairs in the back of a pickup truck. I take eight trips, the metal of the folding chairs refreshingly cool against my arms.

The sky is dark now, but not black enough for stars. Re-Be's bright perimeter lights cast long shadows. The crew dismantling the stage is in the middle of a heated conversation.

"I'm not going to play the heavy," Ginsberg is saying. "That's not the job of the board. You say you know how to run programs as a collective, fine. But how do you deal with messes like this? Doug. Too sticky. You have an executive director, he or she plays the heavy. That's—"

"We get the point," interrupts Shannon, halfway under the stage with a wrench. She was as instrumental as Kisa in organizing the banquet. "But you—"

"Let me finish," says Ginsberg. "You're opposed to a hierarchy, so what happens? Who plays the boss? The board? Me? I have a full-time job. I have a family. I have a finite amount of time. I want someone on staff, who's here *every* day, to play that role."

"So to make your point," says Shannon, "you're going to sit on the sidelines while we destroy ourselves from within just so—"

"Hey, he didn't say that," says Kisa. "He—"

Shannon turns and snarls at Kisa, who's kneeling under the stage, a cordless drill in her hands. "Kisa, you might want to stay out of this. We all know you're itching to be ED. You—"

"You don't know *what* I want," says Kisa. She sighs, but it's so overstated, I feel embarrassed for her.

"You're not fooling anyone with your coy attitude," says Shannon. "You don't think everyone *knows* you want to be ED? You do, don't you?" Shannon starts off enraged, but sounds more sympathetic with her question. In the shadows, Shannon, with her short brown hair and slight frame, looks like a twelve-year-old boy, with a voice to match.

Kisa pauses with the drill a few inches from a bolt. The crickets keep up their racket and the freeway hums. I've seen plenty of conflict at Re-Be, but never between Shannon and Kisa. I thought they were tight.

"OK, I want it," says Kisa, her voice slow and measured. "Or I did, before tonight. Part of me did anyway. Now can I fire up the drill?"

Ginsberg has stayed silent through this, but he slips in the last word.

"I'm not saying it will be a picnic to fire Doug. It will be brutal and I'm willing to do it. But if we had a hierarchy in place, it might not have come to this."

The drill squeals. I snap a photo of Ginsberg standing with a pile of hex nuts nestled in his cupped palms, looking down at Kisa as she loosens another bolt, his eyes much more those of the worried dad than the lustful swain.

I stay with Kisa after everyone else leaves. After the platforms and tabletops are loaded, the chairs all folded, the dish racks stacked. She and I drink beer in silence. Beer never tasted so good. It soothes my throat and my frayed nerves.

"You up for talking?" I ask. She had promised an interview after the banquet, but that was before the trouble.

"I might say something I regret."

"OK, nothing for publication."

"You promise?"

"Here's what I promise. Anything you say tonight that I'd like to use, I'll come back to you and ask specifically if I *can* use it. If you say no, I'll respect that."

She finishes her beer and opens another one, and tosses the empty underhand into a big blue bin a few feet away. It lands with a plink.

"Shannon and I put months of effort into this event. We were so damn proud of how it came together. We had the TV cameras, the perfect weather, everybody looked so elegant. Just two hours ago, I was thinking about how lucky I am to actually get *paid* doing stuff I love. That feeling's gone. Doug's like a reverse King Midas—he poisons everything he touches. I'd like to poison *him* is what I'd like to do. At least Barb's award was the last of the night."

She takes off her glasses and wipes her eyes. She's changed into a loose-fitting baby blue smock dress with big black buttons and just below the neckline is the word "tolerance" in white lower-case letters. Her fatigue and vulnerability give her face more personality. She looks better than when she was all dolled up. With her curly hair unpinned and her glasses on, she looks like an intense young art student after a long night attacking a canvas.

"Unless we prove otherwise to the board, they're going to force an ED on us. You remember Shannon's line—'the best thing about working in a collective is not having a boss, but it's also the worst thing.' I am really trying to make things work. We all are. Most of us anyway. Losing Barb is huge, but she's still helping us. She was here a few days ago, though she doesn't want anyone to know. She feels guilty leaving us in the lurch." Her shoulders slump. "As if this executive director stuff matters. We could be evicted any day now. I could—"

"Tell me more about the eviction. Any day now? Really?"

"It's a game of chicken. We're three months behind in the rent, but the city is holding up something like five months of reimbursements for curbside. They say we haven't submitted proper documentation. We've already borrowed from somewhere to make payroll, but I shouldn't be telling you that. Anyway, Doug, lunatic Doug, our revolutionary hero—he says it's an empty threat, that the city would look foolish evicting us when they owe us more than we owe them. I dare them, he says. Anyway, there was a deadline of October 1 for resubmitting the reports, and I got us a ten-day extension and then another one. But whatever we turn in won't be good enough because it's a bullshit showdown. The 20th is Tuesday. No more extensions, they say. I guess we're calling their bluff. Damn, I should have known Doug would pull this stunt."

"Don't be blaming yourself," I say, climbing down from the seat of the forklift.

"Is this OK?" I tentatively start massaging her shoulders. I'm not exactly a massage guy, but it's a Re-Be ritual—lots of folks giving each other back rubs. It's one of the things that attracts me to Re-Be. Lots of touching.

"His behavior makes sense now," she says, leaning into my hands.

"The dead dog makes sense?"

"No, no, you see, he was adamantly opposed to us hosting this thing, he said it gave the suits too much legitimacy. Then he let it go. I was so relieved, I didn't think to question his motives. Then he stopped showing up for work. Oooh, that feels good."

She smells so feminine and soft I have this urge to lift up her curly mop of hair and kiss her salty neck.

Barb said to find someone else, and Kisa is cute and smart. But she's opening up to me because I'm listening, not because she wants me to come on to her. She's doing her best to play Barb's role here at Re-Be, but she's not Barb.

"Maybe it's time for me to bail," she says, leaning her head back and resting it on my forehead. "It's too emotionally exhausting. I was so looking forward to tonight. Press harder right below my neck. Can you feel the knot?"

As I press my thumbs into her upper back, a truck pulls into the front entrance.

"It's Doug," whispers Kisa. She sits quietly on the bale that's on the forklift tines. "Let's lay low."

I climb back into the forklift seat, worn and torn and held together with peeling duct tape that tickles my legs.

Doug jumps down from his truck, then struts into the hut.

He flicks on the light switch, then comes out a minute later with several manila folders under his arm. He spots us as he climbs into his truck.

He strolls over, surprising me again with how different he looks without his hair. He's changed from the hazmat suit into black jeans and a white t-shirt.

"What the fuck are you doing here?" It's not a question.

"I work here, Doug," says Kisa, "and I'm happy to inform you, you don't. You're fired."

"Oh, I'm scared now. And who put you in charge?"

"We had an emergency meeting tonight and decided it's time for you to go."

"I don't think so."

"Doug, you ruined our awards banquet. You disappeared for a week. Why do you even *want* to work here?"

"I can see it now. You blame it all on me. You apologize to the corporate criminal. Hunter, you getting this down? 'Re-Be sells out, proffers its ass to Con on a platter.' You'll be out of a job too, sister."

"I am not your sister." Kisa speaks firmly and without restraint, but I hear the alarm bubbling inside her. "If you think we won't—"

"Kisa, he's baiting you," I say. "You can't win unless you don't play."

"Hunter checks in with a devastatingly insightful comment—"

"Doug, I'm not with you on this. *No one* is. What you did was *cruel*—"

"Brian." Kisa interrupts me, gives me a look. Oh yeah, practice what I preach.

Doug's not finished. "Hey Hunter, you see Barb tonight? She looked pretty hot, don't you think?"

I squeeze the forklift steering wheel with my hands.

"You move on her yet? She's got to be horny and ravenous by now—she probably hasn't been fucked in months. You know, now that I think about it, she'd be too much for you. Too huge an appetite."

I swallow. Out of the corner of my eye, I see Kisa clasping her hands tightly, pressing her thumbs together. In the distance, I hear the rumble of a train approaching.

"Well, I'm glad we had this talk." Doug folds his hands like a preacher, then saunters back to his truck and climbs in. I jump off the forklift and chase him.

"Doug, you're totally unhinged," I say when I get to his truck. "You're acting like a truly crazy person. You do know that, right? I'm telling you this because I'm your friend. You're letting your—"

"You don't know anything."

"I know you're hurting."

"She's so cold to me. Like ice. I couldn't melt her with a blowtorch."

His shoulder slumped. "She took Einstein. That dog loved me more than she did."

10.

Boot in Bale

A black-tie awards banquet at a Berkeley recycling facility erupted in violence this evening when a group of hazmat-suited protesters interrupted the festivities by attacking one of the award winners with a dead Labrador retriever in a black plastic bag. We'll be back with live footage after this.

—KRON-TV, October 17, 1998

The Berkeley I live in is a far cry from the mythical "People's Republic of Berzerkeley"—that wacky trapped-in-the-60s city that the mainstream media loves to trivialize. Of course, many of the developments once ridiculed in Berkeley are now civic virtues, right up there with being on the PTA. Like recycling.

Certainly there are more vegetarian bicyclists, Celtic fiddlers, communist poets, lesbian lawyers, disabled activists, and philosopher/general contractors in Berkeley than in your average city in Iowa. And how many Berkeleyans have been arrested for civil disobedience? Arguably thousands.

But pick one of the city's 110,000 denizens at random, and chances are he or she climbs out of bed in the morning, drives to a full-time job, then comes home to eat dinner and zone out in front of the idiot box. Different, but also the same.

And the local TV news, well, what's the word I'm looking for? Awful, that's it. We've got your usual crime stories and "how news promos can be hazardous to your health, tune in at

11" coverage. When Re-Be introduced the "Recycle and Win" program, the only station that covered it gave the usual condescending "only in Berkeley" treatment. At the end of the newscast. The Consolidated Scavenger versus Re-Be battle that I've been writing about hasn't received a second of airtime.

Until Saturday night.

Every news report I catch gives heavy play to the awards protest, mostly the clip of Doug heaving the dead dog.

The cameras caught Barb in a closeup as she broke down. It's heartbreaking to watch. That sequence is played so many times, it wouldn't shock me to see some station play it in slow motion with color commentary. "Here, the dog carcass slides onto the table amidst the dessert plates. Barb Genessee turns away, steels herself, and charges Spaulding. There's teammate Kisa Bettis running interference, setting up for the block. But wait, Genessee's knees are buckling. She's about to collapse. Let's look at it from the reverse angle."

In their wildest dreams, Kisa and Shannon could not have imagined this much coverage. Of course, the awards themselves and the black ties and tabletops on bales of newsprint serve as no more than colorful backdrop to Doug's toxic theatrics.

By Tuesday, the aftershocks have subsided, but Doug is still AWOL, and Barb isn't returning my calls.

In all the coverage, Barb is clearly portrayed as the victim and Doug the heartless aggressor, but the footage is so intimate and humiliating, it's no wonder Barb has cloistered herself. The video clip makes my 200-word Barb-Doug fight sequence in the *Beat* look tame.

I try to reach Doug, but can't. He's been "officially" terminated, but if his unwillingness to accept Barb leaving him is any harbinger, he's not likely to go gently into the night. That has everyone at Re-Be on edge.

Turns out no one knows where he lives. Until he stopped

showing up at work, Doug was at Re-Be all the time, even many evenings and weekends. When Barb booted him from their house, he house-sat in the Oakland hills for a former Re-Be board member, but no one knows where he went from there.

His van, which used to be at Re-Be all the time, is missing too.

I leave him two messages at work, try him on email as well. I also send him an email from my studio neighbor's account, with a return receipt attached so I might fool him into opening it. He doesn't.

I send a letter to Doug's box at the West Berkeley Post Office. Tuesday morning, there's mail in the box. By late afternoon, it's gone. I don't have the patience to lurk at the post office all day.

Tuesday night before I go to sleep, there's an email from Doug. "Check out Re-Be ASAP. More rat-fucking coming."

When I arrive at the Re-Be yard early Wednesday morning, I don't see anyone outside, except some guy I don't recognize over at the buyback scales. I peek in the hut. It's empty, so I drift over to Doug's desk, which is uncharacteristically neat. On the right side of the desk a single stack of file folders and papers is piled four inches high. The top sheet, under an unwashed "Recyclers Do It Over and Over Again" coffee mug, is a things-to-do list with about twenty items. When I click on the desk lamp, nothing happens, but the sun is bright enough I can read the page when I lift it. "Call Rodriguez at BPD for poacher data," says the first item. Next it says, "Check with S&S re: rerouting on Shasta."

The top of the page is neatly printed, in block letters, all caps. As I skim down, the printing deteriorates and it's mostly scrawled in Doug's tiny, tight handwriting.

I open the top right drawer, see a yellow ruled pad. The door hinges squeak.

"What do you think you're doing?"

I whip around. It's Renée, who does outreach for Re-Be's

job-training program.

"Oh, hi, Renée. I didn't hear you come in. I missed you at the awards banquet."

Renée is tall and snooty with short-straight blond hair, and a clump of earrings in one ear. When I first met her and her hair was long and lush, I thought she was beautiful—the hair softened her. Now with her severe cut, she's striking, but not as pretty.

"Out," she says. "Get out."

"You don't understand," I say. "Doug sent me this email, urging me to come by—"

She glares at me, her eyes unblinking.

"I don't get it," I say. "Doug hasn't shown up in more than a week. I know you're trying to fire him, but how can you fire him if you can't find him. I mean, aren't you concerned about where he is? I don't mean you personally, but—"

"You're right. I don't care. Let him stay missing. But I do care that you vacate the premises now."

"You're not speaking for the collective," I say. "I'm sure this is fine with Kisa." I'm not sure, but even though I don't fully grasp the rules at Re-Be, or lack thereof, I know that one person is rarely empowered to speak for the group without a tacit agreement. Never stops Doug, of course.

But then Kisa rushes into the hut followed by Shannon and Ray. "You know how the fax wasn't working," she says to Renée. "Bunch of electrical wires got cut. By the circuit box."

They race back across the yard, and I follow them, after slipping the yellow pad from Doug's drawer into my pack.

On a wooden post behind the scales, four fat wires dangle from the bottom of a rusty metal electrical box. Freshly cut, the copper wires sticking out of the plastic sheathing are still shiny. Two red, two black. Kisa leans closer, her hands clasped behind her back, her nose a few inches from the wires.

"Easy enough to fix, I suppose," she says, "but we'd better

call the police."

Then it gets crazier. We're walking back toward the hut when Miguel strides toward us, his long-limbed body pumping, his jaw taut. Apparently, several reporters just called asking for Re-Be's reaction to a Consolidated Scavenger "takeover memo." One from KCBS, another from the *Contra Costa Times*. Kisa suggests an emergency meeting.

"Sounds like Doug's takeover conspiracy is coming down," Shannon says. "But he was the only one who was following this closely."

"Actually, I've been covering all this recycling wars stuff," I say. "I could—"

But Renée thrusts her hand in my face. "You are not invited."

"Look," I say. "I've been writing about this for two months now. If KCBS has this takeover memo, what I write isn't going to matter much, but—"

Kisa interrupts. "Brian, Renée doesn't want you at the meeting."

"But I—"

"And I agree with her."

They convene in the hut. I turn a bucket over, sit on it. It's too hot. I find some shade and move there. I hate waiting.

I pull out the pad I took from Doug's desk. The notes on the top of the first page are in blue.

POACHERS + MAP + ENFORCER (?) = LESS POACHING IN OAKLAND, MORE IN BERKELEY. CREDIBILITY? MONEY?

ENFORCER = OLD OAKLAND DISPOSAL THUGS? OMBUDSMAN? JONO RETIRED?

WHERE DO NFBs FIT IN?
WHAT ABOUT PLANS FOR RE-BE PARCEL?

Below are a couple lines in black.

RAT-FUCKING:
JULIAN? >> ENFORCER >> KNOW-NOTHING THUGS?
(COULD JIMMY BE PLAYING BOTH SIDES?)

The next several pages are ripped out. I see the impression of writing on the next blank page—Doug pressed hard with his pen. I try to decipher the words. Can't.

Despite interviewing dozens of people and researching far more than my $200-a-story job can justify, I feel like there's a deeper, darker story going on underneath that I'm missing. I can only see its shadow. Maybe it's just a delusion hatched from Doug's paranoia, but I don't think so. Doug seems intent on destroying Re-Be in the guise of saving it, but that doesn't mean he isn't onto something.

OK, the wires got cut. How did the intruder get in? I walk along the fence, look up at the top, maybe there's another scrap of fabric speared on the shards of glass. Rabbit has roused himself and he follows me around several stacks of bales. I heard on the radio this morning that the longshore workers called a strike and I wonder if that's why there are so many bales piled in the yard. Re-Be sells a big fraction of its aluminum and paper to China.

I'm restless and impatient, but order myself to go slow, to pay attention. The sun keeps getting hotter. Every few steps, I stop and look around, trying to see this familiar recycling yard with fresh eyes, as if I have parachuted into a foreign country. I look for the telling detail that I can use in my story, push myself to "see."

That's when I notice the flies buzzing around a bale of aluminum, and, when I walk closer, an inch of black shoelace hanging from the edge of the bale. Rabbit approaches the bale, sniffs, then barks. I swipe at the flies and tug on the lace. A flattened Pepsi can clatters to the ground. Behind the can I see a tiny patch of black, the size of a quarter. I touch it with my finger. It's not aluminum. It's softer, warmer, more like plastic or rubber, like the tread of a tire, the sole of a shoe.

I find a brick by the fence and hammer it on the side of the bale. Several more cans loosen and fall. I probe with two fingers. Now I can see the tread of a boot.

I hammer several more times with the brick, the sharp corners digging into my palm, then pry away a few more flattened cans with my fingertips. I used to have callouses when I played the guitar, but my fingers feel soft and tender. This could take all day.

I poke my nose into the cavity and sniff. Just the usual sticky sweet soda smell.

I need something more efficient than a brick and my uncalloused fingers. I run over to the nearby shed and search the closets. Nothing. I find a white plastic bucket and swing it against the side of the bale. The bucket cracks. I grab the brick again with both hands and strike the cans with a downward motion, and enough cans fall that a heel becomes visible. Inside a dirty yellow hexagon is the letter "R" in a black slab serif.

I run to the hut and knock on the door.

Kisa answers.

I tell her I found a boot in a bale. "This might be nothing, but, you know, with the wires cut and everything, I think it might be more than nothing."

We walk, then run across the yard. When we get to the bale, she pulls a utility knife from her belt, opens a screwdriver blade, and wiggles it under the heel of the boot. A few more cans shake loose, but the boot doesn't budge.

"We should wait for the police," she says. "Miguel called them about the cut wires."

I know we're thinking the same thing.

"Should we tell the others?" I ask.

"Let's wait until the police take a look."

But she changes her mind, because after she returns to the hut, everyone else rushes out. But they don't know where to go. There are bales all over the yard.

"The police should be here any minute now," says Kisa, who's standing in the doorway. "Let's wait here, by the hut."

"What, are you nuts?" says Renée. "We're supposed to stand around and make small talk. Brian, where is it?"

I start to point, then stop at the sound of tires crunching down the driveway into the yard. A black and white Berkeley police cruiser rolls into view.

I remember I have my camera in my pack. I take a shot of Kisa and Shannon conferring with the two officers who get out of the car, a beefy young white guy with red hair and a thin Asian woman closer to my age, with short black hair and glasses with black frames, the Laurel to her partner's Hardy.

Kisa leads them first to the buyback area to show them the cut wires. It's on the way. She has to convince them not to linger there, but to follow her to the bale. "We saw a boot stuck in there and we're afraid there might be a foot inside it." That gets the officers moving.

Everyone crowds around the bale and the stocky officer waves his arm to keep us back. I take one picture, then realize I only have five or six left, so I stop.

"I've got a crowbar and some hammers here," says Shannon, who has run back to join us. "And we can lift off the top two bales if you like."

Kisa drives the bale clamp in, lifts the top two bales, and places them a few feet away. She moves the adjacent stacks so the bale with the boot stands alone on top of a stack of three. At eye level.

My stomach gurgles. A crow caws. Sweat drizzles down my back. I want to be wrong about this.

The beefy cop snips the wire strap around the bale, then wedges the crowbar below the heel of the boot and pulls it toward him, opening up the cavity. I stand behind Renée and two others on my tiptoes, but the officer, built like a linebacker, blocks my view. I hear the voices in front of me gasp in harmony.

I crane my neck and catch a glimpse of a red sock sticking out of the top of the boot.

"Back up everyone, please," the officer says. "This is now a crime scene."

The policewoman nudges us back and speaks into the radio on her shoulder. Then she goes to the car and pulls a roll of yellow do-not-cross tape and marks off an area around the bales.

Two plainclothes officers, both middle-aged black men with mustaches, arrive a minute later, confer with the uniformed officers, then expand the cordoned off area so we're the width of a basketball court from the stack of bales. Through my telephoto lens, I watch them don plastic gloves and cut a hole in the sock with metal clippers, revealing a patch of gray-pink that I assume is an ankle. Two more uniformed officers arrive with suitcases.

It takes about ten minutes—five in conference, then another five with the crowbar, hammer, and cutters—before they break the block open and a body tumbles out. I take my last two pictures.

11.

Recycle or Die

"When recycling re-emerged in the 1970s," says Re-Be's Spaulding, "the organized crime cartels that were hauling trash just slapped a coat of green paint and some recycling logos on their trucks and carried on with business as usual."

—Brian Hunter, "The End of Garbage,"
East Bay Beat, October 21, 1998

I can't see his face, but I know it's Doug.

Because of his long, gangly limbs, which sprawl on the pavement when he falls from the bale. Because of his oil-stained "Recycle or Die" t-shirt. Because of his shaved head.

Because I knew already.

I inhale through my nose and I think I detect a hint of decay, and then realize it's the rich, earthy bouquet from the compost facility on the far side of the yard. I don't see any blood, though the back of his head looks purplish.

I've never seen a dead body before. It's surreal. I don't know what I'm feeling.

For a few seconds, it feels like someone has pressed the mute button and the yard is silent. In Aquatic Park on the other side of the railroad tracks, children are whooping in play. A motorcycle squeals. A police siren gets louder.

Police officers with gloves, clipboards, and cameras surround the body. One mumbles into a radio on his shoulder. The rest of us strain behind the yellow tape. Next to me, Kisa takes deep breaths, removes her glasses, and rubs her eyes. Miguel makes a small sign of the cross with his index finger and mutters under his breath. "The poor bastard."

The sun, directly overhead, sizzles.

One of the plainclothes officers approaches us. He pauses before he speaks.

"Any of you know who this person is?"

Lots of nods.

"I'd like one of you to come with me to make a preliminary identification. Is someone in charge?"

Kisa looks to Shannon, then Miguel. "Can two of us do it?" she asks.

The detective shrugs, lifts the yellow tape and Kisa and Shannon duck under it and walk around the body, keeping their distance. Kisa points toward us.

A few minutes later, another police officer introduces himself to me as Roberto Puma. He asks me how I found the body. He's lean and wiry, the same build as me, but older, darker.

I ask if I can get something to drink first. "My throat's really dry." We walk to the portable where I fill a mug with water from the sink. "Do you want some water, too?" I ask.

"I'm fine," he says. Then he wipes his forehead. "Actually, yes, it's a scorcher out there."

We sit on folding chairs in a corner of the trailer next to a table piled high with books and papers. On the wall are maps of Berkeley with pins and flags and post-it notes with numbers written on them.

"My first thought about the flies," I tell him, "was that maybe a rat or possum had been trapped. A while back, someone found a nest of baby possums in a corner by the baling shed. Then I saw the shoelace."

"You knew Doug Spaulding?"

"I did."

"At what point did you think it might be him inside the bale?"

"Well, there's been a lot of tension around here lately, and Doug was just fired, and he hadn't returned my phone calls, so I guess the possibility was there pretty quickly."

I tell him about the dead-dog incident, which he's heard about. "So the guy who threw the dog, that was Spaulding?"

"Right."

He asks a few more questions, stopping after each one to write. The clock on the wall ticks. I bite my fingernail. But I stop after one. Puma writes left-handed, and slowly. He asks me to read and sign a statement. As we head back out to the blazing sun, I mention I've been writing newspaper stories about the conflict between Recycle Berkeley and Consolidated Scavenger and give him copies of two recent clips.

The body's been moved. I walk toward the hut tentatively, assuming that others have gathered there, but not sure if I'll be allowed in. I see Shannon shake hands with two police officers outside the baling warehouse and I wait for her.

"How are you holding up?" I ask.

"Not so hot," she says. "I showed them how the baler works. They wanted to know if someone could accidentally fall in."

I follow Shannon to the hut. I decide not to tell her that someone *could* fall in, that I had, though it wasn't exactly accidental.

Inside, I spot Barb, across the crowded room, leaning forward with statue-like stillness, resting her chin on her hands. How did she get here so fast? I guess if there's no traffic, it's only a ten-minute drive from downtown Oakland. (Because I don't have a car, it's easy to forget that most people do.)

Though she's sitting by her former desk, she looks out of place in her business suit and black-rimmed glasses. Shannon goes over and hugs her. I want to, but my feet won't take me there. I hang back, sit on a file cabinet. I don't want to call attention to myself, don't want anyone to ask me to leave.

Shannon explains that the police wanted to know how many people knew how to operate the baler and there were so many she couldn't name them all. Re-Be hosted several open houses and invited guests to run some of the equipment and the baler was second in popularity behind the forklift. Barb's idea. Just about every city council member climbed into the baler "cockpit" and pushed a few buttons. I did too.

When she finishes, no one says anything.

Renée rushes in to fill the void.

"I feel terrible about this," she says, "especially because the last couple times I've connected with Doug have been so yucky. He was being mean and snarly, I mean, it feels like there's all this unfinished business with him and now—"

"Hey, girl, you're not the only one," says Shannon. "I called him some nasty names after the stunt with the dog."

Kisa jumps up and looks at Renée, then Shannon. "Can you hear yourselves?" she asks, her arms lifted in a what-kind-of-bullshit-is-this gesture. "This is not about *you!* So what if you had a fight with him? We're supposed to feel bad for you? You never even liked him." She starts out talking to Shannon and Renée, but directs that last sentence to Renée.

"If anyone should—" then Kisa stops abruptly. But not before she's rotated her head ever so slightly toward Barb and carried the rest of the room with her.

All eyes turn toward Barb, then, almost as quickly, turn away. No one looks at her directly.

The refrigerator in the corner growls. Apparently, the cut wires knocked out two circuits, one in the hut. An extension cord and a power strip have been rigged up to get everything running again.

Barb's face is ashen, her body slack. Even in the crowded hut, it seems like everyone is giving her extra personal space.

If the eyes are the windows to the soul, Barb has drawn the curtains. She's clutching her knees to her chest and staring into space. I've been trying, without success, to make eye contact with her. Kisa and Shannon sit together, shoulders touching, heads down.

Everyone seems to be moving at half speed, as if underwater, speaking deliberately, pausing between words, looking at each other. Interrupting is the norm at Re-Be, so the politeness is eerie, the way the freeway is when it's empty on Super Bowl Sunday. The silences get longer.

So when we hear footsteps and muffled voices coming toward the hut, we eagerly turn to the door. David Ginsberg and fellow board member Mitchell Yong carry in pizzas, sourdough baguettes, and bottles of wine and mineral water. Jenny, Miguel's wife, arrives a few minutes later with a basket of cantaloupes and mangos.

We descend on the food. There's a lot of talk about how perfectly ripe the fruit is. The bubbly water calms my stomach. I'm surprised how good it feels to grip the cool glass bottle.

Pretty soon, there are twenty-five of us jammed in the hut, sitting on desks, leaning against file cabinets. The ceiling fan keeps it cool, but does little to dissipate the smell of too many warm bodies in too small a space. The phones, which were unplugged earlier, now ring incessantly.

I've seen far too much contention and chaos to romanticize Re-Be, but in the darkness of that impossibly bright and blazing afternoon, everyone seems to have dropped their personal agendas as easily as unbuttoning their shirts. For at least a long moment, the potential for community that Re-Be so often fails to realize blossoms. The food helps. I don't feel like an intruder. I feel like I belong, like I'm part of the family.

I was a friend of Doug's and he didn't have many actual friends. Now he's gone, but instead of grieving for him, instead of missing him, I'm savoring the feeling of being included. I convince myself that doesn't make me self-centered, just normal.

The hut's thick walls insulate us from the heat, and it feels like we're in a secret clubhouse in the bosom of a cool, leafy tree. Light from the picture window and six tube skylights floods the room.

One of the uniformed officers, a tall and wiry black woman with short reddish hair, knocks on the open hut door and asks for our attention. She introduces herself as Marion Falls and speaks in a low, rich voice.

"We've talked with some of you already, but we'd like to talk with all of you. Unfortunately, you're going to have to leave because this facility is now a crime scene. We've received permission to search the premises for potential evidence, so we're going to adjourn to the police bus substation parked outside the gate. We'd like to conduct more interviews there. As you leave, I'd like to get your name and contact information and your relationship to Mr. Spaulding or Recycle Berkeley. No one here is under suspicion, but we do need your help. At this point, you know more about the victim than we do."

Barb rises slowly, stiffly. As she approaches the door, I step in front of her and give her the hug I wanted to give her earlier. "I've been thinking about you," I whisper. "I'm sure this must be hard for you." She wraps her arms around me and pulls tight, then lets go almost instantly. She looks at me solidly in the eyes, her face solemn. I see a glimmer of connection—I'm not just some stranger—but it might only be what I want to see. Then she lifts her shoulders and walks past me, her stride firm and purposeful.

Miguel has blocked the door and is demanding to know

who's given the police permission to search the yard. Apparently, they don't have a warrant.

Falls looks at her clipboard.

"We have a 'consent to search' signed by a Mr. David Ginsberg, Recycle Berkeley board of directors president, and witnessed by Shannon Goss and Kisa Bettis, executed 1:45 pm."

"But wait, who gave them—?"

But before Miguel finishes, a TV cameraperson and reporter rush through the door of the hut.

They're looking for me.

Over the next hour or two, I repeat my story about finding the boot in the bale six or seven times. I've got a pretty polished narrative by the time I'm finished and I manage to implicate Consolidated Scavenger without making any unsubstantiated claims: "With all the noise Doug Spaulding was making about Scavenger's plans to take over Re-Be, I would think the police would want to look into how this murder might be connected."

It's exhilarating, but exhausting.

In front of the police bus outside the Re-Be gates, Daria Reeves, the *Chronicle* reporter, asks me if I have photographs of the body and practically leaps into my arms when I say I do.

Fortunately, one of my bookkeeping clients is a struggling young photographer who's been developing my film in exchange for me keeping her books. I find her at home, in her loft a few blocks from Re-Be, and after the briefest of pleasantries and explanations, she grabs my camera and says she'll have scans in my email box in half an hour, how's that for right away?

I reach the photo editor at the *Chronicle*, tell her Daria Reeves has referred me, that I have shots no one else has. I have no idea what the going rate for photos is—I'm about to ask for $250 when I get a sudden case of confidence and tell her $500. "Let me see what you've got," she says. She doesn't shriek about the price.

The first photo that comes in over email is my last shot—

Doug's body crumpled on the pavement in front of the bale. But the next scan, which shows the boot poking out of the bale, framed by two officers wielding crowbars, is far more chilling. I forward them both to the *Chronicle* editor, say more are coming. She calls me immediately and says how about $600 for all of them.

Then I bicycle to the police station downtown. Puma, the detective I talked to earlier, had asked me to answer a few more questions and I agreed to come up. The entrance to the station is like a fortress—I'm buzzed through two doors before I get to the receptionist, then a few minutes later, Puma comes out a steel door and beckons me to follow him.

We sit in a small conference room with a window that opens into an airshaft. The air smells stale. A young blond man with a neatly trimmed goatee joins us. I didn't see him at Re-Be in the morning. He slips into a chair next to Puma, across from me, and opens a spiral notebook.

"Officer Wallace here is going to take notes," says Puma. He pauses. "Pretty wild day, huh?"

I nod.

Then Puma asks some innocuous questions like my address and occupation, my relationship with Doug, and so on. Some of this I answered earlier in the portable.

Wallace passes his partner a photocopy of my *Beat* story—"This Time It's Personal"—the one Barb got so justifiably angry about. I cringe. I know what's coming.

"You observed Mr. Spaulding and Ms. Genessee argue at her office. Were there other times?"

"They had an argumentative relationship when they were together, and he was angry with her after they split up, but I can't believe she would get violent."

"Did they physically fight?"

"No, it was verbal sparring. They would disagree with each

other at meetings, for example."

Puma asks me about the breakup and how that played out. He's brisk and businesslike—he doesn't smile, just nods, pauses, then asks the next question.

"Would you characterize their relationship as abusive?"

"Why are you asking all these questions about Barb and Doug, and none about Consolidated Scavenger and their takeover plan? That's far more likely to be where you'll find the murderer."

"Would you characterize the relationship as abusive?"

I don't know if Doug ever hit her—it's not that I can't believe he would as much as I can't believe she would stay if he had— but "abusive" is the *exact* adjective I would use to describe his treatment of her.

"No," I say. "They argued a lot."

"Are you sure you didn't see them fight other times?"

"No, only that time in Barb's office."

The detective puts down his notebook and looks at me. I look down at my hands, and when I raise my head, he locks onto my eyes and holds them as tightly as if he had grabbed me by the ears.

As he stares at me, a Re-Be meeting I attended when I was helping with the bookkeeping flashes through my mind. This was an earlier instance when the public works department was holding back its reimbursements to Re-Be, and Barb threw up her hands in exasperation. "The city would not be on our ass," she said, "if Doug weren't perpetually late with the tonnage reports."

Doug retorted, "Thank you, Mother Theresa. We sinners look to you for guidance."

Barb said, "Fuck you."

Doug said, "Oooh, the wit rises in the east."

I was aghast, but Barb didn't blink. Nor did anyone else. And this was *before* they broke up.

Puma snaps me back to attention. "Look, Mr. Hunter, we

know you're holding onto something you're not telling us. You're a material witness because you found the body, but you're not on the witness stand. You're not a suspect. I read your stories. You seem like the kind of person who believes in doing the right thing. You have a strong sense of morality. You're protecting someone."

Well, yes, I am the kind of person who believes in doing the right thing, but I've promised Barb I won't write about her personal squabbles with Doug again, and the right thing to do is extend that promise to talking to the police.

I speak slowly and respectfully. "I'm happy to answer your questions, but there's a much bigger picture here that you're ignoring—I mean, Re-Be is being threatened by Consolidated Scavenger, by the Berkeley City Council, by the city public works department, and Doug was speaking out against all that stuff. The stakes are high—if Scavenger gets the Berkeley contract, and they run a few other competitors off, they'll have a Bay Area monopoly worth tens of millions of dollars. Millions, anyway."

Puma and Wallace remain impassive. Wait.

"What I mean is that Doug was a prickly personality. He clashed with a lot of people. He was leading the charge to expose this takeover attempt. He's made enemies."

Again they wait. So do I.

"Some people you have in mind?" asks Puma, quietly. He slides a piece of paper to me, then a pen.

"I'm not suggesting these people would kill someone. Scavenger is a large company and I've only talked to a few people."

Puma doesn't say anything.

"I don't feel comfortable naming names."

"We're only looking for people to talk with," he says.

I look past him to a wall full of photographs of old men. Puma looks at me, unwavering.

"What if they ask who told you to talk to them?" I ask.

"We don't answer that question."

"OK, well, there are two men at Scavenger who have had run-ins with Doug. Julian Allard is one. He works in Oakland. The other is Tom Herman. He's a vice president, based in Walnut Creek. There's also someone Doug called 'the enforcer.' I don't know his name, but he's some old-timer who's been around since way before Scavenger bought the company and he used to rough people up when, well, I don't know, when they didn't pay or something. In the old days, the garbage biz was linked to organized crime, and it's cleaner than it used to be, but there's still less than legal stuff going on. In Ohio, there's documented evidence that two operatives from this private security firm poured sugar into gas tanks of strikers. Whether or not they'd kill someone is another story."

Wallace is not writing this down.

"Ms. Genessee works for Consolidated Scavenger," says Puma, "is that correct?"

"Yes, that's true," I say, trying to mask the hesitation in my voice, "but she just started, so she wouldn't have any power to design a takeover."

"Mr. Hunter, in your newspaper account, you show Mr. Spaulding trying to make Ms. Genessee feel guilty about working for Consolidated Scavenger, correct?"

He keeps circling back to the Barb-Doug conflict, and there's this newspaper story right in front of him with the snippet from Barb's office, and I can't believe I convinced myself it was OK to write about it.

"And your relationship with Ms. Genessee?"

"We're friends."

"No romantic intentions?"

I hesitate.

"I like her, but we've never, you know, gone anywhere with that."

Puma raises his eyebrows. I feel like the cliché in the movies. My lips are dry, my forehead sweaty, my underarms clammy.

"I wouldn't be writing about the petty squabbles she had with Doug if I was romantically interested, would I? Plus, I was married until recently, until July."

Then Wallace looks up from his notebook and speaks for the first time.

"Detective Puma says we've eliminated you as a suspect. But if you're protecting Ms. Genessee, you are an accessory to a murder."

His reproachful tone catches me by surprise.

"Barb couldn't have done it," I say. "I understand the ex is always a suspect, but you don't know her. She's a peace activist. She facilitates nonviolence trainings. Yes, she might argue with Doug, but it's all words. Making distinctions. Barb would say it was hot and Doug would say it was only 67 degrees, that's not hot. I never, *ever,* saw *any* indication that she would physically hurt him."

They ask me about Doug's relationship with other folks at Re-Be, specifically Ginsberg, Kisa, Shannon, and Miguel. I say he infuriated everyone with his stunt at the awards banquet, but I don't know much beyond that.

Then Wallace asks me: "And you, where were you last night?"

The same severe tone. I speak calmly, carefully.

"I was at home, at my studio, where I've been staying. You said I'm not a suspect. What's going on? Was last night when he was killed?"

"You live a few minutes away from the Recycle Berkeley facility?"

"Yes, but—" I pause to take a breath. "It's four blocks."

They grill me about what I was reading, the music I was listening to, whether anyone could corroborate that I was home.

I prepared myself. Rehearsed what to say if they threw my

past at me. I had an explanation for living in my warehouse, but I hadn't prepared to be treated like a suspect. I was looking forward to giving them leads about the Scavenger takeover, imagining they would be grateful. I don't know if I'm more upset because of how they're treating me or because of what they're insinuating about Barb.

"I'm telling you the truth. I came here to help. I have no reason to hurt Doug. He had enemies out there. I was one of his friends."

"How did it come about," says Wallace, who appears to be enjoying my discomfort, "that you showed up at Recycle Berkeley at such an opportune time this morning to find the body? Convenient timing, wouldn't you say?"

"Doug suggested I come by. I forgot to mention that. I got an email from him last night, suggesting I come by the yard because there might be some sabotage. Those cut wires, remember?" Now I'm angry. "I've been to Re-Be many times. Mostly nothing happens. No, he didn't say sabotage. He said 'rat-fucking.'"

Wallace stares at me.

"I'm not going to answer any more questions." I push back my chair and stand. "I came here on my own time to provide information and you're making me feel like I'm under suspicion. You had my goodwill. Not any more."

"You do have a police record," Wallace says, holding up a piece of paper. His tone is less harsh now. "We're looking at all the possibilities."

"That's ancient history. Charges dropped. An aberration. My only encounter with the police. Ever. I've never even gotten a moving violation. Why is that still on my record?"

12.

Bad Habits Die Hard

Police say death was caused by a blow to the head with a blunt instrument, probably a piece of wood, and that Mr. Spaulding was dead before he was crushed in the baler.
—KTVU News, October 21, 1998

Once, while we were unloading groceries from the car on a rainy afternoon, Eileen said to me that she had mistaken my unhappiness for depth.

Ouch.

So I *know* Eileen is *absolutely* the *last* person in the universe to seek comfort from. But bad habits die hard.

She lives in the rented house we shared for six years, a humble bungalow with lots of windows and not much insulation. Two yard signs flank the front walk. "Holden for School Board" in turquoise and orange, and "Yes on EE" in lime and black.

She answers the door, opens her arms wide, and gives me a hug.

"B, oh God, come in. I heard the news. Good to see you, *glood* to see you. You look like you could use a drink."

Glood, that's an encouraging sign. An oldie. Her young nephew used to mix up glad and good, and we adopted the new word for ourselves.

"Are you OK?" She puts her hand on my shoulder. I pull away. I keep forgetting that she's not angry with me, she's just *done* with me. We're still married in the eyes of the state of California and the county of Alameda. Not in hers.

"I hope it's OK to stop by. I didn't know where else to go."

She walks into the kitchen, opening and closing her hands. Because of her chronic wrist pain, she's always doing wrist exercises. Short and well built with hair between brown and blond, she can look foxy or mousy depending on how her hair is behaving and whether she's wearing glasses or contacts. Today, she looks pretty, but weary.

She gives me a whiskey sour in a blue tumbler and sits across from me at the café table in the kitchen. "Tell me what happened. I only know what I saw on TV."

I don't want to start with the body falling out of the bale—that feels too melodramatic—and I don't assume she's read my stories, so I start at the beginning, with the recycling wars and how Doug demanded I expose Con's imminent takeover and impending monopoly. I'm all over the map and backward and forward, but she's following. I tell her how shaken up I am by the police interrogation. "They kept asking me about whether I'd seen Barb and Doug fighting and I remembered so many arguments, but I just couldn't tell them. It felt like I would be betraying Barb."

I study my thumbs, twist a napkin around them. Eileen pours me another drink.

"You like her, don't you? Barb."

"Yeah, I do." I start to qualify, but then I don't.

"You've liked her for a long time." It's not a question. "You know she's in my Pilates class."

"I didn't."

"I'm in *her* class, actually. I just started going. I like Barb too. Though I never respected her until she left Doug. What took her so damn long? The police are certainly going to be knocking on her door."

"You think she did it?"

"How would I know? But I mean, Doug practically *tortured* her, didn't he?"

"Doug tortured a lot of people."

"Like who?"

"I feel like I'm back at the police station."

"I bet they didn't serve you whiskey sours."

"I might have told them more if they did."

I tell her about Herman and Julian, but when I mention the alleged organized crime connection, and how Doug was convinced Con hired thugs to puncture his tires, she rolls her eyes.

"Let's put it this way," I say. "Doug's on a lot of people's enemies lists. Not just out there in the world. At Re-Be, too. Especially Kisa. And Ginsberg maybe too."

She tells me she heard Doug threatened Ginsberg and accused him of being an infiltrator.

"How do you know all this?"

"Small world, B. I'm helping out with Gluckman's campaign, remember?" I know Gluckman and Ginsberg are cousins, but don't know how close they are. I rarely see my cousins.

I start to tell her about Ginsberg taking me aside at the banquet, but realize I've been talking almost nonstop, and that now might be a good time to thank her for listening so patiently and ask how she is.

When I do, she leans back in her chair and smiles. "Guess who called me."

I give her a quizzical look.

"Joaquin. He asked me out."

"*My* Joaquin?" The other singer/songwriter in the band. The one who almost burned down the warehouse. That Joaquin.

"He heard I was unattached."

"You're going out with him?" I say, with as much incredulousness as I can.

"No, of course not, but I was flattered he asked."

"That's the kind of shit that drives me crazy. You know him. He's totally irresponsible. He's a flake. He's—"

"I turned him down. Relax."

"You said you were flattered."

"Brian, you really don't get it, do you?" She throws up her hands. "I can already hear you whining, 'Women don't appreciate nice guys. They only like assholes.' *Wrong!* We do prefer, I do prefer nice guys, but men, not babies. Joaquin told me straight out he found me attractive and interesting and wondered if I wanted to get together sometime. I can't even *imagine* you saying that."

"That's not fair or true."

"Maybe not fair, but it's true."

"You'd be surprised." But I say that under my voice, more for myself than for her. "But tell me this—and I don't know why the hell I'm asking *you*—but why would a self-respecting woman go out with Joaquin? He's dishonest and untrustworthy. Yet he's always getting laid."

"It's simple, B. He asks. Without apologizing. He leads with charm, not weakness."

"You might call it charm. I'd—" I watch her as she licks her lips after finishing her drink.

"You look good," I say.

"Huh?" She wraps both hands around her empty glass, as if to keep warm.

"I find you attractive," I say. "Please note: I am asking you if you want to make love. Now."

She laughs. "I didn't mean for you to take me so literally. You haven't finished your drink."

I finish it, then summon my best Humphrey Bogart lilt. "There's thousands of bars I can get a drink in. But you are one of a kind."

"I'm flattered, B, but let it go. You've made your point."

"Is that a no?"

"That's a no. But I'm not offended you asked."

"I'm not offended you said no."

Truth be told, I'm relieved. I don't know why I propositioned her. Our sex life, the intercourse part of it anyway, had soured. That's an understatement. She said to me once, and I quote: "You come too soon and you don't satisfy me."

Not what I want on my tombstone.

"How about a massage?" I say. *Just* a massage.

Sex with Eileen was good when we first met, but then got awkward and complicated. When she got pregnant, we decided to get married, but then she miscarried. We went ahead with the wedding, and ironically, one of our biggest problems then became *trying* to get pregnant. She monitored her cycles, we had sex on schedule. Sex became a chore.

But she always liked massages.

"*Just* a massage would be excellent."

Her bedroom walls are still painted the creamy beige I slapped on shortly after we moved in. Where there used to be a photo of Eileen and me in front of Yosemite Falls, now there's a Picasso print. One of his blue women.

On her bedside table is a stack of books and a bottle of Johnnie Walker Red. One side of her bed is covered with a pile of folded clothes, which she scoops up and drops into a basket.

I reach behind a curtain and push up a window. The neighbor's dog barks and rustles in the bushes. All of a sudden Eileen feels like a stranger. I'm not sure why I offered the massage.

She spreads a floral sheet across the bed, then goes to her dresser to get a white bottle of almond oil. She undresses and stretches out on her stomach. I start kneading her back.

"You are getting very relaxed," I say, rubbing oil in small circles on her neck and shoulders. "You're body feels heavy, but not because you're fat, he hastens to add, but because you are sinking into the welcoming arms of mother Earth. Your body is at peace. Just imagine I can keep doing this without laughing."

Eileen has led me through guided visualizations many times, but I've never done one for her. I feel like I'm spouting gibberish, but she's sighing in what seems to be pleasure, so I continue. She has a tight spot next to her shoulder blade that I work on for a few minutes with my thumb and fingers.

I press with my palms on the knot. Her elbows are bent along her sides and she's arching her back into my palms and moaning. She wriggles like she's trying to shake the knot loose. I bite my upper lip and squeeze my eyes shut as I lean into her with more of my weight.

I haven't had this much touching since forever, other than some quick hugs and those all too fleeting kisses with Barb. I want so much to lie down and wrap myself in Eileen's arms. I squeeze my eyes shut, push out everything but the sweet almond fragrance and the feel of Eileen's back.

"Brian, Brian, stop, you're hurting me."

I open my eyes, relax my arms.

She twists her back, turns her face. "Are you crying? Are you OK?"

I see a teardrop slide down her back.

"No, no, I'm not OK."

"What is it?" She says it as if she cares.

"The poor son-of-a-bitch. Doug. He alienated everyone, burned bridges with abandon. I'm not saying he deserved it or anything, but he was headed for a wreck. Something was going to happen. Someone was going to get hurt. I saw it coming, but so did anyone paying attention. No one did anything."

"It's fine to cry," she says. "Good even. *Glood.*"

I shake my head. "I've changed," I say. "I mean, I'm changing."

"Good luck with that." She touches my cheek. "Really."

13.

Where Does It Hurt?

"Could a rivalry between a Texas-based garbage conglomerate and a scrappy local recycling collective be linked to the grisly murder discovered yesterday morning in a Berkeley recycling facility? We'll be back with more after this."

—KCBS News Radio, October 22, 1998

When I return home, I get drunk and watch myself on TV. Before I left for Eileen's, I programmed my video and audio recorders to tape as many news broadcasts as possible. Reminds me of what Dick Cavett famously said of Andy Warhol: "He has two tape recorders on at dinner. One is recording the other."

There are some short snippets of me on most stations, though the main event is the video clip of Doug heaving the dead dog onto Barb's table last weekend. Death occurred in the twenty-four hours before I found the shoelace, the reports say, most likely Tuesday night, at Re-Be. The police found Doug's blood on the pavement and in the baling shed. Traces of blood were everywhere—cuts are part of the deal when you work daily with broken glass and sharp metal.

I forgot all about the fax/takeover memo, which gets more airplay than I expect. One station says, "Before the body was discovered, media outlets received a fax outlining Consolidated Scavenger's unorthodox strategy to win the $1 million-a year contract Re-Be has with the city of Berkeley. Later the fax was revealed to be fabricated."

I check my fax machine and find two sheets. The top one says:

> *Dear reporters and editors:*
>
> *I work for Consolidated Scavenger. I saw the story about the demonstration against Scavenger, and the claims that we were going to take over Recycle Berkeley and swallow other smaller companies. I have come across an internal memo that may interest you. (No matter what my beliefs are about the takeover, I do abhor the protesters' use of a dead dog to make a point, whatever point that was.)*
>
> *The attached sheet is a printout of an email message from Tom Herman, the vice president for Northern California, to three employees in our Oakland office. As has recently been alleged, it appears there really is a plan to take over Re-Be.*
>
> *I urge you to investigate further.*

The second page looks like it was faxed, run over by a truck, copied, then faxed again. It's not easy to read.

> *To: Allard, Genessee, Zellner*
> *Fr: Herman*
> *Re: Re-Be, Womack*
>
> *Time to rethink our plans. First, let's back off until the heat fades. Second, muzzle Womack. She's jumped the gun. Tell her to hold off on any statements about Re-Be until after Election Day. She underestimates public sentiment for Re-Be.*
>
> *Bob, push her, but not too hard. The slush fund accusations, the eviction threats are too much. Wait until the contract renewal. Make sure Brady, Wilcox, any others like them don't talk to reporters, like Hunter from the weekly. Don't*

want to read about campaign contributions in the papers.

Barb, you've got to neutralize Spaulding. He's a one-man wrecking crew. No talking to the press either. Any press. Refer everything to the media shop.

Julian, lay low on the rat-fucking. You don't have to stop everything, but be careful. Slow it down. Ramp it up after November 3.

The spotlight on us will fade, especially if we can keep Womack on the reservation. We can crank it up once the elections are past.

—Tom

"Rat-fucking"—who else but Doug uses that word? But how could he have sent this? Wasn't his body already crushed in a bale?

There's another fax, from Consolidated Scavenger. I guess I must have bugged them enough I'm now on their press list. I skim a long introduction. Then:

We suspect this memo was fabricated by Recycle Berkeley to divert attention from the fact that Recycle Berkeley is facing eviction from the city for nonpayment of rent, is under investigation for an illegal slush fund whereby taxpayer money is funneled to allied political candidates, is unable to meet its contractual obligations to the city, and is suffering from high turnover, low morale, and staff conflict, as evidenced by the ugly disruption at the California Recycling Association awards banquet on October 17.

I play my voicemail again—reporters want to talk to me, and there's an editor asking about my photographs. But I'm already questioning selling those photos to the *Chronicle*. It doesn't feel *wrong*, but it certainly feels weird.

There's no message from Barb. I write her an email telling her I'm sorry for her loss and I apologize again for writing about the fight I witnessed with Doug.

I'm exhausted, but I can't sleep. I watch the tapes again, find an old movie on Channel 44, but can't stop thinking about Barb.

"One day I'm going to snap."

I unfold my futon and tuck in the sheets and blanket, then stretch out and close my eyes. I don't know why I bother. Despite all I've drunk, my mind thrashes with a thousand thoughts. Why did I publish all that personal shit between Barb and Doug? Was I sabotaging myself? Was I just stupid? I mean, it was a good story, but that's all it was, a story. Did I need the byline and money enough to blow my chance with Barb?

I think about Doug, try to remember him before he got so crazy. A couple years ago, we got high together, sitting in the front seat of his truck after one of those tedious finance meetings when I was helping move Re-Be from the abacus to the Mac. Doug was softer then. This was before Barb left, before he got on the "Scavenger is Satan" path. He cared so passionately about the work. "We're going to reinvent this planet, Hunter, don't let the cynics tell you otherwise. Look at our composting program. We've got fourth graders bringing food waste from home to school to feed worms. Those kids are never going to see organics as waste again, but as dinner for the red wigglies. We're transforming how people think, how people live. It's a beautiful thing."

I remember I told him about Eileen that night, about how we tried to get pregnant and were having sex on schedule and how I said to her once, in a moment of candor, that I wasn't sure I was ready to be a father. And that Eileen never let me forget I said that.

"That sucks, man," Doug said. "Sure wish I could disappear some of the shit I said."

I need to call someone, but who? It's two in the morning. Who are my friends? I read in a magazine that most men spend more time maintaining their lawn than their friendships. Not me. I don't have a lawn.

But why do I need to talk to someone? Can't I sit with this? Read a book? Breathe deep and take it one hour at a time?

There's Dan. He once called me in the middle of the night. Years ago. It's five in New York. Too early.

My sister? I can't imagine her listening. Then I decide that's not fair, that if I call in the middle of night with disturbing news, she might respond with the appropriate empathy.

She answers, lets me talk, doesn't interrupt like I expect her to, doesn't even berate me for waking her.

But then I pause, take a breath, and she jumps in. "That reminds me of this time that Mike and I found this deer dead in our driveway, with a bullet in its skull. And then that other time when—"

"Thanks for listening," I say. "I'd better let you get back to bed." I drink more whiskey, watch the tapes again, try to close my eyes.

I don't even consider calling my parents. And not because it's the middle of the night.

I've been sending them my clips, but they haven't responded in any way. They were actively critical of me being in the band, and they've used the word "underachiever" enough times that, for a while, I thought it was my middle name.

With some therapy and time, I've managed to let go of *some* of my resentment about how overprotective they were, my mother especially. They taught me to avoid fighting, not out of pacifist leanings, but because the world was a scary place for them, and they didn't think I could manage out there on my own. For too long, I believed them.

When Eileen and I split up, I fretted about telling my mother, knowing how she disapproved of divorce. When I finally did call her, she said I brought it on myself.

"Mom," I said, "it wasn't exactly my decision."

"Well, it's no wonder she left. Women don't respect indecisive men."

"Mom, I don't think I need marriage advice from a woman whose marriage is unhappy."

She gasped.

"I'm sorry, Mom. That was uncalled for, but I don't respond well to advice."

This was my mother, who, a few years earlier, had called my father "emotionally retarded." I remember that I didn't say anything, and she filled the silence by saying he was a consistent provider, headed off to his job in the printing plant every day for decades, never missed a day of work.

At three, I call Dan. It's six in New York.

He answers. Sounds awake.

"Dan, hi, it's Brian. You up?"

"Barely. Water's cooking for coffee. What's going on? You alright?"

"Yeah. No, I mean, I can't sleep. I can't close my eyes. I can't even explain why. No, I can. I just can't do it linearly. Is that a word? Linearly? I guess I'm drunk. But I have my reasons. Yesterday, I found a friend of mine who was murdered. I found his body. That's only part of it, there's so much more, but that's at the bottom of it. Doug. I've told you about him, from Re-Be."

"Can't place him. He was murdered?"

"The guy who was with Barb."

"That's Doug? You didn't like him. Can you hold for a sec?"

I pace from my futon to my desk. Four steps. Five if I take baby steps.

"I'm back," says Dan. "It's getting chilly here. I had to put on a bathrobe. I only have a few minutes. Got a hearing at 8:30 in

Queens." Dan's a public defender.

"Hey, I'm grateful even for a minute. Really. I am so exhausted, but my mind won't shut down. Can I ramble here? I mean, I can't do it any other way."

"Be as nonlinear as you want. I'm pouring milk into my coffee. Talk to me."

"OK, Doug is dead. You're right. I sort of didn't like him, but we hung out now and then, talked about what was important to us. But now I can't stop thinking about Barb, and how the police think she did it, and I'm in love with her, but she's not interested in me, not enough anyway, and I have this delusional idea that I can win her love by finding the real murderer. What do I know about tracking down murderers? Maybe it's infatuation, not love, but we did go swimming together and we kissed so it's not a total fantasy." I tell him about the story I wrote that pissed Barb off and the photos I took of Doug's body, but everything spills out at the same time. Dan stops me.

"Forget the details. Tell me why you're so upset. What made you want to call me in the middle of the night? Where does it hurt, man?"

"Where?" I pause. "Everywhere."

"You found this body, he was your friend. Or he wasn't your friend."

"Here's what it is, Dan, and thanks for asking. Doug dies, and all I can think of is myself. Eileen used to accuse me of being self-absorbed, and I don't think that was fair, but it's more on the mark than I'd care to admit. Doug was messed up, but he cared about much more than himself. How did my life get so small is what I want to know? If I died, could I fill a room with mourners? How did I get to be forty-one years old and camping out illegally in a warehouse studio, counting money for a living, my guitar gathering dust in my closet, my nights spent alone on this thin futon, and this happy life—Eileen and me and a couple bambinos in the sandbox and a cute puppy licking up the food that falls from the high chair—what happened to that life? I didn't get it. I don't have anyone except you to call in the middle of the night, and I was scared even to call you until it was dawn there and I figured you'd be up."

"You did the right thing to call me, man. I'm honored. You're going to be OK, but I know it doesn't feel like that now."

"No, it doesn't. I feel like crawling into a cave and sucking my thumb. Hey, did I tell you I was on TV and everything today, well, yesterday? For finding the body. Everyone wanted a piece of me."

"So you had your fifteen seconds, huh?"

"*Seconds?* I thought it was *minutes,*" I say.

"Seconds, minutes, it's like a snowman. The sun comes out and he melts. Remember when I was all over the papers and the radio, when I was working on the Livermore Lab stuff? Ancient history. Enjoy it while you can. Scratch that. Doesn't sound enjoyable."

"It has its pleasures," I say. "This is helpful. I feel more grounded. I'm going to let you go to work and fight the good fight. Some other time I'll tell you why I'm so obsessed with Barb even though she's so obviously trouble."

"Ah, yes, the lure of the woman who's trouble. Now you get to the good stuff when I've got to run."

"One more thing, Dan. The police said I could be charged with accessory if I lied to protect Barb, I mean, if she was guilty, which I don't believe is the case. Is that true?"

"Did you dispose of bloody clothes? Drive the getaway car? Then you'd have to worry."

"I did nothing but *not* tell them about arguments I witnessed. It couldn't have been Barb."

"You think she's innocent."

"I do."

"And your assessment of her innocence is based on?"

"She wouldn't do something like this."

"And you, you wouldn't either."

"No, I wouldn't, I—I get your point."

"There are bad people, and then there are good people who make mistakes and some of those mistakes are doozies."

"I got it the first time," I say.

"Now I really need to go. Call me tonight."

"Wait, why do they still have that Joaquin thing on my record? Those charges were dropped, right?"

"They didn't drop the charges. They never filed them. But the incident report never goes away."

14.

Opportunistic? You Bet.

Were it not for the longshore workers strike, Doug Spaulding's body might be undiscovered still, stacked in the cargo hold of the Pinyung freighter, sailing for the world's largest aluminum smelter in South Korea.

—Daria Reeves, "Recycling Activist Found Dead in Aluminum Bale," San Francisco Chronicle, October 22, 1998

I lie awake listening for cars in the street. Most mornings, even half asleep, I hear the newspapers arrive—the clanky cars with their incompetent mufflers, the fuzzy bass lines bouncing out the car windows, the slap of the papers on the pavement. All I hear this morning is the hum of my little refrigerator.

But then I fall asleep and the papers are there when I wake up. My photo of the boot sticking out of the bale is on the front page of the *Chronicle*, above the fold, spanning three columns. The tiny band of bright red sock at the top of the boot jumps out of the picture. Doug had a flair for the dramatic, but even he couldn't have anticipated the impact of the socks he pulled on that morning. Or that those would be the last socks he ever wore. Makes me think I should pay more attention next time I get dressed.

I push the clutter on my desk to one side and make a list on a yellow pad. A long list. Everything I want to do, need to do. Some items seem like ridiculous long shots, like finding Doug's van or getting Tom Herman to admit to manipulating community groups. Nothing seems easy.

I don't limit myself to my journalist-cum-detective world. I write it *all* down. Long-term and short. Find the murderer and expose Con. Win a Pulitzer for investigative reporting. Tell the truth. Win Barb's heart. Fuck her brains out. Save Re-Be from its city council opponents. Earn a decent living. Make some friends. Get a life. Make the world a better place. And do it all by Election Day.

I look for the business card Tom Herman gave me at the awards banquet. It's in my top desk drawer, the first place I look. Last time I called, I got rerouted to his secretary and she was as pleasant as she was unhelpful.

This time he answers.

"Mr. Herman, this is Brian Hunter, friend of Barb Genessee. We met at the awards banquet. I'm a writer for the *East Bay Beat*."

"Please, call me Tom. What can I do for you?"

"Like I said before, I'd like your perspective on this alleged takeover of Recycle Berkeley by Consolidated Scavenger, especially in light of Doug Spaulding's murder." I'm hoping the police haven't been to see him yet.

"Yes, I'm sorry to hear about that," he says. Yeah, I'm sure. "What a tragedy. I know I promised to squeeze you in, but this time of year, I'm overloaded, I'm sure—"

"How about lunch today? I've heard some fascinating stories about Scavenger's alliances with community groups that I'd like to hear more about."

He doesn't say anything.

"The thing is, *Tom,* the thing is, I've heard some accounts of how Scavenger has infiltrated and manipulated grassroots groups to oppose that landfill expansion of yours, and I thought, *Tom,* you might like a chance to comment on that before I go to press—"

He starts to interrupt me, so I stop. He stops too. I hear him exhale.

"Can you come out to Walnut Creek?" he asks. "I do have to eat lunch."

Herman's office, a short walk from the BART station, is in a new building that combines the high-tech mirror and metal look with Southwestern pastel. The landscaping might look natural in five years, but right now the trees are still too puny in relation to the slabs of metal and stone. Red and pink flowers in huge pots line the entryway. The guard at the front desk says to go on up to the third floor.

I take the stairs, as is my habit, and I see Herman waiting for me in front of the elevators. I approach him from behind. He's a tall, husky guy who probably played football in college, which must have been close to forty years ago. He has a full head of wavy white hair.

On our way to lunch at Chihuahua's, I lob him some softball questions, like how he got where he is and he rides that train until our meal shows up. He tells me he got bored with banking and jumped to what was then called Environmental Industries of Texas, just as the company was embarking on an ambitious growth spurt, mostly through mergers and acquisitions. Herman's job was to raise money for those deals.

"Back then," he says, "I knew zero about landfills or burn plants or recycling, but I found I was more interested in what we *did* than how we financed things, so I got myself set loose from the money game and hired into planning. It may seem strange to someone like you, but inside Scavenger, I'm *Mr. Recycling.*"

I've studied several of Scavenger's annual reports, so I know the company has grown one-hundred fold in the past decade, from a regional hauler to a multi-billion-dollar international conglomerate that operates incinerators, paper mills, recycling facilities, landfills, even an electricity generating wind and solar farm in the California desert. But Herman's story fills in some blanks.

When the waitress brings him his Huehuetenango, he hoists the brown bottle in a toast and winks. "To the recyclable bottle and the magic potion inside it. Sure you don't want one?"

"That beer does look pretty enticing," I say. He lifts his bottle to get the attention of the waitress, and holds up two fingers.

He continues his spiel, about how Scavenger is the world's largest recycling enterprise, how advanced its landfills are, and so on. I ask about Barb and he's full of praise for her. Then I say that some people have characterized hiring her as "opportunistic."

"Opportunistic? You bet." He leans back in his chair, stretches his legs under the table. "That's how this company was built. We bought other trash haulers. We bought landfills. We're getting into composting and methane generation. But we can't do it without hiring the best people with the best experience. If you call that *opportunistic*, we plead guilty."

"Weren't you concerned about hiring someone like Barb, from her background, someone who hasn't worked in the corporate sector?"

"You Berkeley liberals sell yourselves short. We ignored recycling. We resisted it. We thought it was a fad and we didn't want to set up an infrastructure that wouldn't last. But we were wrong. So what are we supposed to do? Throw up our hands and watch from the sidelines? No, we wanted to be players. But we didn't have the experience. We had capital. Trucks. Relationships with city and county governments. So we hired the experience. Barb wasn't the first—we've been hiring people like her all over the country, all over the world. We'd be foolish not to."

He stretches his long frame and smiles. Damn, this guy is way too pleased with himself.

"How did you find her? Barb?"

"Her name kept coming up. I saw her give a presentation last year in D.C., all about economic incentives, integrating the recycling mentality into an overall waste-reduction, efficiency approach, etcetera, etcetera, etcetera. Practical, not rhetoric. Plus she talked about building the program from the bottom up, not just having management issue an edict. I was impressed."

He takes a bite of his enchilada, slowly chews it. I savor a sip of beer.

"So I took her to lunch and told her we were looking for someone to manage our recycling program in Alameda County. Turned me down flat."

"She did?"

"She blasted us for preying on small companies. She might even have called me opportunistic. But she was intrigued. A few weeks later, I called her and asked her if she'd lead the search process, as a paid consultant. 'Of course, we'd rather skip the whole process and hire the best person, which is *you*.' She came around."

I drain my beer, fold my hands together, and look Herman in the eye.

"Sources have told me," I say, "that Consolidated Scavenger, in its zeal to monopolize the Bay Area market, has created or infiltrated various community groups."

"Sources other than Spaulding?" Herman says, and looks down for a second. "With all due respect, look, Spaulding puts us on the grassy knoll in Dallas in '63. He says we're in bed with the mob. Look, we're a $17-billion global corporation. We've got a fiduciary responsibility to our shareholders. We've got bond obligations. We've had three straight losing quarters. Why would we engage in petty crap like that? It'd be like Bill Gates sticking up a lemonade stand. We play in the big leagues and follow the rules. We take our competitors to court. We lobby elected officials. We try to get the EPA to give us some flexibility."

"Maybe so," I say, "but speaking of following the rules, I've talked with some people in Bay Point, right up the road from here"—I start to point, but realize I don't know what direction north is—"people who say you created and funded a fictitious community group and used charges of racism to fight a competitor's landfill. I'm going to press with that story tomorrow. What can you tell me about that?"

I deliberately say Bay Point instead of Pittsburg—it's the neighboring community, formerly called West Pittsburg—hoping he'll correct me. I wish I could say his face is full of fear. It's not. But he does pause before answering.

"Oh, that again. I thought that went away." He wipes his mouth and pushes away his plate.

"You know that old Mark Twain line about how lies can travel all the way around the world before truth puts its boots on? That's what this is. Wild fiction. More Spaulding conspiracy theories. There was some bad blood during those landfill fights a couple years ago, accusations that we manipulated the process. But this is really fallout from a schism among environmental groups. You know, the environmental movement is pretty white—my guess is that this racism claim was part of some broader agenda."

"I've got some pretty damning evidence," I say, "that you bankrolled these community groups."

"Bankrolled?" He laughs. "We made a few donations. We helped out a few groups whose interests coincided with ours." He pulls out a business card from his pocket and writes on the back. "Here, you check with Reverend Charles Johnson, Leland Baptist Congregation in Pittsburg. Charles Johnson. He'll set you straight."

"What about Scavenger employees joining environmental groups? What can you tell me about that?"

"We encourage that. That's something we're proud of, not

something we would hide. We *want* to be green. We're not pretending."

After blustering through a short choppy patch, he's sailing smoothly again, picking up speed.

"Anyone from Scavenger join Re-Be?"

"Couldn't tell you."

"I'd think that with wanting to expand, and with Re-Be being a vocal opponent of your expansion plan, it would be a logical place for you to have someone be your eyes and ears. I'm not suggesting that you had anything to do with Doug's murder, of course."

"Of course." He gives me an icy glare.

"I go to print Tuesday, so if you'd like to comment, I'll need something by Monday morning. That work for you?"

"I can give it to you right now: 'Consolidated Scavenger is committed to fully involving the community in any landfill siting or garbage and recycling collection or pricing that affects local citizens. We're responsible and accountable to the communities we work and live in."

"Sort of long," I say. "You can do better than that."

"How about this: The allegations are false, fabricated by our opponents." He looks at his watch. "Gotta run. I've got a 1:15 call with the feds."

He whips two twenties out of his wallet, slips them under his plate, and raps the table with his knuckles as he leaves.

I jump back on the phone when I get home, and on my first try, reach a man named Johnny Farina, who testified in a price-fixing case against Scavenger in Solano County several years ago.

"I read up on the case," I say. "You said in court that you were doing your route, picking up garbage and recyclables from business parks in Vallejo and Fairfield and some guy would follow you and go to your clients and offer to haul their stuff for half what you did, and you said that no one could make a living at those prices, that they had to be offering below-market rates."

He doesn't say anything.

"Are you still there?"

"I'm here."

"So that's what you testified. I see that Con got convicted of price-fixing. Did you recover your business, get back those clients?"

"It's sort of complicated." He speaks so quietly I can hardly hear him.

"Tell me about it. I've been reading these long legal documents. Complicated I can do. Can you tell me what happened?"

I can hear him breathe and I wait him out. Ten seconds. Fifteen seconds.

"I work for Scavenger now," he says. "All that stuff in court is ancient history."

"But it isn't. It's happening again in Alameda County. There are people here that are trying to hold onto their businesses. Like you were."

"Sorry, I can't help you."

Oh, but you have.

15.

Jimmy the Scrap Metal Guy

Sources within the police department this morning said they are looking into the relationship Spaulding had with Recycle Berkeley's board of directors' president David Ginsberg, that at a board meeting, Spaulding had reputedly threatened to "hang Ginsberg from roof of the baling shed."

—KGO News, October 21, 1998

After a short nap, I feel rejuvenated, if still tired. I take my Re-Be route map, block print the buyback addresses I remember from Wilson's map, fold it, photocopy it on my pathetically slow office copier, and fold it again a few times more. I smudge it with a crusty garden glove and spill some salsa on it just for fun. Then I bicycle down to Jimmy Pawlowski's scrap metal yard, in the shadow of the Oakland harbor and its army of stark white container cranes that look like erector-set giraffes designed by Picasso.

The streets in this forgotten sliver of West Oakland are wide and empty, strewn with broken glass, home to pickup trucks held together with yellow twine and cardboard. Jimmy's yard is one of a dozen or so recycling and scrap metal facilities, with their corrugated metal roofs and mounds of colored glass.

I bring a six-pack of beer in my front basket. Doug characterized Jimmy as a disciplined drunk—he starts his days before dawn and his evening drinking early in the afternoon.

He's easy to spot. Just inside the wide-open barbed-wire topped gate is a short man in a dark olive jumpsuit smoking a cigarette and leaning against a pale blue car with fins, but no wheels or windows. From a distance, with his strawberry blond hair and freckled face, he looks like he stepped out of a gas station advertisement in the 50s. Up close, he looks less wholesome. The jumpsuit is ripped, his teeth are crooked, and his hands are scarred and leathery. He has a pleasant boyish face, however, and when I hop off my bike and lift the six-pack of Weltanschauung from my basket, he lights up with a grin.

"I got some cans for you to recycle," I say, "but they have to be emptied first."

"I'm your man." He has a quizzical look on his face, like he recognizes me, but has no idea of who I am.

"I'm Brian, a friend of Doug's. You heard?"

"Gruesome man. Done in by a baler." He pops open a can. "You can find a boatload of beer in the empties, but yeah, you know, I like it better fresh."

He takes a big gulp. "Aaahhhhhh." He stretches it out. Then he wiggles his shoulders, like a dog shaking off water.

Usually I'm mindful to tell people from the start that I'm a reporter, and I remind myself that I need to tell Jimmy, but it never comes up. I think he already knows. If not, he doesn't seem to require a reason for my visit.

On the plywood wall behind him is a cardboard sign that reads, "A big enough pile of anything is worth something."

He drinks two beers within fifteen minutes while he leads me on a tour around his yard. Between the spaces of a confusing narrative about the international garbage conspiracy and how it's out to crush little guys like him, he gives me a show and tell. This sculpture is rebar from the I-80 overpass that collapsed during the '89 quake, that iron eagle up there on the fence was soldered together from pieces of old railroad cars. He says he does good business with local sculptors, and sells some of his pieces as garden ornaments.

"You think the killing might have anything to do with this turf war with Con?" I ask.

"I'm a fucking artist, you know, a metal sculptor. I've got iron in my veins, muscles of steel. I'm, like, one with the aluminum, one with the, well, I got this piece of airplane wing, you know, from a wreck. I don't need to *do* anything. It's *already* art. I just need to, you know, give it a title."

He continues rambling as we walk through the yard, occasionally lapsing into lucidity. He's speedboating, racing across the water and only touching down here and there. There's a rhythmic, poetic charm to his speech, which is punctuated by a mantra of "yeah, you know."

The awards banquet protest, he suggests, and other belligerent moves by Re-Be, like not paying its rent, were all part of Doug's master plan to force Sheila Womack and her Neighbors and Families allies to show their hands before the election. "Doug was onto their shit, man. He was, like, digging a tunnel right into Con's secret bunker. Womack keeps quiet, she can ride to re-election, then get Con in once the contract ends. But see, if Re-Be and the PJs get Womack to say out loud she's going to shut down Re-Be, well, shit, she's blown her wad. You know, I want to get a cushy grant and collect stuff. This is my art, you know, having a junkyard. Someone should be *paying* me for doing this."

We've circled the yard once and are approaching the front gate again, where I left my bike. No customers in sight.

"Jimmy, your address was on the flyer you passed out at the protest." He leans against the fence, next to a stack of windshields, and lights a cigarette. "At the awards dinner. Is this the headquarters or something? What's your role?"

He exhales, coughs. "This is ground zero, man. This is where we make our stand."

"So is Con after your business, too?"

"We gotta be like guerrilla fighters, like the Viet Cong, you know, hide in the tall grass, sneak up behind the big guys at night."

Jimmy's scrap yard does not seem a likely candidate for Scavenger's acquisitions list. He's more packrat than businessman. But I know that Jimmy also picks up cans and bottles from some busy restaurants, which is now technically illegal because Con signed a "flow control" contract with Oakland, giving them exclusive rights to all such materials within the city limits.

Under a similar law, Con sued two small operators in Las Vegas for collecting cans and bottles from hotels, thereby, as the legal documents said, "skimming the cream of the crop."

Only a small fraction of the recyclables are valuable enough or concentrated enough to make a reasonable profit on their own. Curbside collection doesn't pay for itself—outfitting and staffing the trucks costs more than the collected materials are worth—but it makes economic sense for cities because they save on landfill fees. One smart guy with a pickup, however, can identify where the cream is and make a decent take just picking up cans and bottles from a couple bars and hotels. More and more, Con is pushing for exclusive contracts, making the guys with the pickups, like Jimmy, essentially poachers.

Jimmy seems to relish being an outlaw, and at the scale he does it, he's under the radar. If I understand correctly, however, part of Barb's job is to expand commercial pickup, which eventually could mean going after Jimmy's modest pickings.

"Jimmy, did you see Doug after the demonstration?"

He shrugs, rubs his hand through his hair, takes another gulp of beer. He's walking ahead of me, stroking with tenderness first a radiator grill from some ancient car, then a black wrought iron railing lying on its side so it looks like a wide ladder.

"Heard he was going to get his ass fired for that stunt," he says. "Guess they don't need to do that now."

"How do you know that?" I ask. "I mean, not that anyone wouldn't be fired for that."

"You hear things."

"He disappeared from Re-Be for more than a week. Do you know where he went?"

"Said he was hanging with some anarchist printer in the city."

"Do you know where?"

Jimmy walks over to my bike and pulls another can from the plastic rings. "I'm going to need another one of these beers."

He drains half of it in one gulp. "Yeah, you know, Doug was saying maybe he should just disappear. Go to Canada and pick apples."

"Jimmy, I was out one morning a week ago and ran into a guy named Wilson, one of those guys with the shopping carts that—"

"Wilson, yeah, he's cool"—and here Jimmy smiles and makes a circle with his finger around his eye—"the marble-eye guy."

"Does Wilson bring in his cans and bottles here, to you?"

"Once or twice. Mostly I get guys in trucks. It's a long walk down here from Berkeley."

I pull the salsa-stained Re-Be map from my pocket. "Funny thing," I say, "there's this Berkeley route map I got from Wilson that has your address on it, like someone is saying, 'Hey poachers, bring your recyclables to Jimmy, no questions asked.' Did Doug know about this?"

Jimmy furrows his nose like a dog about to snap. "What this all about? What does Doug have to do with this?"

"Well, it looks like your scrap yard is one of the places recommended for poachers to bring their stuff stolen from Re-Be. Don't you think Re-Be folks might be pissed about this? Especially Doug. I mean, when you buy the stuff the poachers bring in, you're helping rip off Re-Be. You *know* these guys are coming in with stolen stuff."

"Hey, snoopy, I don't, like, check IDs or nothing. They want cash. I want cans. It's not stealing, it's, you know, business. Am I getting rich here? South of Market, that's where the printer was."

"Huh?"

"Where Doug was hiding out."

Jimmy sits down on a stack of tires and tosses his empty beer can into a nearby shopping cart and puts his forehead in his hand. He looks like he's about to take a nap.

"Can we look at your buyback setup again?" I say. "We zipped by it and I didn't get a chance to take a photo."

He leads me over to a scale set in the pavement, a shiny but scratchy steel platform about four-foot square. I step on the scale and watch the needle jump to 140 pounds.

On the wall by the scale hangs a sign with a few numbers still legible. Most have been crossed off.

"So if I were made of aluminum," I say, "I'd be worth, let's see—"

"Three-fifty," says Jimmy, before my math wheels finish turning.

"Pretty quick calculation," I say. "Do you do them all in your head?"

"Nah, knew that already. I weigh the same. If I was made of cardboard, I'd get almost six bucks for myself."

Jimmy pays 2.5 cents a pound for aluminum, 1.5 cents for clear glass, and he doesn't take glass bottles in mixed colors. "They're almost worthless," he says. He pays less than Re-Be and he's harder to get to by shopping cart, but he pays in cash. Re-Be pays by check—the city requires that—which means that the guys with the shopping carts have to wait in line at check-cashing places, which take a cut off the top.

"So Jimmy, I saw some notes of Doug's, on his desk, and one said, 'Jimmy, is he playing both sides?' What do you think Doug meant by that?"

"Both sides of what?"

"I don't know. That's why I'm asking you. You've got your address on the anti-Con flyer, you've got your address on the map the poachers use. Whose side are you on?"

I try to pose my question like I have no stake in it, but it comes out more accusatory than I intend. Jimmy stands up slowly, grabs my shirt and pulls me toward him. I can smell cigarettes and beer and something chemical I can't identify.

"You seem like a nice middle-class boy with soft hands," he says. "You might want to be more careful about, you know, what you're saying."

He doesn't raise his voice, but he tightens his grip on my shirt. It's as if he's shrugging his shoulders as he talks. There's menace there nonetheless.

I shake loose. Jimmy keeps glaring at me. I don't feel scared—whether I've grown a new layer of courage since lunch or all the arguments and altercations in the past week or two have thickened my skin, I don't know. Maybe I'm underestimating Jimmy. He has no loyalties except to himself. Backed into a corner, he could hurt someone. What if Doug badgered Jimmy the way he did me?

"Look, Jimmy." I'm pacing back and forth in the narrow pathway between piles of junk, so I'm seeing Jimmy like a bird, one eye at a time. "I don't give a shit about the poaching. Like you said, it's business. What I care about is that someone killed Doug and I think it had to do with him exposing Con. You've got your eyes open. You know things I don't. Doug used to talk about how Con had—he called them 'enforcers'—people who roughed other people up. I also learned that Con 'hires' people to go and get jobs or be volunteers at places like Re-Be. You must know about this stuff. You have some sixth sense."

"I'm like invisible, man. No one thinks I'm paying attention on account of I'm a drunk. On account of me being a flaky artist. You don't think I know what people say about Jimmy. Jimmy the Scrap Metal Guy. Burnout Jimmy. Yeah, you know. Jimmy's elevator don't go to the top floor."

Once I promise Jimmy I'll spring for a round of drinks, he's quick to invite me to meet his crew. Friday night at the Lost House in Emeryville.

16.

Golden Handcuffs

"We're running a clean and legitimate operation in a business that has long been plagued by corruption and criminal activity," says Consolidated Scavenger Vice President Tom Herman.
—Martin Skeel, "Police Say Organized Crime Link to Recycling Murder 'Unlikely,'" *West County Times,* October 22, 1998

Friday starts poorly. I wake up at eight, angry at myself for missing my early morning "appointment" with Wilson. I already missed last Friday for the same reason, but I was hoping that Wilson's schedule was regular, and tracked the Re-Be pick-up schedule. Since seeing Jimmy, I'm even more curious about Wilson and his offer to be my sponsor.

So much for "getting started" on a rewarding career in poaching. Guess I'm going to have to make do with bookkeeping and journalism.

Waiting in my email is a note from *anonymous245@yahoo.com,* alerting me to a secret meeting in downtown San Francisco Friday evening. Tonight. That perks me up faster than my coffee.

"You may be interested in this meeting," the note starts, "which will have in attendance Tom Herman from Consolidated Scavenger, Gill Sykes from the city of Berkeley, and others. I can't tell you any more, except that some participants have taken elaborate measures to keep it secret."

I start tackling my long to-do list, and surprise, surprise, I get a real live answer on my second call. Gino Anconi, a Scavenger old-timer Donna told me about, says he'd be happy to talk with me, except he's not allowed to give interviews.

"Maybe you could give an informal tour of the transfer station to, say, a friend of your cousin?"

"You know my cousin?" he asks, but then the light bulb clicks on. "Yeah," he says, "come on by." I almost hear him smile.

The transfer station is down in South County, so I take my bicycle on BART and ride there from the San Leandro station. It's easy to find. I follow a stream of garbage trucks, pickups, hatchbacks, and vans through the front gate. After I lock my bike to a post, I walk toward the office, then take a quick left. I breathe through my mouth.

Back when I was a rookie reporter, a long month and a half ago, I came down here for a tour of the recycling center, which is similar to Re-Be's, but far bigger and more automated. The trucks pour mixed recyclables onto a conveyor belt, where materials are separated by bursts of air, magnets, and about ten workers on a catwalk fifteen feet above the ground. We learned from Betsy, the perky young tour leader with the blond ponytail and blue fleece vest, that the conveyor belt system was manufactured by a roller coaster company.

Searching for Gino, I approach the mammoth transfer station, a hangar-like structure where dozens of garbage trucks back up to a football field–sized pit thirty feet below and dump their loads. In front of me, a lean guy in cowboy boots and a baseball cap climbs out of his pickup, and a man wearing an orange vest and hardhat rushes over and slaps two triangular blocks behind the front tires. Then Baseball Hat and Hard Hat bump heads as they confer amidst the roar of engines and the throb of bass from someone's radio.

Then Baseball Hat pulls on gray work gloves and heaves scraps of paneling and roofing and bulging black garbage bags over the edge. As I walk closer, I see a dozen more variations of that same theme, mostly pickups, a couple hatchbacks, and down at the end, several garbage trucks tilting up their backs so the compressed muck slides into the pit.

"You must be the nosy reporter," says a voice behind me. I turn and there's a big man with a neatly trimmed beard on his tanned, lined face.

"Yeah, Brian Hunter." I reach out my hand and wait until he removes his glove and offers his. "I thought I was a friend of the family."

"No suits here today. You can be whoever you want. But you still have to wear this hard hat."

I can hear every word Gino says, but only because he has a booming voice and he's shouting in my ear.

He's eager to talk. I ask him how he got started and hardly have to ask another question. With so many of the people I've been interviewing, I feel like I'm extracting wisdom teeth. (Well, Jimmy liked to talk, but he didn't answer my questions.)

"Used to be a family business, my uncle's family," Gino says. "He's gone now, retired, rich. Me, I didn't get rich. I'm making a living, not a killing."

We climb several flights of stairs to a catwalk high above the pit. The roof is just a few feet above our heads.

Below, bulldozers roam the pit, even out the piles. From here, they look like toys. One of the huge "possum-belly" trailer trucks drives down the ramp and disappears into a tunnel under the pit where it loads up for the drive to the landfill.

"My dad had a chance to go into the business, but didn't want to, thought it was beneath him. He drove a hauler in the morning, went to college in the afternoon, and got a gig as a P.E. teacher and football coach. He was a big guy like me, played ball in high school. But not in college, cause he was collecting garbage to pay the bills. The college girls were not impressed.

"He got out, and he did not want me to go in. Stay in school, he said, but I didn't listen. I wanted a car. I wanted money. I started washing garbage trucks when I was fifteen, was driving them a few years later. Quit school. But then I hurt my back and that was the best thing that ever happened to me. Other than my kids. My wife convinced me to go back to school and I ended up at Merritt College, back in the '60s, when there was a big Black Panther scene. Here I was this working-class dago going on thirty hanging with these militant black dudes. Smoking a lot of dope anyway. Learned a lot too, and got it in my noggin that I could be an engineer. I was always fixing things, making things. There were ecology types running around then too, the old dumps were getting full, the new ones had all these complicated rules for leachate collection and I went to San Jose State to study landfill engineering. Got a job out at Solano Sanitary in Benicia, owned by another Italian family. Up here, it was Italians doing the garbage hauling. In L.A., you had the Armenians. In the valley, it was the Irish. It was an honest living. Before the suits showed up."

He points down to what looks like three tollbooths inside the front gate. "That's where they come in, only one open now. A guy with a pickup, he drives onto that scale, gets a ticket, gets back on the scale on the way out. They subtract the weight of the truck after he unloads from what it was before, and he pays $48 a ton. The city trucks come in that far lane, get weighed when they're parked to unload."

"So how'd you get back here?" I ask. We've walked halfway across the pit on the catwalk and I can see the whole transfer station, recycling yard, and truck parking lot stretching down to the shore of the bay. The facility is at least ten times bigger than Re-Be's. From here, I can see the familiar San Francisco skyline from an unfamiliar angle. The roof cuts off the top of the Transamerica Pyramid.

"Alessandro, my uncle, hires me before he sells, so I get some stock, but not enough to retire. Then Con brings in their own people to do what I already know how to do. They can't fire me—that's part of the deal. Man, that whole sale was fishy."

"How so?"

"My uncle got rich, like I said, but I don't think he had a choice. Con had already picked up a couple of companies out in East County. They expanded this landfill out near the Delta, a dozen miles from ours. Undercut us. Started snapping up indy truckers hauling from businesses."

Gino is the kind of source I've been aching for, disgruntled and talkative, but even for me, this is getting to be—as Eileen used to say—"way more information than I need." I let him talk. You never know what random fact will be important.

"Once Con gets a foothold," he says, "they turn the screws. We used to be the big daddy in those parts. We had residential in South County, Oakland, Richmond, and a sweet slice of the commercial sector. So we're paying this franchise fee to the cities we service. A million bucks a year in Oakland. But the city budget was tight, there was clamor for recycling, and some wise guy in Oakland came up with the idea of raising the franchise fee from five percent to ten. We got it down to eight, but shit, there went another half a mill out of our pocket. The same kind of thing happened in Fremont and Hayward. Meanwhile, the tipping fee at the landfill—owned by Con—doubles. We're squeezed in both directions. Perrini, the guy in Hayward, sold to Con. Then, mysteriously, a few months later, the franchise fee increase in Hayward got reversed. By then Con had the license."

"So what are you saying? Con gets the contract, then renegotiates the franchise fee?"

"That's what happened in Oakland. That's what happened in Hayward."

Gino tells me more, but it's the same story. Con comes in, squeezes its competitors, and then makes them an offer. I ask him if he knows anything about an "enforcer" from the old days.

"My uncle used to talk about a guy at OD—"

"OD?"

"Oakland Disposal, what it was called before Con bought it. There was this guy called an 'ombudsman.' There was some rough stuff—other companies trying to muscle in, union shit."

We've reached the end of the catwalk and we're walking down the other stairwell. I'm not noticing the smell as much now.

"So, about this enforcer. What did he do? Can you remember any stories?"

"Mostly it was petty shit, like when some workers were organizing to bring in a new union, they would, like, puncture their tires. I remember right when I got back on the job after school, we got a visit from the state. This Mexican woman—what a piece of work, one of those affirmative action gals, I'm sure. She had us nailed on some technicality about groundwater contamination at our old dump in Newark. Said we had to shut it down or retrofit it. But it would have cost more than it was worth to bring it up to code. So Jono fixed it."

"Jono, huh? What did he do?"

"Don't know. Probably threatened her. Or gave her some money. We kept that dump open four more years, and then capped it. Now it's a wildlife park on the bay, looks pretty nice."

"So is there still an enforcer?"

"They say that strong-arm stuff is history. With the suits here, this white-collar crime is, like, practically legal. You got a problem, you go to this Allard guy in Oakland."

"Julian Allard, he's the enforcer?" I stop on the stairs for another look into the pit.

"No, no, he jobs it out. But the guy who pulls the strings, he's out in Walnut Creek."

"Tom Herman?"

"You know him? Yeah, he's the man. Mr. Smooth."

17.

Secret Meeting

With the exception of the "dead-dog" demonstration at the recycling awards dinner on October 17, Doug Spaulding had not been seen at the Recycle Berkeley yard for ten days before he was murdered, and he had no known address.

—"Police Expand Search for Murder Victim's Truck,"
Bay City News Service, October 23, 1998

Before I head to the city, I check out the situation at Re-Be, which seems to be boiling over. Officially, the threatened eviction can be carried out at any time, though no one really believes the city will dare. In the meantime, the yellow crime scene tape is serving as a de facto eviction. The police have cordoned off more than half the Re-Be yard, including the hut, the portable, and the shed housing the baler and conveyor belt. The police said they would reopen the area today, but the yellow tape is still there mid-afternoon.

When I arrive in San Francisco for the "secret meeting," and climb up from the Embarcadero BART station, I hear a cacophony of whistles and police sirens and amplified voices bouncing between the tall buildings lining Market Street. At street level, I hear the rumble of a helicopter overhead. A steady stream of bicyclists, six to eight abreast, clogs two lanes of the street, heading toward the Civic Center. The fog has slipped in and there's a snap to the air.

A group of bicyclists are chanting in a self-mocking, zombie-like dirge, a mantra adapted from *Animal Farm*:

Two wheels good. Four wheels bad.
Two wheels good. Four wheels bad.

It's Critical Mass, an "organized coincidence," as the flyers put it, where hundreds of bicyclists take over the downtown streets. More like thousands today—it's the last one of the year before daylight savings ends and darkness starts falling in late afternoon. According to a flyer an earnest cyclist hands me, it's a "xerocracy"—that is, anyone who makes copies of their ideas, or a map of the proposed ride, is a potential leader. One rider carries a flag that says, "We aren't blocking traffic. We are traffic."

It's not only bicyclists making a ruckus. Moving in the opposite direction, taking up the other two lanes, is a boisterous "Justice for Janitors" rally, picket signs waving and megaphones blaring. As the two processions pass, they cheer each other on. I see a driver, waiting on Fremont Street in his bright red convertible, mutter to himself, then give the finger, whether to the marchers or the bicyclists, I can't tell.

I find the building where the meeting is scheduled and make my way to the fourth floor. Both doors off the small landing are locked. Through the open window of the lobby, I can hear the whistles, sirens, and the whomp, whomp, whomp of the helicopter. I want to get in position early before the meeting starts, but I have to wait fifteen minutes before a woman comes out the door. She turns her head toward the noise coming from the street, and doesn't notice when I catch the door before it closes. I rush down one corridor, then another, then there's Suite 410. "O'Meara, Connelly, and Associates," it says in black capital letters on the translucent white glass. No lights are on in the office.

Ten feet from the door is another bend in the hallway.

Around the corner, a marble bench sits at the end of the hall.

There are four doors in this leg of the corridor. Doesn't look like anyone is around. A lone bulb hangs from the high hall ceiling. Cobwebs cover the molding. The floor is carpeted and looks like it's vacuumed regularly, but the cleaning crew doesn't bother with anything above the doorways.

I hear the elevator open and it's Gill, speaking in his distinctively low voice. "They're mostly anarchist assholes, but they make some good arguments. If you're stuck in traffic behind a car, you begrudgingly accept it, but if it's a bike, you're pissed. Here we are." A key clicks open the door. "Let me get some lights on."

Then comes a female voice. "What charming windows. Look, you can—" The door closes and muffles the end of her sentence. I can't place the voice, but it's not Sheila Womack. This is a more girlish voice. Though I only hear a few words, they have that sing-songy rise in pitch at the end of the sentence. And Gill sounds like he's talking down to her, sharing his vast wisdom with a young greenhorn. Not how he'd talk with his boss.

I put my ear to the wall. I hear voices, but not words. I go to the window, but even the union march and the bicyclists are in the distance, there's still too much din to hear anything from the office.

Below I see the changing of the guard on Market Street. The workforce is retreating to Berkeley and Mill Valley and Concord, the bicyclists and marchers have moved on, leaving the tourists, the hotel guests, the barhoppers, and the street people.

I feel exposed on the bench at the end of the hallway. My heart beats fast. I've never eavesdropped on a meeting before. Unless I count hiding at the top of the stairs as a kid and listening in on my parents. I'm tense, even a little scared. Excited too. Danger is more interesting than I realized. Though I don't suppose the danger level here is that high.

This could be a dead end, but that's what reporting is all about. Getting lost is how I find the way.

A few minutes later, I hear footsteps down the hall, then a knock on the door. "Tom, come on in," says Gill. Well, that saves me some detective work.

Then come more footsteps, this time a man and a woman. He's talking. "It might be good to act surprised if he brings it up. Just in case."

"Come on in," says Gill.

While I wait, occasionally putting my ear to the wall, the sky drains to black. The moon rises high over the Oakland hills, just left of the ferry-building tower.

I try listening at the door and hear a random word here and there. I'm pretty sure I hear Gill say "Spaulding." I have to pee. Too much coffee again today. I've been waiting half an hour. I wander down the corridor and dig out a wide-mouthed iced tea bottle from the trash and relieve myself in that. I crumple some newspapers in the neck of the bottle to create a plug so it won't spill on the janitor. I wedge it upright at the top of the trash.

I'm still buzzing from my visit with Gino this morning and his mention of Tom Herman and Julian Allard as the fix-it guys for Con. Gino didn't corroborate any wrongdoing, though if I can explain it more succinctly than he did, the story has promise. But Gino affirmed that I'm looking in the right direction. I know I'm not being objective, but I so much want to nail Con for Doug's death. Of course, a corporation can't kill someone—maybe through its pollution, but not by hitting someone over the head and crushing him in a bale. An individual has to do that.

Julian Allard? Tom Herman? They'd be far more likely to delegate than do any whacking themselves, but that's almost worse. Is this where Jono comes in? Didn't Doug mention that name to me once?

But I keep on circling back to Barb. Wondering if she could have murdered Doug. Wondering if this "find someone else" talk is code for "I'm going to build this wall and warn you not to climb it, but I hope you do."

What was it Barb said? *"Someday I'm going to snap."*

What if she did? Doug baited her incessantly. But then, Doug baited everyone. Including me. He antagonized everyone at Re-Be. Ginsberg's been a target of Doug's wrath, but if things were bad enough, wouldn't he just quit the board?

But what if this alleged affair that Ginsberg is having with Kisa is part of the package? People do crazy things for love. And Kisa, didn't she say something like, "I could kill him," after he disrupted the awards?

Not that we haven't all said that in a fit of anger.

As for city officials who've had a run-in with Doug, you'd need an organization chart to identify them all. No one has been more outspoken in criticizing Doug than Sheila Womack, but as much as I disagree with her politics, she seems above reproach. Gill Sykes has had his share of squabbles with Doug at solid waste commission meetings, but I never get the sense that Sykes is all that invested in Womack or the Neighbors and Families crowd. But he does seem to be the host of this secret meeting.

And then there's Jimmy, who I can easily imagine getting violent. He seems to have a pretty loose sense of right and wrong, but like Sykes, it's tough to imagine he cares enough about anything to go so far as murder. Maybe he was cornered—I don't pretend to know what makes him tick.

I told the police Barb couldn't have done it, but I know that's not true. She's capable of anything, Doug once said, and I believe that. That's part of why I'm attracted to her. She doesn't live life halfway.

The night we went swimming, she did her best to convince me that she was no saint. Could she have been anticipating what was to come?

What doesn't make sense, though, is that she knows everyone's fingers are pointing at her. Especially after her well publicized fights with Doug. I keep berating myself for including those paragraphs about Doug's visit to her office—*what was I thinking indeed?*—but the TV clip of Doug throwing the dog at her has been seen by thousands more people. And was far more vicious.

Barb, after all, is the woman of the flawlessly produced grand gesture. Like the street theater she pulled off when the city council was set to cut funding for Re-Be's composting program, claiming it was extravagant. She brought ten Re-Be staffers to the council chambers wearing burlap bags with price tags, showing everyone's very modest salary. Very modest—they ranged from $32,300 to $39,500.

"Citizens and councilmembers," she said, with a flamboyant sweep of her arm, "may I present to you, the city of Berkeley's best bargain. These people, who earn less than *any* full-time city worker, plus our volunteers and interns, who earn nothing, will implement this program, which also includes an hour-long interactive educational component. Once we reach 50 percent participation, the program pays for itself." And then she whipped a conductor's baton from inside her burlap sack, extended it to its full length, and, to the tune of "I've been working on the railroad," led the Re-Be staffers in a chorus.

> *I've been working at Re-Be, all the livelong day.*
> *I've been working at Re-Be, to keep the garbage trucks at bay.*
> *Can't you see the green bins overflowing, rise up so early in the morn?*

If the world were fair, the TV cameras would have recorded that for posterity, not her knees buckling under her after the dead dog slid onto her plate. (A photographer from the *Oakland Tribune* was there for the burlap bag revue, but the photo the next day didn't capture the magic of the moment. I kick myself for not bringing my camera, but at least I was there.)

So what am I saying, that she couldn't have murdered Doug because if she did, she would have done it better? Good thing I'm not her lawyer.

I hear chairs scraping on the floor, interrupting my reverie, and I leap back to my hiding place. But I stop before I turn the corner. Why hide?

I pivot, and pull my camera out as the door opens. Tom Herman steps out, his back to me, heading for the elevator.

"Mr. Herman, Brian Hunter from the *East Bay Beat,* good to see you again." I approach him. "What did you discuss in this secret meeting with city officials? Is Scavenger going to take over Re-Be?"

Gill pokes his head out the door.

"What the fuck are you doing here?"

I snap a quick photo of Gill's head, with Tom Herman behind him.

Herman looks at Gill, then back at me. Doesn't say anything. Mr. Smooth loses his sheen.

"Mr. Sykes, great to see you again, too," I say. "You're a city employee. I'm wondering if you can tell me why this meeting was held in secret in San Francisco? Doesn't that violate the Brown Act? Don't all city meetings have to be open to the public?"

I walk to the doorway, which Gill is blocking, and peek past him into the office. Standing next to a cluttered wooden desk is a man I don't recognize. Public works department from the city, that's my guess. Next to him, sitting in a red wooden chair, her back to me, is Renée Moraine from Re-Be. She's wearing a pantsuit, more formal than her usual jeans and button shirts, but her tall lean carriage and short blond hair are unmistakable.

"Well, hello Renée," I say with a smile, hiding my surprise. "Are you representing Re-Be here tonight?"

She shrinks into her shoulders. I take another photo, but only get her back.

"This is a private office," says Gill. "Out." His voice is matter-of-fact, but he's pissed. "You're trespassing."

"Renée, what's in this for you? I hope you're getting a bundle. You don't want to sell out your friends unless the price is right."

That's mean. I see her cringe even though her face is turned away. Her shoulders tighten, then slump. Out of the corner of my eye, I see Herman, who froze when I first called his name, slink away.

"Renée, I'm going to publish a story tomorrow saying that you were participating in a secret meeting with Consolidated Scavenger and city officials. Can you tell me what transpired at this meeting?"

I hear her slowly inhale through her nose. In the distance, a police siren wails.

I turn to Herman, who's inching down the hall.

"Oh, Mr. Herman, this story I'll be writing"—I shout, so I won't lose my power spot in the doorway. "I'm going to say you were meeting in secret with city officials to arrange for the takeover of Re-Be. Earlier, you've denied that. Do you deny that now?" I'm tempted to throw at him some of what I learned from Gino, but it's too complicated.

"We were just having our monthly Great Books discussion," he says, as he reaches a bend in the hallway. "We're reading *Cold Mountain.* I recommend it. Have to get home and finish that last chapter. Cheers." Then he's gone. Not before I snap another picture.

When I grow up, I want to be cool under pressure like that.

Renée moves to the window. I turn to the man by the desk. He meets my gaze without fear.

"Sir, can I ask you your name? I'm Brian Hunter, a reporter for the *East Bay Beat*.

Gill gives him the slightest of nods.

"Lincoln Payne, city attorney's office."

"And your role here?"

"As you know, for a variety or reasons, Recycle Berkeley is not able to meet its contractual obligations to collect and process materials, so we were discussing contingency plans."

Spoken like a true bureaucrat.

"Why the secret meeting?"

"Who said it was secret?" says Gill.

"Well, you told *me* not to tell anyone," Renée says. She doesn't turn her body, just her head. She's about to burst into tears.

18.

Diablo Winds

A century ago, the haulers in Berkeley sold the wet garbage to hog ranchers, but too many hogs died from ingesting broken glass, discarded phonograph needles, and razor blades.
—Brian Hunter, "The End of Garbage," *East Bay Beat,*
October 21, 1998

Early Saturday morning, Renée knocks on my door. I wonder how she knows where I live.

I've been up for hours, but still dressed in pajama bottoms and a sweatshirt. As I pad toward the door, I can feel the chill of the concrete floor through my socks. I turn down the radio and run my fingers through my disheveled hair. I haven't showered.

She has. Her hair is still wet.

"I was wondering if we could talk."

"Coffee?" I ask, waving her in. I fill my kettle and plug it in.

She unzips her orange fleece jacket. Underneath, she's wearing a tight black top. I offer her a seat, but she stands, her arms clasped behind her.

When she doesn't say anything, I do. "I was surprised to see you last night."

"How did you find out about the meeting?" she asks.

"What would be more interesting," I say, "is how you found out."

"Are you writing a story?" She gestures toward my monitor,

which has a dense screen of my notes showing.

"I am. About Con's employment of infiltrators or double-agents or whatever you call yourself. Did they give you a job title?"

"You don't like me, do you?" she says, with a defiant voice and hesitant smile.

"I thought it was you who didn't like me."

"I haven't been friendly." She takes a small step toward me, and tilts her head in a shy and deferential way, like a dog who doesn't want to be put out. I get the sense she's trying to flirt, but is convinced I won't buy it.

"So you're being friendly now?" I smile broadly, daring her.

"You've become a celebrity of late. You must feel good about that."

"Beats working."

"Why do you think I don't like you?" She takes another step toward me, licks her lips. Her green eyes, wide and naked, are less than a foot from me. She's almost as tall as I am. "You're cute, you know that."

"Thank you." Her lips are moist and tempting. I feel her breath on my cheek. I squeeze my hands together behind my back. She lifts her hand to touch my shoulder, then drops it and steps back.

"You can't bring yourself to come on to me, can you?" I say. "I must not be very tempting."

"Well, you're not helping me out any." She pouts.

"I might if you were being genuine. You're a lovely, intelligent woman. And you could be in big trouble. Once word gets out you're a spy for Scavenger, the police are going to be asking where you were the night Doug died."

"*What?* What are you saying? I had nothing to do with the murder. How could you even think that? *Oh my God!*"

She looks genuine now. Like it never occurred to her that

she might be considered a murder suspect. She shifts her weight from one leg to the other.

Last night, during my restless sleep, I built a case for Renée as the murderer—if Doug had found out what she was doing and threatened to expose her, well that's a powerful motive.

"I don't know why I came." She zips her vest. "I'll call you later, promise. Will I see you at Doug's memorial? We can talk after that." She comes toward me again. "I was hoping that—" She stops mid-sentence, looks at the floor, then boom, she's gone.

The kettle whistles. I unplug it.

I hurry to the Y for a shower and just as I'm walking back into my studio, I get a phone call from Doug Fontana, a friend of Doug's I've been trying to reach for weeks. He's a rabble-rouser from Toxics Action, based in Milwaukee. Doug told me Fontana's been monitoring Con for years, and knows more about the company than anyone on the outside.

He hasn't heard about Doug. After I tell him, I say that if Doug were here today, he'd be blaming his death on Con.

"I so much want to believe that Con would waste someone who got in their way," Fontana says, "and I wouldn't put it past them, but I have never found any evidence they've gone that far. I'm looking. That's what makes Con so fascinating. They've got a rap sheet a mile long full of fines and violations from here to Timbuktu—and I mean Timbuktu literally—but they do it with lawyers and accountants and bribes. They rob you with a fountain pen, like Dylan said, not a six-gun. Whereas the old garbage haulers had guys with baseball bats."

"Woody Guthrie," I say, "not Dylan, but you were saying—" I immediately regret correcting him, but he doesn't seem to notice.

"You could argue the big companies like Con are an improvement. In some respects. Before Con, there were haulers that picked up the garbage and dumped it in the river. They dumped bodies there too. In New York and New Jersey, the haulers were controlled by organized crime. Every company had its turf and if you were a city or business, you couldn't hire anyone else to pick up your garbage. When Con first started in those parts, trying to get a foothold, one of its salespeople went to the mailbox, and found, just like in the movies, the head of a big sheepdog with a note taped to its mouth. 'Welcome to New Jersey.' God's truth. Life imitates art and all. Con didn't back down and now it's the one doing the intimidating."

"With fountain pens?"

'Yeah, it's funny. Con gets all ruffled by words like 'organized crime.' You can accuse them all you want of white-collar crime, just don't accuse them of having thugs with shotguns. You know the saying: 'We don't want to break the law. We just want to write it.' That's Con. With the pen, like Woody Guthrie said."

"So they're not breaking the law?"

"Of course they are. Predatory pricing, for example, but that's a bitch to prove,"

"Explain that to me. I think I know, but pretend I don't."

"OK, you see, the road to monopoly is paved with under-bidding. With predatory pricing, which is when a company purposely charges a fee that's a money-loser for them in order to take business from a competitor. The big cartels take profits from one area of the country to drive out competition in another, then when the competition is starved out, they increase prices and use the profits to dominate somewhere else."

I tell him Donna's story of infiltrating community groups, and my sense of what's going on with campaign contributions from people like Lynn Brady in Emeryville.

"Oh sure," he says. "Those are both right out of Con's playbook. Chapters one and two."

"What about strong-arm tactics? Like murder? Are they

in the playbook?"

"They farm that stuff out. To these private security firms. Plausible deniability and all. In some places, where they've purchased one of the old mob-influenced firms, there might be a thug network still in place."

"Like Oakland?"

"Like Oakland."

I race to the memorial, afraid that I'll be late, but of course it doesn't start on time. Fittingly, the service is on the waterfront at Cesar Chavez Park, where Re-Be got its start, where the city established a dump about a century ago, where the Costanoan Indians piled their garbage before the Europeans arrived.

In the 1970s, the first generation of ecology true believers donned work gloves and picked through garbage for reusable goods, like construction materials, lawnmowers, sinks, and toilets. That initial salvage operation spun off into what later became Re-Be.

The city closed the dump in the early 1980s, capped it and landscaped it. You can tell the park is sitting on a landfill by the big smokestack sticking out of the grassy field. That's where the methane gas, a byproduct of decomposition, vents. Without a smokestack, the methane would build up and explode or burn.

No explosions yet today, but it's wild out here by the bay. The Diablo winds are whipping in from the inland valleys, blowing hot air toward the ocean. The wind almost always comes from the west, bringing fog in summer and rain in winter, but because of low pressure over the Pacific and butterflies flapping in the southern hemisphere or something like that, on a few rare occasions, the wind reverses directions. As I near the picnic site for the memorial, I recall a famous Raymond Chandler quote about the Santa Anas, the more well-known southern California equivalent of the Diablos: "Every booze party ends in a fight. Meek little wives feel the edge of the carving knife and study their husbands' necks. Anything can happen."

I do feel on edge. My senses are heightened. I've misplaced my sunglasses and I almost can't look up because the achingly blue sky is so dazzling and clear.

On the hillside, a dozen or so kite flyers bend their knees and lean their bodies backward to fight the wind. Some have big sophisticated box kites that look powerful enough to sweep the flyers into the sky. The walking path is littered with wind-blown tree branches.

There's a huge turnout. I count ninety-three at one point, and more arrive after the service starts. Most are part of the Re-Be extended family—board members, former and current volunteers and staff, colleagues from sister recycling organizations. Kisa and Shannon organized the memorial because Doug's parents scheduled a funeral in San Diego and how many of us are going to head down there? I thought it was going to be a small, private affair, but word got out—Doug *was* a public figure of sorts. I see Gill Sykes and Tom Herman are here. Not together. Sykes, looking sharp in a black shirt and crisply pressed black pants, avoids my eyes. He promised last night to call me this morning, but hasn't. Herman nods at me and smiles. There's Jimmy Pawlowski on the outskirts, his hair slicked back, looking uncomfortable in a brown suit that's too small.

As I peruse the crowd, I remember that I learned from some cop show that the murderer often makes an appearance at the funeral. The Berkeley police must have watched that same show because they're here too. At the back of the crowd are two officers I recognize from the day I discovered the body. They're dressed in civilian clothes. One still looks like a cop, but the other blends in with the Re-Be folks, laid back in a middle-aged hippie earth-mother sort of way.

Of course, Barb is here, standing next to Kisa. I don't approach her, but nod and lift my finger in a tiny wave. She nods back, but breaks eye contact quickly. Renée slips in after the service starts.

The tables are covered with colorful cloths, anchored by rocks. One is stacked with food, the other displays mementos of Doug—photographs, newspaper clips (including one of my stories), a megaphone, a collection of toy trucks and moving equipment, rubber lizards, and a composting how-to book called *Worms Eat My Garbage.* A boombox plays some ethereal song by Enya. Doug would not have approved of the music.

David Ginsberg acts as master of ceremonies. "This is not an official service," he says. "We have no agenda. If you'd like to share any stories or thoughts about Doug, just come on up here and do so. Then we'll eat."

The Doug described today is a different beast than the one I've experienced over the past month. Many of the stories come from the past, before, well, no one says this, but before he started acting psycho.

I stand with my hands in my pockets, fingering my keys and coins, allowing a few tears to slide down my cheeks. The wind dries them instantly. I was so furious with Doug for treating me like shit that I forgot I had seen him as a potential friend. No, an actual friend. Maybe not a kindred soul, but someone more lost than I was. Someone so lost he didn't know he was lost. I no longer think he was really trying to kill me when he pushed me into the baler. Of course, he would have hit the emergency stop button—he wasn't that deranged.

I'm surprised to see Tom Herman stride to the front.

"Good afternoon. My name is Tom Herman. I work for Consolidated Scavenger, which I know is considered to be the enemy in these parts. Doug was a thorn in my side. He once got in my face at a board of supervisors' meeting in Martinez and accused me of shutting down independent recyclers. He made my life difficult. But when I heard he died, I remember thinking, 'What a horrible loss.' Doug Spaulding was not about to let me get away with a thing, and the world needs more people like that. They keep us on our toes. Keep us honest. So I join you in recognizing his contributions and mourning his loss. God be with you, Doug."

Shortly after Herman, Barb takes a turn in front. She takes off her sunglasses before she starts.

"I'm Barb Genessee. Until this past summer, Doug and I had been together for ten years. I've never known someone as passionate and full of life and creative energy as Doug." She hesitates, fiddles with her sunglasses. As she talks about Doug's boundless ideas, I recall Doug saying Barb could lie like a champ, but he could always tell. Can I? She seems natural and vulnerable up there. It's hard to believe she's not sincere.

"I was trying to think of a story to tell on the way over here. There are so many. But the one that sticks with me is from about seven years ago when Doug and I visited India and I got sick. I couldn't get anything down. I had a high fever. I couldn't sleep. We were in a cheap hostel in Delhi. Doug found a store that sold applesauce and he kept shoveling spoonfuls of it in my mouth. Making me drink water and tea. He kept a cold washcloth on my forehead. And he read me an entire book. *Grapes of Wrath.* The whole thing. Hour after hour. That's how long I was sick. He stayed awake almost all the time I was awake. He made up stories about why I was so sick, said there was a contentious Re-Be budget meeting going on inside my stomach and that's why I couldn't keep food down. I got better, but now he's gone and I can't imagine a world without him. Last night, I found the copy of *Grapes of Wrath* we brought back from India and I couldn't read a page without drenching it in tears. Thank you, Kisa, Shannon, and the rest of you, for putting this memorial together."

Once the service is over, Ginsberg suggests we reconvene at his house. It's not exactly picnic weather here on the waterfront. Despite the warmth, the raging wind keeps us all off-balance.

Miguel and I take the rocks holding down the tablecloths and throw them into the bay.

Renée asks me to give her more time before I do anything. I'm not sure what I'm going to do with the information I have anyway. My next print date isn't until Wednesday. What do I do in the meantime? Tell Kisa? Ginsberg?

"We're scheduling an emergency meeting tomorrow," she says. "Re-Be, that is."

I ask her what I get for being patient.

"I'll get you into the meeting," she says.

19.

Bad Dog

"There's been a paradigm shift in the past five years," says Re-Be Board Chair David Ginsberg. "Recycling used to be what we saved and separated from the garbage. Today, garbage is what's left over after we recycle and compost."
—Brian Hunter, "The End of Garbage," *East Bay Beat,* October 21, 1998

Renée gives me a ride up to Ginsberg's. I ask her how Con recruited her, but she turns up the volume on the CD player, talks about how much she likes the song that's playing. I'm not familiar with it, but we like some of the same bands. Newt Crossing. The Hemorrhoids. She's stalling for time. I don't press. I'm not used to having this kind of power over anyone.

Ginsberg lives in a charming old house in Strawberry Canyon, behind the Cal football stadium. He apologizes for the mess when we arrive, but I wish I had that kind of mess to apologize for. The dining room and living room are a riot of color. A yellow and green Mexican rug covers the back of one couch. One wall is painted the color of red wine. Another wall, a creamy gold, is covered by two wide abstract art canvases, one with an orange corkscrew spiral pattern in the middle. There's a warm, worn wood floor, but you can hardly see it under all the rugs. The coffee table is piled with magazines.

Food is set out on a round dining table with a white pumpkin in the center. The place is hopping already, although it's a smaller crowd than at the park, mostly the Re-Be extended family. No police, as far as I can tell. Miguel is arranging the mementos on the mantle in the living room. A few people are on the deck, but it's as windy here as down by the bay.

Ginsberg has been a reassuring presence since the murder, so unruffled—not in the callous and slimy-smooth way of Tom Herman, but with a confident "yes, this is hard, this murder and turmoil, but we'll deal with it." He seems comfortable no matter where he is, with a bunch of rag-tag hippie recyclers or humorless city officials. He's very affable as he shows me around the house, but when I ask him if the police have talked to him, he says yes, and then brusquely excuses himself.

I gravitate toward a corner where Kisa, Miguel, and other people I know are congregated. Miguel is talking about how Doug got into recycling.

"I just landed here, but Doug, he sought it out. He supported the environmental movement, but thought it was too genteel, too much middle-class office worker stuff. He wanted something hands-on, gritty, industrial, an actual service—"

"All that may be true," says Kisa, "but I heard a different version."

She hesitates before starting. Miguel waves his hand. Go ahead.

"It wasn't long after Barb started at Re-Be, in the late '80s, I guess. Doug had been working at some cooperative moving company in the city—"

"Oh, sure," says Miguel. "Movement Movers."

"So he met Barb, I don't know, at some political event, and Barb told him about Re-Be, and he talked himself into a job even though there wasn't an opening or funding or anything. He never gave a thought to recycling before then, but he was taken with Barb."

Kisa smiles. *I wonder where Barb is.*

"But Barb had a boyfriend. I forget his name, but he was a regular, reliable guy, a lawyer, I think, or maybe in law school. They're at this party, Barb and her boyfriend and Doug, the three of them standing there, and Doug says to the boyfriend, 'You know what would make me happy is you stop seeing Barb so I can.'

"The boyfriend was stunned and looked to Barb for help, but she wasn't about to rescue him. Finally, the guy said, 'If that's what she wants.'

"That was the end of him and the beginning of Doug."

Later, Shannon introduces me to Doug's parents, who got lost and missed the service. By the time they arrived at the park, we were packing up for Ginsberg's. We'd heard they were hosting a memorial in San Diego, so we weren't expecting them to make it to Berkeley.

Berto and Dorothy—that's what they insist we call them—look terrible, their eyes puffy behind thick glasses, their crisply pressed clothes practically holding up their slumping bodies. I'd heard they were vigorous for a couple in their late seventies, but they don't look it at the moment. Bowed heads. Tight lips. When Berto stands to greet me, he stiffens as if he has to lock his knees so his legs won't buckle under him.

Doug told me about his parents once, how they expected big things of him, and weren't shy about expressing their disapproval. Doug rebelled by aiming low, rejecting status, and embracing the underground. It was the '60s in southern California, so he had company. His parents were liberal lawyers who defended draft resisters and Black Panthers, and romanticized the working class. They wanted their son, however, to aim higher.

"We pushed him too hard," says Dorothy. I'm on my third glass of wine, but I'm behind her. She's pouring it down, talking to herself as much as to us. "He was a smart boy, but he didn't want to follow in our footsteps. Maybe if I hadn't lived for work, taking on everything and anything that came my way, I would—"

"Don't blame yourself, honey, he was a grownup," says Berto. He strokes her hand.

"But if I had paid more attention—"

"A fifty-year-old man is not living his life to spite his parents," Berto says, "If he is, it's his own damn fault."

Dorothy starts talking about Doug's childhood. I study Berto. Behind his heavy glasses, he squints like Doug. He cheats like an actor on stage, his head at a forty-five degree angle from Dorothy, looking at her out of the corner of his eyes, so even though I'm next to him, I can see the front of his face. He nods his head almost imperceptibly, folds his hands tightly, breathes quietly through his mouth, his lips loose and swollen. Suddenly, he winces, as if wracked by a spasm of grief.

But a few seconds later, his eyes widen and his mouth opens into a smile. I look behind me. It's Barb. Berto stands, walks toward her, opens his arms. Barb falls into his embrace.

"I'm *so, so* sorry," she mumbles into his chest. Dorothy stops talking. Barb backs up, nods to the rest of us, then walks behind the couch and puts her hand tentatively on Dorothy's shoulder.

"I'm so sorry," she says. "This must be impossible for you."

An empty wineglass in her hand, Dorothy stares off into the distance.

No one is saying anything. I feel extremely hungry all of a sudden. I have an insatiable need to check out the paint job in the kitchen. I excuse myself to get some food. So does Shannon.

I eat, walk around, drink more wine. I drink water in between glasses of wine. Everyone seems to be sitting or standing in a group, but I don't feel social. I notice a cute, dark-haired woman in the kitchen schmoozing with a couple of people I don't recognize—her arms and hands do a graceful dance as she speaks, and she leans forward with intensity as she listens.

I don't know if it's shyness that keeps me from going over there or maybe I feel like it's inappropriate. I recall some TV show where some cad hits on a woman at his wife's funeral and I don't know why that should stop me from talking to someone, but it does. The person I really want to talk to is Barb, but she seems to have vanished.

When I spy her emerging from a room with Doug's parents, and gathering her purse to leave, I rush over and ask if I can walk her to her car. She wraps her arms across her chest and gives my question some thought. "That would be nice," she says.

Her dog, Einstein, is in the car, and he makes up for whatever enthusiasm Barb lacks. She opens the door carefully, to keep him inside, but he pushes his nose through the opening.

"How about we take him for a walk?" I say.

Einstein may not be as smart as his namesake, but he knows the word "walk" and he tries even harder to nose his way out the door. Barb holds her body against the door for a few seconds, then exhales with a long sigh and lets him out.

We're a couple blocks from Claremont Canyon, which has a ridge trail popular with dog walkers. We walk up a concrete stairway between two big brown-shingled houses.

"I had a great time with you when we went swimming." I wait, two steps above her. She's letting Einstein sniff a tree. "But with Doug's body showing up and all, it seems like that night never happened."

"Yeah, I know what you mean."

"I was wondering why you haven't returned my calls." That's not how I wanted to say it. "I mean, I guess I do know, what with the police asking questions, and all the media attention. I just—"

"Just to save you the strain of having to ask the question, the answer is no. I did not kill Doug. End of discussion."

We walk in silence. Einstein sniffs every few seconds. It feels like everything I want to ask Barb is off-limits, but then I remember the distressed look on her face when I saw her with Doug's parents. I ask about them.

She seems to approve of the question. "Did I ever tell you about the first time I met them?"

I shake my head.

"It was after we'd been together for maybe a year. Doug got high in the car on the drive down—I still had my old bug then—and when we got there, to La Jolla, his mother asked him how he was and he started talking about Re-Be and didn't stop for half an hour. Then he said, 'I'm tired, I've got to go lie down,' and he went up to his old room. There I was, still standing, with his parents, and he hadn't even introduced us. His dad looked at me sideways and said, 'Douglas tells me that you're good for him. Is he good for you?' How do I skate with that one? I said yeah, mostly, but he's been stressed out lately.

"And Berto says, 'Lately, you mean like the last thirty years?' Anyway, I really appreciated that Berto immediately wanted to know how I was doing, and he's become very fond of me. Dorothy, however, is convinced I corrupted Doug, that he'd be a prominent legal scholar if I hadn't come into the picture. I didn't look forward to coming up here today because I was afraid Dorothy would give me her usual spite. She did, though she had the courtesy not to do it in front of everyone. I was trying to be friendly and cheerful and she said I didn't seem distraught enough, and I took the bait. I told her about not sleeping and people acting weird with me at work, whispering behind my back. Mistake. She clapped her hands and said, 'Bravo, bravo. Her pain is bigger than my pain.' She talked about me in third person the whole time, as if I weren't there. 'She lost someone she's already discarded and I lost my only son.' I was good, though. I didn't fight back. I was even empathetic, and then she burst into tears and wanted me to hug her."

"Sounds pretty heavy."

"Yeah." She changes the subject, starts talking about how unsettling these dry Diablo winds feel, how long the hot spell has lasted, how much she likes these unusually warm nights. We both have nostalgic memories of shirtsleeve midwestern summer nights, so rare here. Barb tells me how confused her tomato plants are. "They're putting out new blossoms, not realizing there won't be time for the fruit to ripen."

"Kisa says you're still helping with the reporting paperwork for the city," I say.

"Well, I said I would. I haven't been there in weeks."

"I thought she said you were coming regularly."

"I think I would remember if I was." She doesn't say "end of discussion" this time, but I hear it in the cool tone of her voice. "Actually, I feel bad I haven't," she says, her voice softer and more intimate. "I promised I would."

The warm wind chills me in a funny way. It's not cold, but it's not soothing the way warm evenings usually are. "You really looked stunning at the awards banquet," I say. "I've never seen you look so glamorous."

She smiles. It feels like a game here. Pick the right question or comment and I'll be friendly. Another bulls-eye.

"It was fun to try that on. I probably wouldn't have if it weren't for the dress code that Kisa came up with. The glamour thing was like this corporate job I have. Make-believe. I'm not sure if it's me, but maybe it is. I mean, do you ever feel like you're trapped by other people's perceptions of you? That's why I'm so insistent you don't idealize me."

"Well, if you meant to dissuade me by dressing all sexy and glamorous, you failed miserably."

"Don't take this the wrong way, but I dressed that way for myself, not for anyone else. Reminds me, I knew this woman in the dorms at college, not exactly a friend, but she would confide in me about her man troubles now and then. Who would have ever guessed? She was a beauty queen in high school—great figure, perfect skin, luminous blond hair—and she got all this attention from an early age and she got to like it and got all bitchy and superior and she said the only guys she really liked were those who weren't intimidated with her, and they were usually assholes. I don't know why I'm telling you this except that when I got dressed up for the banquet, I remembered her and I thought, oh, this is what that feels like. I was really self-conscious at first. I'm almost forty after all."

"Good thing I had my camera to hide behind. You couldn't see me drooling over you."

"Don't kid yourself." She stoops down to pet Einstein. I start to ask her about how it feels to 'act corporate,' but she cuts me off.

"Why are we only talking about me? What about you, your reporting adventures. I know you got those photos published and I heard you on the radio and everything."

I can't pass up that offer. I tell her about getting whacked in the thigh by Wilson, about my conversations with Jimmy the Scrap Metal Guy, even about meeting Donna. I don't mention my lunch with Tom Herman. Einstein's getting a longer walk than he expected, but he's pulling us along happily and sniffing all these new smells. The trail is dusty. The sun is setting.

I feel like I can talk forever. Maybe she's only trying to avoid answering my questions, but she seems interested. I tell her I want to get a staff job at the *Beat*, where I'll actually get paid every week instead of writing on spec. "Assuming they don't catch on that I'm an impostor," I add. "So far—"

"Brian, why do you do that?" Her voice is scolding, but I hear caring too. "You're forever talking about how you used to be. But that's not who you are now. You're stuck in the past.

You've got this desperate, longing, almost feminine quality in you and that's going to make it hard for the woman of your dreams to sit down for a cup of coffee with you, knowing so much is riding on every sip."

Ouch!

"I *have* been changing, even though my old self is still lurking underneath. It's like I've brushed a new coat of paint over poorly prepped walls. I'm afraid it won't last."

"So what? Here you are gallivanting along on this investigative reporter path, and you've got those photos published, and that was all you being assertive. You've been plenty aggressive with me, despite my warnings." She touches my arm. "You remind me of the Wizard of Oz characters, like the tin man and the cowardly lion. They don't realize they have brains, a heart, courage. You're a wonderful man, but you don't know that yet."

"Could you repeat that? I'd like to hear that again."

She laughs.

"So you're saying I'm not confident?"

"Exactly."

"But that I have every right to be?"

"You're so unlike Doug. His confidence was far out of proportion with what he had to offer."

I tell her more about other leads I've been following, feeling more cocky than apologetic for the moment, then I ask her if she knows anything about the "anarchist printer" Doug was allegedly hanging out with in the city. She doesn't. Pretty soon, I'm grilling her about Con's infiltration and manufacturing of grassroots community groups. She stops me.

"Brian, there you are in your reporter mode again. You know what I think about that."

"But wouldn't it bother you if you knew that Con was manipulating community groups?"

"Brian, I don't need you or Doug or anyone to poison me

about what Scavenger did wrong today. I know the score. Doug sent me five copies of every report or newspaper story ever published about Con's misconduct. I had to get away—from Doug, from Re-Be, from the whole self-righteous, self-flagellating 'save the goddamn planet' scene. But no one will let me. Kisa keeps calling and asking for help. Doug kept throwing whatever doubts I had back in my face. You won't let me either. You've turned me into this archetypal character for your own devices, this idealist turned mercenary. I don't want to be a metaphor for anyone's grand hypothesis. I'm just a girl with a dog. Get over it."

I lean over to Einstein. "You hear that, fellow. She's talking about you."

"Everyone acts like I've got cooties," she says. "Or they tiptoe around me like I'm some ancient Egyptian urn, about to crack."

"That's why I was so surprised you went ballistic about my story—because you *are* tough."

"Well, that was horrible judgment on your part, and if I'm so tough," she sighs, "why is everything so goddamn hard?"

I reach over to touch her, but she bends down to pet Einstein between the ears. I can't see her face.

"Doug told me he was hurt you took Einstein," I say.

"I'm sure he was, but he wasn't the one who took care of him. He barely knew how to open a can of dog food."

"Really?"

"That's an exaggeration. When I was away, however, he would forget to feed him, or let him out. I'd come home to find poop on the kitchen floor."

We walk in silence for a few minutes. Through the trees, I see the purple and orange of the sunset.

"You know Doug accused me of working for Scavenger to spite him and that's not the case at all, but there could be the tiniest sliver of truth there. I mean, where else could I work that Doug would hate more? But I didn't pursue it. The job found me. And I know it's a good thing to get some experience in the private sector. It's not like I've signed my life away. I'm trying it on for size. Does that mean I have to carry the weight of Scavenger's criminal record on my shoulders? You oppose U.S. foreign policy, right? Does that mean you wouldn't work for the National Park Service? I need the money. I'm sending a check every month for my mother, to help pay for her caregiver."

Barb only told me a little about her family, but Kisa filled in some missing pieces. At ten, Barb's father walked out on her mother and three kids and she didn't see him again until she was an adult. At sixteen, her license still shiny in her purse, she bungled a turn driving her younger brother to a soccer game and swung the car, passenger side first, into an oncoming car. He was wearing a seatbelt, but was killed instantly. Her mother never let Barb forget.

"My goal is to prevent materials from being wasted, and I feel like I can do more of that at Scavenger than anywhere else. I can help make Scavenger better. For Doug, making them better is postponing the revolution. But the revolution is not at hand, and if it is, Re-Be is not at the center of it. For Christ's sake, the dump in Mexico City 'supports' ten thousand people, and they're not rummaging through there to save anyone but themselves and their families. But here I am defending myself again. End of speech. I'm tired of that."

Her lightness is gone. We turn onto a narrow uphill trail that leads us back to where we started. It's steep and rutted, with tree roots serving as steps. We're both breathing hard.

"With all this talking about my work and yours," I say, slowing down for her to catch up, "I've left out the main thing going on with me, which is that I'm thinking about you. Hung up on you, if I may be so honest." As soon as I say it, I feel the urge to apologize, but I hold my tongue. It's not like she doesn't already know this.

"How long are you going to live in your office?"

"Where did that come from?"

"Well, if you're going to want to date women and things like that, you might want to get a real place."

I feel a little defensive, but she's teasing me, I think, and I'm flattered that she's even noticed my living conditions.

"Going to the Y to take a shower is starting to get old."

"Brian, I know you have an anti-materialist streak in you. So do I. But you're forty years old and you have to get real. You meet a woman, she sees you living in your office, not having a car, doing freelance writing and accounting, she's not going to stick around long enough to succumb to your charms."

"This is temporary. It's been three months, going on four. I've got to make this reinvention as a reporter happen, and I'm cutting all the corners I can with money. This woman you're referring to. Is that you? Do those things—the house, the car— do they matter to you?"

"Brian, there's nothing wrong with wanting nice things. Regardless of what Doug and his purist ilk say, the working class, the third world, 'our brave brothers and sisters who hold up the sky,' they want nice stuff too. What's not to like about a comfortable bed, a good shower, nice furniture? But don't you go running to fix yourself on my account. I told you, I'm on the disabled list."

I search for a wisecrack, come up empty.

She pauses in midstep, then Einstein jerks her forward on his long leash. We walk in silence for a few minutes. We stop. Einstein noses around near a pile of dog poop.

We've leveled out. We're facing the Oakland harbor, where the huge white cranes dominate the skyline. I hear Einstein grunting and turn around. He's gone back to that mound of poop and now he's rolling in it, squirming with abandon.

"Damn dog," Barb yells, yanking the leash. *"No, no,* get out of there. Einstein, come here."

He leans his head back, his tongue hanging out, his legs in the air. Barb grabs him by his collar and pulls him away.

"Bad dog. *Bad dog.* Shit, shit, shit."

Einstein's back is covered with the poop. There's a dollop on his ears, another above his eyes.

Barb lets go of his collar, squeezes her eyes shut. She clenches her fists and jumps up and down, has a mini-tantrum right here on the trail. Then she starts crying. "Damn dog. That's just what I need."

I hold her. She's shaking.

"We'll clean him up. Together. I've got a utility sink in my studio that's big enough for him to stand in. It's going to be OK."

She leans her head against my chest.

"I'm feeling so *fragile* lately," she says. "Every little thing upsets me. Maybe I'm too quick to defend Scavenger. But it's hard not to get defensive when everyone is attacking you."

We walk back to the car without much talking. It's a long ten minutes. She composes herself, but as she drives me home, she looks like she's about to cry again. Einstein is whimpering—Barb has lashed him tightly against the inside of the hatchback so he won't get dog shit all over the car. She drives fast.

As she approaches my building, I offer again to help her wash the dog. She accepts, and we have a reasonably good time goofing around with Einstein in the sink, as good a time as you can have with a dog who's rolled in shit and a woman who's roiled in melancholy. There's even a little laughter in the mix.

It takes about five towels to dry Einstein, and then we have to clean out the back of the car, but in an odd way, it feels more intimate than our swimming adventure.

"Would you like to stay here tonight," I ask, "even though it's not a proper apartment?" I say it in a light enough way that it sounds like a what-the-hell offer, not a request.

"Thanks, but no."

"I'll call you tomorrow," I say, as she climbs into the driver's seat.

"Please don't," she says. I—"

"OK. I won't. No need to explain."

I lean in, holding the door for balance and give her a quick kiss. She lifts her face to me, and I feel a small, but real kiss from her. If there were a meter that could measure the energy of the kiss, it would read 90 percent me, 10 percent Barb. But 10 percent is encouraging somehow.

I walk around the back of the car and Einstein follows me with his eyes. I wave at him. He's wet and constrained in the back of the car, but I can see the sparkle in his eyes. You can't keep a good dog down.

20.

Paid Protesters

Two dozen sign-carrying demonstrators from churches and neigh-borhood groups in Pittsburg, in Contra Costa County, marched in front of Sierra Club's national headquarters in San Francisco yesterday, challenging the organization to uphold its stated support of environmental justice by opposing a proposed landfill in Manza-nita Canyon south of Pittsburg.

> —Scott Burnett, "Protesters Charge Sierra Club with 'Callous Lack of Action' on Controversial Landfill," *San Francisco Chronicle,* May 14, 1996

Sunday morning, I take BART to Pittsburg and visit five churches before I find anyone who gives me more than a shrug. She gives me a snarl. The streets are ghostly quiet. I walk three blocks and see only a few passing cars.

Pittsburg is an uneasy mix of sleepy slum and bland bed-room community. An industrial magnet during World War II, it attracted blacks from the segregated South with good-paying jobs in the factories and shipyards. But the shipyards closed and as the Bay Area boomed, the suburbs pushed east and the outskirts of Pittsburg blossomed with subdivisions. So though it's far smaller, it reminds me of my hometown of St. Louis, with its bleak central city, full of boarded up storefronts and mission food kitchens, ringed by middle-class and affluent sub-urban areas.

When I find Leland Baptist Church, where Reverend Charles Johnson preaches, there's a small sign about services on Wednesday night, but nothing seems to be happening this morning. There's a handwritten note about Sunday services at a nearby church.

I haven't been to Pittsburg before, so I'm taking it all in, which distracts me from rehashing my conversation with Barb again. She was infuriatingly inconsistent, sometimes genuinely kind, other times shutting me down. We covered a lot of ground, both walking and talking, but the walk was at least a loop, while the conversation jumped backward and forward, between intimate and chilly. That maddening combination sucked me in—it seemed like when she let down her guard, she came closer, and then once she noticed that, she pulled back. But I'm losing my conviction that she had nothing to do with Doug's murder. It's not that I think she actually did the deed, but I'm starting to wonder what happens if my desire to win her heart and my pursuit of the murderer collide with one another. I'm aghast that the possibility she may have killed Doug doesn't dissuade me in the least from pursuing her. I want her more than ever and I'm afraid that when she says she's not ready what she really means is she's not interested.

I even strapped on my guitar last night and started writing a love song for Barb. I came up with a chorus for a song I am *not* going to finish.

> *She's the woman of my dreams and I want us to have sex.*
> *The police seem to think that she murdered her ex.*

I arrive at Christ the Redeemer Baptist Community Church as the service ends. The church was once a corner store. Its large window has been replaced with white plywood and the name of the church is stenciled in black. I wait while the minister greets his polite and well-dressed parishioners, and when I ask him about Reverend Johnson and the protests over the landfill, he gives me a brief, "I don't know what you're talking about" response and excuses himself. I turn to leave, and almost bump into a large, round woman with small eyes. She wears a dark purple choir robe and nestles a newspaper under her arm.

"Whenever some do-gooder white person comes to see us," she says, "my first question is, what's in it for him? Cause I ain't seen a lot of do-gooders doing good for us."

She speaks in a booming voice, although I can tell she's only using a fraction of it. I've only run into blankness and indifference so far today, so her sharp words jolt me awake.

"I'll tell you what's in it for me," I say. "I'm writing a story for a weekly newspaper in Oakland about the misdeeds of a big garbage company, Consolidated Scavenger—I believe they do your garbage and recycling pickup here—and I will spend a week doing interviews and writing the story, and *if* they accept it for publication, which there is no guarantee of, I get paid two hundred dollars. So I'm not getting rich. You may not believe this, but I'm trying to find out what *actually* happened and to tell the truth. I think that this garbage company lied to Pittsburg residents and committed illegal acts. I'm trying to prove that."

"Illegal. My, now I'm impressed."

I hold my tongue.

She smiles. She's clearly at home with this contentious repartee. She may even be having fun.

"You do look sincere," she says, her voice softening for a second. "Could be a good acting job."

"I am sincere. To a fault. If there's any acting I'm doing, it's acting like I'm comfortable and confidant talking to you when I'm not."

I look down, and when I look up again, her eyes are right

there waiting for me. The lobby smells musty. I try again.

"Let me tell you what I know." I'm polite and resolute. "Someone who used to work for Scavenger told me that the company organized a group of Pittsburg residents, mostly through the black churches, to oppose a nearby landfill. And that maybe these churches, these ministers were used. Were manipulated."

"You think that's news?" she jeers, her eyes narrowing. "You think that doesn't happen eight days the week out here? Tell me something new, honey, tell me something new." But her tone is softer now, less caustic.

"I imagine that happens far too often, and I'm sure I'm oh so naive, but what I heard is that Scavenger practically created this opposition group, and made it look like it was the community speaking out when it wasn't. I came out here today to see Reverend Charles Johnson, from Leland Baptist Church, but there's no service there today. Do you know him?"

She notices the huddle of parishioners hovering in the doorway, pretending not to listen, and motions me to follow her. We walk down a steep staircase into a low-ceilinged room where a couple of dozen other people are congregating. She leads me to a silver percolator and offers me coffee. I say yes and she fills two white foam cups. We sit in folding chairs. I thought I was the only white person there, but I see a small redheaded woman who looks like she's there with her husband and little boy.

I introduce myself. "Mary Willis," she says. "I'm the pastor's wife. And assistant." She sits erectly and sips her coffee. Her thick body dwarfs the chair.

"We didn't involve the congregation," she says. "We're not a political church. We're trying to take care of our own families."

Her voice is earnest now, almost demure. She's speaking so softly I have to lean closer to hear her. A couple stands nearby, their backs to us, eating pastries off paper plates. "A landfill outside town? Why not stop whatever we can. They're always putting the things no one wants in our neighborhoods. I put in some time."

"There was a demonstration outside the Sierra Club headquarters in San Francisco, in the Tenderloin, about two years ago. Were you there?"

"I was. We drove about a dozen people out there. Reverend Johnson asked us."

"I recently spoke with someone who told me that Scavenger opposed the landfill outside Pittsburg because it was proposed by their primary competitor, and they, Scavenger, wanted to build one of their own, out near Antioch. Expand the one they have, that is. So they started calling this one the Pittsburg landfill, even though it was closer to Concord."

The coffee is undrinkable. I've laced it with some non-dairy latex whitener—but it's still weak and bitter. You live in Berkeley long enough, you become a coffee snob without intending to.

I continue. "So this person at Scavenger helped create a fictitious community group to oppose the so-called Pittsburg Landfill. I can't give you a name because I promised confidentiality. The idea was to frame it as a fight against environmental racism. The big bad garbage company locating its landfill in a poor minority community."

"What do you mean, created a fake group?"

"According to this person, it wasn't a true grassroots group started by community members in Pittsburg, it was paid employees of Scavenger who started it. That's why I'm here asking questions."

"So you want me to tell you I fell for it? Is that what you want?"

"No, Mrs. Willis, that's not what I *want*." I pause. "I'm trying to confirm that this story about the fake community group is true. I know it's confusing. You said you were recruited by Reverend Johnson?"

She nods, looking uncomfortable, but she's not leaving.

"This doesn't mean your concerns weren't legitimate," I say, turning up the volume on the sincerity. "You are absolutely right about big companies running roughshod over communities like Pittsburg."

She leans back in her chair and folds her hands.

"My husband and I are positive, life-affirming people," she says. "Reverend Willis, he preaches hope. We look for what is good and praise that. I believe we all have Christ inside us, every one of us, even those young men who hang out on the corner drinking malt liquor. I try not to be negative. But that does not mean that when a stranger comes in and gives me a song and dance about how we are being taken advantage of, I'm not suspicious that maybe he's just one more person about to take advantage."

"I understand." I take a tiny sip of coffee and put it on the floor. It hasn't gotten any better. "I'm going to be totally honest with you and you decide whether to trust me," I say. "I mean, I have been honest already." I take a breath and regroup.

"I would very much like to publish a carefully checked story that says Consolidated Scavenger did illegal and unethical things, like create and manipulate this community group, and I would very much like to quote you and use your name. But I do not want to embarrass you or your husband or your fellow ministers. I don't want to portray you as dupes."

"Even though we were." She stops. "We showed up at the event because Reverend Johnson asked us."

She asks me not to use her name—damn, why won't anyone go on the record?—but gives me the names of others who were at the San Francisco rally. I use the bathroom before I leave and pour the coffee down the drain.

Late afternoon, back in my studio, I follow up on the names Mary Willis gave me. I get an answer on my third call.

"Hi, I'm looking for Leroy Washington."

"Hey, that's me," he shouts.

He sounds drunk.

"Leroy, my name's Brian Hunter. I got your name from a minister in Pittsburg. I'm looking for people who were part of a rally in San Francisco, about a year or two ago, about a landfill in Pittsburg. There were a couple dozen folks marching with signs outside the Sierra Club office in the city. Ring a bell?"

"I was there. Yeah." I hear a television in the background. He sounds pleased he remembered.

"Do you remember how you became part of that?"

"I got paid." Then he yells and claps. "Yes, yes!!"

"Football?" I ask. "What's the score?"

"Chiefs 24, Raiders 10. Just lose, baby!"

"Can I ask how much?"

"I told you, guy, 24 to 10."

"I meant how much did you get for going to that rally? Do you remember?"

"Fifty dollars. Plus lunch at some Vietnamese place. Had me some spicy chicken. With those fat noodles. Still remember the noodles."

"Did other people get paid too?"

"We all had lunch. We crowded into this tiny space."

"Did you know anything about the landfill you were protesting?"

"Hey, I can be against anything if you pay me fifty dollars."

I tell him I want to use his name in the story. He's never heard of the *East Bay Beat.*

"For fifty dollars, I'm your guy."

"I can't pay you anything."

"Fuck that."

I pause for a couple of seconds, giving him a chance to say more. He doesn't.

"You're rooting for the Chiefs?" I ask.

"You got a problem with that?"

"No, no, I used to root for them. I used to be from Missouri. I mean, I still am from there. But I live here."

"K.C.?"

"No, St. Louis, but I rooted for both teams. Newspapers don't pay people who are in stories. That's not the way it works. You're part of the news."

He's chewing on something crunchy. "OK, you just say if they's looking for someone to carry signs, Leroy's your guy."

21.

Confession

There are plenty of myths to be debunked, not the least of which is that recycling is virtuous. In fact, recycling is just perfect for our consumer culture. You can buy as much crap as you want, but that's cool because you're recycling the cardboard packaging.
—Brian Hunter, "The End of Garbage," *East Bay Beat,*
October 21, 1998

Sunday night, fourteen of us crowd into the basement family room in Kisa's childhood home. Her two moms live here, in an old four-story building at the base of the Berkeley hills, in the shadow of hundred-year-old redwoods. The uphill wall is below ground, the opposite one, a row of wide windows, faces the bay and the tall buildings in Emeryville and downtown Oakland. In the corner, a green and white sign proclaims, "Sarah Gluckman: Government for the People, by the People."

"Sorry to be so mysterious about the meeting," Renée says, from a stool in a corner. "I know the eviction threat is on everyone's mind, and the murder, but I'm sorry I have to add to that."

She looks pale. No earrings or jewelry. Tired eyes.

"Someone asked why Brian is here. I'll get to that." She squeezes her fists. "Wow, I knew this would be hard, but—"

She has everyone's attention. Kisa sits backward on a chair, gripping the top slat. Miguel slumps on the couch, hands folded tightly. Other than me, only staff members are present.

No one from the board.

"I'm not a murderer. This is not about Doug." Renée looks down at her legs. "But I am here to confess something I'm ashamed of. I don't expect you to forgive me. I expect you to fire me. I screwed up big."

She's been studying the back of her hands. She looks up.

"We're here, Renée. We're listening," says Shannon.

Renée takes a sip from her water bottle.

"OK, five weeks ago, I sort of—I'm just going to blurt it out. Five weeks ago, I accepted a sort of consulting gig with Consolidated Scavenger. I was—" She raises her voice to run over the rumble in the room, then stops and buries her head in her chest until it calms down. Shannon bolts up as if to speak, then sits back down. Kisa shoots me a dirty look, as if I'm the one who took the job at Con, or maybe it's because I didn't immediately come to her with what I knew.

"I was annoyed with this place. With Re-Be, I mean." Her voice is quaking. "Everyone was fighting all the time." She covers her eyes with her hand for a second, then takes a deep breath and sweeps the room with her eyes. "But it gets worse. Scavenger wanted me to stay here at Re-Be and 'monitor' what was going on. I agreed to do that. Please, let me finish."

I try to write down every word, but I'm running a sentence behind. Now she's crying, and it's hard to tell what she's saying.

"...Doug said there was a 'spy' at Re-Be. That was me."

We're all silent now, and the only sounds are her sniffles and the tinkling of a piano from next door.

"All I had to do was tell them about the people who work here," she says, regaining her composure. "Let me skip to the end. I'm not telling you because I'm brave. I got caught. By Brian. That's why he's here. Friday night, I went to this meeting in the city. Tom Herman was there. Gill Sykes was there—he's Sheila Womack's aide. There were two people from the city public works office. The meeting was sort of about how, if Re-Be got evicted or shut down, how there could be a temporary arrangement for Con to do the curbside collection and processing. They asked me what Re-Be would do if the city repossessed the trucks or baler. I didn't know they could."

"They can't," says Miguel.

"Whatever. They were talking about seizing the moment while the crime scene tape is still up and doing the eviction now, but I think they're afraid of the backlash. I wished I weren't there. I felt like I was betraying Re-Be. Because I was. I pondered quitting and leaving town, moving back to Boston. But I was found out. Brian here"—she gestures toward me sitting in the back furiously scribbling away—"he found out about the meeting and was in the hallway and he asked me what I was doing there. I didn't have an answer."

"That's because—" Shannon starts to speak, but Renée cut her off sharply.

"Let me finish. This is hard enough."

"It should be hard." Shannon looks furious, her eyes narrow, arms folded across her chest.

"I was used," Renée continues. "Willingly. I sold out Re-Be for money. I'm so ashamed. But I'm finished with Con. I resigned today—by phone and fax and email. It's too late, I know—"

She pauses, but no one says anything.

"I can't undo what I did, but I did not run to the airport. I'm here. How can I help? I'm willing to go public with this, uh, statement, this confession. I will help you fight these bastards in the city and Scavenger who are trying to put us down. However I can. I've been frustrated here, you know that—this is a messy, disorganized place full of headstrong people—but you guys are here because you care, and these Scavenger people, the city hacks, I feel like I have to take a shower after being with them. That's it. I'm done. You have to fire me, I know, but you might want to wait until I finish the training. We have a few more interns ready to go. If we stay open. Is that what we talk about next?"

She sits, then after about ten seconds of silence, Kisa speaks up, first addressing Renée, then the others. "Thank you for telling us." She enunciates her words crisply, almost exaggeratedly so, in a calm, measured tone. "I would like to suggest that we go on to our discussion about the potential eviction, let this Renée situation percolate, come back to it later. We've got a lot of things to figure out."

They agree pretty quickly to follow Kisa's suggestion. That's when they ask me to leave.

Renée walks me outside. She looks calm. Obviously, it's been a relief to unburden herself.

"Thank you for letting me do it this way," she says. "I hated you for showing up at that meeting, but you forced me to do what I should have done in the first place. It's so bizarre. I lie and I betray, but somehow telling the truth makes it better. Feels like some parable from the Bible or something."

She shakes her head. "I still want to get on that plane."

I ask her who at Scavenger hired her. A man named Bob Zellner, she says. What about Tom Herman, I ask. Where does he fit in? She says she never met him until Friday night.

When I tell her the *Beat* might want a photograph of her, she's surprised, then tries not to appear pleased. "Whatever," she says.

As I'm unlocking my bike, Kisa and the others rush out the door.

"What's going on?"

"One of our neighbors down by Re-Be called," Kisa says, climbing into her truck. "The eviction crew is there right now locking down the yard. We're going to stop them."

22.

Mosquito Fleets

Re-Be spokesperson Kisa Bettis called last night's eviction a "naked power grab" by the Neighbors and Families for Berkeley Party. "The city owes us more than $60,000 in reimbursement for residential curbside collection of recycling, work we've already done, and we owe only half that in rent. There's no legitimate reason for the eviction."
—KPFA News, October 26, 1998

I'm up early Monday morning, but not as early as Kisa and Miguel, who have already set up a screened tent canopy in the driveway in front of the Re-Be gates, which are chained and padlocked with three thick rubber-coated fluorescent orange locks. A security guard slouches in a car in front of the gate, reading the newspaper, seemingly unperturbed by the five Re-Be staffers huddling around a card table under the canopy. A four-page eviction notice is tacked to the wooden "Welcome to Recycle Berkeley" sign, the paper rustling in the light breeze.

The winds are still blowing from the east, but they've calmed down. I wander around, take photos, ask questions. No one seems to know anything. A reporter from a radio station interviews me, but all I can do is speculate.

Back in my studio, I call the city and get shuffled around to a rattled Elizabeth Cortland. She says she'll have to call me back, and when she does, she reads a terse statement that reveals nothing new. Re-Be was evicted because it didn't pay its rent and refused to negotiate in good faith. Why now? I ask. She reads the statement again.

I phone Donna at work planning to ask her about her Scrabble competition, but jump straight to my adventures in Pittsburg. I guess I'm afraid I'll lose my nerve and not press her. Three times she tells me I can't use her name. Three times I tell her I've already promised I won't. She pumps me for information about the people I interviewed in Pittsburg—I can see she knows how to be a reporter. I ask her if she was involved in the so-called environmental justice rally in San Francisco.

She doesn't say anything. I ask if she's still there. Repeat the question. "Not 'involved' per se," she says. "But, uh, I was there."

That sounds pretty involved.

"I wasn't in any leadership role or anything. I—I told you this was bad. But I was surrounded by people saying that Solano Sanitary was shoving their landfill down the throats of low-income minority residents and we had a responsibility to help them." Now the words are gushing. "It sounded like there really was a community movement and we were just helping out. I thought I was doing the right thing. We made a $3,000 donation to their group, and the deal was that they would get forty protesters to the really. They ended up with about twenty-five.

"Who paid who?" I ask, softly.

"I don't know, but we gave the money in advance. They needed it to recruit people to come."

"They? Was that Reverend Charles Johnson?"

"I can't say any more," she says, her voice quivering. She sniffles.

"Are you OK?"

"I don't know why I didn't say anything at the time. We gave them cash, in ten- and twenty-dollar bills. What was I thinking? I have to get back to work."

I walk to my studio door and open it to let in some fresh air. I sit at my desk making notes. My story was due today at noon, but I got an extension until tomorrow. I had way too much material even before the eviction, even before going to Pittsburg. I don't know where to start. I feel bad for Donna. I want to give her comfort, but I'm about to write a story that will make her feel worse. Even without mentioning her name. She'll know.

The reporter in me is thrilled about the eviction. More action. More conflict. But I have to wonder: why is the city evicting Re-Be now, less than a week after the murder, a little more than a week before a hotly contested election? It looks *exactly* like the "undisguised power grab" that Kisa called it on the radio. I suppose the eviction could have been scheduled for this weekend all along. If Sheila Womack is behind it, and she certainly has been the one making the most noise about Re-Be misdeeds, why is she risking such a dramatic move now? She's the incumbent. Sure, she's expected to win, despite Sarah Gluckman's headstrong challenge. But if she wants Re-Be out and Con in badly enough, why not sit tight until the current contract expires in the spring? Maybe they went forward with the eviction because I crashed that secret meeting Friday night. Could I have unintentionally set some wheels in motion?

Whether the eviction is legal or not, it's a slap in the face to the Re-Be crew, and they are not likely to sit idly by.

They don't. All morning, they summon reporters and friends. The city calls a press conference in the afternoon. Once again, there are a lot of empty words and not much information, but I do get to question Sheila Womack in front of one TV crew and four other reporters.

Not your typical Berkeleyan, Womack wears black pleated pants and a gray sweater. She carries herself regally, leading with her chin, her silvery blond hair pulled into a tight bun. Her lips are thin, her eyes small and deep, her reading glasses hanging on a plaid cord around her neck.

She has a bit of Berkeley in her, though. I learned through the grapevine that she keeps bees on the roof of her house, and gives honey in tall glass jars as presents to city council colleagues. I've even seen one of the tall honey jars in her office at City Hall, when I met Gill Sykes.

I sit in the first row, and after her short statement, stand up and say that Re-Be seems to be in a catch-22 situation. It can't pay the rent because the city keeps holding up reimbursements that it owes Re-Be.

"That is a legitimate problem," she says, "but this town is full of banks that are in the business of loaning money."

"Yes, but the city owes Re-Be $60,000 in reimbursements. Why have those payments been held up for four months?"

"The documentation justifying the reimbursements has not been completed satisfactorily," she says. "We can't just write checks willy-nilly without proper accountability."

I know Re-Be has borrowed money before to get through short-term cash-flow crises. Maybe this is all part of Doug's plan, to orchestrate a standoff, dare the city to follow through with the eviction. But Doug's not here to lead the counter-attack.

Doug argued, years ago, against signing a contract with the city in the first place, saying it gave the city too much power. But money and benefits won the day. Until four years ago, when the first two-year contract kicked in, Re-Be workers didn't have health insurance. Lifting bins was tough on the back. Bottles and cans can be heavy even when they're empty.

One of the TV reporters asks who will pick up the recyclables while Re-Be is shut down. Womack says the city has contracted, temporarily, with Scavenger and another hauler in the North Bay. She repeats the word temporary four times.

Nothing permanent has been decided, she emphasizes.

I slip in one more question as she steps away from the microphone.

"Councilwoman Womack, do you know Lynn Brady and James Wilcox?"

She gives me a blank look.

"They each gave five hundred dollars to your campaign."

She lifts her chin and stiffens. She has a small flabby web of wrinkles at the base of her neck, just above the top of her sweater. They tighten, but her face remains stern and impassive.

"I don't personally know everyone who contributes to my campaign," she says.

"Wilcox and Brady are Consolidated Scavenger employees," I say, "not highly paid either. It looks like it's not their own money they contributed, but Scavenger's. That's a violation of state campaign finance laws. I spoke with Lynn Brady at her house last week. She's not even registered to vote."

I pause, then pounce. "Are you going to return the money?"

That last part, about Lynn Brady not being registered, I make up, but it works. Womack opens her mouth, but nothing comes out. She toys with the microphone.

"If Scavenger is financing your campaign through those people," I say, "it looks like your support for the Re-Be eviction is payback." I say it too soon. I should have waited, let her break the silence.

She tightens her left fist, loosens it, then says, in a measured voice, "If the contributions are determined to be illegal, I will return them."

"It just seems too coincidental," I say. The TV camera is turning back and forth between us as if following a tennis match. I wish I'd taken a shower this morning. "You've spoken out against Re-Be mismanagement, and you've threatened eviction publicly, all since these contributions came to you, all since this initiative by Scavenger to get the recycling contract."

She gathers herself and speaks sternly, as if reprimanding a rowdy child. Her eyes drill into mine.

"There was no bargain struck here, Mr. Hunter. My record is solid. I did not become an advocate of privatizing city services last week. I've been calling for more efficient use of city funds since my first campaign. It is the corrupt and unprofessional behavior of Recycle Berkeley that has brought this to the fore."

"So you're really in favor of putting them out of business?"

"I have never said that and you know it. Curbside recycling is only part of their bailiwick. What I am concerned about is that city money is spent efficiently and I believe that in the case of curbside recycling, we can do better. Thank you."

I bicycle back to my studio. The story keeps moving faster than I can write it. Reverend Johnson of Pittsburg calls. I've left three messages for him. He doesn't sound cheerful.

"I'm publishing a story on Wednesday," I say, "saying that Consolidated Scavenger paid you and your group of phony protesters $3,000 to go to San Francisco and stage a rally outside Sierra Club headquarters, and that you paid cash and lunch to various individuals to show up and carry signs."

I think I hear him gulp. I hold my breath.

"I don't know...what you're talking about," he says, feigning puzzlement. His words are halting. For a second, I feel sorry for him.

"I have this from several sources. Do you have any comment?"

"This is outrageous. Someone is trying to frame me. Who told you this?" Now he speaks sharply and harshly, loud enough that I pull the headset away from my ear.

"You were the leader of this group, do I have that right?"

I flip to a fresh page on my notepad, careful not to rustle the paper.

"I was not in charge of anything. It was an ad hoc association. Nothing official. This is just one more example of scapegoating the black community."

"In the *Contra Costa Times,* back about a year ago, you were quoted as the spokesperson for the People of Color Against the Pittsburg Landfill. And Tom Herman of Consolidated Scavenger—he told me you were the man."

"I'm afraid I'm not going to be able to continue this conversation," he says. "I have an evening service to prepare for."

"Fair enough. But I'm going to press tomorrow and I thought you might like a chance to defend yourself. I'm not sure it's going to look so good, taking three thousand dollars from a big multinational garbage company to create a fake group and make phony charges of environmental racism. Sounds to me like you were used big time."

Outside dogs are barking. I sit on the edge of my chair, my pen hovering above my pad.

"I. Am going. To have. To think. About this. And get back to you." He speaks quietly, solicitously, so slowly I have to resist the urge to interrupt. It sounds like he is holding back physical pain, though I wonder if this is some trick preachers know to give weight to their words.

Cornering Reverend Johnson gives me no pleasure. I want him to parry with a good explanation for his actions, wriggle out of the trap as smoothly as Tom Herman, but he doesn't. Uncovering wrongdoing and writing about it sounded better before I started doing it. These are real people with real regrets, not cardboard bad guys. Well, maybe Leroy Washington in Pittsburg sounded pretty one-dimensional, but I only talked to him for a minute.

I didn't even enjoy making Sheila Womack uncomfortable, and she's nobody's victim. And I hated putting Donna on the spot. I had some inkling there might be some romantic possibilities with her, but I probably screwed that up.

My story is due Tuesday morning, but I don't want to miss anything at Re-Be, so Monday night, I write a few paragraphs, look at them with displeasure, then run over to Re-Be to see what's happening. I repeat that combination several more times until after midnight. I can't sleep anyway. I keep thinking Barb might show up, but why would she?

When the drama unfolds, I miss it. I'm home writing, and by sunrise, when I finish my bloated first draft, it's out of date.

When I arrive at Re-Be, a bleary-eyed, but animated Kisa recounts what happened. At four in the morning, eleven Re-Be "guerrillas" snipped a four-foot breach in the chain link fence at the far side of the yard, skulked across the yard in soft-soled shoes and black clothes, and built a barricade out of overturned dumpsters, bales of aluminum, and a decommissioned Re-Be truck.

No one thought to turn off the power or the phones, though the city had taken the starter box out of the baler. "Did they think we didn't know how to call an electrician?" Kisa asks with a defiant look.

The police show up shortly after I do, and Kisa tells them that Re-Be has retaken the yard and is going to stay. She says the eleven Re-Be staff and volunteers are unarmed and nonviolent, but will actively resist being removed, and at nine, a lawyer will be filing a brief asking for a temporary injunction against the city's eviction. The first TV crew arrives as she's completing her statement. She repeats it for the camera.

Dozens more police arrive, and they mill around the gate, huddling in groups of three or four and talking into the radios on their shoulders. By this time, there are three or four dozen Re-Be staff and supporters in and around the hut and the barricades, expecting to be arrested and forcibly removed. A number of folks arrive with chains and cables, prepared to attach themselves to fences or dumpsters. A local cheese collective has donated four thermoses of coffee, a couple dozen baguettes, and a huge wheel of Sonoma goat's milk cheddar that got smuggled in through a new breach in the fence. Meanwhile, a few of the Re-Be staff are trying to operate as if it's just another day, collecting and sorting bottles and cans. The police don't try to stop them, though they warn everyone through megaphones that they are trespassing and can be arrested at any time.

After I update my story and email it in, I bicycle around to see what's happening with the curbside collection. Yesterday, Scavenger sent out two trucks to cover the Berkeley streets, but only after they completed their Oakland routes. There wasn't much to collect. I heard that Re-Be made a bunch of phone calls to people like Jimmy the Scrap Metal Guy, and unleashed what they called the "mosquito fleet," the ramshackle pickup trucks held together with plywood and bungee cords and duct tape. As Miguel put it, Re-Be essentially "deputized" poachers to collect the Monday routes.

I find and follow the one Re-Be truck, which had been parked outside the yard when the eviction came down, and at the corner of Parker and California, I see a Scavenger truck coming toward us. Renée, who's driving the Re-Be truck and who's been in the thick of everything for the past two days, screeches to a halt, jumps off, and runs over to the Scavenger truck. She hops on the ledge of the cab and leans in to talk to the driver.

I catch up with her when she returns to the Re-Be truck.

"What was that about?" I ask.

"I told him there was double coverage today, that we would do north of Parker, they could do south, and we could both go home early. The Con drivers—they aren't the bad guys."

Tuesday night, three dozen people sleep inside the Re-Be yard, including me. But even with two foam pads, the bed of paper bales I spread out my sleeping bag on is as unyielding as a cobblestone street, and we're all too wired to sleep anyway. At four in the morning, the police announce they are coming in, are going to retake the site, and will arrest anyone who does not voluntarily leave. I leave, but stay close and take notes as best I can with the dim light of my headlamp. Fifteen people are arrested. That takes an hour. The police are prepared with bolt cutters and enough reinforcements from other police forces that the yard is cleared, the breaches in the fence closed with plywood and barbed wire, and the arrested individuals carted away before nine. It's a circus, with TV cameras and photographers and reporters wandering all over, getting in the way of the police. One photographer gets arrested by mistake. But it's as peaceful and congenial as a bitter eviction can be. It's theater. I hear more laughter than I expect. There's even a soundtrack—reggae music blasting from a second floor window in the printing plant across the street.

All this takes place after the *Beat* goes to press. It prints in Fremont on Tuesday night and trucks are delivering it to newspaper boxes as the police take back the Re-Be yard on Wednesday.

Now I have a new eyewitness story, but won't be able to publish it until next week, after the election. Unless I can find another venue.

23.

Hunt for the Anarchist Printer

As dramatic as the murder, lockout, and reoccupation of the Re-Be yard were, they are only a chapter in a larger "recycling war" between Re-Be and multinational garbage giant Consolidated Scavenger over who gets the million-dollar-a-year contract to collect recyclables from Berkeley residents, and the broader fight between independents and multinational chains.
—Brian Hunter, "Murder. Eviction. Aluminum."
East Bay Beat, October 28. 1998

After all the arrests Wednesday morning, I walk back to my studio and crash. On the way, I pass by the newsrack where I usually pick up my copy of the *Beat,* but it's empty. I still get a thrill out of seeing my story in print, but after six stories in six weeks, the urgency to see it first thing in the morning isn't as strong. Plus, I'm exhausted. And I know the story is already out of date, even if the ink is barely dry.

I set my alarm for noon, but wake up in the dark, at seven. I jump up, distressed that the day has disappeared, then decide to slow down, read through my notes, and rest until tomorrow.

I go back to my newsrack for a couple copies of the paper and it's empty again. I go to three other locations before I find a copy. Front page! Yippie! I grin to myself and pump my fist in triumph, then look around to see if anyone is watching. As if they care. Or would recognize me.

I learn later that thousands of copies of the *Beat* were stolen from all over town, that is, if you can steal a free paper. Someone called the *Beat* office to report that a white man in a purple jogging outfit removed the entire stack of copies from a newsrack outside the Ashby BART station, tossed them in the trunk of a dirty white Honda, and drove off.

So the theft of the papers becomes part of the story, and gives it more legs. The TV stations all cover the turf battle at the Re-Be yard. The murder continues to be the anchor story, but because the police have not announced any breaks in the case and the shutdown and civil disobedience and newspaper theft are "so Berkeley," the murder coverage morphs into the shutdown/takeover drama. The story keeps circling back on itself—I'm telling the story, but I'm also in it. Several news reports focus on the two sentences in my story when I mention the possible organized crime connection. Renée gets her fifteen seconds, and blasts Scavenger for their deceptive practices. One television reporter speculates that perhaps the murder is tied into the larger political struggle over the "chain gangs" taking over Berkeley. *Yes! Yes!*

I feel like I am discovering the truth and creating it as well. And I feel a pang of jealousy that the other reporters are stealing my words, my work, while I'm home watching them on TV. But then didn't I steal all this from Doug? Isn't it all recycling of a sort?

My story from the *Beat* starts showing up on telephone poles as part of Sarah Gluckman's campaign literature. She's jumped on the eviction story, taking the chance that even in her hills district, voters will support homegrown nonprofits and be suspicious of Texas-based multinationals.

By now, the Re-Be yard is sealed tightly and there are four security guards, plus alarms set up around the perimeter. It looks like they're guarding plutonium, not bales of old newsprint and bins of broken beer bottles.

Doug turns out, posthumously, to have been a pretty good strategist. At a certain point, he said, no one cares that much about the daily operations of Re-Be—if the city wants to shut down Re-Be, it can. But if enough people are watching, it makes it all that much harder. One flyer I see says, "The whole world is watching." I doubt that, but of course there are more people watching than a few weeks ago.

I may even deserve some of the credit for that.

Thursday, I decide to look for the anarchist printer Doug had reportedly been staying with before he was killed. It gives me an excuse to call Donna, who lives in the city, south of Market, not far from where the new Giants stadium is under construction. This time I make sure to start with some small talk about Scrabble, and I don't say anything about the fake Pittsburg community groups. She does, however, thank me for leaving her name out of the story. She gushes about how dynamic the story was— well, when you have a murder, an eviction, a spy, and fabricated community organizations, it's hard not to be. I only had room for four paragraphs on Pittsburg, what with all the other drama, but I'm sure it still must have pained her to read it.

She says she'd be happy to join me for my wild goose chase. I'm sure it helps that I promise a game of Scrabble afterward. She even offers to take the afternoon off.

We start in the South Park area, which used to be full of printers, but has lately become a mecca for web designers and multimedia enterprises.

There are a bunch of digital pre-press shops there and we can't tell from the company names if they're printers. We go into one, and I say, "How's it going? My name's Brian, this is Donna, and we're looking for a guy named Doug, who was supposedly hanging out around her with some anarchist printer friend. I'm guessing that's someone in his forties or fifties.

Sound familiar?"

We show them a photo of Doug from the *Beat,* before he shaved his head.

The first person we ask is young, disinterested, and contemptuous of printers. "Not only do we not practice 19th Century technology," he says, "we don't have any aging hippies around here."

"That's a no?" I want to say more, but I pretend to write a note instead.

He rolls his eyes and goes back to his monitor, which has some animated game on it.

Most people, however, are friendly. Curious too. A couple peg us as cops, which amuses me.

"Why are you looking for this guy?" asks an orange-haired woman wearing horn-rimmed glasses. "Maybe he doesn't want to be found."

"Maybe so," I say, "but it's a little late for that. He's dead now and we're trying to figure out where he spent his last week."

At one brightly lit third-floor office, a muscular young guy with a shaved head ignores me and gives Donna all his attention. "Why do you care about this guy?" he asks.

"He seems to have disappeared," she says, and here she whispers, "with proprietary information."

When the guy asks what kind of business, Donna smiles. "If I tell you, then I'd have to kill you." And she winks.

After six places, we have no leads, but we're having fun, improvising together, and elaborating on the story. We no longer mention the guy we're seeking is dead, but at a print shop on Folsom Street, a man who tells us he's going to be a cyber-lawyer—"Intellectual property, that's the battleground of the 21st Century"—recognizes Doug's name.

"The body they found in the recycling place?" he says. "Same guy?"

"Same guy," I say.

"I'm actually working on a related project," Donna pipes in. "Dissertation about people who change their identities. We think he may have been doing that."

Outside, back under the hot sun, I make a face at Donna. "Dissertation?"

She grins. "That could have been my life. I majored in sociology before I went for the big bucks in journalism."

"Let's do a couple more," I say, "then let me take some of my journalism big bucks and get you a coffee. I'll even spring for one of those mocha-cappa-dappa-cinos with organic lowfat goat's milk if you that's what you go for."

"I'm a black coffee with sugar girl."

Pretty soon, I stop worrying whether we'll find anything. Donna *is* a lot more fun when she's not talking about her time at Consolidated Scavenger. I misread her. She has more imp in her than I guessed. As cute as she is, maybe because she's so cute, I thought she'd be more of a lightweight. But then everyone is, compared to Barb. I haven't laughed this much in months.

Right after our coffee break, we find our man.

"Anarchist printer, huh?" says a fortyish designer with a goatee and a Café Helvetica t-shirt (only the typeface is some classical serif like Bodoni with a little teardrop on the arm of the "a"). "Try Red Star Press. They're syndicalists, or actually Wobblies. By the Toys 'R' Us, near the freeway overpass." He points toward the Mission.

There's no answer when we ring the bell. A note directs deliveries around the corner.

We walk down an alley, spot an open door. I recognize him immediately—I know I've seen him before. And he looks the part—mid- to late-fifties, with an unruly gray and white beard, a leather fisherman's cap the color of coffee with cream, and a red ink-stained apron over a blue work shirt. He slumps in a chair with a half-eaten sandwich and the *Chronicle* in his lap.

As soon as I mention Doug, his body gives him away.

"Can't help you." His face is blank, but he looks like he's gritting his teeth. He shakes his head.

"Come on, I saw you react when I mentioned Doug." I stop. "That's it. I saw you at Doug's memorial. On that windy day by the bay."

He picks up his sandwich and takes a bite. A yellow pepper is hanging out between the slices of dark bread.

We wait while he chews. Then he takes a drink from a thermos.

"Who are you guys? Really."

"I told you. I'm a friend of Doug's. Really. And a reporter for the *East Bay Beat,* from Oakland. Doug's been murdered, you know that."

He looks down at his newspaper. "Yeah, I've been reading about that. So those stories are yours, huh?"

I nod. He stands up. "You want to sit down?" He leads us to the adjoining room. There are several plush, but threadbare chairs facing a wall-sized window that looks down onto the floor of a printing plant.

A green and black Heidelberg press, a king-sized version of what the *Beat* is printed on, is rhythmically whooshing and whomping away. The vibrations rattle the floor.

"Shit, man," he says. "Shit."

He walks over to the window so all we see is his back.

"I don't want to talk about this," he says. "I'm not going to pour it out for you one cup after another." He sounds educated and articulate, but with a working-class affect. I can detect a slight accent, but can't place it.

"Easy question first," I say. "What's your name?"

He turns to face us. "François. And that's not as easy as you think."

"Doug described you—I got this second hand—as an

'anarchist printer.' What's that mean?"

I look to Donna and give a tiny nod, not sure what I'm asking, other than let's play him carefully, not scare him away.

"I'm a printer who's an anarchist, that's all. I'm still part of Red Star, but this place here is where I make my living, cranking out sex weeklies and supermarket circulars—whatever comes in. I'm night floor chief. I'm here during the day a lot too."

Then, as if he caught himself, he stops.

"So Doug was here, what, a couple weeks ago?" I ask.

"Look, I'm a printer. I believe in a free press. I support the free weeklies. Even with the hegemony of television, if you have a printing press, you have a stage, a megaphone. But you *must* understand: I don't want to be *in* the paper."

"Listen, François," I say. "I don't mean *any* insult by this, but we're not interested in *you*. We want to know about Doug."

Then Donna says, "Can you tell us when Doug was here and what he was doing?" Her voice sounds warm and agreeable.

"I didn't want to see him. I told him to stay away. But he didn't let up."

"Why not?" I ask. "See him, I mean."

"I don't know how he tracked me down. He said it was through my brother, who lives in San Diego, but I haven't seen him in years. See, I knew Doug back in southern California. Through surfing. He was still in high school. We partied a lot together."

I sit back down and so does François.

"And so Doug found you?"

Again, he hesitates.

Goddammit! Why is everyone so afraid of speaking the truth out loud? Why can't anyone go on the fucking record? The only guy who seemed to want his name in the paper was Leroy Washington, and he wanted fifty dollars for it.

"He won't print anything about you if you don't want," says

Donna. "Brian grilled me and I was afraid to talk. But he kept his word, kept my name out of the story."

François gives Donna a sideways look. I sit back in the spongy chair, let her draw him out.

"Why don't you want to be found?" She leans forward, her elbows on her knees. "Are you in trouble?"

François leans his head on his fist, seems to zone out and forget we're there. I notice the floor here has the same scruffy gray-white linoleum as the church basement in Pittsburg. Come to think of it, the offices in Berkeley City Hall have them too. Must have been a big linoleum sale thirty years ago.

"So Doug did find you," says Donna.

He's back at the window again. "He kept calling. I didn't return his calls. Then he shows up here. Well, next door. I told him to leave me alone."

Not only can I feel the rhythm of the press, I can smell the sweet scent of warm ink.

"I got in some *situations* a long time back, so I slipped back to Quebec, where my people are from. I hung there for seven years—learned new skills, printing, pre-press, digital imaging. I got tired of the icy gray winters.

"So I come back to California, here I am, doing a little political work on company time, but earning my keep, practically living in the print shed. I help people do their zines, do some web shit, charge some of the costs to the big clients, slip in some small jobs at the end of big print runs. Nothing big. I'm ninety percent legal."

François is looking at Donna as he talks. As smoothly and slowly as possible, I slide out my notebook and pen and begin writing, snippets at first, then as many words as I can.

"When Doug arrives, I think, no fucking way, no one is supposed to know who I am, where I am. But, you know, Doug is persuasive. He said he wanted my help to monkeywrench

Con. I said forget it. I'm clean. But it's like I was waiting for something like this to happen. We fired up some weed, reminisced about the old days, and how we might still throw a few wrenches in the gears. It was a wallop, man. Doug was frantic, like a squirrel on speed, with more juice than that Heidelberg downstairs. Never seen him so wired. He had all these ideas for sabotaging Con's trucks, their transfer station, the elevators in their headquarters.

"He needed a place to crash, but I just have my studio, and I've got a kind-of girlfriend, so he stayed in his truck and used my shower and printer. We cranked out some fake Con stationery and phony reports and press releases. Then, bang"—he snaps his fingers—"Doug's gone."

"The phony memo about the takeover," I say. "You guys did that? It looked convincing."

"When I read about the murder, I hung low, didn't want any stinkin' badges barging into my life."

"The police are looking for his van," I say. "Do you know where it might be? Did Doug leave anything behind?"

He stands up, taking a few seconds to lift his head, then motions for us to follow him. We walk outside, up the alley, and back to the door we first knocked on. Red Star Press. He turns a corner, open a door, and lifts a banker's box from a shelf.

I extend my arms to take the box, but he pulls it away.

"The price for this collection," he says, "is to keep my name out of the papers."

24.

Make Sure They Spell Your Name Right

Re-Be supporters say they expect thousands of participants this Saturday, Halloween, for a street party and rally in front of the padlocked gates of the Re-Be yard. Word on the street is that the rally will be followed by civil disobedience.

—Brian Hunter, "Murder. Eviction. Aluminum."
East Bay Beat, October 28, 1998

I'm playing music loud and tapping my foot. On my first pass through the banker's box, I look for that significant and telling piece of evidence that jumps out at me and illuminates every dark corner of my studio. Doesn't happen. But that's because almost every piece of paper in the box warrants a second look.

One printout lists forty-three ways Scavenger has purchased, shut down, discredited, or bankrupted its competitors. Next to many are Doug's handwritten comments, noting their relevance to the Re-Be situation.

There are dozens of pages about industrial sabotage from an Australian anarchist website—*www.stickinthespoke.au.* Doug has highlighted passages in a yellow-green marker. "The small and incremental can be more effective in shutting down the system because discovery takes much longer," reads one sentence.

Another is a list of Re-Be board members, volunteers, staff, and colleagues, and Doug's notes on whether they might be the suspected infiltrator. I'm near the bottom of the list: "Refuses to carry water. Sincere but faint of heart. Hides behind 'search for truth' bullshit."

While these scattershot notes confirm the depths of Doug's paranoia, his blunt character assessments are surprisingly perceptive, and of course, he was correct about the existence of an infiltrator. Doug seemed to think Kisa was the most likely candidate: "Corporate mentality hiding behind hippie facade—stop her at all costs."

He didn't suspect Renée: "Unreliable, but unlikely. High cheekbones, low scruples. A lightweight."

I'm listening to a tape Doug made for me, full of political songs. Here's one of my favorites starting up, by Hugh Masekela, a wailing, sluggish dirge about weary miners taking the "coal train" to Johannesburg, and here comes the bright piercing trumpet. How can the world be so sorrowful when music is this moving?

I copy phone numbers and other leads into my notebook, and study what appears to Doug's to-do list before the awards banquet:

> *[ ] borrow hazmat suits from K*
> *[ ] retrieve dog from G*
> *[ ] call Jimmy*
> *[ ] check in w Barb (Friday?)*

No date on the page. I turn it over. Blank. That's when I see the drawing. It's a gray photocopy of an architect's rendering. Some of it I can't read and I don't recognize all the symbols, but I can tell immediately that the location is the Re-Be yard.

On the bottom, it says, *"nothing.but.net"* and below that,

"Chase & McAuliffe, Architects."

I stare at the drawing for a long time. Seven structures are spread around the yard and adjacent properties. The abandoned red brick warehouse across the street from Re-Be is part of the plan. The two dead-end streets on either end of the Re-Be yard are gone. There are sidewalks winding through the site, clumps of plants and trees, and what looks like a roof deck on the printing plant across from the front gate. It does not look like a recycling facility anymore.

I try not to get ahead of myself. Doug faked the takeover fax—he could have invented this, too. Besides, if this is real, how did he get it? Why haven't I seen it? Why didn't he shove it under my nose? I've been living and breathing this story for weeks and never came across a hint of anything like this.

I find Chase & McAuliffe on the web, but the site is bare bones. Just two pages. I also look up *nothing.but.net,* but can't exactly tell what it does. It's in a partnership with Roaring Routers and has offices in El Cerrito and downtown Berkeley. I've never heard of them, but they seem to be growing like crazy. There are nine jobs posted on the website, all technical— javascript programmer, network security director, and so on.

I take a break to watch the news. Nothing new on the Re-Be situation, though one station airs a brief report from the site. I sit up another hour until my eyes start closing, then I get ready for bed.

I brush my teeth for a long time, lost in thought. What a good day. Found a secret treasure. Had fun with Donna. Barb told me to find someone else. Maybe I have.

But Barb continues to haunt my thoughts whenever things slow down. I keep replaying that tentative kiss she gave me after we bathed and toweled off Einstein. I felt at least an inkling of desire from her. Small, but real. I didn't imagine it. Whether it was an intimation of some deep reservoir of passion or just her gratitude for helping her wash the poop off the dog, I can't say.

I've been writing Barb emails over the past few days—short and light, nothing heavy, no questions about Con. She wrote back a couple times, also short. I'm trying to keep the flame burning, but not overwhelm her.

Barb certainly was emphatic with her pre-emptive declaration of innocence. Would I have asked her point-blank if she killed Doug? I don't know. But I'm having a hard time keeping my suspicions at bay. She said she hasn't been at Re-Be to help for ages, but didn't Kisa say otherwise?

And I can't get that one item from Doug's to-do list off my mind. *Check in with Barb.* I thought they weren't talking. Well, it could have been Barb not talking with Doug, but not the other way around.

One day I'm going to snap.

Maybe something will happen with Donna. We laughed a lot today. She barely beat me in the Scrabble game we played after finding François. She seems to like me. Why is that so surprising? I've been charming with her, and we certainly had a stimulating adventure. (I'm sure it helped that we didn't discuss Pittsburg at all.)

Donna doesn't have the gravitas of Barb, but who's to say that's not a good thing?

I climb into bed with the banker's box beside me and keep reading. I'm having a hard time keeping my eyes open. Then I find a photocopy of a handwritten letter to Barb.

> *Dear, dear Barb,*
>
> *I miss you so much. You can't imagine how much.*
>
> *I know how difficult I am. I know I've attacked you enough times you don't trust me. I know I've promised to stop and I did, but then I didn't.*
>
> *I can't live without you. Nothing has any meaning*

without you around to share it. I can't concentrate on any-
thing unless it has something to do with fighting for you,
though it must seem to you like I'm fighting against you.

I'll do anything, and I mean anything, to get you back
and keep you. I'll go to a shrink, get some meds—I'm scared
shitless to do that because, well, you know—but I will. For
another chance with you.

I didn't mean to explode like that with Brian there the
other day—I couldn't help it. I was jealous and it got the
best of me.

Then come two paragraphs crossed out so fiercely and completely I can't distinguish a single word. He wanted to be sure
no one could read those lines, but how could they be any more
private than what I just read?

I look for the next page. I look for the original. No luck.

Did he send this to Barb, crossouts and all? This would have
been written sometimes after my visit to Barb's office, on October 12, a Monday, and October 20, eight days later, the day the
police say he was killed. But there's no reference in the letter
to the awards banquet, where he was far more vicious than in
Barb's office, so I assume he wrote it before then. And it looks
like he spent most of that time living in his truck and using the
facilities at François' print shop.

I read over Doug's letter again and I'm surprised that tears
start streaming down my cheeks. I let them.

I'd like to think I'm crying for Doug, and not myself, but
either way, it feels good to be sad. I've been so engaged and
stimulated since Doug's murder that I haven't been feeling sorry
for myself like I used to, and it feels weird that somehow Doug's
death has energized me. So the sadness feels right, like I'm not
as selfish as I fear.

Friday morning, I hardly have the patience to read the newspapers, though I do read a follow-up story about the stolen copies of the *Beat*. Apparently, half of the print run was taken. Another eyewitness saw the same white car following the *Beat* delivery truck, and empty the rack outside REI.

I skim the paper, but mostly I'm waiting for it to be late enough to call Chase & McAuliffe. I try them a few minutes after eight, but the voice mail says the office opens at eight-thirty. I wait until nine.

The receptionist puts me through to Jack Chase, who's just walked in. I tell him what I call a "partial-truth lie." I say I'm a freelance writer—that's where the truth stops—and my name is Lorin Palmer and I'm working with Chuck Brinkman, the *nothing.but.net* CEO on an investment prospectus. I tell Chase that Chuck suggested I get a couple sentences from him about the proposed development in West Berkeley and the direction the company is going.

"Chuck told you to call us?" Chase asks. "That's, uh, interesting. What does he think we can tell you that he can't?"

"He suggested that the architects' themes might be effective metaphors for his company's strategic vision."

"That's what he says? Our themes?" Chase gives a little snorting laugh, and then the mumbling equivalent of the shoulder shrug. "He's got cart before horse. We designed the campus, then shoehorned the themes from his mission statement into our write-up. But don't quote me on that. I suppose there was some intuitive stuff going on that we only grasped afterward."

"Sometimes telling the story backward captures the truth better," I say. (Oh yeah, capturing the truth, I'm all about the truth.)

Then comes an uncomfortable silence. I let five seconds pass, counting them out on my fingers. Most people step in to fill the void before then, but Chase doesn't.

"Look," I say. "Chuck told me you might not know what to

say, what with all the controversy, but rest assured, this document will be massaged till the cows come home and the final draft won't see daylight until all this unresolved stuff has shaken out."

"How this?" Chase says. "If the plans evolve the way we'd like, the combination of the open architecture, the eclectic buildings, and the gentle curves of the walkways that connect the structures will reflect the company's goals. To be open, multifaceted, to support the independent inventors and at the same time maintain the existing product line. And unify it all by making it easier to connect. Geez, that's either not bad or total nonsense."

"Any reference to the recycling yard that's there now?"

"Totally. I'm getting there. Done right, the campus will mirror the company—in its balance of innovation and tradition. No, no, not tradition. Fundamentals. Innovation and fundamentals. Tried and true with wild and untested. In one of the buildings there are no walls at all, just posts and pillars. It's all open. And then, like you say, this was a recycling facility. Now we're repurposing that, making the old new."

He continues to ramble. I can't shake the nagging question of how Doug managed to find out so many things that have eluded me. I always heard he was an idea guy, but he didn't follow through. He procrastinated. Barb executed. That was why he wouldn't let her go. But maybe without her, he rolled up his sleeves and got down to business. He didn't lack for passion. Or maybe that was where François came in. Maybe Doug needed a partner.

Chase is on a roll, but when he repeats himself for the third time, I interrupt and say I have to get to a meeting.

"One last question," I say. "This isn't for the annual report, just my own nosiness. Chuck was mysterious about the project. I know it's just preliminary—they don't have the financing or the land yet—but is he being upfront with you? I mean, I feel like I'm only been given half the story."

"Can't help you there, my friend. It's up in the air, like you said. We're used to that. We draw a lot of plans that never get built."

I don't get the concrete details I'm hoping for, but I get what matters most. Which is that the plans are real. As real as plans are. Doug didn't fabricate them.

Next I flip the scenario around and call *nothing.but.net* as a writer doing the quarterly newsletter for Chase & McAuliffe. But I can't reach anyone who knows anything.

I go back to the list of phone numbers I wrote down last night. I call them. No cover story here. I say who I am and that I've come into possession of some of Doug Spaulding's papers and I'm trying all the numbers. The fifth one is Sheila Womack's office at City Hall. I don't leave a message.

I look for the paper with Womack's number. It's scribbled in the margin of the front page of the *Chronicle* sports section. To the left of the phone number, it says: "mtg w S noon." The date of the paper is Tuesday, October 20. Doug was murdered that night.

I eat some shredded wheat with banana for breakfast and then walk up to City Hall. Womack's office is locked when I arrive. I walk down the hall and poke into another council member's office. I ask an elderly black woman if she knows when Womack will be in.

"Usually Mr. Sykes is here by now. Is there anything I can help you with?"

I tell her who I am and that I want to talk to Womack about the Re-Be situation.

"There's been a lot of commotion down there these past few days," she says.

"I imagine, with the Re-Be eviction and the election and all," I say.

"That young man of hers, Mr. Sykes. A lot of people think he's a model for the community, with his sharp suits and educated bearing. But he thinks way too much of himself."

Sykes. Hmmm. Why did I assume the "S" stood for Sheila? Doug was a last name guy. He called me Hunter.

Turns out the woman is mother and aide to Councilmember Rodney Robinson. I ask her if she knows anything about a proposed development on the Re-Be site, but she doesn't. While we're talking, I hear footsteps climbing the stairs, getting louder. I retreat inside her office. It's Sykes.

He's dressed casually, in black jeans and a short-sleeved blue and gray checked shirt. There's a laptop in one hand and a shopping bag in the other. His lips are moving as if he's talking to himself. He shuffles over to his office and unlocks the door. The back of his head is shaved from the neck to the big bone at the base of the skull. Though he's a wiry man, his neck has a thin ripple of fat. One flap of his shirt is untucked, hanging over his belt.

I wait until he's entered the office before I charge toward him. He kicks the office door closed behind him, but I catch it before it hits the jamb.

"Mr. Sykes. Brian Hunter with the *Beat*. I've got some questions for you."

"Not now, Hunter." He drops his things on a chair and pushes his glasses up with his knuckle. His expression is easy to read. *Get lost.* But there's a hint of the put-upon as well. Why is this happening to me?

"It's just that *now* is necessary." I step inside. "See, I've found a blueprint of a development on the Re-Be site in Doug Spaulding's papers, and evidence that you and he met on October 20. That's the day the police say he was killed."

He doesn't move, though I can see his Adam's apple rising, then falling. "I'm going to the kitchen," he says calmly.

"Destination: caffeine. Want some?"

Bingo. No denial.

"Sure. I'll walk there with you." Score one for surprise. Out of the corner of my eye, I see Edna Robinson inching back into her office.

He apologizes for the mess in the kitchen, but there are only a couple of dirty dishes in the sink.

When we return to the office, Gill closes the door behind him. I sit down and take out my notebook. He stands in front of the door. The coffee is a lot better than what I gagged on in Pittsburg.

"Look, I had nothing to do with his death," he says. "And, for the record, I never learned to run the baler."

"You were there, at the open house. It's in the minutes."

"I wasn't paying attention. Never took my turn."

"Measuring the yard for the architects instead?"

"What are you talking about?"

I don't answer. He glares at me, takes off his glasses and rubs his eyes with his thumb and forefinger. He takes a sip of coffee.

"You don't publish again until next Wednesday, right?"

"Wednesday as in after the election? Well, the *Beat* doesn't publish until then. But I am a stringer for the *Chronicle*."

He takes a step toward, locking his eyes to mine. His earring glints in the shaft of sunlight that shines through the small south-facing window.

"I bet *you* know how to run the baler."

"I do."

"And you've fought with Spaulding."

"Your point?"

"The police could make life difficult for you."

"They already have. They thought I might know something." I pause, smile. "Turns out I do."

"You live in a warehouse in West Berkeley, don't you? Alone?"

"I do. How about you? Where do you live?"

"We're talking about you right now."

"You know, the *Chronicle* is going to be very interested in the architect's drawings of the software campus on the Re-Be parcel. And of course, Berkeley voters will as well."

"How long would it be before someone noticed you were missing?"

He puts his coffee on top of a file cabinet and folds his arms across his chest.

I sit back in my chair as if I don't have a care in the world. "Where did you pick up this tough guy act? From the movies? Look, Sykes, don't pretend to be a gangster. I know all about you, how your father was president of the Berkeley Black Property Owners Coalition, how you went to private prep school. You can't scare me. I live in a cold warehouse with concrete floors and winter's coming. I don't have a job or a girlfriend or a dog. You know *Invisible Man,* the Ralph Ellison book? There's a passage in there where he says there's no one more dangerous than a man who has nothing to lose. I'm that man. You, on the other hand, have a lot to lose. A job, a beautiful woman, a promising future. And whatever happens to me, these software campus plans are out of the bottle. You can't pour them back in."

He walks slowly back to his desk and sits down behind it. I turn to face him.

"None of this changes the fact that Re-Be has been mismanaging its funds and breaking the terms of its lease," he says.

"You expect me to believe you *care* about that?"

He puts his chin in his hand.

"What did Spaulding want?" I ask.

"I told you. I had nothing to do with his death. I was shocked when I heard."

"So I'm sure you told the police you met with him the day he died."

"I have no motive to kill him. He was pushy, but that's

politics. The campus. It's merely an idea. There's no financing. There's no permit. The land is not available. They didn't even survey the site—they used the county parcel data. You're making way too much out of this. So did Spaulding."

I look up from my notebook, doing my best to look like he just told me what he had for breakfast.

"What did he want?"

"I don't know. That's the truth. To tell me he knew what we were doing next? Even though we didn't. To wave the plans in my face."

"Who's we?" I ask.

Then he launches into the already familiar accusations that Womack has made about Re-Be's financial irregularities, as if that somehow justifies everything else. He knows I'm not buying it, so he recites the words like he's reading a press release. Then he shoos me out.

By the time I plop myself down on a bench outside City Hall, I feel deflated. Here I am with another big investigative scoop and I don't know what to do with it. I have an exclusive, but I work for a weekly, and the timing is all wrong. I told Sykes I'm a stringer for the *Chronicle*, but the *Chronicle* doesn't know that. Even worse, I can't think of anyone to tell about all this. Except Eileen. And I try not to make the same mistake twice.

Well, there's Donna, but I still hardly know her.

I can go to Re-Be, of course, but where? With the yard closed, they're meeting in various people's houses, and I can't very well barge in like I used to at the yard. They'll go ape-shit over the development plans, that's for sure. The police might be happy to hear me out, but they're going to want all the papers in the box.

The sun feels warm on my shoulders. Teenagers in Halloween costumes saunter down the sidewalk by the high school. A group of four boys stumble along together with their legs in irons and chains, but instead of convict stripes, they wear suits with corporate logos—Starbucks, Wal-Mart, Nike, Blockbuster. The chain linking them looks real, but makes soft pings as it drags on the sidewalk, not the clinking and clanking of metal. On their back is stenciled "corporate chain gang." Ah, Berkeley. I write it all down. Doug would love it.

On the way home, I notice the juxtaposition of Halloween decorations and political signs. Yes on 5. Rodney Robinson for District 3. Gray Davis for Governor. A pair of pumpkins sits on a bale of straw. On a fat oak, a witch on a broom is wrapped around the trunk as if she smashed into it going at warp speed. And on almost every telephone pole for blocks are flyers plugging the Halloween night rally and street party in support of Re-Be.

At home, I call Shannon and Kisa and leave messages. I try Donna, but she's away from her desk. Then I call the news desk at the *Chronicle*. I say I've been writing stories for the *Beat* on the Re-Be controversy, and that I recently uncovered new information, and I want to write a story for them. The first person I speak with seems interested, but he passes me on to someone who says that won't work. "We have a reporter on that story," he says.

"But I've uncovered new information that could impact the election next week."

Ten minutes later, I get a call from Daria Reeves. She remembers me from discovering Doug's body and helping me sell the photos of Doug's boot in the bale. I tell her I want to write the story, not be a source. I tell that I understand it's her beat, but that I'm also in touch with the *Tribune* and *Examiner*.

"Mr. Hunter, I get you want this story, and I know you don't want to hear this, but if you've got breaking news, you have to let it go. You'll still have your own story in the *Beat* next week. Those stories have been excellent, by the way. But the *Chron* is not going to put you on a news story. You're an advocate. You're too close. You can be a source—I'll quote you in the first or second graf—if it's good."

"Oh, it's good."

I want this story. She's got that right. I've already constructed the lead:

"The morning before he was murdered, Doug Spaulding met secretly with Gill Sykes, aide to Berkeley Councilmember Sheila Womack. Spaulding had uncovered an architect's drawing of a proposed development on the site of Recycle Berkeley. And Spaulding had scribbled Sykes' phone number in the margin of the *Chronicle* sports section dated October 20."

No, no, that's not it.

"Less than 24 hours before he was murdered on October 20, Doug Spaulding met secretly with Berkeley city council aide Gill Sykes. Spaulding had discovered an architect's drawing of a development plan on the Re-Be site, which Sykes has helped shut down."

OK, it's not there yet, but I have it in me.

"When's your deadline?" I ask Reeves.

"I need it now if we're going to run it tomorrow."

"Give me half an hour."

I call Barb again. She's out. I try Ginsberg. So is he. I call my editor at the *Beat,* somehow hoping she'll say, "Oh, we'll put out a special edition on Sunday." She doesn't.

I reach my friend Dan in New York, but he says he only has a minute. I give him the short version.

"Give it away," he says. "As many places as possible. You said you wanted to make the news, not just write it. Here's your chance."

"But I've been working on this for months. I can't give it away. It's not fair."

"You want fair? Come work at the P.D. office in the Bronx for a week and you'll learn about fair."

I sighed. "I hate it when you're right like that."

"Make sure they spell your name right."

25.

Pour the Boy Another One

Police investigators found the van belonging to recycling yard murder victim Doug Spaulding inside a garage in West Oakland this morning, parked inside a former cardboard recycling facility. Inside the van were bolt-cutters, which had been used to break into the locked garage.
—KCBS News, October 30, 1998

I wash up in my utility sink and walk to the Lost House in Emeryville, about two miles from home. To meet Jimmy the Scrap Metal Guy and his crew. I planned to go last week, but there was too much going on. Tonight, I'm totally primed for it.

As soon as I walk in, I see this is not my scene. First off, it's smoky. There's a new state law banning smoking in bars, but this place is pretending otherwise.

Mostly, it's a young crowd. Longhaired white guys in t-shirts and jeans. It's no yuppie bar serving microbrews made with organic cold-pressed hops. Pretzels are piled in red plastic baskets. Above the bar are two TVs, one playing a football game, the other a gaudy cartoon in saturated primary colors.

I don't see Jimmy, so I take an empty seat at the bar between a woman with screaming red hair and a big man stooped over his beer. I pull the stool under me, put on a smile, and say hi. The woman is talking with a man to her left. The hunched man grunts. He's in his fifties with a wrinkled brow and tired eyes. His glass is almost empty.

"What are you drinking?" I ask.

He points to the Weltanschauung coaster.

"Another?"

"Sure." I hold up two fingers to the bartender and point to his glass.

"What's up?" I ask. "What brings you here tonight?"

"Stool's got my name on it. Course the name's worn off cause I've been parking my ass on it so damn much."

He's feeling the beer. It's radiating from his pores.

I learn quickly that he spent a year in jail for transporting stolen goods. "Well, shit, I knew I was losing my job, and I had this container trailer full of TVs from Korea and I knew a guy who knew a guy, and we had a plan that almost worked."

I look around again for Jimmy and I'm startled by a haggard face in the mirror that I think I recognize, and then I realize is me. *Shit, shit, shit.* I look older than my forty-one years, that's for damn sure. Well, a couple weeks of deep sleep would help. Fortunately, I don't feel as bad as I look. I've got a nice buzz on. I'm still high from all the interviews this afternoon, with Daria Reeves at the *Chronicle* and the three radio reporters who returned my call.

When I spot Jimmy, I grab a chair and squeeze in next to him, at a crowded table by the front door. Next to me, I soon discover, is a young Irish guy who used to be a muscle man for Solano Sanitary, a company Con purchased a few years ago. What luck. It's Jimmy's sixth sense. How is it I walk into a bar I've never been in before and as soon as Jimmy shows up, I stumble into a guy who can practically write a story for me?

Irish is sloshed already, slurring his words. I tell him I visited Jimmy's scrap yard a few days ago and I find this whole garbage and recycling world fascinating.

"Shit, we had it good," he says, swirling his beer and looking at the bottle meditatively. "Did some heavy-ass lifting, but lots of time to rest. We'd have to rough someone up now and then, scare the shit out of them."

"What, did you, like, get an assignment? Here's this guy, give him a working over. Did they give you a photo? An address?" I ask the question straight up, anxious that he's going to think I'm too nosy, but there's more swagger than secrecy in his response.

"An address. Me and the Baker, we knock on the door of some dude and tell him we come to collect. Mostly, we were collecting."

"What for?"

"Whatever. Disposal. Services rendered. These dudes were scared. They knew they owed us."

He ends his sentences with a weird five- or six-syllable chuckle. "This place is like home. They cash my unemployment check so I can waste it all on beer, hee, hee, hee, hee, hee." Then the next outburst is lower, like a series of grunts. "Ain't no market for honest physical work no more. Everybody's got to have a fucking email or www-thing, huh, huh, huh, huh, huh." All this with an Irish accent.

"What do you do now?"

"Some hauling. Pick up shit and dump it somewhere. But now I'm the one owing money. Last month, I had some goon knocking on my door wanting to get paid. I chased him off with a crowbar."

We're all drinking and it's noisy and everyone is talking and no one is listening. So I talk about my writing. It's not like I'm undercover or anything.

"See, I was writing these stories about how the big garbage companies like Scavenger are getting into recycling, and, like, how many people really give a shit about that, not many, right? Then there's this murder and shit, and, you know, I'm no crime reporter, what do I fucking do now? Nobody wants to read about the fucking commodities price of aluminum. They want to know about how this guy's body got crushed in a bale and who whacked him. You know how to run a baler?"

Irish raises his hand and so does Jimmy. I didn't realize he was listening.

I ask Irish. "Is it hard?"

"It's easy, man, but if you never done it, you're not gonna know what to do, huh, huh, huh."

"So the person who crushed this guy in the baler, he must be in the business?" I say. "Or she. Or could someone who'd like, done it once or twice figure it out? Cause the whole fucking city council learned how to do it at some open house. But if I was going to dispose of a body and I'd run a baler only once, wouldn't it make more sense to put the body in a bag and dump it somewhere? Isn't that the way bodies used to be disposed of?"

Well, *that* gets the conversation going. Everybody's got a story about some body they found. Everyone's an expert on disposing of corpses.

Many rounds later, a little before closing time, Jimmy says he and a couple pals are headed to a private club, tells me to come along.

Jimmy drives. There are four of us in an old Ford clunker with a front seat like a couch. It's a longer drive than I expect. We're somewhere along the bay in East Oakland or San Leandro. Once we leave the freeway, I don't recognize where we are.

We're bumping along a rutted unpaved road, a barbed wire fence and cinder block buildings on one side, a stand of eucalyptus trees on the other. I smell the brackish water. Through the trees, I see the white cranes of Oakland Harbor. Irish and another pal of Jimmy's are laughing and shouting in the back seat. They're drunker than I am. I've had a good time tonight, but as we barrel into the dark and deserted waterfront, I'm starting to feel dread in my stomach. Be careful what you wish for and all that.

We climb out next to an old one-story boathouse on a cove

next to a short fishing pier. Paint is peeling from the clapboard siding. There's a blue tarp on the roof, anchored with cinder blocks. Inside, it's roomy and cozy, the worn paneling an orangey knotty pine. Shelves are filled with upright liquor bottles and upside down glasses, but there's no bar or bartender. A couple tall windows open onto the bay. The putty around the panes is cracked and it seems like the glass is attached to the frame with masking tape.

There are four of us from the car, and another five who are there when we arrive. We're all sitting in overstuffed chairs drinking shots of whiskey and Jimmy introduces me to a leathery old man with white hair and thick glasses. He cups his shot glass in the palm of his hand. Jimmy tells him I've been asking about the old days of Oakland Disposal. It's Jono, the enforcer Gino told me about. I don't know how I know, but I do. And it scares the shit out of me.

"Why are you interested in garbage?" He twirls the glass in his fingers. He sounds more cautious than menacing.

I sit back, take a sip of whiskey. An hour ago, I was drunk, but felt light, like I was leaping on the moon with no gravity. Now I feel heavy, my limbs sluggish.

"I used to live near the dump," I say. "I know people who work in the recycling world. I read some books, talked to some people." Not much of a cover story, but at least it's true. In my condition, I don't want to weave some elaborate ruse and have to remember what lies I've told.

"That's not much of an answer."

"Well, there's something that resonates for me about, you know, recycling things that still have value, transforming them. You know Jimmy was friends with Doug, the guy who was murdered a couple weeks ago. I knew him too."

On Jono's left, a young man in a green t-shirt and leather jacket slouches in the chair, his eyes heavy-lidded, his chin on his chest. Jono clears his throat and the guy jumps up, grabs a bottle of whiskey, and moves to fill up my glass. I cover the glass with my hand, but he keeps on pouring. The whiskey spills on my hand, my pants, on the floor. He keeps on pouring. I remove my hand, let him fill the glass. No one makes a move to clean the puddle on the floor. I look at Jimmy, but he averts his eyes, shifts his chair so his back is to me and he's closer to a cluster of four guys, including Irish.

Jono tells me he's met Doug. "That boy had a mission. Take down OD. Came looking for me."

"Why?" I lift the shot glass, take a sip. What I really need is some water.

Jono says Doug had this idea that he was connected to some of Oakland Disposal's "freelance activities." Then he urges me to drink up, the party is just starting.

"So you work for OD?" I ask.

"Do I look like I'm still working? I'm an old man. I'm retired."

"You may be retired, but you don't look that old. Or tired."

"We both know that's a crock of shit. I can't even wrap my fingers around a baseball bat anymore. Good thing I've got loyal assistants."

He glances to the guy slouching next to him, whose eyes are locked onto mine. I turn away.

"You seem to know a lot of people," says Jono. "You wouldn't happen to know this guy who's writing the newspaper stories about how Con is trying to take over. Jackie, pour the boy another one."

"I've had enough. It's been a tiring week."

"Nonsense. It's Friday night. Time to unwind."

"I don't think I could get much more unwound than I already am."

As Jackie returns with the whiskey bottle and pours again. I place my glass on the floor. Jackie pours whiskey in my lap. The other group stops talking.

Jackie sits back down, opens his jacket, and pulls a gun out and centers it on a little café table. The barrel faces me, about four feet away.

I make myself breathe. My testicles retreat as if I've jumped into cold water. Behind me, I hear a lock slide into place. Irish, the guy I felt so lucky to stumble into a couple hours ago, leans against the door with his hands in his pockets. I've never had a gun pointed at me before. The fact that it's sitting on the table and not in someone's hand makes it even scarier.

"Um, what's going on?" I say.

"Good question," says Jono. "Maybe you can answer that."

I stand up. My legs feel wobbly, but they hold me up. I feel whiskey dribble down my leg.

"OK, I'm the guy writing those stories, but you already know that. What do you want? I'm not out to get you. I mean, don't you feel like you're being used? Con is all suits and lawyers these days. They've got muscle that writes checks and lobbies legislators. Don't you feel squeezed?"

"We may be retired, but we like our privacy. We don't like being in the newspaper." I alluded to "enforcers" in one sentence in my last story, but never mentioned Jono by name, not even Oakland Disposal.

"Jackie?" Half-awake Jackie picks up the gun and licks his lips.

"We want to know who told you about us," Jono says.

"You already know. Doug did."

"Doug's not around anymore, is he? So sad."

"I don't really know anything. I just read some stuff."

Jackie takes a step toward me and swings at my head with the gun handle. I twist, but the guns whacks me in the back of the head. I hit the floor, groaning with pain.

I'm on my knees and elbows at Jackie's feet. My mouth is a couple inches from his pointy red cowboy boots. They're polished so shiny I can almost see the reflection of my terrified eyes. I start to lift my head to see if he's going to hit me again, but there's a stab of pain in my neck. I grab his legs and wail.

"Please, I'll do anything you want. Don't hurt me."

He tries to knee me in the face, but I grab him tighter and blubber like a baby. I'm over-acting, but not really.

He jerks his legs to shake me loose. I'm on my stomach now, my arms around his ankles. He kicks me again, in the chin, and I lose my grip. I lean back on my knees, look up at Jono, who sits impassively in his chair.

"I'll never say anything. Whatever you want. Just don't hit me again." I bend my toes under my legs.

Jackie steps back, looks down at his boots as if I've contaminated them. As he shifts his gun from one hand to another, I push off my toes, lunge directly at the gun, jarring it loose. I spin away, my elbows whirling, then race toward the window, and leap into it, my arms long, my hands clasped together in a tight fist in front of me as if I'm diving. Which I am. The window shatters and I plunge into the water. It's so cold I can hardly breathe, but I push deeper and swim underwater as long as I can. I come up, gulp for air. A bullet whizzes by my ear. I dive back under, my shirt billowing over my face. I pull it down and bite on it, swimming toward the darkness in front of me, away from the shouts behind me.

Next time I come up for breath, I start swimming the crawl, faster than ever before. The only time I've swum with clothes on was lifesaving class in junior high. I can't hear anything except the splashing of the water and the pounding in my ears. I'm exhausted, but don't dare stop. Ahead, I see lights, but can't tell what direction I'm facing. No matter. I can't swim that far. The boathouse is behind me. I veer right, swim closer to shore, then parallel to it. My arms feel like cement blocks. I head for land, feel for the bottom. There it is. I stand. Rest. Breathe.

The adrenalin is gone. I'm freezing. Depleted. Stiff with pain. But also exhilarated. I won't say happy, but it's in that ballpark. A few weeks ago, when Doug pushed me in the baler and I yanked myself off the conveyor belt, I felt like a victim. Now, I feel more like a hero.

My feet make a sucking sound as I pull them out of the muck.

26.

Halloween Street Party

The Berkeley recycling yard murder case took a new twist with the discovery yesterday of an architect's sketch of a software campus on the city-owned land that Recycle Berkeley was recently evicted from, and a meeting between city council aide Gill Sykes and murder victim Doug Spaulding the morning before the murder. Sykes' lawyer says his client may be guilty of having ambitious ideas for developing West Berkeley, but he had nothing to do with the murder.
—Daria Reeves, "New Developments in Recycling Murder,"
San Francisco Chronicle, October 31, 1998

I wake up to the smell of coffee. I'm in a sleeping bag in the living room of my old house. Eileen's house. The sun is streaming through the windows.

There's a note on the kitchen table. "I'm glad you called last night. Have to help a friend move. Maybe I'll see you tonight at the rally."

I feel stiff when I stand up, but remarkably whole for someone who got drunk, crashed through a plate glass window, and dodged bullets while swimming in the icy bay. My neck is throbbing, but not as sharply as last night. My head is cloudy, my mouth as dry as cotton. I've got cuts and scabs on my knuckles and the back of my hands. But I slept more soundly than I have in weeks. I'll have to make a note of that: For better sleep, get drunk and exercise vigorously before bedtime.

I vaguely remember walking through deserted streets of East Oakland and calling Eileen collect from a pay phone outside a liquor store. She came right away, no hesitation, with warm clothes and thick wool socks.

Maybe Doug wasn't so paranoid after all. I don't know if Jono and his pals are coming after me again, or they were just trying to scare me. They did that. The only thing they seemed to want to know was who told me about them. Should I go to the San Leandro transfer station and warn Gino? I didn't identify him in the story, but there may not be more than a few potential sources.

I don't know why they were shooting at me. Maybe it's like if you run from a bear, it will chase you. I made a dramatic exit and so they went after me.

The newspaper's in the kitchen and Daria Reeves' story is on the front page, lower right corner. My name is in the second paragraph. Spelled right.

I read the story twice. She not only covers the development plans, but also includes some of what I told her about Con's infiltration of community groups and its history of crushing competitors. All the threads I've been following seem to be coalescing into an epic story, like a bunch of small streams feeding a mighty river. It's *my* story she's telling, though she's clearly done additional reporting. This is the first time any-one but me has done any significant excavation of Scavenger's activities.

She's got Tom Herman denying infiltration charges and call-ing Renée Moraine a "publicity-seeking impostor." Scavenger has no record of hiring her, he says. No one has ever heard of her. Yes, the company donated money to the Pittsburg com-munity group, but Herman characterized it as part of its stan-dard charitable outreach. "We strive to be good neighbors."

I know it's irrational, but I look for a story about my

boathouse adventure. I guess I'll have to write that one.

The newspaper also says rain is coming, but the sky is clear and blue as I walk home. Indian Summer has lasted far longer than usual. The air smells of dusty sidewalks and car exhaust. A band of brown smog hugs the horizon across the bay.

All over town, there's a buzz about tonight's Halloween street party and rally outside the barricaded Re-Be yard. At the produce store on San Pablo, the woman in front of me is chatting with the checkout guy about it. "Can I take my kids?" she asks. There are police cars prowling the empty streets near my warehouse.

When I get back to my studio, there's a message from Donna. I call her and tell her about my harrowing escape in East Oakland last night. "I'm a better swimmer than I realized and either braver than I thought, or crazier."

She's so sympathetic, it's embarrassing. And then she deconstructs the story in the *Chronicle* and wants to know all about the Halloween street party. There are even posters up in her neighborhood in the city. I don't have to sweat about inviting her—she practically invites herself.

I'm thrilled, then immediately start worrying about what to say if Barb sees us together. Totally irrational, I know. A few days ago, I called Barb to ask if she'd join me for the party, but she hasn't returned my call.

I borrow a Santa Claus suit from my puppet theater neighbors, so I'll be in disguise. It was used for a life-sized puppet a few years back, so it's sewn into one piece and I have to wiggle into it from the back. But it was originally made for humans, so it fits snugly once I wedge a pillow in front of my stomach.

Donna laughs when she arrives. "Aren't you a little early, Santa?"

"Oh, I'm just checking out the chimneys," I say, my voice low and gravelly. "Last year, I got stuck in a couple, so the wife put me on this low-carb diet." I croon from my throat with a raspy baritone. "Chipmunks roasting on an open fire…"

She gives a friendly punch to the pillow and rolls her eyes. "My friend's sister works in a lab at San Francisco General," she says, pinching the sleeve of the green hospital scrubs she's wearing. "This is the best I could do."

I tell her she looks beautiful and sexy. I mean it. I really do, but if feels like such a line, and I deliver it in a light way that feels like self-mockery. Like it's something I would never say. Donna doesn't know that. She smiles and says thank you.

Maybe it is something I would say after all.

Fifteen years ago, when I was regularly going on bicycle trips—along the East Coast, around Vancouver Island in British Columbia, through the rolling hills of Arkansas—one day I piled my camping gear on my bike in Berkeley, barreled out of town, then took a U-turn and headed back in, pretending to be a tourist. I stopped a dozen people to ask where to camp for the night, asked about the town as if I'd never been there before, and talked to far more strangers than I would have in a month of regular jaunts through town. I noticed how the Spanish-style bungalows got bigger as I headed north on Peralta, how the troubled neighborhoods were marked by the "drug-free zone" signs. Mostly, I noticed how bold and liberated I felt by my pretense.

Tonight I feel the same way—expansive behind the Santa suit, trying a new persona on Donna, the jolly romantic. I know this isn't the real me, but there's nothing wrong with acting as if it is.

Earlier, on the phone, Donna called me "refreshing" again. I get the sense that she's dated one too many corporate golden boys and she appreciates my modesty. Whatever the reason, I'm flattered by her interest and when I tell her that, she says she's glad. She's so straightforward compared to Barb, but I can't help wondering if she's slumming it—she might like to *visit* this quirky and refreshing Berkeley world where we care about saving the planet and all that, but she's not going to settle in. No matter. Savor the moment.

Ahead, four or five spotlights fan across the sky, and I hear snatches of amplified singing by a man with a low voice. In one side pocket I have my skinny notebook and a pen, in the other my smallest camera. I'm not relaxed at all. My mind and body are throbbing with the drama of the past few days, and I have no clue of what's ahead—with Donna, with the Re-Be street party, with the election on Tuesday, with the next week, or year, or decade. But something is bound to happen and I'm damn well going to show up to find out what it is.

Big clouds hang in the sky. They slipped in late afternoon, like the fog, but they're more like the ominous Great Plains summer thunderclouds from my childhood. There's a hint of Missouri summer in the air—a sluggishness, a thickness, with that ephemeral sugary ozone smell you get from lightning storms or running the vacuum cleaner for too long. Plus, there's the sweet and skunk-like scent of pot floating down the street.

We're still a couple blocks away, but I hear snatches of a singer keening the Grateful Dead song, "Friend of the Devil."

"Do you like to get high?" asks Donna.

"Sure, sometimes. How about you? Doesn't that impact your playing Scrabble?"

"Yeah, it does, but in a good way. I mean, I never play competitively when I'm high, but it's nice to play without the edge. I still play pretty well. I see the board differently. You probably think I'm straight as an arrow."

"You're full of surprises."

"Thank you," she says. "Believe it or not, I used to go across the street in Lodi to my neighbor, this old lady, and she had a hookah, like the kind they have in Turkey, not like a bong or anything, and we would sometimes get high and watch TV. We played Scrabble a time or two, but she didn't have much aptitude or vocabulary."

I try to tell Donna more about my boathouse adventure, and

she's very interested, but as we get closer, it's so noisy I have to shout into her ear. It's not the time for involved narrative.

"Hey Donna," I nudge her gently with my elbow. "You too big to hold Santa's hand?"

She pokes her finger into my spongy belly. "I don't know, Nick. Depends on what kind of presents you have in your bag. Hey, you don't have a bag."

"Maybe later you can sit on Santa's lap and tell him what you want for Christmas."

"Well, he's tall, dark, and handsome, and I don't think he's going to fit in a bag." Then she gives me her hand. I take off my white gloves. It's too warm for them.

The front gate of the Re-Be yard is strung with chains and barbed wire and standing in front are ten guards in dark blue uniforms. There's a logo in yellow script on their front pockets. Eight fold their arms in front of them. Two hold them behind their back. All wear sunglasses—the floodlights are that bright. Searchlights chase each other across the sky from a makeshift platform, hooked by a fat yellow extension cord to a gas generator behind the dead end sign. In the center of the street, a lanky, goateed singer on a flatbed truck wails away about Wal-Mart. His red t-shirt says, in strident black ink, "1. Arm the Peasants. 2. Seize the Factories. 3. Smash the State."

There must be at least a thousand people here, and more keep streaming in. Hundreds are in costume—a few elaborate, but most are simple plastic masks. I see at least a dozen Bill Clintons, almost as many Monica Lewinskys. And Nixon never seems to go out of style.

Twenty feet from the flatbed truck is a station wagon with a sheet of plywood on the roof and hundreds of flashlights taped together in a pyramid, all shining on the singer. There are a couple dozen flashing green and white bike lights as well.

Out of the corner of my eye, I think I see a bolt of

lightning, but I assume it's another wandering searchlight. A few seconds later, I hear thunder rumbling. My armpits are sticky with sweat. Santa's overdressed.

Hanging from cars, streetlight poles, building windows, are painted bedsheets and hand-lettered signs. "Take Back Re-Be," "Consolidated Scavenger Out of Berkeley," "Con Go Home." A row of tombstones parallels the Re-Be wall along Sixth Street, each with a flashlight shining up on it from below—"Re-Be Will Rise Again," says one. "R.I.P. Scavenger," says another.

Across the street I spot Jimmy, dressed in stained jeans and an untucked button shirt. I ask Donna to wait, and stride toward him. He has an aluminum can of Weltanschauung in one hand and he's grinning and swaying. I'm sure he won't recognize me. "Hey, hey, Santa, yeah, you know." He gives me a gentle jab in my belly. Not as gentle as Donna's. "Gonna bring me some beer for Christmas? Better be cans, so's you can drop 'em down the chimney. Good enough."

He throws his arm around my shoulder, as if for balance, and shakes his head, his grin falling into a grimace. "Man oh man oh man," he says, "Jimmy's been naughty this year. I am way wasted."

He pulls his arm away and faces me, cold sober in recognition. "You alright, man? I'm so fucking sorry. I didn't think they would, you know—"

"Try to kill me?"

"They were just trying to scare you, man," he says. "I had to bring you there, I swear, I owe them so much money. Shit, are you a good swimmer."

It's hard to be too angry with Jimmy. He's like a child.

"Did they waste Doug?" I ask.

"Don't ask me that, man. Don't ask." And he slips into the crowd.

I'm not too modest to notice, at a table stacked with flyers, a pile of reprints of my latest story in the *Beat* and Daria Reeves' story from this morning's *Chronicle*.

In between musicians are speeches from the truck bed, mercifully short. Kisa stands on stage, holding the microphone, her face covered by a ghoulish hood. "We're here to celebrate Halloween, but also to send a message to City Hall and Consolidated Scavenger that they picked a fight with the wrong people, trying to shut us down. Back to music in a minute, but one announcement first. At nine thirty, we're going to march to University Avenue. Please join us, and remember, we do not have a parade permit. It's only because there are so many of us and that we are peaceful that the city is letting this party happen. We want to send a message, but we also want this to stay peaceful. Thank you. Now here's my colleague Renée Moraine, to tell you a story."

Renée wears a simple light blue summer dress, down to her ankles. Not much of a costume, but then I've never seen her in a hippie dress like this before.

"I owe it to Re-Be, and to myself, not to hide behind a costume," she says, "especially on Halloween." Her mouth is too close to the mike. "I'm a Re-Be staff member, and some of you know from the newspapers, I betrayed Re-Be, before coming to my senses." She does a pretty dramatic rendering of her covert meetings with Scavenger and then she mentions me. "I didn't come clean on my own. Brian Hunter, a reporter for the *Beat*, and a former volunteer for Re-Be, caught me in the act, and I thank him for that."

Donna nudges me in the ribs and grins. After Renée comes Miguel, who rails against Scavenger's criminal record. The crowd near the stage is getting riled up and I steer Donna to a spot outside the floodlit area where it's dark enough I can't see the green of her scrubs.

"Have you ever wished you could kiss Santa Claus?" I ask.

"Now's your chance."

I take her hand and place it on my beard. "Might be kind of scratchy, but I can pull it down."

We slowly lean forward until our lips graze each other's. She pulls back for a second, then returns for more.

"Mmmm," she says.

I step back. She grabs me by the pillow and pulls me toward her.

While Miguel continues his rant—I hear every word, though I try not to—I lean against the brick wall of the print shop and Donna leans on me and we make out like teenagers. My belly pillow keeps our bodies apart. She's a hungry kisser, but she keeps her eyes closed or averted.

After Miguel comes a woman with a high voice singing an Irish ballad. Donna pulls me closer.

"You're fun," I say. "Scares me a little."

"As much as being fired at by bad guys?"

"Much more."

"Well, there's good-girl Donna and bad-girl Donna. Good-girl Donna stayed home tonight."

"I like both Donnas," I say. "Maybe someday we could do a threesome."

"Don't get any ideas. It would get pretty crowded in your tiny studio."

I'm about to give her another kiss when I spot Barb in the crowd thirty feet away. She's leaning her ear toward a tiny woman with gray curly hair. A teacher friend of hers. Can't remember her name.

I turn my head, pull the beard back up on my face.

"What's wrong?" Donna asks.

"Nothing. Just feeling shy."

"You weren't shy a minute ago."

I feel Barb's eyes on my back. I nudge Donna toward the

railroad tracks. "The march is starting."

I steer us in a wide arc away from Barb. We walk up Sixth Street without talking. I can tell that Donna is put off, but I don't know what to say. There's no good way to spin it. Just ahead of us, the flatbed truck inches up the street, carrying the searchlights and the generator that powers them. Two young women are singing the Sweet Honey in the Rock song, "We Are the Ones We Are Waiting For."

The security guards stay in front of the fortified entrance to Re-Be, but police on bicycles and horseback follow the marchers. I see officers from Oakland, El Cerrito, Albany, even the California Highway Patrol. Behind the truck is a small contingent carrying torches. Hundreds of people are carrying flashlights, but Santa forgot to pack one.

Miguel is on the sidewalk leading chants through a megaphone.

Hey, hey, ho, ho, Scavenger has got to go.
Hey, hey, ho, ho, Scavenger has got to go.

Ginsberg from the Re-Be board, dressed as a scarecrow, in a red flannel shirt, is on the sidewalk flailing his arms and yelling at Kisa. She's holding her hands in front of her face as if to defend herself physically from his words. He is livid, his neck muscles bulging and his face flushed. I grab Donna by her sleeve and scurry toward them. Kisa is gone, running toward the front of the march. I pull down my beard.

"Dammit," Ginsberg says. "Dammit."

The chanting gets louder.

"You'd think I was the enemy, not an ally."

He adjusts his straw hat. Every time he talks to me, he's so guarded, worried about how he'll sound on the record. But he doesn't seem to be thinking about that now and I'm not about to remind him.

"I would love to be wrong," he says, "but watch. It's going to backfire. Civil disobedience is theater. You have to rehearse. They're not prepared. They're not disciplined. There are too many free agents wandering around, with masks on. This is a nightmare waiting to happen."

Ginsberg starts talking about the protests against the Persian Gulf War in '91, when roving bands of "so-called anarchists" in Berkeley broke windows, set fires, and overturned a police car. "I hate that they call themselves anarchists," he says. "They sully the name of an honorable and disciplined radical tradition. They just want to tear things down, show how screwed up the system is, lash back at everyone and everything. They'll be here tonight. Count on it."

Then he stops and appears embarrassed by his outburst. I introduce Donna. We slip back among the marchers. As we approach University Avenue, Donna stops, pulls down my beard, and gives me a quick peck on the lips. I almost jump. "Thanks for inviting me," she says.

That's when the sit-in starts.

When the stoplight changes to red, several dozen people in costume dash into the street and sit down facing the University Avenue traffic. The flatbed truck and a couple of other trucks roll in behind them. Burly Ray Robbins, a former Re-Be staffer, hops out of the driver's seat, climbs on the hood, and raises the ignition key high so the crowd can see it. Then he heaves it onto the roof of the futon store across the street. The light changes and honking starts at the same time as the crowd cheers Ray's throw. He takes a bow, jumps off the truck, and sits down in the street.

"Join us. Sit down with us," shouts one of the masked women in the front row. Soon there are more than a hundred people sitting in the intersection. Horns blare. The protesters are surrounded by dozens of police, many walking next to their bicycles. It's too crowded to ride them. One barks through a megaphone.

"If you do not disperse, you will be arrested. I repeat. If you do not disperse, you will be arrested."

The order is met with cheers and more honking. The driver of a car at the front of the line, a bald, gray-bearded man wearing a leather jacket and blue jeans, turns off his ignition, climbs out, and raises his fist as he sits down in the street. The crowd roars its approval. The searchlights fan back and forth across the sky. The young man who was singing "Friend of the Devil" earlier climbs up on the truck next to the generator and leads a chorus of "We Shall Not Be Moved."

Two helicopters hover above, stark in front of whitish storm clouds. A cameraman steps carefully between sitting protesters, followed by a reporter who leans over and sticks her microphone in someone's face.

"Were you expecting this?" Donna shouts into my ear.

"No," I say, "but then I wasn't expecting to be kissing you either."

"Wait till I tell my friends I made out with Santa Claus."

After another warning, the police wade into the crowd and start making arrests. But every time someone is lifted up and escorted—or dragged—over to the police bus on Addison Street, someone else takes their place. There seem to be hundreds of police here, but they're overwhelmed by protesters. Shannon from Re-Be is one of the first to be arrested. She waves her Hillary mask as she's led off. I pull out my camera and try to get closer.

A bolt of lightning streaks across the sky, and a second later comes a rumble of thunder.

I used to tell people that I was arrested once for sitting down all night in front of a Wells Fargo ATM machine protesting the bank's investments in South Africa, but it's just a joke. I've never done civil disobedience. I'm feeling a sudden urge to do so now, to sit down in the street and get dragged off by the police in plastic handcuffs.

I want to take sides, not stand on the sidelines as an observer. Sure, I'm on the side of the truth, but it's not the truth that's going to determine whether Sheila Womack and Gill Sykes and Tom Herman boot out Re-Be in favor of dot.com development and Consolidated Scavenger's monopoly. I pause momentarily to wonder what Donna will say, but another voice chimes in quickly: "Don't let her make your decisions."

I pull down my beard and speak into her ear. "I'm going to sit down here in the street," I say. "I might get arrested. Do you want me to walk you back to your car, or can you get there yourself?"

"Wait a minute," she says, "I thought you were a journalist. You're going to hurt your credibility."

"I'm not so sure that whatever credibility I have has ever made any difference."

"How can you say that?" she says. "Why do you think you were in the *Chronicle* this morning?"

"Because I found the blueprints. The plans. They weren't interested before. And that wasn't because I was a journalist. I wanted to write the story, but they said no." I pause. "So you think I shouldn't do it because it might compromise my integrity, but you're not mad at me about leaving you on your own on a Saturday night?"

"I'm a big girl, but thank you for thinking of me. Seriously, Brian, there are plenty of people who can sit in the street and get arrested? Who's going to write the killer story about what happened here tonight? Who's going to tell the truth that you're so big on? Keep taking pictures."

Before I can deliberate further, I hear an explosive crash behind me and turn to see the shattered glass window of the Bombay Sari Palace fall to the sidewalk. Then comes a sharp "whhhhhup" and a burst of flame from a garbage can a few feet from the window. Six or seven revelers wearing capes and black masks whoop and dance around the fire.

Then I'm crushed in a mob of people going in opposite directions. A cluster of police race toward the fire and the broken window. Everyone else is running the other way. A short Asian woman with a clenched jaw is pulling a child by the hand and smacks right into me as I turn. Before I can help her to her feet, I get bumped from behind and hit the curb with my left shoulder. I raise my head to look for Donna. More glass breaks and then one of the helicopters dips lower and the wind whips around me.

There are so many sounds at once. Horns honking. The police bullhorns. The throbbing base from a car stereo. A high-pitched howl of pain. The deafening helicopters. The crackle of fire. I smell plastic burning, acrid diesel exhaust, the grainy earthiness of horse manure, Thai food from the corner restaurant. Ducking and leading with my head, I wiggle away from the crush of bodies and find myself next to the flatbed truck, which is empty. In the distance, a train whistle shrieks, and then comes the clanging bells of the crossing gate. As if any traffic is moving. Behind me, a man bays like a wolf.

I swing up on the stage, about three feet off the ground, feeling a sharp spasm in my shoulder as I push off. I pick up the microphone on the bed of the truck and tap it. It's live.

OK, brave boy, you want to make the news. Go for it.

I straighten my beard and lift the mike to my mouth. "Listen up kids, it's Santa Claus, eight weeks early." I haven't stood on a stage and spoken into a microphone since the band's last days seven years ago. I curl my fingers tightly around the mike, feeling the metal grooves with my palm. Can anyone hear me? Is anyone listening?

"I'm not really Santa Claus, but you know that. I'm actually a member of the big, bad media we all love to hate. I'm a news reporter who's been covering the Re-Be fight for several months. And let me tell you something else you already know. What the story on the TV news is going to be tonight. How Re-Be is standing up to the city of Berkeley and Consolidated Scavenger? No, the story will be: 'Riots rock Berkeley. Unruly protesters break windows and burn trash cans.'"

From the back of the crowd comes a cheer. Or is it a jeer?

"The television news," I lift up the mike for emphasis. "The people watching the news. They're going to say, 'Oh, it's Berzerkeley.' They'll ridicule what should be a great moment of people rising up and stopping the takeover of an important community institution." My God, I sound so preachy.

"Let's stop with the vandalism. You know what Santa says, 'Peace on Earth.'"

"Fuck Santa," I hear from the back. "Fuck off." And then comes a chorus of jeers. I think they're shouting down the hecklers, but I'm not sure.

As I turn my head, a rock the size of my fist flies by my face. It smashes the front windshield of a black and blue Berkeley police car. The glass shatters, but doesn't break. The rock rolls onto the hood.

I feel the first droplet of rain on my wrist. Then another on my cheek. Kisa is looking up at me from the edge of the truck bed, her hood off her face, her eyes wide. I reach out my arm and pull her up to the stage, feeling another spasm in my shoulder.

"Santa's done now. Please, I want you to listen now to Kisa Bettis from Recycle Berkeley. She's one of the organizers of tonight's protest. She's good people. Kisa Bettis."

When I hand her the mike and carefully lower myself off the stage, there's a roar of cheering and clapping, whether for Kisa or me, I don't know. I hear the same voice at the back yell, "Fuck Santa," but he sounds hollow, and the cheering drowns him out.

"Let's go back," Kisa says, her voice calm. "Let's walk peacefully back to the Re-Be yard." The drizzle is falling more steadily now. Kisa turns and faces the protesters sitting in the street. One of the spotlights turns to illuminate her. She's taken off her hood and her hair is wild and frizzy and pointed in three directions. One strand is stuck on her cheek and seems attached to the hood twisted around her ear. She flings up her arm in front of her face to block the light, but keeps talking. "We've made our point. The rain is coming. Dozens of our courageous brothers and sisters have been arrested. We've inconvenienced enough drivers. Let's open the streets back up, go back to Re-Be, and continue our party. And be peaceful."

Her exhortations are greeted with a mix of applause and boos. Mostly boos. A group of protesters chants, "Hell, no, we won't go." But four or five people blocking the intersection slowly stand up, then a few seconds later, another two, then a clump of about six. For a brief moment, it seems as if there's a hush in the din and all eyes are locked on the protesters rising to their feet in slow motion. As if practicing tai chi. It's quiet enough, for a split second, to hear raindrops bouncing off the hood of the flatbed truck. The police pull back. The helicopters seem muted. One large man dressed as a clown gets up, then falls back down and has to be helped up. He grins. Others laugh. There are still dozens of people sitting defiantly when a police officer speaks through a bullhorn in a calm voice. "We will give you five minutes to clear the intersection. Anyone remaining on the street in five minutes will be arrested."

Ray, who flung the key of the flatbed truck onto the across-the-street roof, must have a spare, because he climbs back into the truck and slowly backs it into a driveway as the crowd retreats. A couple police officers and some costumed civilians push and wiggle the garbage can back to the curb. I stand on my toes and scan the crowd for Donna in her green scrubs.

With Kisa still standing on it, speaking quietly into the microphone with the patience of a kindergarten teacher, the flatbed inches down Sixth Street in the middle of the throng of marchers. The drizzle is gentle and soothing.

But the slow motion is shattered by another rock-meets-glass explosion, then war whoops and police bullhorns and honking cars. Now everyone is running. I try to get over to the sidewalk so I can stand on something and look for Donna. But as I turn my head to make sure I don't get run over, a light mist stings my eyes and they sizzle with sharp stabs of pain. I scream, rub my eyes, fall to my knees. Around me, I hear an awful chorus of shrieks and moans. I curl up into a ball and wail.

27.

Full House

Riots rock Berkeley tonight as costumed protesters shut down University Avenue, set fires, and vandalized local businesses. Police made more than one hundred arrests.

—KCBS News, October 31, 1998

When I shake my head clear and open my eyes, I see the traffic moving slowly on University Avenue. Two rows of police officers stand back-to-back and shoulder-to-shoulder across Sixth Street, one row facing University, the other down Sixth. The rain falls in sheets.

My throat tickles. I gulp the wet air greedily, grab my red hat and beard, and stand on wobbly legs. My Santa suit is soaking.

A loose column of protesters is walking down Sixth Street, looking more exhausted than festive. There's the grim reaper, his cardboard and foil scythe wilting. Clumps of people sit on the curb in a daze, and, like the expression goes, they look like I feel. I totter over to an elderly man in a brown monk's robe, who's lying on the grass next to a driveway.

"Are you OK?" I ask.

"No," he says, "but I will be if I just lie here for another week."

I offer my hand to help him up, but he waves it away. My eyes are still teary, but the sharp, searing pain has faded into the more recognizable feeling of rubbing my eyes after cutting jalapeños. I lift my face to the sky and let the rain wash out my eyes.

As I pass the locked-down Re-Be yard on my dazed walk back to my studio, Renée calls out from across the street. She asks if she and her friend Sean can dry off and watch the news at my place. It's almost eleven, she says. "You remember what Doug used to say after demos. 'The revolution will not be televised? Of course it will be. It'll be fucking syndicated.'"

"How do you even know I have a TV?" I say.

"Oh, come on, everyone has one, even if you never watch it."

"It's black and white," I say.

She tilts her head and shoots me this give-me-a-break look.

"OK, there might be color," I say. "Since I only watch black-and-white documentaries, I'm not sure."

Kisa catches up to us and I invite her as well, and she in turn invites Barb and her teacher friend, who have somehow joined us walking toward my studio.

"Man, what a night," Renée says. "You wouldn't happen to have any towels and booze there with your black-and-white TV?"

I do. Plenty of alcohol anyway. Nowhere near enough towels.

I run ahead, my wet black sneakers squishing like sponges. I need to straighten up my studio, I say, but mostly I'm wondering if Donna is waiting for me. I hope she is, and I hope she isn't. I don't want to be dealing with Donna and Barb at the same time. But she's sitting in the front seat of her Toyota, the window partly open and country music playing. She swings open the door and gives me a hug.

"You're soaking. Are you OK?"

"I got gassed, but I'm fine now. A little nauseated. How about you?"

"Still buzzing. Not too wet. Your Santa speech was awesome."

Kisa and the others are waiting at the front entrance to the warehouse. "Hey, it's almost eleven," she shouts. "Let us in."

I try to tell Donna I had a delightful time with her, but please go home now. The words don't come. I unlock my studio door. She invites herself in, introduces herself to everyone.

I pass out all the towels I can find and some dry shirts and socks and sweatpants, pretty much empty out my dresser. Then I haul out the booze. Before our breakup, Eileen and I did a lot of drinking, and then I kept that up for the first few weeks I lived in the studio. I still have almost a full bottle of whiskey, another of brandy, and five bottles of a very drinkable red table wine from Portugal. I dump my soggy Santa suit in the utility sink and slip on some dry clothes.

While I'm hunting for more towels in my storage chest, Donna figures out she's met Barb before.

"I used to work at Scavenger," Donna says, "in the Broadway office, and I remember Tom Herman walking you through the place. He introduced us. You probably don't remember."

Barb nods. Her eyes dart from me to Donna and back to me.

"Some networking thing, I can't exactly remember," Barb says quickly, grabbing the towels from me and passing them out. "I got a tour of the office and met a bunch of people."

She turns to me and speaks quietly—for my ears only. "The truth is, Tom Herman was wooing me to work for Con long before I could ever imagine doing so."

The TV shows live footage of traffic flowing on University Avenue. A reporter standing in front of the shattered Sari Palace tells the story of what he terms a "riot." There's film of the fires, the broken windows, the blaring horns and megaphones. A helicopter shot of freeway traffic backed up on the University exit ramp all the way to Emeryville. Lots of protesters in costume. The news anchor uses that ubiquitous trivializing phrase, "reminiscent of the '60s," as if to say, "oh, it's just a bunch of aging hippies rioting for old times' sake."

The media loves to trivialize Berkeley. Time and time again,

Berkeley proves to be ahead of the curve, and many of the embryonic movements and trends nurtured here—from free speech to recycling to divestment from South Africa—have become mainstream, but the "only in Berkeley" gibe never seems to go out of style.

A long-haired young man named Robbie, looking like he's homeless, tells the reporter, "We're here to send a message to the city to reopen Re-Be." Maybe not the right messenger, but the right message.

Then Robbie's statement is "balanced" with three clips of angry motorists. "Berkeley thinks it can play by its own rules," says the last one.

The newscaster also says that City Councilmember Sheila Womack, reached by telephone at her home, says those arrested should be prosecuted to the fullest extent of the law, especially those who instigated the violence. She says that security around Re-Be will be tightened and that the city will not tolerate any more violence of this sort.

Kisa hasn't stopped pacing since we came inside, not that there's any room to pace. She grabs the remote and switches to other stations, but none have local news. There's a movie on Channel 7, and we catch a teaser between commercials. "Halloween riot in Berkeley closes down University Avenue. Seventy-five arrested. News at eleven thirty."

I've never had this many people crammed into my studio before. Fortunately, I cleaned up this afternoon, before Donna came, and folded the futon into a couch. That's where Renée, her friend Sean, and Barb sit. Barb's friend Marion is in my desk chair, Donna's on a folding chair next to her. Kisa, when she stops pacing, leans against the studio door. I've pushed aside some papers on my desk and perch there, my weary legs dangling.

I'm wiped. I'm not the only one. Kisa, however, is bent on revisiting every episode of the evening. Sean suggests that maybe the violence helped the cause, "put the demo at the top of the news."

Kisa snaps at him. "Sure, yeah, *you* try talking into a microphone while hoodlums are throwing rocks at you. *You* stand there and let David Self-Righteous Ginsberg lash out at you with his oh-so-articulate Stanford debate club arguments. *You* try and reach consensus with a bunch of purer-than-thou radicals. And then you have to worry about what mister-watching-from-the-sidelines Hunter is going to say about you in the newspaper."

"That's not true," I said. "I was not on the sidelines."

"Oh yeah, *you* stepped up. Just in time to pull me up on stage to get pelted with rocks. What a night. How am I going to sleep? Do you have any Advil? I've got a headache, I'm nauseated, and I didn't even get gassed."

Turns out everyone and their sister has been venting at Kisa. Miguel gave her grief because she called off the civil disobedience unilaterally, without consulting others.

"Even Jimmy Pawlowski lectured me," Kisa says, "gave me a piece of his mind, however marinated it might be. 'The revolution,' he said, he actually said this. 'We had the revolution in our fucking hands and you gave it away. The pigs were shitting in their pants.' Does he know what he sounds like?"

She downs another shot of brandy, looks to Barb as she speaks. "I tried to do the right thing. No one else was taking responsibility, so I said, let's march to University. People were cheering as we headed up there and we could have had arrests go on all night. Every time someone was led away, someone else took their place. But all anyone is doing is yelling at me or expressing their disappointment. I stepped up to the plate, but I certainly get no credit for that. I wish Ginsberg had just yelled at me, but he shook his head in disapproval, like I was a stupid child who didn't know any better."

Barb lifts her shoulders and speaks sharply. "Kisa, what do you want from me? You want me to hold your hand? You think you're the first person ever trashed for making an unpopular decision? For making a decision, period? You think you deserve special treatment?" She says "speckle" instead of "special."

Kisa sits down on the arm of the futon. "Why is everyone ganging up on me?"

"Look, Re-Be isn't just some innocent victim here," Barb says, her voice softening. "They never would have shut us down if we hadn't screwed up the reporting, if we hadn't given the city the finger every time they wanted us to be accountable. You wanted the money, you wanted to be treated like adults, but you acted like teenagers who wanted freedom without responsibility—"

"Don't you lecture me—"

"Maybe you're just now figuring out how fucked up Re-Be is. Everybody has to contribute to every decision. Everybody's opinion is equally valid. That's bullshit. Re-Be's got the worst case of Berkeley-itis I've ever seen. I didn't jump ship to Scavenger for the money. I became an expert on recycling after many years of hard work, but Re-Be couldn't handle experts. 'Experts are elitists. Expertise is bourgeois.' Any moron stumbling down the street has an opinion that's just as valid as mine. What did you expect, Kisa? Sure, you tried, hooray for you, but for how long? Six months? You want a medal? I did it for ten years. Did I get a medal? Yes, I did, but I didn't get a chance to accept it before I was attacked with a dead dog, for Christ's sake. Blame everyone else. The city's full of meddling bureaucrats. Con is evil incarnate. The collective is somehow holy, but every individual in it is suspect. The board is overreaching. I don't know what pronoun to use anymore, we, you? Stop whining. Deal with it."

Kisa is stunned, her mouth wide open. We're all frozen for a second. Is this rapier-tongued Barb the same woman I've been swooning over for years? Whew! She's ice cold and searing hot at the same time.

Renée leans forward and faces Barb.

"You're being way too harsh," she says. "Sure, Re-Be is all those things, but we're also family, and this family did a much better job forgiving me when it mattered than—"

"You got a free ride, Renée," snaps Barb. "You betrayed the organization. You lied. You only repented because you got caught, yet you were welcomed back like the prodigal daughter, flying high on the freedom of your public mea culpa."

I raise my hand. "Whoa! Can't we, maybe, all get along? We could check the news on the radio—"

Barb storms over me. "I didn't betray anyone. I gave months of notice. I explained myself repeatedly, but I've been given so much shit about leaving. Endless shit. Then I hear Kisa whine about a tiny fraction of the problems I endured for years. I'm supposed to be sympathetic? Shannon's the only one who said to me straight, 'We'll miss you, but you need to do this.' Everyone else called me a whore, a sellout, leaving Re-Be in the lurch. I kept helping even after I left, though I don't know why."

Kisa stands up again, tears streaming down her face. "Hold on. You're painting us all with one brush here. I never criticized you. I defended you. Over and over again." She's pleading, her voice high, trembling. "You're not talking about Re-Be. You're talking about Doug. He's the one who trashed you. He's the one who blamed you. He's the one who was obsessed with making you into the devil. A lot of us defended you, maybe you didn't know that, but we did. I did."

There's a few seconds of silence, then Barb sighs and bows her head. "Oh, Dougie."

She slumps there looking at her hands folded in her lap while everyone else in the room holds their breath. Kisa put her finger on it. Doug is here with us tonight. His manic madness. The free-floating anger and agitation churning in my studio tonight and in the streets of West Berkeley a few hours ago, the floodlights and the armed guards in their sunglasses, the impromptu sit-in on University, the violence, the tear gas, even my own voluble Santa Claus—the tortured and mercurial spirit of Doug is twisted through all of it.

Donna has hardly said a word since we arrived—when has she had a chance? I haven't said much of anything myself. The drama is unfolding without any help from me. Other than changing the channels and the volume on the TV, which now has a story about Halloween in the Castro.

Then Barb starts talking about Doug, in a slow, dispassionate voice that I have to lean in to hear.

"I can't believe how long I stood for him denigrating me. I can't believe it."

She looks down at her hands, twists her hair in her fingers. Her glass is empty. She reaches across Renee's knees to pick up the whiskey bottle from the floor and fill her glass.

"Whenever I tried to break up," she says, after taking a drink, "he would get all apologetic and vulnerable and say he had a hard time with me finding my power. He supported me, he said, and I would melt. He was sincere. In that moment. We had some stretches where we broke up, and there was this big emptiness because he took up so much space in my life, and when he crawled back and begged me to give him another chance I did. Three times I did. But not four. That enraged him. He thought he could win me over. I had to be cold to him or I would succumb again. I was ice cold. A brick wall."

The rain pelts the skylight. After a minute of silence, there's some small talk, then Donna stands up and says she'd better be going. That starts a mass exodus.

We say our goodbyes and I walk Donna to her car and kiss her goodnight. The rain has softened to a drizzle.

"Maybe next time," I say, "we can have a more traditional date—dinner and movie, not civil disobedience and a riot."

"I'd like that," she says, "but don't apologize. Tonight was... stimulating. Really."

"We'll have wine instead of tear gas next time, I promise."

I watch Donna drive off and lean my head back to drink in the cold, bracing air.

When I push open the door to my studio, there's Barb slouched on the futon, her feet tucked under her, an empty shot glass in her hand, and a look on her face somewhere between come-hither and stop-the-world-I-want-to-get-off.

28.

Creating My Own Truth

At the recycling awards dinner, Barb Genessee never got a chance to deliver her acceptance speech, and she fled after the protesters' attack with the dead dog. But she left behind a scrap of paper with a list of people to thank. One name on that list was Doug Spaulding.
—Brian Hunter, "Murder. Eviction. Aluminum."
East Bay Beat, October 28, 1998

My first impulse is to slam the door and run.

I squeeze the doorknob, take a deep breath, and look around the studio and down the warehouse corridor. "Did Marion leave?"

Barb nods. "Did you kiss the lovely girl good night?"

I close the door and walk across the room to my desk. I want to sit, but can't figure out where.

"What is it with you, Barb? You resist my advances. You don't return my calls. You tell me to find someone who's available. You give me advice about how I need to find a real place to live and a car, and now I hang out for one evening with a woman who likes me, who is not a *'girl,'* who laughs at my jokes, who, by the way, *used* to work at Scavenger, then decided she didn't have the stomach for it. Yes, I kissed her. You did everything but rent a billboard to discourage me. Why are you here?"

"A girl is allowed to change her mind."

"I can change mine too."

Actually, Barb's been giving me mixed signals all along. I remember what some advice columnist said, that when someone gives a mixed message, it's actually a message that couldn't be clearer—I'm trouble and you should stay away from me. Too late for that.

Barb drapes a fleece blanket over her shoulders, and stares intently at her hands. She's laced her fingers together, and is pressing her thumbs together so hard they're trembling with the pressure. After all the larger-than-life storminess of Halloween night and the restive crowd crammed into my tiny studio, Barb seems so small sitting there by herself. Not the same woman who lashed out at Kisa twenty minutes ago. She shifts her legs again, sways side to side.

For too long, I've been thinking that Barb was somehow too "big" for me, too charismatic, but it's not so much that she's big as I'm small. *Was* small.

"You're drunk," I say.

"I'm relaxed."

"You know, I'm not the kind of guy who takes advantage of a woman who's drunk. Maybe now's the time to change my ways."

"Maybe I'm not that drunk. Yet."

I laugh. Or is it a sigh? A little of each. "So what are you saying, Barb, give me more whiskey and then fuck me?"

She cringes, her eyes closing for a second. My heart is beating fast. I steady myself against the file cabinet. Then I sit on the other end of the futon from her.

"That came out wrong."

"I'm not sure why I'm here. I told Marion she should go without me."

She looks warm and cozy, but not comfortable. "I think about you a lot, Barb, especially since we went swimming, and after the walk with Einstein. Actually, I've been thinking about you since the day we first met, but you probably don't remember that."

She shakes her head.

"When my band played a Re-Be benefit. I sort of came on to you, but then Doug came along and I slinked away."

She looks up at me and I see a tiny tear in the corner of her left eye. I swallow. So does she. Her defiance is gone. I feel my entire body opening to her. She looks so vulnerable.

I slide closer to her and run my fingers through her hair. She doesn't flinch or move away, so I do that again. Then inch closer. She looks down.

I gently lift her head and kiss her on the forehead, then I take her hand in mine and we sit without talking for a few minutes. I tell her I'm going to get a glass of water, my mouth is dry, does she want one too? Or does she want whiskey? Water, she says.

There's so much I want to ask her, so much I want to tell her. "I'm glad you stayed." I'm shaking as I say it.

She closes her eyes and I kiss her on the lips.

"Can you turn the lights down?"

I twist the snaky arm of my desk lamp so it's an inch from the desk, then I turn off everything else. The room is dark, but the glow from the desk is enough to see Barb's face.

"Let me open the futon so it's flat," I say. "We'll be more comfortable."

She helps me flatten the futon and spread out the sheets. "It's still too bright," she says.

"I want to see you," I say.

"Do you have any candles?"

"No, but I'll get some, after I get a house and a car."

She half-smiles. "I don't mean to complain."

I turn the desk lamp off and I can barely make out Barb's silhouette a few feet away.

"That's better. Thank you."

"I can't see your face. Guess I'll have to feel my way around."

Raindrops tap dance on the roof and air whooshes through the aging ventilation tubes.

I find her lips, first with my fingers, then with my mouth. We kiss for a long time. And grope. I start undoing the buttons on her shirt. She strokes my arm. I can't seem to undo the third button.

"That's why I like zippers," I say.

"Take your time, Brian. There's no fire."

I slow down to an exaggerated slow motion. She laughs. That melts some tension.

I slide her pants off an inch at a time—that takes a couple of minutes—pausing to kiss her stomach and her breasts. When we both have our clothes off, we slip and slide our bodies together, clinging tightly to each other.

"Mmmm, bare skin on bare skin," I say. "So delicious."

I trace my finger down her stomach, then up the inside of her leg. "You know that old polka song," I say, "'I used to kiss her on the lips, but it's all over now.'"

She pulls my chin up to her face and places her hand on my cheek. "Be gentle with me," she says. "I'm not as tough as you think."

I can see her face now. Just barely.

"Gentle I can do," I say. "Wild and exciting I might need some practice with."

"Excitement is overrated," she says.

We make love slowly and tenderly. I've never gone so slow in my life before. I bury my nose in the back of her neck and breathe in the musky sweetness of her hair. She bites my ear. Then it gets wild and we roll onto the floor, under the desk, and we have to crawl back into bed with the sheets tangled in our legs. Her moans turn to sobs.

"Are you OK?" I ask.

"Just keep fucking me."

I've wanted Barb for so long, and now I'm making love to her and it's thrilling and feral and terrifying all at the same time—as if I've jumped out of an airplane into the chilly, cloudless sky with a borrowed parachute.

My body is clenched, anticipating a crash into hard ground.

When we finish, the sheets are damp with sweat and tears. She rolls away and turns her back. "Are you OK?" I ask again. She nestles her head below my chin, her hair grazing my Adam's apple. She's stopped sniffling.

"I'm just feeling really emotional. I'm fine. Better than fine."

Her body radiates so much heat, I pull away and lie on my back. We rest silently holding hands. I feel calluses on her palm, at the base of her fingers.

"You were gentle," she says. "I liked that."

"You were wild. I liked *that*."

She sits up, downs the water in her glass, then nudges me with it. "Please?"

I fill it from the utility sink.

I want to sleep but my mind is racing. Barb sits up and drinks more water.

I start talking and I can't stop. I tell her about my boathouse adventure, about finding François, about the banker's box. I hear voices in my head shouting questions I'm afraid to ask. I tell her about confronting Gill Sykes, about telling my story to the newspapers. I'm stalling, circling, waiting for an opening. I want her to do the work for me, but I know she won't.

I take a deep breath, swallow, lick my lips.

"You left Doug before you left Re-Be, right?"

I hug my arms to my chest. She hesitates.

"I pretty much had to do them both at the same time. I couldn't work with him. It was hard enough when we were together."

"I'm a little confused about what happened when. Earlier

tonight, Donna said she recognized you from a visit you made to Scavenger, but that had to have been last year. I thought it wasn't until this summer that you started that dance."

Barb is lying on her back, her face to the ceiling.

"It was more complicated than that. I had some conversations more than a year ago, nothing real. Back then, I could talk with Doug, even about leaving Re-Be, and he could listen. He would argue, but we could talk. We did talk. Ending the relationship—he wouldn't discuss that. I just had to do it.

"He was always telling me how terrible it was that I abandoned Re-Be, but that wasn't it. It was leaving him that was so terrible, though he would never admit that. He was so out of touch with his feelings, I'm not sure he even realized that. Then all that anger would come screaming out of him at all the wrong times and in all the wrong ways."

She stops and we don't talk for a few minutes. I want to melt into her, but I keep my distance. Her body burns with heat. I have the sheet over me, but she's moved it down to her ankles. Twice I start to say something, then I tell myself, stay with the tenderness. Like Barb says, there's no fire.

But I'm too awake, too excited, too afraid I'll lose my nerve.

The third time I get it out.

"I told you about the banker's box. There was so much in there—Doug wrote down everything and he didn't exactly file things in an organized fashion. Anyway, there's one thing that got me thinking. It was a note about me visiting you at Con on a Tuesday. That day I came to your office. How did Doug know about that? In advance?"

"Can't you leave your reporter hat off for more than a few minutes, at least in bed?"

"See, the thing is, he didn't seem surprised to see me. At first I thought it was because I was a meaningless piece of nothing to him, but then I thought no, that's not it."

"What's gotten into you, Brian? Can't you just enjoy the moment? We just had some really intense sex. I've really let down my guard. I want to stay in this peaceful place, not get interrogated."

She's right. I've waited so long for this moment, to be lying with Barb in my arms. I've imagined being thrilled, content. I'm not.

"I told you he had been trying to reach me," she says. "I suppose I might have mentioned that you were coming to see me."

"So you're saying that you and Doug were, sort of in contact during this time he disappeared, even though you weren't speaking to each other?"

"Oh God, we were never not speaking to each other. I was *trying* to not speak with him, but he wouldn't stop badgering me. He'd leave voice mail. He'd write email. He waited for me outside my work one day. He even bought stationery and wrote notes and sent them through the mail."

I massage her upper back. Her neck is stiff, her shoulders pulled toward her ears.

"You've got a big knot here by your shoulder blades." I press harder with my thumb. "You're holding tension there."

"The booze has worn off."

"You knew I was going to write about the fight in your office, didn't you?"

Two seconds. Four seconds. I feel my life turning upside down.

"What do you mean? How could I possibly have known?"

"And you knew Doug was going to do that protest too. At the awards. You were so nervous when we were talking. You kept looking out of the corner of your eye like you were expecting something. And I heard from a reliable source that you arranged to shuffle the lineup so you were the last award."

Barb turns over, sits up, pulls the sheet and blanket around her shoulders. My eyes have adjusted to the dark, but I can't make out her eyes. I can tell she's looking at me.

"Brian, you were accusing me of sending mixed messages before. I'm getting some very mixed messages from you." Her voice is sharp.

"Of course, they're mixed." I start out matching her sharpness, but then ease up. "I care about you, I really do. There's nothing mixed about that. But I want you to tell me what's going on."

"We're here, now, together. There's nothing more to tell."

"You can trust me."

I can tell by the tilt of her head that she's studying me.

"Brian, I know you care about me. I'm touched. Truly. It's hard for me to hear this, this distrust from you."

She takes a deep measured breath, runs her fingers across my chest. I expect to feel tension in her body, but instead she seems to relax.

Oh, that's how she does it. She plays the vulnerability card. Woos with her authenticity.

"I can tell when you're lying," I say.

"Come on, lover boy. Romance is not interrogation."

"See most people get tense when they lie, but you, you get all heartfelt and heavy. Direct and honest. Except you're not honest. You tell it like it isn't."

She grabs me playfully by the hair and pulls me to her. "Come on, stop playing Inspector Clouseau. I thought you wanted to be more passionate."

I squeeze her and kiss her deeply, passionately, then I bury my head in her hair. I sit up.

"Barb, I already know more than I want to know." My voice is firm, but I try not to be cold.

She takes a drink of water.

"No newspaper stories," I say. "None. Nada. Zip. Everything stays here."

She puts the glass down. Rubs her eyes. Sighs. Something shifts. I wait.

"So you know how Doug would not let go of the idea that Con was going to take over Re-Be?" She speaks haltingly at first, then picks up a rhythm. "I didn't believe that, at first. I don't even know if Doug did, but he had to believe that Scavenger was evil so he could demonize me. He did convince me that in other parts of the country, Con had gained monopolies by buying up or taking over competitors—you know all about that. So I agreed to stage what we called 'preemptive strikes' against a possible takeover. It was his idea, but I was a willing participant."

I'm wide awake now, my mind racing ahead, trying to figure out what's coming.

"We decided to enlist you to be a messenger, to write these stories about the possibility of a takeover. Keep Con honest. You'd already written those book reviews and we knew you wanted to be a reporter. So Doug pitched you the whole garbage/recycling wars idea—"

"Sure, sure, I knew he wanted me to track the takeover stuff, but you too? You and Doug talked about this? How could you ever have this idea that I would write these stories before I did? You hardly even knew me. You—"

"You talked about it. You told me you were going to pitch the idea to your editor. That time we met on Shattuck, when you were on your bike."

"No, no, that was after Doug bugged me about it. He was relentless. So...man oh man, did I...I mean—" I can't string a sentence together. Barb touches my shoulder tentatively, like she's trying to gauge my level of agitation.

"So did I do what you wanted?" I ask.

"Beyond what we'd imagined. But things got out of hand. Doug abandoned the script. He pretty much did what he wanted."

"So let me get this right—you staged the fight in your office so *I* would write about it? And then you got all pissy and self-righteous when I did? What kind of bullshit is that?"

"The fight was Doug's idea and I did not want to do it, and then it turned out to be vicious. I was shaken. That was no act. It's just that I sort of did know he was coming and he did know you would be there. It was supposed to be light. We wanted to create some drama for you."

"You did."

"I guess I took it out on you when the story came out. That wasn't fair."

"No, it wasn't."

"I couldn't very well praise you for the story."

I wait. So does she.

I lift my head and lean on my elbow so I can see the side of her face. Barely.

"I'm having a hard time believing this. And the demonstration? At the awards?"

"Doug rewrote that script too. I thought there was just going to be some parading in front of the stage with signs, for the TV crews. The dead dog thing—Doug was deranged. He never went that far before. He wanted to punish me, and I didn't understand how deep his desire to do that was until, well, by then I had a pretty good idea. The dramas we scripted were supposed to be small. Once he started improvising, getting hostile, I couldn't reach him anymore. He disappeared. He would contact me, but I couldn't reach him. There was no dog in the script. And don't think I didn't notice what kind of dog Doug found. For all I know, he found a live dog and killed it. I wouldn't put it past him."

I walk over to my sink again and fill my glass. I go to my dresser and pull out the long-sleeved button shirt that Eileen bought for me. It's soft and comfortable and, except when it's hot, always the first shirt I wear after my laundry is clean. I slowly button it up, breathing deliberately. I stroke the worn fabric along one arm, then the other. I'm not cold, but I want the softness, the comfort. I fill Barb's glass and sit down on the edge of the futon. Barb folds the pillow under her head. The red numbers on my alarm clock say 4:23.

"You met with Doug the day before the awards."

She doesn't answer.

"It was in his notes. In the banker's box. 'Check in with Barb on Friday.'"

Barb lies there breathing deeply. Even in the darkness, I can see the rise and fall of her chest.

"There's another thing I don't understand," I say. "Well, there's a lot I don't understand, but, well, let me just ask it straight." I take a breath. I'm jumping off the cliff. "How did you get Doug's van to West Oakland? Or maybe what I mean is how did you get back?"

Barb's shoulders stiffen.

"You must have heard. They found Doug's van yesterday. It was on the news."

She says nothing.

"It was in West Oakland. Near Jimmy's. Jimmy the Scrap Metal Guy."

Barb bolts up. "Remember the night we talked at Bolshevik Café?" she says, leaning toward me with a conspiratorial whisper, touching me affectionately on the wrist. "We did more than talk."

"Of course, I remember. I've thought about it millions of times. I feel like I got to know you that night. But what's this have to do with Doug's van?"

"I thought you were going to make a move on me."

"I thought I did."

"I was disappointed you stopped."

"I was too. But I was married. For all practical purposes, you were too. And we were parked across the street from where Eileen was sleeping. If she was sleeping."

"You know that's what I like about you—you wouldn't have an affair because it's wrong."

"And you would."

"Would and did," she says. Then, after an awkward silence: "You're horrified, aren't you?"

"I'm done being horrified, or surprised, by you. We were talking about Doug's van."

She tugs at the pillow she's sitting on, then throws it at me. I deflect it, then reach down and pick it up off the floor. "I don't want to flirt." I wish I could see her face better.

"I'm not finished talking about *us*. In my car. Why you stopped. I was not giving you mixed signals."

"Changing the subject, are we?" I aim for lightness, but it feels phony. Dark as it is, I can see the whites of her teeth open into a playful smile. I feel like I've imagined, or maybe dreamed, having a pillow-fight with Barb, though it was silly and sunny.

I so want to be playful.

But it's too late. I hand her back the pillow.

She lies back down. "Can you come down here next to me again?"

"No, Barb, I can't." I'm not sarcastic, but cold sober. Almost apologetic.

Then I do it anyway. Lie on my back. She rests her head on my chest.

The drizzle on the roof is soothing, rhythmic. Barb clears her throat.

"Even after we broke up, Doug was still renting space in my head. I'd have imaginary conversations, trying to figure things out, explain to him why I had to do what I did. I still talk with him." She pauses between sentences, sometimes between words, but the pauses get shorter as she continues.

"In real life, we could not have a calm conversation. He would escalate it. But in my mind, we could slow things down and I could make him understand that it was just something I had to do. The breakup, I mean."

I start to tell her that I know all about imaginary conversations, that I have been having them with her. But I bite my tongue. I hear the building breathing.

"For all that manic, energetic bravado, Doug had a depressed soul underneath. I loved that part of him, but he wouldn't let it show. The poor guy. I felt for him. I really did. Once he said he couldn't bear living without me—because I understood him. I don't think anyone else ever did. It was such a bizarre thing—he would say he missed me so much, then he would tell me what a shit I was, a sellout, a hypocrite, a narcissist, a bitch. I had to set boundaries. I had to protect myself."

She stops.

"So Doug clipped the electrical wires, right?" I ask.

"Always with the questions, huh? Is this how you woo women?"

"Apparently so."

Everything I know is suddenly wrong. Yet I've seen this coming for a long time and now it's here and why am I surprised? The pieces have been here all along, but I haven't put them together. I haven't wanted to put them together. I've been looking for new pieces instead and building alternative scenarios.

I created my own truth, just like Doug urged me to, but it's a lie.

She takes my hand in hers, lies on her side facing me.

"He was sabotaging Re-Be. To spite me, to blame me, to make me feel bad for leaving him, leaving Re-Be. It was all going to be my fault. I couldn't believe that he had it in him to be so...obsessed with revenge. I used to tell friends that he would have been a better boyfriend if he had been jilted a few more times in the past. He was so spoiled. So selfish. And so full of energy. Always so tireless and relentless. He used to wear me out. His intensity was unreal."

Barb stops talking. I try to relax, let every thought and feeling pass through me, make way for the next. If the wind keeps blowing, nothing can take root.

"OK, so it's nine at night, it's dark, you're working at Re-Be," I say. "You've promised Kisa you'd finish something or other. Reports for the city. And then, what?"

"I'm feeling depleted. I can't."

"Start at the beginning."

She's breathing rhythmically, her head buried in her chest. I wait. I'm afraid she's fallen asleep. Then she starts talking.

"You're right, it was a little after nine, like the police said. Kisa had already run the data for the report, but she wanted me to review it. She's still new at it. Can you at least hold me?"

I reach one arm around her midsection, but I keep some space between our bodies. My breaths come in short pants, from the back of my throat. I pull my head down into my shoulders like a turtle, try to push my breathing into my diaphragm.

"Thank you," she says.

"So I had turned on the computer and had opened Excel, but mostly I was looking at the hard copy Kisa left for me. I got rid of it later because it had my fingerprints all over it, but I don't think anyone missed it. There were other copies. I heard Rabbit barking.

"He stopped, and then I heard noise from out in the yard, a clanking sound. I took the flashlight from the drawer and walked outside the hut. I picked up a two by four. It was about three feet long, heavy. I took a few steps into the darkness and said, 'Anybody here?' It wasn't that dark, but my voice sounded really small in that big night sky.

"I kept talking. I didn't want to surprise anyone. I figured it was some homeless guy who had snuck in to sleep. Mostly all I could hear was the freeway. And the crickets that live in that thicket by the tracks. That's good, crickets in the thickets. It was muggy, like tonight before the rain. I swept the flashlight across the yard. I relaxed a little, telling myself I was just tense from everything going on and it was a raccoon or something. I called for Rabbit, and when he got there, I shined the flashlight on him and noticed how old he was getting, how his eyes were so droopy and sad. But he was wagging his tail.

"He limped away and looked back to see if I was following. So I did.

"I swept the area in front of me, left to right and back again, and I caught this split-second image of a tangle of wires hanging out of the circuit box on the metal pole by the shed. I walked over there, thinking maybe old paranoid Doug was right after all, there was sabotage going on. I switched arms so I had the wood in my right hand and then I heard the sound of a glass bottle hitting the pavement and breaking. I turned the flashlight toward the sound and there was Doug standing there with wire cutters in his hand. First he squints in the light, then he folds his arms in front of his chest and looks defiant.

"'What the hell are you doing here?' I ask him.

"He took a step toward me and said, 'I work here, remember. Who invited you? Did your corporate masters send you here to rip off Re-Be's office supplies?' He has the gall to say this while he's holding wire clippers in his hand. And yet I felt defensive. I asked him what he was doing with the clippers."

"'You're trespassing,' he said to me. 'You don't work here anymore.'

"'From what I hear, neither do you. You've been fired, and you haven't been showing up for work anyway. This place is going down the tubes and the city is breathing down our neck.

That's why I'm here, to help Re-Be.'

"'Our neck,' he said, with his trademark sneer. 'Our neck? Who asked you to play savior?'

"'Kisa did, and the board.'

"It wasn't until then that I realized how ludicrous the situation was. He was standing there with the wire clippers and making *me* defend myself. So I let him have it—verbally, I mean.

"'You couldn't find evidence of sabotage, so you created it yourself, is that it? You answer me or I'll call the police right now.' Or something like that. I remember every word he said, but not what *I* said. If I would have called the police like I promised, things would have been different.

"'I'm here to bring you down,' he said, and then went on one of those rants that I will spare you about me being in my mighty corporate tower sucking the big Con dick, nothing I hadn't heard before. 'When Re-Be goes down, you're getting the rap, honey.' He was so hostile, so full of vitriol. It was as if I represented all the evil in the world.

"I told him he needed help, that wanting to hurt Re-Be and blame me for it was sick. 'You hate me so much,' I asked, 'that you'd destroy something you've worked on for ten years?'

"'You've already destroyed it,' he said. And then he took a step toward me.

"I raised the two by four over my shoulder and told him to stay where he was. The wood was heavy. My arm was tired. I didn't know what he was going to do. I didn't know what I was going to do. I really didn't.

"'Oh, are you afraid of me?' he said. He made some face at me, like he was sticking out his tongue, but it wasn't that. I can't really describe it. 'Little miss corporate whore with her big salary and her martial arts classes and her billy club is afraid of a skinny guy with a pair of wire cutters. What are you going to do with that club? Hit me over the head with it?'

"'I'd like to kill you with it, put you out of your misery.' I said that. I actually said that. But it was only words.

"'How efficient,' he said. 'You could kill Re-Be and me with one blow.'

"'Oh, that is a laugh. Like you're holding this place together.'

"'You can say it was self-defense, that I was attacking you.'

"He even told me how to dispose of his body. 'After you hit me,' he said, 'drag me over to the baler, pack me inside some aluminum, and ship me to Korea. They won't find me for weeks.' It was almost like he won this battle of wills with me by making me hit him. Doug reveled in people being angry at him. If no one is angry, he used to say, we're not upending the system, we're only shuffling aluminum and glass around.

"'Get out,' I said. 'Get out however you got in.'

"But he didn't leave. He crouched as if he were about to pounce, and then he did this fake lunge, like he was going to tackle me by the knees."

I felt a wave of relief sweep over me. She told him to leave, but he didn't. He attacked her. She wasn't a cold-blooded murderer. She—

"I jumped forward and whacked him. It made a thunk and he went down."

"It was self-defense. You—"

"Brian, he didn't hit me, he taunted me. This is why I keep trying to disabuse you of this notion that I'm a saint."

"Oh, I think you've cured me of that." It comes out sharper than I expect.

"I hit him over and over again and then I sat down on the ground next to him and put my head in my hands and wept." Her voice trembles, but there's not a hint of tears now. "If only I had called the police."

She presses against me, and pulls my arm tighter around her. I can feel the in and out of her stomach. I can also feel myself stirring below. What a dog I am. I pull away.

"I heard the train rumble by. I checked for a pulse, but knew I wouldn't find one. Not much blood really. I was appalled at what I'd done, of course, but I also felt clean, light. Justified somehow. How weird is that? My eyes had adjusted to the dark. There was just a little light from the streetlights over on Sixth Street and I walked over to the baler and I could make out the colors of the cans, the bright ones anyway, the green of the Sprite cans. I snapped open the wire on one of the bales using Doug's wire cutters, and then used the forklift tines to knock it open. I dug a cavity to fit Doug in, lifted him in with the forklift. Turned on the baler. I slid the bale in the back way. I was in an altered state, a daze, but part of me was thinking clearly, like there was a bright light shining in my head and I was looking at everything through a glass window that had just been sprayed and squeegeed. No streaks or dirt. I scrubbed the ground where I hit him. With bleach. Then I found some cans with beer or pop in them and poured them on the pavement."

I sit up, put a pillow behind my head and lay back down, barely touching her. I pull my shirt closer at the collar.

"I know you're going to tell me to turn myself in. Plead self-defense. But he never attacked me. I lost it."

"You snapped, like you were afraid you would. It's still self-defense even if he wasn't attacking you in the moment."

"And what law school did you go to?"

"But it was. You can't just live with this. Don't you think you'd have a hard time holding onto such a heavy thing? I can't imagine."

"Brian, you would never have done this in the first place, but if you did, you would turn yourself in. You would. You're an honorable man. But that's you. What do I gain by doing that? Yes, I did something wrong, something horribly wrong, but going to jail isn't going to make it right. I'll be miserable no matter what."

"But I did do something like this," I say. "I'm no saint either." I've never told her what happened with Joaquin, but it's too complicated to get into now, and it's not the same anyway. "If you turn yourself in, you might get off entirely or get a light sentence."

"A light sentence? What? Ten years? Twenty years? We're in a law-and-order state, Brian. If I had caused some industrial spill that killed hundreds, I might just get a fine, but clubbing someone with a two by four? I mean, there's a guy I know from college who's serving twelve years for driving a dope dealer to a buy. See, I'm channeling Doug. Doesn't that sound like him?"

"So if it weren't for the strike, the longshore workers' strike, that bale would have been on a ship to Korea?"

"They have no evidence. Yes, I bungled the Korea thing. Another mistake. I slapped a bar code from the manifests onto the bale, assuming it would be shipped out in the morning. Used to be we'd ship all our metal to the East Coast, but Kisa lined up this new contract with a Korean broker. The biggest aluminum smelter in the world. I found out about the strike the next day at work. Con also had to shift some shipments, from boat to train.

"But I covered my tracks. I didn't save any of the work I'd done on the computer, so there was no record of me being there. My fingerprints are everywhere, of course, but I worked there for ten years. And I had work gloves on for, well, the baler part and all that."

"Do you have any sort of alibi?"

"I told the police I stayed home, finished reading the Sunday *New York Times,* and went to bed early. There's a bunch of people who can run the baler. There's another of Doug's ideas, 'Let's teach all the board members and solid waste commissioners and council members how to run the baler.' We had a couple of great open houses where we did that. You put that in your story."

I remind her that one lesson isn't enough—it may not be as complex as piloting a plane, but it takes practice. I stop mid-sentence. I feel protective of her.

I feel afraid of her, but I've always been afraid of her. And that excites me.

My penis is hard and pressing against her back. I pull her toward me and climb on top of her.

"What are you doing?" she says.

"My body has a mind of its own," I say, pulling her closer.

She groans. "I am wiped, Brian. It's been quite a night."

"I want to come inside you again." I lift her up and slip a pillow under her.

"Be gentle," she says.

I'm not. I'm selfish. Only interested in my own pleasure, in blotting out everything but the physical sensations.

She turns her face from me. I grab the underside of the futon to keep from falling off, and feel grit on my fingertips. Here I am inside her, where I've dreamed of being since forever, but she's not who I thought she was. I'm angry at her. I'm angry at myself. I'm angry at the fucking universe. Her body finds my rhythm. I bite her neck, pull on her hair. She's ruined everything. For herself, for us. She's fucked it all up.

I come. I roll off. I drink some water. The morning light dribbles in through the skylight. I turn away. I can't look at her.

"It's dawn," I say.

"And who's going to take care of Einstein when they lock me up?" she asks. "He's too old and neurotic for anyone to adopt him. Who's going to take care of my dear old dog, tell me that?"

"Do you want any water?" I ask.

"You weren't gentle."

"No, I wasn't."

She rolls onto her side and pulls the blanket over her head.

"What a night," I say. "I'm going to make some coffee."

Barb sleeps. I sit on the floor watching her upper body rise and fall under the blanket. I drink cup after cup of coffee, and replay the night from a hundred angles. How can she sleep? I can't imagine ever sleeping again.

The newspapers slap on the pavement and there's a snatch of a song in Spanish from the car radio.

Barb is right that I've been deifying her—I've projected all this goodness and nobility onto her. That's what one of my friends, a Jungian therapist, says romantic love is all about. We project all of our saintliness onto another. It's exhilarating, but not real.

I kept making excuses for her. Coming up with alternate scenarios.

Later in the morning, we make love again. I caress her body for a long time. She seems so small and vulnerable, like she's on the verge of tears. Her body arches into mine, and she clings to me tightly.

But she's checked out. We can see each other clearly in the morning light, but she won't meet my eyes. She wrinkles her nose and squeezes her eyes shut. Though her body seems responsive, I don't know if she's feeling pleasure. Or if I am. For a second, when I shift position to rest my arms, I catch her eyes before she closes them. In that fugitive second, I see a shiver of terror in them, as dark and forbidding as the frigid bay I was swimming in Friday night to escape Jono and his henchmen.

She leaves without touching the coffee I pour for her. As she disappears down Eighth Street, I lean against the coarse bricks of the warehouse and gulp the rain-fresh air as greedily as a mountain climber whose oxygen tank has failed.

29.

Election Night

When voters in Berkeley go to the polls on Tuesday, the future of Recycle Berkeley is not officially on the ballot. But with the city's rival political factions so polarized, the Doug Spaulding murder, the eviction last weekend, the recent discovery that developers have plans for the land Re-Be leases from the city, and last night's civil disobedience and riot, it might as well be.

—Luba Voinovich, "How Showdown Over Recycling Could Reshape Berkeley Politics," *San Francisco Chronicle,* November 1, 1998

Back inside my studio, I study the only photograph I have of Barb, a bland, black-and-white headshot that accompanied one of my stories. She looks pretty—her cheekbones are prominent and it's a good hair day—but she's not looking into the camera and her eyes are vacant, as if no one is home. It was taken before the murder.

A week earlier, the same photographer took a dynamic shot of a restless Doug sitting on a bale at Re-Be. You can almost see him fidgeting.

Late morning, after my sixth or seventh or twentieth cup of coffee, I finish reading the newspapers, front to back, including the stock pages and obituaries. They're full of election coverage. Both feature a prominent photo of costumed protesters outside Re-Be on the front page, but only a short blurb. They went to press before the sit-in and vandalism.

I walk like a zombie through the maze of gray corridors to the bathroom. The puppet theater guys are rehearsing and laughing as if it's a normal Sunday afternoon.

Mid-afternoon, I find myself reconciling a bank statement for the salvage yard on San Pablo. My mind knows what it needs, the comforting neutrality of numbers. I catch up with three of my backlogged bookkeeping clients, don't even play music. More than once, I find myself staring at the computer screen, fingers frozen on the keys, not remembering what I'm doing. At one point, I jump up in my seat, startled that the sun has gone down.

That's when I turn on all the lights—my desk lamps, floor lamps, clamp-on utility lights, and the fluorescents hanging by a long steel tube from the center beam of the ceiling. When I strip the sheets and blanket from the futon, I lift them to my nose to see if I can smell Barb. Maybe. I don't know what she smells like. I borrow an extension ladder and clean the panes of the skylight with ammonia, vinegar, and dish soap.

Later, I stuff all the towels and my other dirty clothes into a couple of pillowcases and a backpack and walk to the all-night laundry on University. The rain has come and gone again. The air crackles. Seagulls squawk overhead. Tree branches shake in the wind and leaves flutter to the ground. It smells like the first day of fall. Stapled to almost every telephone pole on University are wet, blurred copies of Daria Reeves' Friday story in the *Chronicle* about the development plans for the Re-Be parcel. I bring home Indian takeout.

When I turn out the lights at around midnight, I'm exhausted, but can't sleep. The studio smells of ammonia. When I open the tiny little window above my desk to let more air in, the hum of the freeway and a bell clanging in the harbor come floating in. I feel snug in the clean sheets, still warm from the dryer, but my mind won't shut down. It bounces all over from Barb to the boathouse to bookkeeping jobs from six months ago. And Donna keeps popping up here and there, as if to say, hey, just because I'm not as deep and disturbed as Barb doesn't mean I don't have something to offer.

But mostly it's the all-Barb channel. I have to do something. But what's more courageous—telling or not telling? Lying or not lying? And what about my promise to Barb about not splashing her personal life all over the newspapers? Does that disappear because she's committed a crime? A murder?

The wind blows the night away and at dawn the skies are as crisp as a snap bean.

After a shower at the Y, I head uphill to the law library on the UC Berkeley campus, and huddle in a carrel, reading up on self-defense and Battered Woman Syndrome. There were a bunch of cases where women who had killed husbands or boyfriends after years of abuse were acquitted. One woman even murdered her husband in his sleep and got off. Self-defense does not have to mean you're in danger the exact moment you kill.

Soon I'm dozing, my forehead pressed to the book, my chin on my wrist. I get more sleep in the library carrel than in my bed at home.

When I call Barb on Monday night, she doesn't pick up.

Tuesday morning, I vote in a storefront Baptist church. There's no city council race in my district—my councilwoman, a Re-Be supporter, has two years left in her term.

Later, Donna drives over from the city to join me for the Peace and Justice Coalition election-night party. The sky is dark when she arrives, but the heavy gray clouds still hold a hint of sunlight. From my desk, I see her drive up in her black Corolla and park in front of the warehouse. She rummages through her tiny purse, looks in a small mirror, and applies lipstick. She musses up her thick hair with her hands and shakes her head before she climbs out of her car. I'm flattered to watch her primp herself before knocking on my door. She looks casual, but chic in black jeans and a black sweater.

"You look lovely." She smiles, hesitates, then steps forward and gives me a quick kiss on the lips.

"Sorry, I'm so late. I would like to blame it on traffic, but the truth is I didn't leave on time."

She kisses me again, this time for a few seconds. She puts her hand on my neck and pulls me close. "We'd better go," I say, breaking free. "There should be some results coming in soon." Well, that was damn romantic. I grab my shoulder bag with my camera and notebook.

As we approach her car, I lift her hair and kiss the back of her neck. "Did I tell you how beautiful you look?" There, a partial recovery.

The election party is only five minutes away, in a former shoe store on Sacramento Street that served as campaign headquarters. The glass double doors are open when we arrive, and a jangly Nigerian pop song, heavy on high-pitched electric guitar, crackles into the street, sounding strangely like California surf music from the 1960s. Inside, display cases that once showcased running shoes are stacked with campaign literature and staple guns.

The front room is crowded with about sixty or seventy people, most huddled around the table with the beer and hors d'oeuvres. Dominating the room on the long side is a mammoth TV sitting on a plywood plank between two wooden stepladders. A man with a bushy beard and a baseball cap is taping wires to the floor of a makeshift stage. A skinny young man in a pink bodysuit and flowing cape weaves through the crowd on a unicycle, giving high fives and a toothy grin to anyone who will indulge him.

"That's Pink Man," I tell Donna.

"You live in a different world than I do," she says.

We peek into the back room, which has floor-to-ceiling shelves on both walls. On a low shelf, next to a label that says "11 Men's," there's a stack of Sarah Gluckman signs and a box of staples the size of a cereal box.

I try to steer Donna back into the main room, but she pulls me into a corner, then, with a giggle, pushes me against the wall and falls into me. "You're pretty cute even without the red suit, you know that?"

I kiss her on the nose first, then the lips. I feel myself getting aroused, but I don't trust my body. It has its own agenda, just like on Halloween night. I wrap her in a hug and pull tight.

"I really had fun with you the other night," I whisper to the top of her head, which smells of vanilla.

She lets go, steps back, and gives me a kittenish closed-mouth smile. "I just have one question. What's the deal with this Barb chick? You've got a thing for her." She doesn't seem angry or jealous, just curious.

"What gave you that idea?" I immediately wish I didn't ask such a dumb question.

"I'm right, aren't I?"

"I like her, but she's not interested in me. We go way back."

"She was Doug's girlfriend, right? She certainly *seemed* interested. I saw her friend leave without her."

She pokes me in the chest and looks at me with mischief in her eyes. "I wonder how she got home. Do the buses run that late? Did you bring her home on your bicycle handlebars? Or perhaps she stayed the night in your luxury suite?"

I kiss her, quickly and lightly. She tilts her head back languidly and gives me a slow-motion grin. "You're cute when you're nervous, too."

We go back to the front room to get some food.

I grab two beers from the cooler, then wolf down a bite-sized taco from a black plastic tray. Wow, that's good. In front of the tray is a business card from "Planet Café" with the words 'duck and avocado tacos donated by" printed in pencil above the restaurant's name.

I hand Donna a beer, take another taco, and eat it slowly, in several bites, savoring it, trying to block out everything but the delicious greasy, crispy, salty taste. Then I wrap two more tacos in a napkin and we head over to Kisa and some of the Re-Be folks. I'm relieved to be in a crowd. I'm guzzling the beer and feeling a wave of fatigue pass through me, like a gust of winter wind.

The first city council returns come in a little after ten. A man with a ponytail announces from the stage that with about fourteen percent of the votes counted, Sheila Womack leads Sarah Gluckman by sixty-three votes. That announcement sobers everyone up fast, but it's early. We don't know what precincts have been counted. It doesn't mean anything, that's what everybody keeps saying.

Because I've been so preoccupied and self-absorbed in my own soap opera, I'm only grasping now how high the level of interest in the election is and how the murder and street party and news about Con's deception and corruption have intensified that.

Yesterday, Sheila Womack fired Gill Sykes and announced that, although she didn't condone the violence of the Halloween protest, she underestimated the degree of community support for Re-Be and would work to reopen the yard immediately. But there's a palpable sense, certainly in this room, that it's too late.

I'm half listening to some architect talking about downtown development and height limits and "knee-jerk opposition to anything different, even in Berkeley," when I see Barb across the room. I feel my neck stiffen, my shoulders hunch. My first impulse is to race over and talk to her, but I resist. I was hoping she would show—after all, she's a political junkie and still very much hooked into the PJ crowd—but I didn't expect her. The architect keeps talking, but it sounds like a foreign language.

I shift position so I can see Barb without turning my head. She's talking to a pensive woman with thick gray hair. Donna seems to be following what the architect is saying.

We hear the next election update on TV. Womack's lead is more than one hundred now and half the precincts have been counted. The room falls quiet. I tell Donna I'll be back in a few, but mumble so she can't understand. In the bathroom, I study myself in the mirror. My hair is unruly, but I don't look as unstrung as I feel.

I take a deep breath, inhaling the lemon and ammonia smell from the mop bucket. What do I say? Hello? Don't script it. Just walk over and be friendly. Something will come out of my mouth. I have my speech prepared, but that's not going to work as an opener.

I walk out of the bathroom away from Barb. My plan is to make a U-turn toward her, so she'll see me as I approach, but ahead of me is Eileen, so I stop and turn around as if I forgot something in the bathroom. I'm grateful to Eileen for rescuing me the other night, but tonight is complicated enough without adding her to the mix.

Barb makes it easy. Before I approach her, she excuses herself and walks up to me. She wears her hair tied back, which makes her look more severe, but as usual a couple strands of gray and black have escaped and she sweeps them to the side with her fingers. As she does, her silver earring flashes. Her face looks puffy, her eyes tired.

"Hi," I say.

She touches me on the wrist and gives me a smile, but it takes a lot of work. "You're here with the girl."

"Yeah."

"So what do you think? It's after ten—is our brave barrister going to come from behind?"

"You care who wins, don't you?"

"Brian, my heart is still with Re-Be. You must know that."

"I don't know what I know anymore."

No one watching us would suspect that we slept together three nights ago. Is this what it's like to have an affair? We don't touch. We stand a foot apart, arms at our sides, but the room is loud enough we have to turn our heads and shout into each other's ears.

"So have you done any more thinking about what you're going to do?" I ask.

Barb lifts her palms to her ears and points to the back room. She leads the way.

I expect to feel angry, but I'm calm. I'm ready to lay down my conditions, give her a chance to do the right thing.

I follow her past the wall Donna pinned me to half an hour ago, then around a corner and through a plywood door to a metal staircase with three steps. The glass on the exit sign is cracked. She props the door open with a brick and sits down on the second step. I sit next to her.

"You know this place," I say.

"Yeah, the PJs used it for their headquarters a couple years ago. Remember, Doug and I were unrepentant PJ 'operatives' for many years. That was not a crime until Sheila Womack made it one."

It's cool on the back stoop, refreshing after the sauna inside. The door rattles with the bass from an Elvis Costello song. I take a sip of beer from my plastic cup. Barb bites her thumb. At the bottom of the steps, a young dandelion grows out of a crack in the pavement.

"Brian, I know you feel like I'm being distant, and I don't blame you for that, but this is not about you. At all. I mean, it is to the extent that you're sweet and kind and I needed that and needed some closeness the other night, but then you were the opposite of sweet and kind. Either way, my retreat is not about you. I'm not open to anyone right now."

"Isn't that hard? To shut yourself off from people who care about you?"

"I can do hard. I warned you about me."

Barb looks at me for a few seconds before returning her gaze to the parking lot. I wrap myself with my arms. I'm cold in my short sleeves.

"Who was it who stayed in my studio after everyone else left, fondling a whiskey bottle, and daring me to fuck her?"

"The truth is I wanted to fuck. Is there a law against that? I thought men were always game for a little catch-and-release fuck."

"You know I wasn't. That's why you warned me."

"Give the man a stuffed animal."

"You know, you are disturbingly good at this parrying and thrusting," I say.

"That's not a compliment, is it?"

This is not the conversation I want to be having.

"I went to the law library today," I say, shifting gears crudely, as if urging an old truck uphill. "California has this law declaring Battered Woman Syndrome scientifically valid so the prosecution can't challenge its admissibility. There was one case in—"

"Brian, please, do you think I don't know about Battered Woman Syndrome?"

"I'm sure you do. I'm just saying, there's this case, People v. Walker in 1991—"

"And then there's People v. Robins, where the defendant gets forty years, and don't forget good old Dolores Sedeño, where after ten years of *documented* physical abuse, she still got a sentence of twenty years. I've done my homework."

"I get it, but it's still your best option, to turn yourself in."

"Not going to happen."

"If I figured it out, so can they."

"You didn't figure it out. I told you."

"No, I knew."

She glares at me. "My best choice is to stay away from the so-called justice system."

I lean back against a metal bar so I can see her. "I don't think you understand. Justice is required. You committed a murder. You have to pay the consequences."

She turns back to me with a pained look on her face.

"I've been paying all my life, just waiting, hoping some day I would get the life I deserved. I watched my baby brother bleed to death before the ambulance showed up. My dad walked out on me when I was in middle school. My mom—look, you met Doug's parents at the memorial. They are a piece of work, but nowhere near as damaging as my mother was. Still is, if truth be told. I'm not making excuses for myself, just stating the facts. I have a cousin who's a therapist and she says the biggest obstacle to people getting better is their unwillingness to accept what is.

"My mother blamed me for the accident, and at the same time, she would tell me that she couldn't manage in the world without me, which was a monster burden for a teenage girl trying to break away and become an independent adult.

"She was the one who insisted I drive Michael to his soccer game. It's not like I was drunk or reckless or not paying attention. Someone was behind me, following close, and we were running late, and I didn't slow down enough to make a clean turn, and I was not an experienced driver, and the man who hit us was going fast. I will never, ever, ever be able to fix what happened and my mother will never, ever stop reminding me of that. She can do it with a raise of her eyebrow or the tone of her voice or one of her plaintive sighs. Now I have another death on my hands that I can never fix, and you think somehow I'll be redeemed by going to prison, that—"

"I didn't say you'd be redeemed. I—"

"I paid my price. I've been paying my price for going on thirty years, and I was just getting myself free this summer, after letting myself be held hostage by a psycho because I was afraid he would hurt me if I left. And then he did hurt me. He was so twisted he taunted me to kill him just so he could destroy my life. Don't be telling me about not paying consequences."

She pants, looking down at her feet.

"My life is ruined. I've fucked up any chance I might ever have of being happy. Do you think I can lead a normal life now? You think I can fall in love? Bear a child?" She shrinks into her shoulders. "You don't know me if you think that."

She rubs her eyes and looks up at me.

I won't let myself get hooked, but this can't be an act. This is the troubled, vulnerable Barb that I've long been so attracted to, though the trouble goes far deeper than I imagined. She looks like she's about to cry. I swallow.

"Doug was abusive. You were afraid. That's why you can claim self-defense."

"Brian, the truth is, I would if I could. I don't believe I can win." She whispers. Her mouth twists as if she's in physical pain. "You looked for a couple hours at some books in the library. Brian, I've been studying this for the past ten days. What do you think I do when I can't sleep? People v. Jennings, 1987. They tried Battered Woman Syndrome and the prosecutor claimed her life was never in danger, and she got eighteen years. Do you know how old I'll be in eighteen years? Do you have any idea what prison is like?"

I lick my lips. I can still taste the saltiness of the duck taco. I lift my cup to my lips, but the beer is gone.

"I thought we had a special connection on Saturday," she says. "You told me I could trust you and I did. I let down those incredibly thick walls I've been hiding behind. It felt liberating to tell you who I am. I cannot understand how three days later, you want to send me to prison."

She looks so sad and small. I want to take her in my arms and make it all better. I inch toward her on the step. She hugs herself, shivers. Maybe we can still soar together, I think. But it's too late. I jump to my feet.

"You know, I have to say that I like this act better than the cold and indifferent act." The words coming out of my mouth surprise me as much as they do Barb. It's as if I've pressed the start button and a different tape than I expected is playing. "This one sucks me in. The vulnerable victim. This act usually works for me. Not tonight."

"Brian, this is no act. You know that."

"Do I?"

"This is who I am. I'm not pretending to be someone I'm not. The cold and indifferent bitch. That's me. The one who feels sorry for myself because she fucked up her life. That's me too. You only want to see the part of me that wins awards and holds Re-Be together. That's me too, but it's only part of me."

"Not true. I've always been attracted to your dark side. But you're darker and badder than I realized, that's all."

She chuckles under her breath and then leans back and gives me that same open-mouthed, come-hither look she did on Halloween, sans empty shot glass.

"I'm liking this take-no-prisoners Brian. Maybe you have more bad boy in you than I realized. It's sexy. Is that who you really are under that mild-mannered Clark Kent costume?"

I don't bite. "The van," I ask. "You never told me about the van."

She says nothing.

"Doug's van. How did you get it to West Oakland?"

"Why do you care about that all of a sudden?"

"I want to know."

She stares at me. I stare back.

"His bike. He kept it in the back of his van. I rode it back to Re-Be, then came back with it in my car. I kept my gloves on the whole time. Satisfied?" She buries her face in her hands.

I get up, walk back and forth on the asphalt and suck in the cool night air.

"Let me think out loud for a minute. How's this? You stop working for Con, resign publicly with some harsh words for Con's predatory practices, then go back to Re-Be." I stop, rethink what I just said. She's not going to turn herself in, and I have to do something. "OK, Re-Be is struggling—let's assume it survives, even if Womack wins. Maybe you can, I don't know, imply that Con was responsible for Doug's murder. No, scratch that. But you can help Kisa succeed as director, use your considerable skills to make Re-Be thrive. Doug is gone. Kisa is capable, if a little green. She won't have to contend with Doug. Ginsberg is dedicated to making Re-Be work. You've had your glory days. You've had your taste of corporate culture. You work behind the scenes."

I nod to myself. Not bad. It's not prison, more like community service. Definite consequences. Some semblance of justice. Barb plays with her hands, squeezing one with the other, then reversing hands. She shoots me an accusatory look. "So what are you saying?" She draws out the words into snarls. "You're going to snitch on me if I don't pick one of your multiple choice answers?"

"I'm just trying to be flexible here."

She gets up and charges toward me. In my face.

"This is blackmail. This is bullshit. Who appointed you sentencing judge?"

I back away. "It's not blackmail. You're twisting what I'm saying. I don't have to give you *any* option at all. But I'm not willing to be an accomplice and, I don't know, what do you want me to say? Let's go to Mexico. I'll drive the getaway car.

I don't think so."

"You really know how to make a girl melt."

"That sounds like a no."

"Brian, you don't know anything. You had parents who over-protected you, poor kid, and you suffered from lack of confidence, such a tragedy. Your relationship with Eileen didn't last, boo hoo, welcome to the club. Get over yourself. You can't compare your existential angst and moral qualms with what I am facing, what I have faced. Please, open your eyes."

"Barb, I don't mean to dismiss your experience or pretend that I know how you feel. I don't. But I know what it's like to snap, to swing a metal folding chair at my bandmate Joaquin. I almost killed him."

"Almost doesn't count."

"It does. I'm just saying I understand how you can snap. I put Joaquin in the hospital."

"And you turned yourself in."

"It was complicated."

"I'm sure it was."

"I was out of control. I'm not trying to diminish the ordeal that your relationship with Doug was, but my bandmate Joaquin and I, we had a major quarrelsome thing going. When the band was on its downward spiral. He was destructive like Doug was. Hurting us by hurting himself. He practically burned down the warehouse and I hit him with a chair. He's fine. Physically recovered anyway. Still an asshole."

She starts pacing. "Do whatever the fuck you want. Go to the police. Sic the justice system on me. Write your story. Get your by-line. Be a hero. Knock yourself out. I thought you were different."

"This is exasperating. Did you and Doug communicate like this all the time?"

"No," she barks. "He would never make veiled threats like you do. He went straight for the jugular. He didn't *pretend* to be nice and sensitive, giving me 'options.'" She spits the last word. "What a crock of shit."

I feel another tug to give in, like an undertow grabbing at my legs, but I squeeze my jaw, puff up my chest, and plant my feet firmly on the asphalt. She's baiting me just like Doug baited me, just like he baited her.

I stand tall, resolute, but inside I feel like an eight-year-old boy with a squeaky voice trying to be a tough guy. "I get it you don't like my community service *option,* but you understand it, right?"

"You want me to go back to Re-Be and be an unappreciated flunky. Hah, why do you think I left?"

"Exactly, this is a penalty, not a prize. It's not supposed to be something you want."

She turns away, twisting her hair in her fingers and pulling, enough so it's uncomfortable to watch. "I need some time. A couple days."

"Twenty-four hours."

"I know I did something wrong," she says, sounding sincere. Sounding. "The desire to hit Doug has been inside me for so long and Doug knew how to play me perfectly. But I cannot see any benefit in confessing."

"I'm not sure that's your choice."

"Brian, you've got to believe me, I would undo this in a second if I could. I'm wracked with guilt. I can't sleep. I can't eat. I can't work. I can't talk to my friends. It was a huge, huge mistake to cover it up. If I would have gone to the police right away and pled self-defense, things might have turned out different. I was arrogant. I thought his body would never be found."

"Twenty-four hours," I say, and then go back inside to find another duck taco. I can't just let her walk, hold on to her secret.

The tacos are gone, but I grab the second-to-last beer from the cooler. I spot Donna talking to a tall young man with a beard. She's grinning and talking with her hands and he's nodding vigorously, arching his neck to look her in the eyes. I decide not to interrupt. I walk over to the TV, where California's newly elected governor is awkwardly pumping his fist in the air.

Donna taps me on the shoulder.

"Hi," she says with a smile. "You were gone a long time. What were you doing, finishing up what you started on Saturday?"

"We talked. That's all."

"About what?"

"You don't want to know."

"Of course I do."

"OK, I don't want to tell you. How's that?"

I like Donna's teasing, but right now it feels like being tickled for too long.

She pokes me. "Boy, you can get serious fast. I don't care. Really."

We're interrupted by an announcement from the stage. Sarah Gluckman, who didn't figure on winning on her first foray into electoral politics, has won by fifty-four votes and is going to be the next councilwoman from Southeast Berkeley. That gives the Peace and Justice Coalition, and Re-Be, the majority on the council. The announcer introduces Gluckman, who has just arrived, and everyone whoops and claps. Almost on cue, in through the front door, come two men carrying cases of beer.

I get a lot of credit from Kisa, from other Re-Be folks, even from some strangers who seem to know who I am. Eileen gives me a hug and says, "you should feel proud." Gluckman mentions my stories in her victory speech.

Donna wraps her arms around my shoulders. "She said your reporting made the difference."

"Hey, she thanked her neighbor's lucky pet rabbit too, so I wasn't exactly singled out."

"The rabbit was a joke, Brian. What is with you tonight?"

"Yeah, I knew that."

I don't see Barb leave, but as the crowd dwindles, I can't find her.

Donna drives me back to my studio and we kiss for a few minutes in her car. A voice in my head says invite her in. I don't.

30.

Love Triangle

"Anyone who doubted the public support for Re-Be doesn't doubt it now," says Kisa Bettis, spokesperson for Re-Be. "It seemed like half of Berkeley came out in support on Halloween."
—Brian Hunter, "Development Plans Galvanize Support for Re-Be," *East Bay Beat,* November 4, 1998

I replay the tape from election night upside down and inside out and from thirty thousand feet as the sleepless minutes dribble toward dawn.

I handled myself reasonably well, I think. Barb kept dangling the hook. I didn't bite. I feel sorry for her, I really do, and I'm not comfortable with the power I have over her. But even after hours of unpacking it, my community service "option" doesn't seem so terrible—as an alternative to prison, anyway. There's some poetic justice there. I'm both impressed with my audacity and unnerved by it. What if Barb calls my bluff and I have to go to the police and squeal?

Maybe a better question is why I hold on to this innocent notion that fairness is doled out like gift bags at a kid's birthday party? We all get the same two plastic toys and five pieces of candy. I know better.

I fall asleep after the sun comes up, then the phone wakes me.

"Are you going to be able to make it?" It's Barb.

"I just walked in the door," I say.

"I sent you an email. Left a message. I'm holding a press conference today. At three. I know it's not much notice."

"Well, if I had something planned, I'd cancel it." I try to be light, but don't hit the right note. "Where?"

"Richmond," she says. "Three o'clock."

"Can you give me a sneak preview?"

I hear her swallow. "It's all in the email. I can't talk now."

"I'll be there."

But she doesn't hang up.

"Brian, I'm sorry. For everything. It could have been different."

I read the emails. The first announces a "press conference to be held by Barbara Genessee and Joanna Rogers, council, to address concerns about the death of Doug Spaulding."

The second is the same announcement, with a personal note from Barb. "Brian, I hope you can make it. Thanks. I've been thinking a lot about our conversation last night."

I grab a shower on my way to Richmond. The ride takes half an hour. The sun keeps peeking out from behind the clouds, then retreating. The air has a bite to it, as if winter is stretching its stiff arms in preparation for moving in.

I have no idea what to expect. I try to put myself in Barb's shoes and imagine her situation, but I can't seem to isolate that from my own moral template. Would she call a press conference to turn herself in? To announce her resignation from Con?

Outside a four-story brick building, a block from the county courthouse, two hand-scribbled signs with arrows point the way to "Genessee Press Conference, third floor." After locking my bicycle to a parking meter, I follow a camera crew from Channel 7 through the front door. I start looking for the stairs, but decide to share the elevator with a scruffy cameraman who's twice my size and a diminutive young woman with perfectly coiffed hair.

"Any idea of what's going to happen?" I ask them.

"I heard the police were on the verge of arresting her," the woman says.

I introduce myself, tell her I've been writing about recycling in the East Bay and how that's turned into a murder story. I'm disappointed she doesn't respond knowingly.

"Might be nothing," says the cameraman. "Lotta news conferences short on news."

As I sign in at an imposing mahogany reception desk, I say hello to Daria Reeves from the *Chronicle*. She asks me the same question I asked the TV reporter. I shrug my shoulders. We walk into a long and narrow conference room with a floor-to-ceiling window next to the doorway.

I don't see Barb, but it's not yet three. An oval table has been pushed to one side, and the chairs are bunched on the right side of the room. The long walls are lined with law books in glass-fronted cabinets, and on the back wall, three double-hung windows open to a sunny atrium. Four TV cameras hug the other wall. I try to pick out the police I know must be there, but I'm too restless to focus. When Barb and her lawyer walk in the room, they have to squeeze by me and several other people leaning against the wall. Barb doesn't acknowledge me as she passes.

She looks like she's had a reverse makeover. She wears a shapeless and oversized blue suit that makes her look gaunt, and black-rimmed reading glasses. No jewelry. No makeup. Her hair is pulled back severely with a barrette and held in place with bobby pins. No loose hairs. She reminds me of a nun without a habit. She's never been a glamour queen, except for that night at the awards banquet, but she usually carries herself with a sexy confidence and wears something interesting, like a turquoise bracelet or colorful scarf. Not today.

In contrast, her lawyer, Joanna Rogers, a few years older than Barb and a few inches shorter, looks sharp and svelte, almost as glamorous as the TV talent. Barb places some papers on the podium and pours herself a glass of water from a gold pitcher that looks like a vase. Then she steps aside and her lawyer stands in front of the microphones until the room hushes. She introduces Barb.

I hear the scratch of pens on paper. I open my notebook.

"As you know, two weeks ago, Doug Spaulding was murdered and I have been identified by the police as a suspect." Barb speaks slowly, precisely, articulating every syllable, snapping the "t" at the end of "suspect."

"Doug and I were partners for ten years, and our breakup was nasty and public, so I understand the suspicion is warranted. I want to start by saying that I am not guilty of that murder."

I'm sitting thirty feet from Barb, but I'm not in her line of sight. She can see me, but she hasn't given any indication that she has. She holds her head high and eyes wide open, looking directly into the cameras. She licks her lips. I thought I hadn't had any expectations, but clearly I do, because I'm surprised by her opening.

The room smells of furniture polish and sweat. The windows behind the lectern are open a crack and I feel a draft on my neck.

"The reason I am holding this press conference is that there are some facts that must be shared."

She speaks in a monotone and looks like a zombie. "This is difficult for me, but I need to do this for my own protection."

I can hear the man behind me wheezing through his nose.

"Some of you may know that one of the people who has been following the murder story and the related story of the recycling wars in Berkeley is Mr. Brian Hunter, a reporter for the *East Bay Beat.*"

Uh-oh. I freeze. Keep breathing. Write every word Barb says, even "the" and "of." I'm sure everyone is looking at me, but no, they don't know who I am. Most of them.

"Recently, Mr. Hunter, who is present today"—without looking up, I can feel her point toward me—"has been pursuing me romantically. He told me he fell in love with me nine years ago, the first time we met, when I was already with Doug. Long story short, this has been a hard time for me and a few days ago, after the big Re-Be demonstration on Halloween night, I was at Brian's studio with some friends and I'd had a few drinks and when Brian came on to me, I let him."

I force myself to take deep breaths.

"I was lonely. Doug and I had been broken up for months, and even though I initiated the breakup, I missed him. I couldn't grasp that he was dead. So I slept with Mr. Hunter because I was lonely and stressed out. He had been pursuing me for years and I thought he would be sweet with me and at first he was."

I squeeze my eyes shut and press my feet on the floor as hard as I can. I want to interrupt, but bite my lip.

"But when the sun came up in the morning," Barb says, "I realized that this was not what I wanted. When I said I didn't want to keep seeing him, he wouldn't let go and he got angry and vengeful. He threatened he would go to the police with this phony story that I killed Doug, tell them that I confessed to him, unless, unless I did what he wanted."

"That's not how it was." I jump up. The cameras turn toward me. I feel like exploding. "She told me she killed Doug, *how* she killed Doug." I speak slowly, emphasizing every word. "And I *urged* her to *turn herself in to the police.* I did *not* threaten her."

"Did she reject you, like she said?" It's a reporter a few feet behind me.

"She didn't reject me. There was no threat."

I feel strangely calm, considering there are dozens of eyes and four TV cameras focused on me.

Another reporter shouts a follow-up question, but Barb's lawyer steps to the microphone and says, "We have more to say."

The cameras return to the front, but I sense that everyone is still looking at me. I can't let my emotions get the better of me. I can't lose my temper. I write in my notebook: "What the fuck is she up to? How could she? Breathe. Don't forget to breathe. Keep my outrage to myself."

Barb stands motionless as her lawyer puts on reading glasses and leans into the stand of microphones. "There are several additional facts Ms. Genessee did not mention that I have an obligation to add. We do not mean to presume to tell the police how to do their job, but there are several facts about Mr. Hunter that shed additional light on this situation."

I keep writing down Rogers' words.

"First off, we have evidence of a love triangle, a rivalry. Mr. Hunter was a rival of Mr. Spaulding for Ms. Genessee's affections." She looks out over her reading glasses. "Let me use first names—it's easier to follow." Then comes a small, tight smile that scares the shit out of me.

"Brian and Doug were rivals, and *Doug*...was angry when he heard that *Brian*..."—she pauses after each name—"was romantically interested in *Barb*. This pre-dated the Barb-Doug breakup. On two separate occasions, Brian...told Barb...that Doug...tried to kill him by pushing him into a baler in the Recycle Berkeley yard. The same baler that crushed Doug Spaulding's body a week or so later."

My whole torso tenses up, as if I'm about to get a shot in the stomach with a long fat needle. I act calm, but I'm not. I have to be smart, not let her hook me.

"Brian Hunter has been obsessed with my client for many years," she continues. "He was relentless in his pursuit of her. Despite her efforts to discourage him, he *stalked* her. Several weeks ago, he waited for her on the street outside her office. This is only one of many documented examples of his obsession. So we have a classic romantic triangle and one of the three has been murdered. So far almost all the suspicion has been focused on my client and not on Mr. Hunter."

"I was not stalking her. I was there to—" Rogers raises her voice and drowns me out.

"When questioned by the police, Mr. Hunter denied any romantic interest in Barb. Fact number two: Mr. Hunter has a history of violent assault. We have here, and I'll be passing these out in a minute, copies of a 1992 police report which describes how Mr. Hunter assaulted a Mr. Joaquin Zepeda in a rehearsal studio in West Oakland." She holds up a stack of papers in her hand, but makes no move to pass them out.

I don't say anything. I can't deny this, though she makes it sound more sinister than it was. I gird myself for more. It's so quiet I hear the cameras whir. For a second, I'm able to detach myself from the hot seat and feel the suspense in the room.

Everyone is holding their breath, not just me.

"Fact number three, and Barb did not want to bring this up today, but I have an obligation to my client to do so. Fact number three: When Barb made it clear that she did not want to continue her romantic relationship with Mr. Hunter, he refused to listen. Mr. Hunter demanded to have sex again and when she said no, he forced himself on her and was rough with her. Legally, this may not be rape because earlier they had had consensual sex. It's a gray area. The truth is she did not want to have sex again and told him so and he would not take no for an answer."

"I did not force myself on her," I blurt, leaping up, squeezing my pen so hard it snaps. "Barb," I say, and then it feels like time stops and I can't get the words from my brain to my mouth. I glare at her in disbelief. "How could you?" I say plaintively.

Rogers interrupts, her voice booming through the room. "I'm passing out copies of the police report about Mr. Hunter's assault in—"

"It was not an assault," I yell over her amplified voice. "It was a fight with a bandmate. An accident. A long time ago. No charges were filed. This is outrageous. Joaquin is alive and well."

Barb steps in front of Rogers. "Let me clarify, please." She waits until the cameras swing back to her. "Mr. Hunter's desire for vengeance is so extreme that he threatened to frame me for Doug's murder." Her voice trembles, her face scrunches like she's in physical pain. "I have to protect myself. I said no when he wanted to have sex. I told him no. Clear as daylight."

I feel like I've been kicked in the balls and knifed in the back at the same time. I can't see straight. Reporters shout questions at me just like in the movies, but all I can hear is harsh noise, like the helicopters from Halloween night are in the room. I stand in front of the chair with my notebook in one hand and my broken pen in the other while the cameras hiss. I feel like my vocal cords have been twisted into a knot. A microphone on a long silver pole pokes me in the ear. I don't remember her saying no. Could I have not heard it? Could I have ignored it?

Maybe she said she was tired, but she did *not* say "no." I'm sure of it. She didn't try to stop me. She didn't say anything afterward. She seemed less traumatized by our night together than I was. A bead of sweat trickles down the front of my neck, then hits my collarbone. I have to say something. Barb and her lawyer have stepped back from the lectern and stand looking down, their chins to their chests, letting all the attention go to me.

Finally, I choke out a few words. "They're making it all up."

"So you really didn't have sex with her against her wishes?" one reporter yells above the other cacophonous questions.

"I'm flabbergasted," I say. "I'm shocked by the sheer audacity of these lies." My voice trembles at first, but as I talk, I gain confidence. "I've been taken totally by surprise by these ridiculous lies, and for my own protection, I have to get myself a lawyer."

Then one reporter directs his question to Barb and her lawyer. "Are you saying that Brian Hunter should be considered a suspect in the murder of Doug Spaulding?"

Rogers takes this one. "Determining who is a suspect is the domain of the police. We are here today to preempt a threat by Mr. Hunter to smear Ms. Genessee. And to share some facts that call his credibility into question. Thank you."

And they head for the exit, nudging their way through the throng.

I jump up on my chair.

"Barb, listen to me. Recant your story. Blame it on your lawyer. Say she urged you to do this against your will."

Barb stops momentarily and looks up and we make eye contact for the first time today. I catch in her eyes that same terrified look I saw the morning after Halloween, while I was making love to her, slowly and gently. I remember how soothing and loving I was—the polar opposite of rough. But I had been rough earlier.

How many times has Barb told me she's no saint? She didn't hide her dark side as much as I refused to see it.

Rogers pushes Barb forward, the door a few feet away.

"Don't let them leave," I say. Daria Reeves is standing next to the door. "Daria, block their way. Please."

She steps in their path.

"Look at me, Barb." All I can see of her is her silver streaked hair and a rust-red barrette. Rogers pushes Barb again, but there are now several people blocking their path.

"It's one thing for you to kill Doug," I say, my voice sounding more assured and confident than I feel. I have no Santa Claus suit to hide behind, but being falsely accused sure helps overcome any faint-heartedness. "That wasn't premeditated. He tortured you emotionally for years. He wouldn't let you go when you broke up with him." I'm rushing. I slow down. One of the cameramen is kneeling in front of me, the camera on his shoulder. The bright lights are blinding.

"He taunted you that night in the Re-Be yard. You thought he was going to hurt you. You snapped. You were scared and you tried to cover it up. You were defending yourself. You had no intention of killing him. It was an accident."

I study Barb's back, looking for a sign that she's listening. How could she not be listening?

"I did not force myself on you and you know it. You know you didn't say no. You know I would have respected that. You know that."

Epilogue.
Chowchilla

After we made love, she told me how she killed Doug.
—Brian Hunter, "When Love Meets Murder,"
San Francisco Chronicle, November 22, 1998

The drive to Chowchilla, down in the Central Valley north of Fresno, takes eight hours round trip. I ask for a rental car with a CD player and bring enough music to last me to Mexico. It's a few days after the summer solstice, so the sun is up by the time I leave and I blast through to Stockton before the caffeine wears off.

I turn the music off once I'm cruising down I-5. I have a lot to think about.

I haven't seen Barb—except on TV—since that fateful day in the Richmond law office seven months ago.

After the press conference, still shaking, I called Dan in New York. He had just walked in the door from work. I talked for ten minutes without stopping. Though I had written down most of what Barb and her lawyer had said, I didn't need my notes. Dan whistled when I stopped.

"Sit tight. Don't talk to anyone. I'll be there tomorrow morning."

I protested—reiterating that I was calling for a recommendation, not for him to come, that he had a job.

"Right now, this is my job," he said.

After he hung up, it hit me that I was in deep shit. What seemed like a desperate gamble on Barb's part was looking ominously like a believable stockpile of circumstantial evidence—pointing at me. I fought with Doug, and I thought, at least at the time, that he was trying to kill me. I pursued Barb with a persistence that could be characterized as obsession. Way back when, I hit Joaquin on the head with a chair and scared myself with the fury of my temper. I lied to the police about my interest in Barb. And I was quick to blame Consolidated Scavenger for everything from Doug's murder to the high price of a cappuccino in West Berkeley.

But there was at least as much evidence pointing to Barb, and of course I had one thing going for me that she didn't. I was innocent.

The next morning, weary from his flight, but focused and serious, Dan questioned me for several hours in his hotel room on University Avenue. After lunch, we walked to the police station under achingly beautiful blue skies and I talked to Detective Puma for almost three hours, told him everything, even the ultimatum to Barb, even the rough sex. Dan advised against that, but it was easier to tell the whole truth than pick and choose.

I tried to leave François out, but Puma pressed me for a name and address and I gave it. If Donna and I could stumble on him in an afternoon, I figured the police would track him down eventually. I promised myself I wouldn't identify Donna as the source of my allegations against Consolidated Scavenger in Contra Costa County. But that never came up. The police weren't interested in corporate misconduct.

My glassblowing neighbor Maya turned out to be a godsend. After Barb's Richmond press conference, the police canvassed the warehouse where I was living and Maya came to me afterward all apologetic about telling them that I asked her to burn a box of papers in her kiln. No one seemed to care about that, however.

The important thing was that the morning after the Halloween street party, Maya had seen Barb in the warehouse, just before dawn, going to the bathroom with a flashlight in her hand.

"I'd never seen her before," Maya told me. "I didn't know who she was. She looked a little lost, like she wasn't sure where she was going."

"Happy? Distraught? Traumatized?"

"I only saw her for a second. She seemed fine."

"Did you tell that to the detective?"

She did.

Turned out Eileen had come to my defense as well. Without any urging from me, she went to the police as a character witness, and said that I never forced myself on her in the six plus years we were together. That she couldn't imagine I would force myself on Barb.

I ran into Kisa a month after my long talk with the police—by then, she had become the executive director of Re-Be—and after we shared a pitcher of Anchor Steam, she thanked me for not writing about her and Ginsberg. She says he had been "a perfect gentleman about it—I mean, if you consider a guy cheating on his wife to be a gentleman." She had ended it, and they parted amicably.

As I stood to leave, she said, "I knew about Barb."

I sat back down.

"I knew she was at Re-Be that night. She told me she was going to be there."

"Did the police ask you about that?"

She nodded.

"And you?"

"I lied. Brian, you know Barb. It *was* self-defense."

"Well, I was going to lie, too," I said. "But it didn't work out that way."

I made a point to call up some of the people I'd talked to in the course of my reporting and offer to buy them a beer or a coffee. Turn some sources into friends. I used to think there was something mysterious about friendship, that there needed to be some spark, some kindred spirit. Maybe so, but sometimes it's as simple as making a phone call.

One of my new friends is the aforementioned perfect gentleman, David Ginsberg, from the Re-Be board. He's only eight years older than me, but successful enough that I feel like a greenhorn next to him. But that's my problem, not his. We think alike about important things. For him, it's important to maintain his integrity and idealism as his career veers further and further into the world of big money. I joke with him about how I haven't had to face that dilemma.

One night, Ginsberg and I had a fascinating conversation about how Re-Be might address its problems with poachers. That got me to thinking about Wilson, and the next morning I set out before dawn, *sans* shopping cart, to find him. No luck that first time, but a week later, I tracked him down, and returned the two dollars he had forced on me. I also gave him forty dollars in interest. That made my day.

As for Donna, I never had to tell her about sleeping with Barb. She heard it on the news like everyone else. A few weeks later, after Thanksgiving, I gave her a call and after some awkward explaining, we picked up where we left off and eased into a sweet, albeit short relationship over the winter.

Maybe because I met her under false pretenses as a phony insurance bureaucrat, and then as an almost-real reporter, she never saw the Brian I thought I was. She saw who I was *becoming,* who I *wanted to be,* and she liked that Brian. So did I.

We celebrated New Year's Eve together at a Scrabble party in a sprawling house down on the peninsula. Dozens of us brought our sleeping bags and stayed up playing into the new year.

"I have a question," she asked that night, as we brushed our teeth in front of his and her sinks. "You told me that you and your ex were trying to have a baby and it wasn't happening and then you stopped trying. Do you still want to have children?"

I kept brushing, motioning that I couldn't talk.

"Did you change your mind?"

I rinsed out my mouth. "It was Eileen who changed her mind. She said that bringing a child into the world wasn't going to make our marriage better, only make it harder."

I remember clearly what Eileen had said after that. "I don't mean to be hurtful, but I read somewhere that the key to a happy marriage is to marry a happy person. I failed on that front."

Donna was brushing her hair and waiting for an answer.

"I think I still do," I said. "With the right person."

"I just don't want to be your getaway car."

Donna was the one who broke things off though.

"You're still hung up on Barb," she said one sunny morning in February.

"Who?" I replied.

Donna said I never let her in. She was right. I had this wild, rich, complicated inner life that I was dying to share, but I kept it to myself.

Maybe I can reach out to Donna again. As long as I was obsessed with Barb, I couldn't give the relationship with her the opportunity to take root. I was able to talk myself into a date with Barb after splashing her argument with Doug all over the news, so it shouldn't be that much of stretch to ask Donna for another chance.

Even if she says no, asking is its own reward. I don't know why it's taken me so long to figure that out.

I never wanted to tell on Barb. I somehow maintained this delusion that we would share the intimacy of her secret, that she would lead a noble life making up for her mistake and that she would be grateful to me for keeping her secret in trust and inspiring her to rediscover her virtue and integrity. And in turn, she would inspire me to rediscover my passion, to fulfill the potential I had never fully realized. All bullshit. The meek do not inherit the earth.

But I had to take my power, save my own life first, and if Barb was sacrificed in the process, well, I was not the one who whacked Doug on the head with the two by four.

About an hour after I stop for coffee, I see the first sign for Valley State Prison for Women in Chowchilla. I've never been inside a prison, never visited a prisoner. I'm as nervous as if I'm on a blind date.

Barb is serving ten years for voluntary manslaughter. I meant to visit her before, but I kept putting it off. I had to rent a car, but how hard is that?

She turned herself in a week after my statement to the police. She was charged with second-degree murder, and there was a buildup to a trial, but it never happened. They made a deal. Her lawyer talked the district attorney into knocking down the charge to involuntary manslaughter. She hit Doug so many times that clearly she had snapped, but then her methodical, and almost successful attempt to cover up the murder made it look premeditated.

My anger at Barb is still there, but it's a shadow of its former self. The questions that have been haunting me since last fall aren't going away. Like why didn't she take the community service deal I offered? Why did she take such a huge gamble and attack me in public? Why not just quietly go to the police with her story?

And why did she, of all people, make a veiled and false accusation of rape? She cared deeply about justice and women's rights and hated those rare instances when women made false accusations of rape because they made the truthful accusations less likely to be believed.

What hurts the most is how she underestimated me. It's not just that she might have been playing me all along, but that she thought she could get away with it, that I would lie down and take it, that I would be so paralyzed by her accusations or my love sickness for her that I wouldn't fight back.

Even now, I give her more benefit of the doubt than she deserves: Doug got the best of her and then she unraveled. That's my spin. Doug got his revenge—if he couldn't have her, no one could. If he couldn't be happy, neither could she. I saw her and Doug more as failed tragic heroes than devious villains.

In Chowchilla, after getting thoroughly patted down and searched, I sit across from Barb on a white plastic picnic table bolted to the floor in the visiting hall. There are ten other tables, four of them with visitors. The room is stark, like a school classroom with all the posters and artwork removed. And with bars on the windows.

Barb tells me how she's started a composting program at the prison, and an organic garden where they grow potatoes, squash, ten kinds of tomatoes, and six kinds of lettuce. She's convinced the cook to create new dishes using the fresh produce and the mess hall now has two bins for garbage—one for compostables, the other for meat and other waste that can't be composted.

"Actually, we've got plans to compost the meat too," she says. "I wrote this grant to get a scarab windrow turner that can get the piles up to one hundred and forty degrees, hot enough to compost anything. Like the one at Re-Be."

Barb is animated, engaged. Sitting across from me in her prison garb, she looks, well, innocent. I express surprise at how quickly she's been able to make a mark.

She shrugs. "I've got to do something with my time."

She also says she might be able to get early release after eight years, and I think, for a second, could I wait for her?

No. No, I couldn't. That window has closed. I closed it.

She doesn't seem curious about me or ask me any questions. She seems happy enough to talk and have an audience.

I tell her I've landed a staff writer job at the *Beat*—three hundred dollars a week—I'm on the Re-Be board, and I even found a legal residence. (I bought some candles too, I joke, but she doesn't get it.) I tell her I went out with Donna for a couple months and we had fun. I don't say that I'm going to call her when I get back home.

I want to give her the impression that I have recovered quite nicely, thank you, from my obsession with her and I'm living a full and rich life.

Which, I'm happy to say, is mostly true.

Barb does ask about Einstein.

"I walk him every morning," I say. "Except today. Because I left so early."

Re-Be "adopted" Einstein when Barb went to prison, but it didn't work out and when I moved to a house where there were already three other people and a dog and a cat, I took Einstein with me. He sleeps on the floor by the side of my bed—I have to be careful not to step on him when I get up to go to the bathroom.

All those questions I've been dying to ask? I don't ask them.

The prison doesn't allow physical contact, so I don't need to worry about whether or not to give Barb a hug when I leave.

THE END

Acknowledgments

I wrote the first drafts of this book long enough ago that I can't possibly acknowledge everyone who helped me make it better. I was part of two overlapping novel-writing groups, each of which helped me shape this final version. They include Clare Willis, Lalita Tademy, Amy Glynn, Yang Huang, Joe Wyka, and Joe Gore.

Others who contributed feedback include Tim Campbell, Shelley Wagner, Nelle Donaldson, Bruce Shigeura, Ed Weisbart, Gail Williams, and Stan Kaufman.

I also want to acknowledge the Ecology Center of Berkeley, where I served as a volunteer and board of directors for a number of years. Recycle Berkeley is a fictional organization, but was informed by my experiences at the Ecology Center.

And special thanks to Nanette Zavala, my wife, for her love, insightful editing, and overall support.

About the Author

John Byrne Barry is the author of *Bones in the Wash: Politics is Tough. Family is Tougher*—a political thriller set during the 2008 presidential campaign in New Mexico.

He's written political comedy, advice columns, musicals, and magazine and newspaper stories. He is at work on a third novel, about a family facing end-of-life choices.

He lives in Mill Valley, California, with his wife and family. (See greennoir.com for more.)

www.ingramcontent.com/pod-product-compliance
Lightning Source LLC
Chambersburg PA
CBHW061011120726
47910CB00006B/1875